INTERNAL AFFAIRS

INTERNAL AFFAIRS

CONNIE DIAL

The Permanent Press
Sag Harbor, NY 11963

For information, address:
  The Permanent Press
  4170 Noyac Road
  Sag Harbor, NY 11963
  www.thepermanentpress.com

Library of Congress Cataloging-in-Publication Data

  Dial, Connie
    Internal affairs / Connie Dial.
        p. cm.
    ISBN-13: 978-1-57962-184-1 (alk. paper)
    ISBN-10: 1-57962-184-8 (alk. paper)
        1. Police murders—Fiction. 2. Police internal investigation—
    Fiction. 3. Police—California—Los Angeles—Fiction. 4. Los
    Angeles (Calif.)—Fiction. I. Title.

  PS3604.I126I58 2009
  813'.6—dc22   2008056097

Printed in the United States of America.

To Jon M. Dial

CHARACTERS IN ORDER OF DEPARTMENT RANKING

Sylvia Diaz, civilian president of the Los Angeles Police Commission

Elaine Miller, civilian attorney, Inspector General (IG), Los Angeles Police Department

Samuel Martin, chief of police

Jacob (Jake) Bell, deputy chief, Chief of Staff for chief of police

Jim McGann, deputy chief, West Bureau

Carl Stevenson, captain, Robbery-Homicide Division (RHD)

Nancy Connelly, captain, Internal Affairs Division (IA or IAD)

Paula Toscano, lieutenant, adjutant for the Chief of Staff

Brenda Todd, lieutenant, officer in charge of the Commission Investigation Division (CID)

Sara McKnight, lieutenant, executive officer for the chief of police

Sally Wolinski, lieutenant, adjutant for the assistant chief in Office of Operations

Mike (Mickey) Turner, sergeant, investigator for Internal Affairs Division

Maria Perez, sergeant, investigator for Internal Affairs Division—West Bureau

Myron (Bill) Nichols, sergeant, adjutant to the Internal Affairs Division captain

Patricia McGann, sergeant, on family leave

Mark (Sully) Sullivan, detective supervisor, Hollywood narcotics' squad

Katy O'Neal, detective, investigates homicides for Robbery Homicide Division

Nick (Monty) Montgomery, detective, investigates homicides for Robbery Homicide Division

Alexandra Williams, police officer, West Los Angeles Division

John (JD) Carter, police officer, Devonshire Division

Department Abbreviations

ADW	Assault with a deadly weapon
BOR	Board of Rights—disciplinary hearing for police officers
COA	Command Officers' Association—representative group for LAPD staff and command officers
CRASH	Community Resources Against Street Hoodlums—gang enforcement
IA	Internal Affairs
IG	Inspector General
ISD	Internal Surveillance Detail—squad of officers who follow other officers accused of participating in illegal activities to determine if the accusations are true
LAPD	Los Angeles Police Department
ME	Medical Examiner—Coroner's office
P-II	Police officer who is off probation
PAB	Police Administration Building (PAB)—Police Headquarters or Parker Center
RHD	Robbery Homicide Division
SID	Scientific Investigation Division (latent prints, photos, evidence testing, etc.)

LAPD ORGANIZATIONAL CHART (PARTIAL)

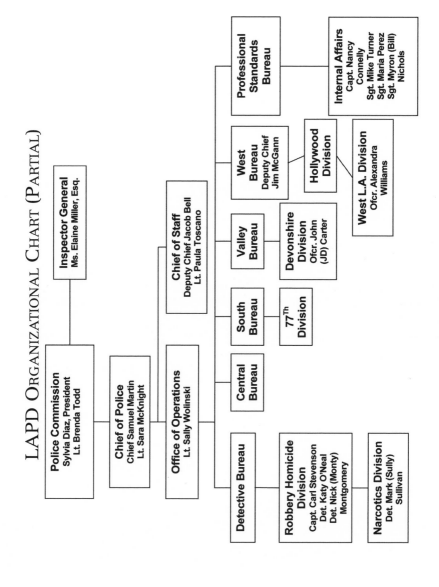

Police Commission
Sylvia Diaz, President
Lt. Brenda Todd

Inspector General
Ms. Elaine Miller, Esq.

Chief of Police
Chief Samuel Martin
Lt. Sara McKnight

Chief of Staff
Deputy Chief Jacob Bell
Lt. Paula Toscano

Office of Operations
Lt. Sally Wolinski

Detective Bureau

Robbery Homicide Division
Capt. Carl Stevenson
Det. Katy O'Neal
Det. Nick (Monty) Montgomery

Narcotics Division
Det. Mark (Sully) Sullivan

Central Bureau

South Bureau

77th Division

Valley Bureau

Devonshire Division
Ofcr. John (JD) Carter

West Bureau
Deputy Chief Jim McGann

Hollywood Division

West L.A. Division
Ofcr. Alexandra Williams

Professional Standards Bureau

Internal Affairs
Capt. Nancy Connelly
Sgt. Mike Turner
Sgt. Maria Perez
Sgt. Myron (Bill) Nichols

9

ONE

As the youngest deputy chief on the LAPD, Jim McGann had a good shot at becoming chief. But he needed the support of the rank and file cops which meant convincing them he was a cop's cop. Laugh with them, work with them, and run with them. He also needed the backing of the police union, but that was no problem. The union guys were in it for themselves and their fat political appointments after retirement. He could handle them with a wink and a promise to put in a good word in Sacramento.

Leaning against the porch railing, McGann carefully stretched his Achilles tendons and did a few toe touches before starting his regular five-mile run. He didn't notice the car parked in front of his house until he jogged down the driveway. There was so little parking in the Hollywood Hills that it wasn't unusual to find strange cars on the street. However, this asshole's car was blocking his driveway. He would get it towed if it wasn't moved by the time he got back.

He reached the bottom of the hill before stopping and looking back. There was something about that car. It hadn't been parked there last night, and it didn't belong on his street, but he was certain he'd seen it somewhere.

McGann circled around and continued his regular route through the hills down to Beechwood Drive, stopping at the Hillside Café, where he grabbed a paper from the rack and sat at his regular table outside the front door, dropping the front section and turning to the local news to find the latest scandal the *L.A. Times* claimed to have uncovered within the LAPD. It was a standing joke among staff officers. They had to read the *Times* every morning to find out what was happening in the department. The chief of police certainly wasn't going to tell them anything.

Today it was good news, meaning no news.

"Coffee, Jimmy?" Judy Taylor, the owner of the café, asked from the doorway behind him.

"Thanks, Judy. Not this morning. I've got to get back up the hill."

She lingered in the doorway and hesitated before approaching the table.

"Jimmy, I hate to bring this up, but . . ." She stepped aside as if she had changed her mind, then stepped back in front of him again. "Hell, I gotta tell you . . . just so you know."

McGann stared at her, waiting for the bad news. Some patrol officer had stiffed her. Her cousin had just been arrested for child molesting. The list of possibilities was endless. He had heard most of the sad tales that always came with the false expectation that he could or actually would do something to help.

She took a deep breath. "Last night, a couple of plainclothes guys," she said, then stopped. "I don't know who they were or where they work," she added, anticipating his next question. "They came in here just before we closed. They was in suits, and I could see their guns and handcuffs."

"So what did they do?" He was in a hurry and wanted her to get to the point.

"They were high."

"You mean drunk?"

"No, I mean high as in strung-out speeders, Meth freaks, crystal junkies." She sighed.

"Don't look at me like I'm nuts, Jimmy. I been living in Hollywood my whole life. I know a tweaker when I see one." She shrugged her bony shoulders. "I just figured you might want to know."

He wasn't surprised. Nothing surprised him anymore. Cops had been accused of drug dealing, murder, bank robbery. Anything was possible.

"Tell you what, Judy. I'll talk to Internal Affairs in West Bureau and have someone call you to get a good description later on today. Okay?"

"Or we could forget the whole thing. Whatever you think, Jimmy. Just figured you'd want to know." She smiled as if it really didn't matter to her.

He was annoyed but tried not to show it. Now he would have to do something. He didn't mind burning a cop when it was necessary, but it was one more piece of business. She'd made him responsible to do something. He left a dollar on the table, did a few knee bends, and jogged back up Beechwood towards home.

As he approached the house, he could see the car parked in the same spot. It was a late-model Pontiac Grand Prix, black with a tan interior. He cupped his hands on the driver's window to cut the glare and looked in, hoping to see something that would identify the owner.

The first thing he saw was a police radio lying on the front seat, almost $2,000 worth of Motorola technology waiting for some strung-out junkie to break the window and steal it. He checked the back license plate and the registration tabs. They were overdue, like on all police cars. He felt his anger growing as he thought about the careless treatment of police property until he noticed several large spots on the asphalt under the rear bumper.

At first he thought it might be oil, but it looked like blood. He carefully examined the ground surrounding the car and found more spots near the passenger side. His hands were shaking as he attempted unsuccessfully to open the locked door, and then he looked in the window again. The tan upholstery on the passenger's headrest was stained with dark-brown patches.

His heart was racing faster than it had been coming up the hill as he dialed the Hollywood watch commander's office.

TWO

Mike Turner didn't like Hollywood. Bad things happened there . . . too many prostitutes, too many drugs, and every parolee who settled in that part of the city seemed to have a death wish and a gun. He took the investigator's job at Internal Affairs to get away from places like Hollywood, but here he was standing in the street under the shadow of that stupid sign, again.

His boss was supposed to meet him here, but Captain Connelly was never the first to arrive. If she were the first high-ranking officer on scene, she'd be expected to take charge and make decisions—something Turner noticed she routinely avoided. The uniformed officers had already established a perimeter around the car, so Turner got as much information as he could from McGann and then wondered why he'd been called out. Until someone figured out how the car got there and what had happened to the driver, it was pointless for IA to be involved. But that was the new LAPD; nobody wanted to make a mistake, so everybody overreacted.

Turner watched Carl Stevenson, the captain from Robbery Homicide Division, struggle up the hill. The guy always looked as if he'd slept in his clothes, and Turner figured his pink face and bloodshot, watery blue eyes were probably as permanent as his red hair. Stevenson was twenty pounds overweight, which straight away put him in a bad mood. He ignored Turner and immediately took control. He told patrol units to block the street at the bottom of the hill and keep the sidewalks clear. He took another roll of the yellow crime-scene tape from one of the supervisors and tied it to the trees and a lamppost, creating a much larger perimeter than the first patrol car officers had. It was common knowledge he was a detective who had been promoted late in his career. His detectives respected him and worked hard for him because he understood their jobs as well as his own.

"Who are you?" Stevenson asked, stopping just long enough to glare at Turner.

"Turner, IA."

"Great. You'll be a lot of help," Stevenson said sarcastically. "Did anybody try to pop the trunk?" he asked, turning to a young lieutenant who was in charge of the uniformed officers.

The lieutenant explained that Hollywood Tow could do it faster and cleaner. He had called them as soon as McGann had notified him. McGann stepped between them and claimed it was his decision to wait for the tow truck. He also tried to explain why his prints would be all over the car. Stevenson seemed to enjoy McGann's obvious discomfort as the sweaty chief tried to explain why it was necessary to touch all the doors and windows.

"How could I know?" McGann mumbled and shook his head.

"SID will eliminate your prints," Turner said, and both men looked at him as if he had crashed a private party, or his comment about Scientific Investigation Division was completely unnecessary. "I've got a tire iron in my car, Captain. You want me to pop the trunk?" Turner asked. He didn't have the patience to wait for a tow truck and suspected Stevenson didn't either; however, at that moment, as if on cue, a tow truck appeared at the bottom of the hill.

"Let's run the plate and see which division this car's assigned to," McGann said, trying to be helpful.

"It belongs to Internal Affairs. That's why I'm here, sir," Turner said, thinking he'd already explained that. "Captain Connelly is on her way. She says the car wasn't checked out yesterday. The garage doesn't have extra keys, and she doesn't have keys to that particular vehicle."

Stevenson excused himself to meet with his detectives. Turner recognized Katy O'Neal and Nick Montgomery. They were respected homicide investigators and looked fresh and eager to work. RHD had the luxury of not handling many cases.

Fresh from South Bureau Homicide, Katy and Nick knew their business. South Bureau was a killing zone. A couple of years on those busy tables had given them a graduate course in murder investigations. They were an odd pairing. Katy was barely five feet tall and weighed about a hundred pounds. Nick was six feet tall, bald, and skinny. He wore trifocals and looked more librarian than cop. Stevenson seemed glad to see them, but Turner couldn't help thinking the RHD callout was more of the "too much, too soon" syndrome.

"Anything from the neighbors? Why isn't the trunk open?" Katy asked as she walked around to the back of the car.

Stevenson shrugged. "The tow truck just got here. They're moving cars and the media's junk so he can get up the hill."

"IA, of course, knows nothing," Nick said. Turner laughed and Nick turned around, noticing him for the first time. "Sorry, Turner, didn't see you," he said, grinning. "No offense."

"None taken," Turner responded and shook hands with the embarrassed detective. He knew Nick had received his share of discipline and had little love or respect for Internal Affairs. It wasn't personal.

"You two know Chief McGann?" Stevenson asked, pointing to the deputy chief, who stood close enough to hear their conversation. Both detectives hesitated for a moment, trying to recall anything they shouldn't have said, and then nodding at McGann.

"You found the car?" Katy asked without any further niceties. She was always in a hurry to work.

McGann explained again when he had first seen the car and how his prints would probably be all over it. Before he finished his story, Captain Connelly and the captain from Hollywood Division arrived. They stood quietly in the street near Turner, listening to McGann. Connelly acknowledged Turner with a slight smile but didn't speak to him. He was grateful. She didn't hide the fact that she never wanted him in her division, and she rarely had anything pleasant or meaningful to say to him. He worked harder and longer than most of her other investigators, but she had a difficult time overlooking his colorful past and his stubbornness when he believed he was right . . . two things that frightened the career-minded Connelly.

By that time, the day watch commander from Hollywood had replaced the morning watch officers with his fresh crew and had appointed a press sergeant to keep the gathering media informed and down the hill. A few of the radio reporters had scanners and had picked up the initial call for additional black-and-whites. The rest of the media had smelled blood in the water when their airships saw all the yellow tape.

Patricia McGann and the twins, still in their bathrobes and slippers, were out on the front lawn. Jim McGann had slipped on a jogging suit over his running shorts and was holding one of the girls. Patricia was tall and thin, with long brown hair pulled back

16

in a ponytail. She was a sergeant on LAPD but had taken a leave of absence to care for the girls until they started preschool. Turner knew her reputation was a lot better than Jim McGann's. She was a popular supervisor.

As the tow truck pulled up beside the Grand Prix, the busy crime scene became quiet. McGann hovered around Stevenson and the RHD detectives. Connelly planted herself at the deputy chief's side, chattering to him while McGann ignored her. She was a stocky middle-aged woman with a henna-colored Veronica Lake haircut. She wore an expensive matronly suit and appeared confused by all the activity. Turner watched quietly and almost felt sorry for the woman.

Hollywood Division's commanding officer was broad-shouldered, with salt-and-pepper hair. He was in uniform and joked with several of his officers as he followed Stevenson around the crime scene. Stevenson directed the truck driver to a parking space and then told the young man what he should do and what he could touch.

"Get that trunk open and get out of the way," Stevenson ordered. He turned to the SID photographer, who had been taking pictures for several minutes. "Do we have photos of the doors and locks?" he asked. The photographer nodded. "Once you get the trunk open, unlock the doors," Stevenson said to the tow truck driver. He looked at the dozen or so uniformed officers who had crowded close to the car. Turner was surprised when he didn't tell them to step back. He seemed ready to move them and then appeared to change his mind. Turner was impressed. These patrol guys were always treated badly by suits, who generally used them as cheap labor and then kept them in the dark and out of the way. Apparently, Stevenson was different.

Turner watched McGann, too. Unlike the other onlookers, the deputy chief had edged away from the car and stood on the sidewalk. Patricia and the kids must've gone back inside the house.

There was that familiar odor as the trunk was opened, the undeniable smell of death. The tow truck driver put his hand over his mouth and quickly stepped aside. Turner moved closer. The victim was curled in a fetal position facing the back of the trunk. He closed his eyes for a moment and had a sick feeling. She looked like a child. She was dressed in a flimsy pink slip and nothing else. Stevenson leaned into the trunk to check for a pulse, but it was pointless. She was dead. Rigor mortis had started, and what was left of her blood had settled. Her skin was purple and yellow. She was a young woman, not a child. Her head was tucked down, her chin buried against a well-endowed chest. Her short blond hair was matted in a sticky pool of coagulated blood. Her arms and legs were caked with blood, but the pink slip was nearly clean.

The SID photographer pushed the uniformed officers aside and stood directly behind the open trunk. He looked at Nick Montgomery for direction.

"Where you want me to start, Monty?" he said, trying not to take a deep breath.

Turner stared disdainfully at the flabby little man dressed in a safari vest and wrinkled baggy pants. Not a second wasted to mourn or wonder at the loss of life in someone so young. This was just another body to photograph and move on to the next senseless waste of life.

"Hold on," Montgomery said, walking away from the photographer and handing a roll of yellow tape to one of the uniformed sergeants. "Extend the crime scene. Make an outer perimeter and start all over again, knocking on doors. Ask about anything unusual, and get names and work numbers. Make certain your log officer has the names and times of arrival and departure for everyone here. Got all that?"

The balding sergeant smirked and didn't answer. He had been an assistant watch commander at Hollywood for more than a decade and had probably handled more crime scenes than anyone there, except maybe Stevenson. Montgomery looked away and took a deep breath. "Sorry," he said. "Even the possibility of a dead cop makes me crazy."

Turner looked around the street for Stevenson and spotted the RHD captain standing on McGann's lawn with the Hollywood captain. Stevenson was attempting to talk him into giving up the resources he needed, including additional detectives to do some of the legwork. McGann stood near them, but he was staring at his wife and kids, who were out on the front porch again. Patricia coaxed the twins back into the house with a woman who looked like the nanny. She started to walk back toward the car, but McGann quickly intercepted her, and after a few words she returned to the house.

Stevenson motioned for Turner to meet with him, Montgomery, and Katy away from the others. Katy was gathering information from officers who had interviewed some of the neighbors. She wasn't happy about being interrupted and didn't bother to hide it.

"Get photos of every inch of that trunk before the coroner gets here. Then wait for me, and I'll walk you through the rest of it," Montgomery shouted at the photographer as he walked toward Stevenson.

"Captain Connelly doesn't recognize the victim as one of her people, but she's not certain," Stevenson said when they were all close enough to hear him.

"What a surprise," Katy said.

"Play nice, children," Stevenson said, looking at Turner. "She has a lot of people working for her. Give her a break. You got a good look, Turner. You recognize her?"

"Nope," he said, but there were a lot of people working IA that he'd never seen. The chief believed in discipline and had doubled the size of the division in the last few years.

"You're right, boss. Who says you gotta have a clue just because you get promoted?" Katy folded her arms and grinned at Stevenson.

"We have no ID, no clothes, nothing to identify this victim. Let's get prints. If she's one of ours, I want to know now. You do it, O'Neal," Stevenson said, looking down at his detective, who gave him a sloppy salute and returned to her car. Turner had to smile. Katy O'Neal wasn't easily intimidated, but he wasn't certain he would have had the nerve to irritate Stevenson that way.

"Smart ass," Stevenson mumbled.

"Yeah, but an excellent detective," Montgomery said.

Where's McGann?" Stevenson asked.

Turner pointed at the deputy chief, who was quietly watching the photographer work. "This is too weird," he said. "A near-naked body in the trunk of an IA car nobody checked out, and it's parked outside his house."

"Wait until the coroner turns her over. Our leader is looking a little green around the edges," Stevenson said.

"You think he knows her?" Montgomery asked.

"Educated guess? Absolutely."

19

Turner wanted to hear more, but Stevenson walked away. For almost another hour, he watched the detectives and a female investigator from SID move around the crime scene, identifying potential evidence, taking photographs and retrieving anything they thought was significant for further examination or possibly for court if they ever captured a suspect. The tedious process was ignored by the neighbors and bored uniformed cops until the coroner's van arrived. As soon as the medical examiner and his assistant, a small muscular Mexican woman, stepped out of their vehicle, everyone inside the perimeter, including Turner, crowded around the car again, carefully avoiding the blood spots and the other evidence marked with numbered and folded index cards.

The ME and his assistant discussed with Stevenson and Montgomery how to lift the body out of the car and where to place the cart to avoid having it roll downhill into the crowd of reporters and television cameras. The ME looked like a used-car salesman in his blue polyester suit and green knit shirt, but Montgomery and Stevenson knew him and followed his direction.

They decided to place a large plastic sheet against her back and roll the body over onto the plastic. Then they could use it like a stretcher to lift her out of the car and not risk losing evidence. The Mexican woman carried a large sheet of plastic from the van and tucked it into the trunk. As she and the ME turned over the body, Turner felt his stomach turn when he saw that the coagulated blood had stuck to the victim's face, arm, and thigh. It was a gruesome sight, made worse when her head rolled to the side, revealing a gaping wound around her neck. Her throat had been cut to the spine.

Montgomery reached over the ME and pointed to the neck wound. "What do you make of this cut?"

The ME shook his head. "Almost looks like the skin was torn, maybe a knife with a serrated edge, or maybe I don't know. It's deep and narrow but not like a knife cut."

"Can you wipe away some of that blood? Are there any other head wounds?" Montgomery asked. "I've never seen a wound like this."

The Mexican woman and the ME grabbed the corners of the plastic and lifted the body out of the trunk. They gently placed the plastic stretcher on the ground. The head came forward, and dead blue eyes stared at the morning sun. The assistant took a towel from her pocket, held the head steady, grabbing a handful of hair, and wiped the face, a pretty face frozen in horror.

Turner had seen enough. He stepped away from the car but had heard Montgomery say that the wound around the victim's neck wasn't like anything he'd seen before. He hoped the autopsy would tell them more. The ME took the liver temperature and more pictures of the body. There was nothing else to do. There were no valuables, no jewelry, and no murder weapon. They lifted the plastic onto the gurney and covered the body with the plastic, a sheet, and the coroner's blanket.

"Couple of things, Monty," the ME said, leaning on the gurney. "Those defensive wounds on her hands were made with something other than the weapon that cut her throat. She's only been dead a few hours based on the body temperature." He shoved the gurney into the van and slammed the door shut.

Turner looked around the crime scene. Everyone was still there. Department brass usually split at the first opportunity, but like him they were hanging around, waiting to find out if this victim was a cop. Stevenson had called Press Relations to help with the media, but the Fourth Estate was becoming impatient with the lack of information. He was, too.

"Boss, any word from Katy on the ID?" Montgomery asked.

Stevenson didn't answer right away. He was looking into the trunk. "Pretty shitty place to spend your last few minutes on Earth," he said and then added, "O'Neal had to drive the print downtown, state-of-the-art police work. Let's get the body out of here and shut down this circus."

The assistant backed up the coroner's van, made a U-turn, and drove slowly down the hill. They had loaded the body facing the television cameras, so every station had its six o'clock sound bite on the unidentified corpse.

McGann had talked to the chief of police twice during the morning. Each time, he came back to the crime scene a little more subdued. He knew this looked bad—a dead cop in a police car parked in front of his home. McGann knew she was a cop. He knew a lot about Alexandra Williams. The only thing he didn't know was why her mutilated body was lying in a car trunk in front of his house.

When the coroner's van was out of sight, McGann called a meeting in his kitchen for Stevenson, Connelly, and the Hollywood captain. When they settled around the table, he told them the identity of the young victim. She was a police officer assigned to West Los Angeles station. They'd been friends, he and Officer Williams—at one time very good friends. The three captains looked at each other. Stevenson's first thought was that it would've been helpful if that bit of information had been shared sooner. His second thought was whether McGann killed her, which he was about to ask when his cellular phone rang with the same information from an excited Katy O'Neal. She tried to tell Stevenson about the reliable rumor of a relationship between McGann and the victim. Stevenson politely thanked her and told her they'd discuss it later. He briefly explained that he was in a meeting with the deputy chief and was aware of the victim's identity. Katy managed to say, "Then why the fuck am I . . ." before Stevenson turned off his phone and shoved it into his jacket pocket.

"Do you know anything about her death?" Stevenson asked McGann.

McGann didn't answer for a few seconds and then said, "The chief of police has given me the authority to oversee the investigation. Apparently, he has more confidence in me than you do, Captain Stevenson."

Connelly looked at Stevenson. They both knew she should state her objection to his involvement from an Internal Affairs perspective. But she didn't speak, and after a few seconds, she quietly stared at the kitchen floor.

McGann explained how the chief wanted a quick and thorough investigation. Stevenson would have any resources he wanted. There would be a daily briefing in the chief's conference room on the sixth floor at Parker Center. Stevenson tried to suppress the groan he felt starting in his brain. Briefings were a waste of time. Every commander and deputy chief who attended would feel obligated to say something stupid or ask something irrelevant just to let the chief of police know they were listening.

McGann set the first meeting for 8 A.M. the next morning. "I want you and your detectives to be there, Carl."

22

"Chief," Stevenson said, hesitating just a beat, "we'll need to formally interview you. If you like, I can do it myself."

McGann's face flushed. Connelly and the Hollywood captain shifted in their chairs. The Hollywood captain put his hand over his mouth, but his eyes couldn't conceal the smile.

"I fully expect to give a statement, Carl," McGann said, recovering some of his composure. "Your primary focus should be finding whoever did this terrible thing. I don't care who interviews me. Just catch this animal." McGann stood unsteadily and pushed his chair away from the table. "That's it, people," he said, turning his back on them. "I'm going to dress and try to spend some time at the office today," he added on his way out of the room.

The three captains knew they'd been dismissed, and they left the house without further discussion. McGann and the chief of police had set the course. Although he relished McGann's reaction, Stevenson knew he had been a touch indelicate with his superior officer. What he couldn't understand was why the chief would let McGann anywhere near this investigation.

Turner was sitting on the porch steps with Montgomery when Stevenson came out of the house. Montgomery was drawing a crime scene sketch. Stevenson sat between them and repeated what McGann had revealed in the meeting. Connelly paused for a moment at the top of the stairs and told Turner to be in her office in an hour. He would be the lead investigator on McGann's IA case. More bad news, Turner thought as he watched Connelly almost run to her car and drive away.

The Hollywood captain laughed as he maneuvered down the stairs. He patted Turner on the shoulder.

"Good luck, partner," he said, and, turning to Stevenson, asked, "What do you need from me, Carl?"

"A couple of homicide detectives," Montgomery answered for his boss.

"I don't have any to spare."

"We need them," Montgomery insisted.

"Just a loan to RHD for a few days. It'll be good experience for them," Stevenson said unconvincingly, knowing the man was too savvy to believe that lie.

"Yeah, like anything could fix this can of worms," the Hollywood captain said, giving his car keys to one of the uniformed officers. "Get it for me, Jerry; it's parked at the top." He turned back to Stevenson. "I know I owe you, Carl, for past favors," he said, winking at Stevenson. "But keep my people out of trouble. This thing stinks." The Hollywood captain's parting words were for Turner. "Watch your back," he said. Turner didn't respond. He was trying to figure out how he could give this high-profile investigation to one of those newbie sergeants who enjoyed being the center of attention and would do anything Connelly wanted.

Montgomery shook his head. "Alice down the rabbit hole," he said, looking at Turner, and then shouted at the Hollywood tow truck driver to hook up the bloody Grand Prix and take it to Central garage, where RHD would have easier access. Montgomery collected statements and interview cards from the Hollywood detectives and patrol officers. It was Katy's job, but she'd never returned from her downtown fingerprint excursion. He was glad she hadn't come back. She would be pissed off that McGann hadn't immediately revealed everything he knew, and she'd make some smart-ass remark that would get her a suspension or worse. He needed her help and more.

It was late afternoon before the crime scene was wrapped up. McGann peered out from his second story bedroom window, watching the tow truck pull the bloody police car down the hill. He saw the uniformed officers rip the last pieces of yellow tape off trees and lampposts as a dozen black-and-whites maneuvered around each other and a few parked cars as they attempted to leave the scene.

He could feel Patricia standing behind him.

"I'll call you later so you can say goodnight to the girls. You've got Mom's number for an emergency," she said calmly. He turned and wanted to say something, but didn't. She wasn't angry or crying. It was worse. She was resigned. She picked up her bags and told the twins to follow her. They started to move toward their daddy, and she scolded them. They quickly ran after her. He smiled at his little girls, but they were gone.

McGann sat on the bed and heard the Suburban start and drive away. He looked around the empty room and remembered how much he hated this house.

THREE

By late morning, the unofficial Police Administration Building hotline was operating at full speed. All the details about the officer's bloody homicide and the relationship between the victim and Deputy Chief McGann were the topic of conversation in every office on the sixth floor of police headquarters *aka* PAB or Parker Center at First and Los Angeles Street.

The power bureaus were on the sixth floor, as was the office of the chief of police. Every deputy chief had his or her adjutant call Robbery Homicide Division and demand a confidential briefing for his or her particular boss. The first secretary who heard the gory details was better than the Internet in sending a vivid description around the building.

The office of the chief of police was in the corner of the sixth floor—the corner pocket, the seat of power. Chief Samuel Martin held court daily from his spacious secure quarters. He had cameras in the hallway and two security officers and his driver, who sat in his outer office as his first line of defense. He was even less accessible than usual this morning, huddled behind closed doors with his chief of staff since he'd received the first frantic phone call from McGann.

The news media had revealed the victim's identification as an unnamed police officer, and the nature of her wounds, before Stevenson and his detectives could drive the fifteen minutes downtown and walk off the elevator to their office on the third floor of Parker Center.

The department's Press Relations office was on the sixth floor, and the lieutenant in charge was working feverishly—preparing a carefully worded news release that didn't tell anyone anything—when he heard three stations on his bank of television screens tell the world every little detail of the morning's events.

Lieutenant Paula Toscano, who was the adjutant for the chief of staff, Deputy Chief Jacob Bell, sat at her desk across the hall watching the television screens in Press Relations. She laughed as the press lieutenant swore and threw his useless briefing paper into the hallway. Every news station had to speculate about how the tragedy had occurred. They knew everything except who did it, and they wouldn't reveal the victim's name.

Paula stared at the in-box on her desk. It was full again. Her boss had been with the chief of police all morning. Work had come to an unfamiliar halt. She stood and walked to the window overlooking the sheriff's detention center. She wore her uniform today, as she did nearly every day, because she knew it looked good on her. She was thirty-eight years old but still slender in all the right places. Also, she was nearly six feet tall, and the Sam Browne didn't let the holster of her .45 caliber semi-automatic hit her knees like it did on some of the smaller women.

"What a joke," she said, hovering over the secretary's desk.

Rose, a serious middle-aged black woman, looked up at her without saying anything for a few seconds.

"You got a point, Paula?" Rose asked, going back to her computer.

"It's immoral to put that man in charge of this investigation. He should be a suspect. What's wrong with Martin?"

"Like I said, you got a point?" Rose asked, grinning.

Paula ran both hands through her short curly hair. "Please promote me and get me out of this loony bin," she said to no one in particular. Chief Martin would promote her to captain in the next couple of months when her name came up on the list. But two more months seemed like an eternity. For the sake of her sanity, she needed to have her own division and start doing some real work. She liked Bell, but being a gofer for a deputy chief for the last year had been the worst job she'd ever had. Adjutants organized other people's lives. They never really did anything worthwhile except try to keep their bosses on schedule and out of trouble.

She would love to be in charge of this investigation. That poor girl had been a police officer only three years. What a terrible way to die. She wondered how McGann had gotten his hands on some-one that young and in an out-of-the-way division like West L.A.

"You better get your mind back on all that work that's about to fall out of that box and kill somebody," Rose said, pointing at the in-box.

"If you'd stop filling it, the problem would be over. Besides, even if I do the work, who am I supposed to give it to?" The chief of staff's office was a paper mill. Hundreds of projects passed over her desk every morning. She suspected that the world would hardly notice if most of them never made it out the door again.

"Go down the hall and get that old man back in here," Rose said. "Don't he know we're too busy for him to be holding the chief's hand all morning?"

"That's kinda like spaghetti supporting linguini, isn't it?" The two women laughed as Paula peeked out into the hallway, looking for her boss. She and Rose were friends and had engaged in many discussions about the lack of backbone on the power floor.

A few minutes later, Bell did return to his office, but he walked directly to his desk without speaking to either of them. Paula shrugged at Rose and leaned across her paperwork to see into her boss's office. He was sitting at his desk with his back to her, staring out the window. Bell was one of the older deputy chiefs. He had more than thirty-nine years on LAPD. His silver hair, pale skin, and slight stoop made him appear older than his sixty-one years. She sat back and took the stack of papers out of her in-box. Before she could glance up, she heard the door to Bell's office close quietly.

The two women looked at each other. Bell was behaving strangely. He was usually friendly and outgoing. He had a hint of Texas drawl and enjoyed playing the wise old country boy. Most of the time, because of his tenure in the department, he did have some good insights. Paula liked him and knew that beneath the organizational behavior that LAPD encouraged, there was a good man.

Throughout the late morning and afternoon, there were several closed-door meetings. Paula watched a parade of commanders and deputy chiefs walk in front of her desk, ignoring her and Rose, and enter Bell's private office. She managed to finish her paperwork but doubted there would be any signing time with her boss that day. She put the folders together, sat back, and waited for him to tell her to go home. It was the unwritten rule for adjutants. You didn't leave before your boss, and you didn't put in for any overtime. If you did a good job, the rewards would be a higher ranking on the captain's promotional list, weekends off, and the opportunity to hear more dirty gossip than a Mafia wiretap.

She called the adjutant for the chief of police, but he revealed little information about what was happening in Bell's office. Chief Martin wasn't telling his adjutant anything, either. Then Paula called every bureau on the sixth floor, but none of the adjutants had any information.

McGann's bureau office was in the Wilshire area. Paula knew his adjutant, whom she referred to as the weasel. Even if he told her something, which he usually wouldn't, Paula knew that no one except McGann trusted the weasel enough to confide in him. She decided against the unpleasant experience of talking to him and resigned herself to the prospect that she wasn't going to get any firsthand information unless Bell told her something before he went home.

At 7 P.M. Bell's office door was still closed. Paula had lost count of the number of staff officers who had gone in and out. The sixth floor was usually empty by this hour, but several of the bureaus had the lights on and the doors open. They knew the chief of police was still in the building and didn't want to run the risk of being the only bureau chief who'd left before the old man.

Rose had gone home an hour ago, and Paula usually wouldn't answer the phone after hours unless it was Bell's private line. But when it rang, she guessed it was Turner, so she picked up. Without saying hello, he asked why she was still there. They had this conversation nearly every night. He got off work every day at exactly 4 P.M. They had been dating and living together for two years, and it wasn't easy to keep their relationship going when their schedules were completely different, but she enjoyed his humor and intelligence and had never been this comfortable with any other man.

"Better eat without me," she said. "I'm stuck here. He's still working."

"I'm still at work, too. I got the McGann thing." He waited, but when she didn't respond, he added, "There's a personnel complaint on McGann now that goes with the criminal investigation."

"You're working with RHD?"

"Looks like it," he said with a nervous laugh. "Lucky me."

"I'm jealous. I'd kill to be running that investigation."

"Great. You take it."

"McGann can't still be in charge, can he?" she asked.

"I guess the chief believes he didn't do it, and he's trying to salvage what's left of the guy's career. For the sake of my career, I wish they'd given this mess to somebody else."

Paula understood his reluctance. Mike Turner was finally on the lieutenant's list in a position where he could eventually be promoted. He had worked hard to overcome a rocky start to his career. It had taken him twenty years to get on the lieutenant's list, and he didn't need this mess to draw attention to himself. Everyone knew you couldn't win with this type of investigation. The subject of the complaint was a staff officer. If you nailed him, his friends in high places would make certain your career was dead. If you didn't find any misconduct, your reputation was trashed among the officers. Every blue suiter would figure you buried evidence because he was a staff officer. Turner told her what puzzled him was that Chief Martin hadn't even hinted at which way he wanted this investigation to go. The chief usually wasn't shy about giving his opinion on the outcome of a case.

The door to Bell's office opened. Paula saw her tired boss walk out and shake hands with the last commander he would speak with that day. Bell stood in front of Paula's desk, and she whispered a hurried goodbye to Turner and hung up. She asked Bell if he needed anything. He took the folders off her desk and told her to go home. He said he would leave notes if anything needed to be done and return the folders by morning.

Paula hoped he would sit down in Rose's chair with his feet on her desk, like he'd done on so many other nights, and tell her what was happening, but he tucked the folders under his arm and turned to go back to his office. Before he could close the door, Chief of Police Samuel Martin entered the office and sat on a corner of Paula's desk.

"Lieutenant Toscano, how are you, young lady?" Chief Martin asked.

She nervously mumbled something that even she didn't understand, and she stood up as Bell returned to her desk. Chief Martin hadn't visited the chief of staff's office the entire year Paula had been there. Martin was an imposing figure who nearly filled the doorway. He was over six feet tall and had jet-black hair and a full mustache. He was in his shirtsleeves and obviously in a good mood. With his neatly trimmed hair and thick mustache, he looked more college professor than chief of police.

Martin asked Bell if he'd met with all the staff officers, and Bell assured him that he'd personally talked to each of them. Paula looked from her boss to Chief Martin. She didn't know if she should leave or stay. Well, she thought, if they want privacy, they can always step into Bell's office and close the door. She wanted to know what was happening, so she sat down and acted like a piece of furniture—a quiet, very curious piece of furniture.

The two men gossiped about McGann's many indiscretions. They agreed he was talented and intelligent, but "he can't keep his pants zipped around a pretty woman," Chief Martin said.

"Patricia is gorgeous," Bell said. "Why risk losing her and the kids?"

"The guy's an idiot. Probably tanked his career," Chief Martin said with a smirk. He didn't like McGann and was obviously taking some pleasure in the man's predicament. Paula knew that several years ago, when McGann and Martin were still commanders, McGann had protested the deputy chief's examination. He wanted the test thrown out on a technicality, and it almost happened. Martin was number one on that list, McGann number fifteen. Martin took it personally that McGann would dare to interfere with his relentless march toward the corner pocket.

Bell had confided in Paula that Martin always wanted to be chief of police and had remade himself several times during his thirty-three-year career to fit the role of chief. Martin's mother was Mexican and his father Anglo. Ten years ago, Martin had officially become Mexican by checking that box on all his applications and department personnel records. He couldn't speak a word of Spanish but saw the long-range benefit of claiming his heritage, with the way things were going in Los Angeles.

He bought his MBA from the finest mail-order institution he could afford and married his plain-looking secretary so she could retype the papers he had cleverly plagiarized from other command officers who had graduated from respectable universities. Everyone knew; no one complained.

The perfect family man, he had two children—a boy and a girl. At community events, he spoke frequently about the responsibilities of being a husband and father. His son was an overweight city garage mechanic who refused to let him see his grandchildren, and his daughter was an alcoholic waitress who lived with her lesbian girlfriend when she wasn't in rehab.

None of that mattered. He was the chief of police for the best department in the world. He commanded respect.

Martin claimed that his real name was Martinez. He said it had been shortened to Martin by his grandfather, a travesty he intended to rectify some day. None of that was true, but he could do no wrong in the eyes of the large Hispanic population in Los Angeles and the president of the police commission. Five civilians appointed by the mayor comprised the commission. They had direct oversight of the police department, and their president was Sylvia Diaz, a wealthy Mexican woman who ran her deceased husband's cosmetic firm and one of the oldest restaurants in Southern California. She had never liked Sam Martin, but he was the only police chief of Mexican heritage in the department's history, and she was determined to make him successful.

"McGann says he'll do anything you want him to do," Bell said. Paula thought her boss looked tired and was trying to end the discussion.

"Damn straight he will. The horny moron still thinks he's got a shot at being chief when my term is done."

"Even McGann's got to figure that this morning wiped out any slim chance he might've had," Bell said.

"I understand people like him, Jake. Deep inside, that guy will never admit to himself it's over. I intend to dangle that hope in front of him, keep him in the fold, and support him unless it starts to crumble. Then it's his problem, and I'll ask him to resign or file charges on him if I have to." Chief Martin grinned at Paula. "Best-case scenario—if McGann's acquitted of misconduct or knowledge of a crime, he'll be forever indebted to me."

Bell closed his eyes for just a moment. Paula caught a flash of disgust on his face, but he was too smart to let Martin see it.

"So, Chief, every staff officer knows they're to refer any inquiry, any information, any source of information to me on your order. Anything else?" Bell asked quickly.

"No, keep me informed. Keep tabs on McGann, and don't let him say anything to the media or do anything stupid. We can pretend he's in charge, but everything gets done through you, Jake."

"What about IA? Will Connelly brief me as well?" Bell asked.

Chief Martin stood. "Absolutely. She's as shaky as the San Andreas Fault. She'll do what you say, but make certain she controls her people. Nice woman. Need a few more competent

31

females I can promote. This one should be home playing with her grandchildren."

Paula shifted in her seat and tried to look as if she were reading something.

"You'll make a great captain, Paula. Know why?" Martin asked, moving toward the hallway.

"I believe so, sir," she said, trying to sound convincing. She didn't have a clue what he was talking about.

"I'll tell you why. You know how to listen without having to say something."

When the chief said good night and disappeared down the hallway, Paula gathered some reading material she'd saved for that night and stuffed it into her briefcase. She locked her desk and walked to the door to Bell's office.

"Think I'll go home, boss, if you don't need me."

"Thanks for everything, Paula. See you in the morning."

She waved at the tired old man, who smiled at her, then quickly returned to his work. Paula had known Jacob Bell for many years and had never seen him this way. He looked like someone had beaten him. Sammy Martin, on the other hand, was nearly giddy.

FOUR

Paula took the elevator down to the first floor. It was only 8 P.M., and she wondered if Brenda was still working. She walked to the small office around the corner. It was reserved for the lieutenant in charge of the Commission Investigation Division, or CID. Brenda Todd was the senior female lieutenant on LAPD. She had made lieutenant from a special list years ago.

The list had been created to give policewomen who had never been allowed to be promoted a chance to catch up. To every male chauvinist's chagrin, Lieutenant Todd proved in a very short time that she was without a doubt the smartest, most qualified manager in the department. She ran CID better than the commander who had had it before her. As a matter of fact, she had been his adjutant at one time and had run the division for him. Everyone knew she was the brains behind his pretty face. When he had been promoted to deputy chief, the chief of police officially put her in charge of CID.

Paula had met Brenda three years before when she made lieutenant. Brenda had educated and trained her on the dos and don'ts of becoming an effective LAPD manager. Brenda not only had institutional knowledge, but more important, she had dirt on everybody, including Sam Martin. She was pretty with olive skin and jet-black hair. Like many of the older policewomen, she had dated several of the command staff. There were no secrets too confidential for after-sex pillow talk, especially after they had consumed two or three martinis. Brenda could drink like a thirty-year detective and remember everything in the morning. Unlike the newer female police officers, she didn't want to be one of the boys. However, she did want to control all of them, including the chief of police.

The office was empty, but Brenda's briefcase was there, and her desk was open. Paula stepped back into the hallway and went to the Police Commission hearing room. It should've been empty at this hour, but there was light coming from under the door. She suspected there might be an impromptu Mafia meeting in the commissioners' comfortable chairs. The Mafia was a group of female lieutenants and captains who helped each other survive in the male-heavy world of LAPD management. They had power but knew it had to be wielded judiciously.

The door was unlocked, so she walked in on Brenda and three other women leaning back in the commissioners' leather chairs with their feet propped up on the pricey mahogany table. They didn't move when the door opened.

"Breathe, ladies. It's just me," Paula said

In addition to Brenda, Captain Nancy Connelly; Lieutenant Sara McKnight, the chief's executive officer; and Elaine Miller, the inspector general for LAPD, were comparing notes and gossip from the day's events. Everyone acknowledged the late arrival, and Sara pointed to the coffeepot near the door.

"Unplanned event, Paula, or we would've sent out the invitations," Brenda said, sitting up and pulling out the chair next to hers.

Elaine raised her cup. "Here's to Chief Sammy," she said. "He's managed, as usual, to take a bad situation and make it worse." She was a diminutive attorney with a pixie haircut who had left a prestigious law firm to take the IG job. She was a star litigator who had accepted a position with LAPD because she wanted a challenge. After a year, she loved the work, hated the department. Mostly she hated Chief Martin, who didn't think the department needed an IG and did everything he could to frustrate her.

"I think you're being too hard on the man, Elaine," Sara McKnight laughed. "Wait till his press conference tomorrow. He can still make it worse."

Paula exchanged greetings with each of them but had a difficult time looking at Nancy.

"So what happened?" Paula asked. "Who killed her? Why isn't McGann suspended? You guys have had all day to figure this thing out."

"Steady, girl. We've got theories," Brenda said, tapping her on the head. "We've figured out that McGann is a male slut, a gorgeous hunk, but a slut. So has Patty. She left him this morning."

"He didn't kill that girl," Nancy said without looking up. "Even McGann isn't that stupid, to leave the body in front of his house for his wife and kids to see. It was some kind of message from the demented scum that killed her."

"But he did date her. He admitted that to Martin," Sara said.

"Now, that's what truly puzzles me," Brenda added quickly.

"Why? He hits on every dickless creature that breathes." Elaine leaned toward Brenda, waiting for an answer.

Brenda laughed. "True enough, Miss Miller. But Alexandra Williams was not dickless in spirit."

"You mean she was a guy?"

"Honestly, Sara, don't you have any sources in that office?" Brenda asked, shaking her head. "She wasn't a guy. She just wanted to be one. She was a dyke. Everybody at West L.A. knew she was a lesbian."

"Well, McGann thinks he had an affair with her," Paula said. Now she was getting confused. "Was he just imagining it?"

"She probably goes both ways or did at one time." Brenda slouched in her chair. She had dropped the best information bomb of the meeting and wanted to savor the moment.

"Do they know about her sexual preference at RHD?" Nancy seemed really interested for the first time.

"Odds are it was still a guy who killed her. That kind of murder is more a man's work," Elaine said. She was the only civilian in the room, but she spoke as if her brief tenure with the department had given her a career's worth of expertise. The others looked at each other, but no one said anything.

Paula thought about mentioning the strategy meeting she'd just overheard between Martin and her boss. She decided it would be prudent to keep that bit of information to herself. At the first opportunity, Nancy would tell Martin everything that was said at this meeting. Nancy wanted to be a commander, and she felt that being a pipeline for the chief would help her. Every woman in the room, including Paula, liked her but knew better than to say anything that they didn't want to go right back to Martin.

"So where's Suck-'em-Dry Sally tonight?" she asked instead.

Brenda spit her coffee on the expensive polished table. "Paula, you know how to change the subject with style," she said, wiping the coffee off her blouse.

"Sorry. I miss all the phony sincerity and the little-girl giddiness that usually comes about now."

"Well, she had to leave early. Her husband wanted her to go to a faculty social with him. She didn't have a date, so she went home to the professor," Brenda said, wiping the table with some paper towels she'd found in a drawer.

Sally Wolinski was a lieutenant adjutant in the Office of Operations. She had a reputation for sleeping her way up the department chain of command to every good job on the sixth floor. Her talent was represented in her nickname. She managed to get close to each boss in a special way until the next good job came along. Paula believed that Sally was smart enough to get the good jobs without the girlish gestures and promiscuity, but Sally hadn't realized that yet.

Paula was annoyed by Sally's giggling and nervous twirling and usually left early whenever she attended one of these get-togethers.

"Did Mike tell you he's handling the IA investigation on McGann?" Nancy asked, changing the subject. She was Sally's friend.

"No, really?" Paula lied, trying not to look at Brenda, who always knew when she was lying.

"Yes. He's been assigned to RHD. You probably won't be seeing much of him for a few months."

"Hey, Paula, you can keep us updated now," Brenda said, smiling at Nancy.

"What makes you think Mike would tell me anything about a personnel investigation? As a matter of fact, I'll guarantee you he won't tell me anything." Paula glared at Brenda. Nancy was paranoid enough without thinking Mike was a conduit from her division to the rest of the world.

Brenda stood up. "Well, folks, I'm beat. Going home now." She grabbed Paula's arm and dragged her out of the chair. "Walk me to my office, Paula." Brenda was half a foot shorter and twenty pounds lighter, but she manhandled the bigger woman, pushing her toward the door. Everyone got up and slowly moved toward the hallway as they exchanged comments before leaving. Paula and Brenda walked down the corridor alone in the direction of Brenda's office.

"Thanks, Brenda. Nancy Connelly would love another excuse to dump on Mike," said Paula, still upset. There were too many nights he'd come home frustrated because Connelly complained he was too aggressive and not a team player.

"Sorry. She's so much fun to screw with that I can't help myself. She knows I was kidding. Relax. I'll tell her I was kidding. So you'll tell me everything Mike tells you, right?"

"What do you think?"

"I knew it," Brenda said. She was quiet for a few seconds before adding, "Elaine shouldn't have said those things about Martin in front of Connelly. You know she'll report every word to the chief in the morning."

"I'd bet that's why Elaine said it. She's trying to get Martin to do something really stupid, and I'm sure he'll oblige. Hopefully this McGann thing will preoccupy him, and he'll ignore her. We need Elaine, but I'm afraid she's on his hit list."

"Just keep your head down. There's something very peculiar about this Alexandra Williams thing. Everybody knows more than they're saying or willing to admit, including Nancy. Tell Mike to watch himself. If I know Martin, he's lining up his scapegoats, and the getaway route has already been planned."

Paula decided to tell Brenda about the conversation between Bell and Martin and what they'd planned for McGann. The older woman didn't seem surprised. Paula left her in front of her office and walked around to the stairs and down to the basement. In the deserted locker room, she quickly changed from her uniform to jeans. She left through the back door of Parker Center and crossed the street to the steel parking structure.

She felt a chill hearing her footsteps echo on the metal stairs as she climbed to the third level where her car was parked. Dead police officer, incompetence, indiscriminate sex, and major backstabbing—what kind of damn organization was this? She longed for the simplicity and hard work of patrol. On the street in a black-and-white, you at least knew who the bad guys were.

FIVE

Turner and Montgomery were huddled in quiet conversation in a corner of the RHD squad room when Stevenson threw his jacket on the table between them. They stopped talking and looked up at him.

"Monty, brief me. It's late. I'm tired of this shit. I'm out of coffee, and I need sleep and sex."

"That stuff you do by yourself, boss, is not considered sex," Montgomery said.

"Tell me your name again," Stevenson said to Turner.

"Mike Turner, your designated IA spy," Turner said, shaking the older man's hand.

"You the same Mickey Turner who rode with Tim Andrews the night he was killed?" Turner nodded. "You did a hell of a job that night, son. You can spy on me any time."

"Thanks. Too bad the use-of-force board didn't agree with you."

"Fuck 'em. You killed the asshole that got Timmy. That's what matters. How'd you ever get into Internal Affairs?"

"Twenty years and fading memories."

"From what I heard, there was a lot more to fade than just that one shooting. You were something of a legend when you worked prison gangs."

"I've mellowed."

"So you want an update, boss?" Montgomery could see that Turner was uncomfortable. He'd heard the rumors about the wild Mickey Turner but didn't care as long as Turner could help him solve this murder.

"Roger that," Stevenson said, sitting on the table.

"Katy started interviewing West LA personnel and should finish up in a couple of days. The Hollywood detectives are going door to door again in McGann's neighborhood, and they're taking a forensics geek to look at the crime scene again. Mike and I will do the post tomorrow morning and then hit Williams' pad with a warrant. We don't know if she was living with anyone, so I got a uniform watching it."

"Any leads from the car?"

"We should have word on prints tomorrow," Montgomery said, exchanging a quick look with Turner. "We want to interview McGann tomorrow night."

"Good start. I'll handle the press conference and the chief's briefing," Stevenson said, adding, "Don't do the McGann interview without me. You copy that?"

"Loud and clear, Captain."

"When we get back from the post, I'll pull Williams' personnel file. There may be something in her background," Turner said.

Stevenson nodded and slowly slid his large body off the table. "Good job," he said. "I'm outta here. Call me if you need anything." He grinned. "Preferably, as usual, just when I start to fall asleep." He grabbed his jacket and left.

Montgomery waited a few minutes. "Sorry about the inquisition. The captain's a great guy but not what you'd call the sensitive type."

"Look, Monty, the stuff he's talking about happened a long time ago, but if you're uncomfortable with me, I'll talk to Connelly and find you somebody else."

"If I were a nicer guy, I'd probably take you up on that offer and get you out of this loser case, but I'm not that nice, and I need all the help I can get. You're a good cop. I need some street sense here."

Turner smiled, but he was disappointed. He'd hoped for a moment that he was done with this business. He'd given Montgomery an opportunity to dump him and send him back to his monotonous, comfortable life at Internal Affairs. Obviously, that wasn't going to happen.

The two men agreed to meet at six in the morning to drive together to the coroner's office for a 7 A.M. autopsy. Both of them had seen a lot of dead bodies, but this was different. This was a cop—a young, pretty cop. What should be routine would be an ordeal.

Turner took the Dash from Parker Center to Union Station. He'd catch the last bus out to West Hollywood, where he and Paula shared an apartment off Melrose. With his regular IA hours, he'd been able to take the bus every day. When he got home, he'd take the tarp off his Chevy truck. He hated that drive downtown, but the bus wouldn't work for a case like this.

Tonight the bus was nearly empty except for him and a tiny Mexican woman who was staring at him from the rear bench seat. She knew he was a cop. Illegals can always tell, but she wasn't worried. LA cops aren't allowed to mess with illegals. Terrorists, factory workers—they all get a free pass in the city of the angels.

Turner could remember a time when an investigation like this one would excite him and keep him awake at night thinking about ways to catch the bad guy. Now he envied the little woman at the back of the bus, unfazed by her circumstances. All he felt about this case was annoyance. He couldn't admit that to Paula, or she'd know what he knew. The fire was gone. He had held his dying partner in his arms over twenty years ago and had done plenty of questionable things after that, none of which he regretted, but he was through with all of it and just wanted to be promoted and be a lieutenant for a year and then retire with a good pension. As he stepped off the bus, he had an eerie feeling that his perfect, well-planned future was slipping away.

When he got to the apartment, Paula had her briefcase open and was editing projects at the kitchen table. She had a glass of red wine in one hand and half a peanut butter sandwich in the other. Her short curly hair was wet, and she wore an old terry-cloth bathrobe that should've been thrown away years before. It was a gift from him, and he knew she'd never part with it.

"Very nutritious, Toscano. Where's the ice cream?" he asked, throwing his briefcase on one of the chairs.

"Had that hours ago. You okay?" She kissed him as he leaned over the table, and he tasted the weird combination of cabernet and peanut butter.

"Of course. Any wine left?"

She pointed to a half-empty bottle on the counter. He poured himself a full glass and emptied the rest into her glass. He sat across from her at the table and quietly sipped his wine while she finished working.

"So tell me what's going on," she said, throwing the last of the papers into her briefcase.

Turner recounted everything that had occurred on the third floor that day and told her what they intended to do the next day.

She told him about the conversation between Bell and Chief Martin and passed along the information Brenda had given her on the victim's sexual preference.

"Somebody's doing a number on McGann," he said when she'd finished. He emptied his glass and sat back. "Monty thinks McGann is involved, but it doesn't work for me for a lot of reasons." He shook his head. "I've been away from real police work so long I'm cold. Nothing's clicking the way it used to."

"You've only had this case an afternoon. Give yourself a break, lover. If you don't solve it by tomorrow, then worry."

He smiled. It was his opportunity to tell her he didn't want the investigation. He wanted to give it back and keep his old life. She was feeding off this new assignment, and he couldn't bring himself to disappoint her.

"Did you know her?" he asked instead.

"Who?"

"Alexandra Williams, the victim—did you know her?"

"Don't think so. I understand she was beautiful but maybe a touch unstable. Kind of like your roommate." He ignored the comment, so she continued. "She was only on the job a couple of years. I can't even figure out how McGann met her, let alone dated and bedded her."

"We'll interview him tomorrow night. Maybe he can enlighten us."

"You gonna be all right with this thing?" she asked, touching his face. "You're looking a bit worn around the edges tonight. If it's too much, tell Connelly to give it to one of those hyperactive baby sergeants."

There it was. She'd given him the opening to graciously bow out of this mess. He wanted to dump it so badly he could taste it. But he could see in her eyes that if he were to admit this weakness, take her offer, she'd surely think less of him. A real cop would never turn down an opportunity to find a cop killer. Paula wanted a real cop, but he didn't think she understood how this investigation might impact their lives. Maybe somewhere deep inside, he was the one who wanted this. It didn't matter. He couldn't see a way out of it without possibly losing her and maybe another little piece of himself.

SIX

The autopsy on Alexandra Williams was finished by late morning. As Montgomery and Turner left the table and finished their small talk with the coroner, they looked at each other without speaking. They tore off the protective masks, head covers, and shoe covers and tossed them with their lab coats into the disposal basket. AIDS protocol had done everything but put them outside the room during an autopsy.

It had been easier than Turner thought it would be to make it through his morning. These paid county butchers couldn't do anything worse to Alexandra Williams than had been done by her killer. Her bruised and battered body had been assaulted first with a knife, superficially cutting her hands, feet, and torso. She had fought off her killer in what must have been a valiant, if bloody, losing battle. She had been stabbed five times and died from a knife wound to the heart. According to the coroner, her throat had been cut with some unknown tearing instrument after she was dead.

"Well, she wasn't raped, so my guess is somebody just hated her a lot," Montgomery said as he and Turner sat in their police car outside the morgue.

"Great. I knew working with you RHD guys would be enlightening," Turner said. He hesitated but had to ask, even if Montgomery thought he was a wimp. "Was it just me, or did those two assistants in there make your skin crawl?"

"You mean more than it usually crawls in the morgue? No, not really. Why?"

"Jesus, two dwarfs in hooded lab coats, hacking away with rib cutters, standing on those stools to reach the table, never saying a word and then leaving like little programmed robots with blood splattered all over them. It was like a bad horror movie. That didn't look weird to you?"

"Maybe from an IA perspective," Montgomery said. "But just another routine day in RHD homicide."

"I'm gonna have nightmares about those midgets. I know it." Turner opened the car window and took a long breath of cool air.

"So what do you want to do, have lunch or go right to Alexandra's apartment?" Montgomery asked, smiling.

Turner's stomach turned at the thought of food. He knew what Montgomery was doing but hoped he never got accustomed to that level of gore. They agreed that lunch wasn't an immediate necessity. Both of them were anxious to search Alexandra's apartment.

Montgomery contacted the Hollywood detectives and directed them to meet him at the victim's apartment with the signed search warrant they had obtained earlier that morning.

Arriving a few minutes before them, Turner had an opportunity to look around the property. Alexandra lived in a bungalow at the rear of a larger house in West L.A. She rented from two elderly sisters who lived in the front house. Turner tried to interview the sisters, who would talk to him only through the screen door. They didn't know their tenant was dead. They never left the house and didn't see or hear anything, ever. Their biggest concern as they stood arm in arm in the doorway was who would clean out the bungalow so they could rent it again. They wore matching housedresses with pastel blue flowers smelling of mothballs and drugstore gardenia perfume. Their hair was styled the same—two white permed helmets. They finished each other's sentences and pretended that Montgomery wasn't standing beside Turner. A black man in a business suit had nothing to do with them.

After several minutes of coaxing, they revealed to Turner that they had a handyman, Phil White, who ran errands and worked on the expansive grounds nearly every day. The ladies thought Phil might know more about their former tenant, and if the police allowed him to, he could eliminate every trace of the dead girl from their bungalow. Turner flirted with them and eventually convinced them it was safe to open the screen door. After charming his way into their house, he made a mental note that Alexandra's bungalow was totally out of view from inside the sisters' place. While Turner was inside, Montgomery slipped away and walked back to the police car. He knew as well as Turner that these little old white ladies from West L.A. wouldn't be nearly as friendly and candid with a tall skinny black man as they were with the handsome middle-aged white guy.

The Hollywood detectives dropped off the search warrant while Turner was in the sisters' house. Montgomery waited by the car reading the warrant until Turner had finished with the sisters. Turner had managed to share a cup of coffee and a stale piece of leftover birthday cake, but the sisters had no real information about Alexandra. They did give him a copy of the rental agreement. They were certain they had never seen anyone, including Alexandra, come to or leave the bungalow. They hadn't heard anything unusual the night of the killing. The property was so large and the foliage so thick that they wouldn't know if someone walked or drove to the bungalow, which had its own entrance at a secluded side gate.

The sisters gave Turner a key to it and its attached garage and made him promise he would come back whenever possible. He assured them he would visit again, and they hugged him before he could clear the doorway. As he walked down the porch steps toward the driveway, Montgomery grinned at him.

"Don't you just love this kinder, gentler police stuff?" Montgomery said.

"You interested in serving this warrant?" Turner asked, snatching the paper from Montgomery's hands. "Or did some detective stay up all night writing this thing and wake up one pissed-off really-ugly-in-the-morning judge for nothing?"

"No, I'm just standing out here because I got nothing better to do."

"I'm interviewing critical witnesses, and you're acting like I was in there having a good time drinking coffee and eating birthday cake," Turner said as he brushed crumbs off the front of his shirt.

"What did your girlfriends tell you?" Montgomery took the bungalow key from Turner's hand.

"Nothing. They're totally out of touch, sweet but vacant. There's a handyman, a guy named White, that we need to interview. According to the old ladies, he's here almost every day."

Montgomery nodded and led the way around the house toward the bungalow. The path was narrow, and they walked single file, with Turner a step behind him. As they approached the wood-slatted cottage, Turner noticed that the front door was ajar. He tapped Montgomery on the shoulder and gestured that he would go around back. Montgomery nodded and positioned himself near the front door.

Turner drew his Smith and Wesson semi-auto as he crouched under a kitchen window. Using the corner of the house for cover, he pointed his gun at the back door and got that rush of adrenaline he always felt when confronting the unknown. After a few seconds, he heard Montgomery kick the front door and yell, "Police." Montgomery was shouting as he cleared rooms and finally, in a loud voice, told Turner that he was opening the back door and not to shoot. Turner stepped onto the back porch and entered the kitchen. The living room was empty, and Montgomery started searching one of the bedrooms. No one else was inside the small house.

While he'd waited outside the back door, Turner had seen a fresh mound of dirt near the edge of the porch. Once the house was secured, he went back and took a closer look. He called Montgomery outside to see it.

"Let's get SID out here and dig it up," Montgomery said. "The house looks clean. We'll each take a room. Look for anything with a name or number." He rubbed the back of his neck. "Shit, just look for anything."

Turner started in the kitchen. After a few minutes, Montgomery walked from the bedroom he was searching across the hall to the other bedroom and then back to the first room. He called Turner to come into the second bedroom, where he pointed to the closet.

"There are two women living here," he said. "The one in this room has really, really bad taste, or my guess is she's a working girl. The other room was Alexandra's. There's uniforms and some nice-looking, expensive clothes in there."

He pulled two skimpy dresses from the messy closet. Turner wasn't a clothes guy, but even he knew that most women wouldn't wear a see-through dress. There weren't many clothes in the room, but they were the stuff he'd seen worn by those cash-'n-carry women strolling on Sunset Blvd. Most of the clothes hadn't been laundered for a while, if ever. The room was cluttered like a crash pad. The other bedroom was clean, everything in its place.

"Look at this," Montgomery said, pointing to a mirror on the dresser. There was a white powder residue on the glass. A rolled-up dollar bill with traces of the white powder was behind the mirror. Turner knew it had been used to snort cocaine. It was paraphernalia every working cop had seen many times.

"Our Alexandra led quite an interesting life," Turner said as he started to put the mirror and dollar into a plastic evidence envelope.

Montgomery took the bag and emptied everything back on the dresser. "Let's wait until SID gets here. We'll have them photo and print this room first."

They finished the search quickly in the sparsely furnished bungalow. The garage was empty.

"What's the matter?" Montgomery asked Turner, who was standing in the living room shaking his head.

"It's too clean. Where are the calendars or date books, magazines, personal pictures, scraps of paper, phone messages—anything with another person's name or number?"

Alexandra's uniforms and gear were in the closet with a few civilian clothes, but nothing else made this place her home. Turner wondered if someone had been here before them.

A team from SID arrived within an hour and took pictures and lifted prints quickly. Several good prints were found in the room with the cocaine residue.

Turner volunteered to dig up the mound of dirt behind the porch while the technicians watched. He'd taken only the first shovelful of dirt when he hit a solid object. He put on a pair of latex gloves and lifted a kitchen knife with a six-inch blade from the shallow hole. Turner opened a large paper bag and slid the knife inside. He continued to dig but didn't find anything else. The area around the mound was covered with leaves and debris. There were no footprints or other tools nearby, no clues that might help them find their killer.

Turner compared the knife with those found inside the kitchen. It didn't match. He opened the bag and studied the dirty flat blade.

"My guess is he used the knife to dig up the ground," Turner said.

Montgomery nodded. "I was thinking the same thing. There's not a drop of blood anywhere. We'll have the lab guys go through it and see if it's been cleaned, but I don't think she died here. Why bury the knife here? It's like someone wanted us to find it."

"Maybe it's not the murder weapon," Turner said.

"No sense guessing. The lab should be able to tell us by tomorrow," Montgomery said, placing the paper bag in a large manila evidence envelope. He left the bag open to prevent mold. "We need to talk to this handyman. Did the old ladies give you an address?"

"Nope. They don't know. He just shows up every day, and they pay him in cash at the end of the week."

"I'm going to ask the Hollywood detectives to come back here and interview this guy when he comes to work. We need to talk to him."

Turner waited with Montgomery until the SID technicians had finished their work and then locked the bungalow. He waved at the two elderly sisters, who stood arm-in-arm in the doorway of their house as he got into the police car. They waved back and giggled as if they were doing something naughty.

Turner and Montgomery didn't talk on the drive back to Parker Center. There was plenty to discuss, but Turner was trying to make some sense of what they'd just seen at the victim's house, and he figured Monty was doing the same. Before they'd reached the PAB parking lot, Montgomery got a call from one of the Hollywood detectives telling him Phil White had arrived, and he had agreed to come to Parker Center for an interview.

From the parking structure, it was a quick walk to the basement of Parker Center, where they could take the elevator back to RHD. Turner volunteered to carry the evidence to the lab and personally oversee the print identification from lifts found in the bungalow's second bedroom. Alexandra's roommate was definitely someone of interest. The elevator door opened on the first floor, and Deputy Chief Jacob Bell stepped into the car between Turner and Montgomery.

"Monty, Mike," Bell said, nodding at each of them. "Missed you at the briefing this morning."

"Sorry," Montgomery said, then added quickly, "autopsy and search warrant. Carl—Captain Stevenson—was there, right?"

Bell grinned. "Right."

"How did the press conference go?" Turner thought it was best to change the subject before Bell told them to attend the next briefing.

"It's scheduled for 1600 hours. The old man wants to go live on some of the channels before the five o'clock news for maximum

47

coverage." He stopped and swallowed as if he had a bad taste in his mouth. "He'll be on at four, five, and six o'clock, not to mention the replays at eleven." By that time Bell was mumbling to himself.

Turner and Montgomery looked at each other and slid off the elevator when the door opened on the third floor. They escaped with a quick chorus of "Talk to you later, Chief" as the door closed again.

Jacob Bell had attended the briefing that morning with Chief of Police Martin, Deputy Chief McGann, and nearly every deputy chief and commander in the department. Stevenson, as the commanding officer of RHD, talked about the investigation. Captain Connelly's civilian boss was there. He answered some procedural questions but wouldn't reveal any information on the confidential personnel investigation.

After several hours of discussion and suggestions ranging from silly to ridiculous, Martin told them what they were going to do. Bell had allowed Paula to attend and take notes. The other deputy chiefs and commanders brought their adjutants for ostensibly the same reason, but Paula knew they were there like she was—to get the sordid details.

Stevenson gave a concise overview of the investigation, which was understandably limited at that point. Several of the staff officers asked questions.

After a few minutes, Paula stopped writing and just watched and listened to the discussion. She was mesmerized, the way one might be by those daytime television talk shows where a mother starts admitting she had sex with her thirteen-year-old daughter's boyfriend.

When there were no more questions and the staff had exhausted the "what if" scenarios, Stevenson thanked them for their input and sat down in the back of the conference room near Paula.

"Shitheads," he mumbled just loud enough for her to hear.

The voices droned on in the background, and Paula's mind wandered. She looked at the charcoal sketches of the former chiefs of police hanging on the walls around the conference room. Sammy Martin's portrait, prominently displayed at the front behind the podium, with his wide smile and arrogant eyes, was of course bigger than the others.

The public relations plan would be simple. Feed the public garbage. Don't tell them anything significant. If the media could actually prove something damaging, deny it. The press release would be straightforward, omitting such key facts as that she had been found in a police car parked in front of McGann's house, practically hacked to death, and that her lifestyle was somewhat suspect, including sex with that same married deputy chief.

Martin would go on television later in the day and say it was a tragedy. He would describe her as a fine young officer and vow to catch her vicious killers and bring them to justice. No mention would be made of McGann's involvement. He and his family had moved out of the house in Hollywood, and his connection to the crime scene shouldn't be that obvious.

During that part of the briefing, Paula, like everyone else in the room, glanced at McGann, whose expression didn't change. He sat staring at Chief Martin with a sick little smirk that struggled to convey a look stuck somewhere between confidence and embarrassment.

Paula knew before the ink was dry on the press release that one of these department leaders would be on his cellular phone to his contact at the *L.A. Times*. Chief Martin had to know it, too. It was common knowledge that before he became chief of police, Martin had a direct line to that newspaper's most notorious muckraker, who routinely broke embarrassing stories about LAPD and the former chief of police. Martin had eliminated his competition and piled up plenty of IOUs with several well-timed calls to Mr. Blue in the city pressroom at First and Spring Street.

Toward the end of the meeting, a girlish giggle made every man in the room turn his head in the direction of the back doorway. Paula groaned. It was Lieutenant Wolinski. The attractive, slender woman, who was wearing a powder-blue suit with a skirt that was slightly too short for office wear, sporting expensive jewelry and sitting with her long legs crossed, blushed when she realized she'd stopped the meeting. It was Wolinski, so everyone looked at her, acknowledged her presence as she had hoped, and then continued what they were doing.

Paula, however, sank in her chair. The woman had no sense, she thought as she avoided looking at her. She did happen to glance in the direction of McGann and was surprised to see him still staring at Wolinski. Several times during the remainder of the meeting, she caught him watching her. On the other hand, Wolinski seemed determined to avoid any eye contact with McGann.

Now there's the odd couple, Paula thought. She made a note to herself to ask Brenda what was going on with that unlikely duo. Two totally self-absorbed users wouldn't seem like a good fit.

Once Chief Martin took over the meeting, the discussion was over. Martin told staff officers to attend the news conference that afternoon and was gone.

Paula always liked to linger a while and pretend to straighten out her notes when these staff meetings ended. She watched and waited for the sub-meetings to begin. There was a ritual dance as deputy chiefs and commanders shuffled their way around the floor. Rumors were spread, information disseminated, and unofficial deals brokered in every corner of the room. Paula knew what some staff and command officers never learned. This was the real source of power on LAPD. Rank was immaterial. The important question was how well you could work the room.

She keyed on Wolinski, who fluttered from one deputy chief to another, giggling and complimenting. McGann stood nearby, moving a few feet from her every time she changed locations. He hovered as if waiting for her to acknowledge him. She didn't. Finally, having no apparent excuse to remain any longer, he left, visibly unhappy. Paula saw Wolinski glance up for only a moment, as if to be certain he was gone, and then she resumed her conversation.

Paula followed the little drama as it played out. She wasn't too engrossed to notice that a few feet from her, Stevenson was another intent spectator.

SEVEN

Phil White, the West L.A. handyman, was twenty years old and nearly six feet tall, with a muscular physique. He claimed to have a genius IQ, but after a few questions, Turner decided that the young man's Ferrari brain was trapped in a Hyundai head. The circuits couldn't translate into making him productive or successful at anything more complicated or stressful than trimming trees or doing other mundane tasks.

The sisters said they liked him because he never wanted to talk to them. They left notes taped to the front door, and he'd do the work. He took his paycheck out of the mailbox on Friday afternoons and never argued about the amount of money or the work.

White walked silently between the two Hollywood detectives as they took him through the public area of RHD and down a narrow hallway. He was told to wait in the first interview room, which was about the size of a large closet. He obeyed without speaking and sat on a chair in the corner. The young man was trembling, looking in every direction as if someone were about to attack him.

"This guy isn't going to give us much," Montgomery said. "He's a wreck—not guilty nervous, scared nervous. Does he have a record?"

"Not exactly a record, but he's been printed and institutionalized twice, once voluntarily, post-graduation UCLA. The second time, his father did it when he found him butt naked in the front yard frolicking with the family dog," Turner said, then stopped Montgomery as he was about to speak. "The detectives got the information from a reliable source. First thing this guy did was give them his father's phone number. Phil White, Sr. said his namesake is brilliant but unstable, not violent."

"Is Daddy coming down?" Montgomery asked, grimacing.

"Nope," Turner said, and when Montgomery smiled, he added quickly, "He's sending his lawyer. Dad doesn't want to see Junior."

Montgomery rubbed the back of his neck. "Have you talked to him?" he asked.

"No, but I seem to have good rapport with the mentally unstable. Want me to ask the questions?"

Montgomery said he wanted an ID on the prints from Alexandra's house first. He wanted to ask the handyman about the mysterious houseguest, but not before he had a name and as much information as he could find. Stevenson joined them and said there were no hits on the prints yet, but he was expecting a phone call any minute.

Montgomery and Turner briefed Stevenson on the morning's events and heard Stevenson's version of the chief's meeting. Turner agreed that McGann's behavior with Lieutenant Wolinski was interesting but not out of character for the ladies' man. After all, McGann had been away from his wife and kids for two days, plenty of time to rekindle old romances.

"He's a predator, boss. It's what he does, and Sally Wolinski is Sally Wolinski."

"Why's she acting like he's got the plague?" Stevenson asked.

"He's not socially acceptable now. He can't do anything good for her career would be my guess."

Stevenson shook his head. "No, it was something else. He looked unsettled, like he had to tell her something. It wasn't lechery; it was desperation."

Stevenson's secretary interrupted them and handed Turner a booking photo and rap sheet. They had identified Alexandra's roommate.

"Catherine Moody, aka Cheri Monroe, Crystal Monroe, and Cathy Arnold," Turner read from the rap sheet. "Your basic street whore and dope addict. Been in and out of jail since she was fourteen."

"Local talent?" Montgomery asked, taking the rap sheet.

"Almost all of her arrests were in Hollywood, except one hype bust in West L.A.," Turner said, smiling. "Arresting officer?"

"Alexandra Williams," Stevenson and Montgomery said together.

"When?" Stevenson asked.

"Last year, and the arrest report says another female working the hype unit, Maria Perez, was her partner."

"Have Katy track down Perez," Stevenson said.

The intercom on his phone buzzed, and his adjutant told Stevenson that Phil White's attorney was waiting and anxious to speak to his client. Turner volunteered to break the ice with the lawyer. If White was going to talk, they needed this attorney to be on their side.

Terry Chernack, attorney at law, looked very young and inexperienced. He was well dressed in a finely tailored suit and carried a stylish leather briefcase that had none of the scuffs and battle scars usually found on one belonging to a hard-working litigator. Turner guessed they could manipulate this guy to get a statement from White. He doubted that Phil White was involved in Alexandra's murder, but he was certainly in a position to have seen and heard a lot. Turner shook hands with Chernack and assured him that his client was considered a witness, not a suspect. The lawyer seemed relieved but kept glancing over his shoulder as if he were expecting someone or something to jump out and grab him.

Turner took Chernack to the small interview room where Phil White sat quietly staring at the wall and ushered him in. Stevenson and Montgomery slipped into an adjoining room where they could watch through a two-way mirror.

Turner was a good interrogator. He put Chernack at ease with a few easy background questions. Turner watched White, who ignored his attorney but stared at Turner, smiling every time he asked a question. Turner spoke to him in a soft, almost fatherly tone. The young lawyer stiffened a little when Turner asked White if he knew it was wrong not to tell the police the truth. White smiled and nodded, and Turner gently led him through a series of questions about what he did on the sisters' property. How often did he go there? How did he get paid?

White seemed to enjoy talking about himself, and Turner massaged each question to keep it personal and nonthreatening. Chernack was quiet. Turner worked like a seasoned car salesman. Don't push. Don't overwhelm. Don't make the mark or his lawyer uncomfortable or anxious.

White told him he was on the property every day until five o'clock. He had seen Williams on several occasions. She was nice to him. He saw people go into her bungalow, men and women, mostly women. Turner showed him the picture of Catherine Moody, covering the booking numbers with his thumb. He had seen Catherine or Crystal, as he knew her, at the bungalow. He thought she lived there, too. She was nice to him.

He knew that Alexandra Williams was a police officer because he'd seen her carry her uniform and gun belt once or twice when she left for work. He'd never seen other uniformed police officers there, but he had seen men with guns. He described what might've been plainclothes or off-duty officers. Would he know them if he saw them again? Yes, he would. At that point, White started to shift uneasily in his chair.

Turner guessed Stevenson and Montgomery were standing close to the glass. Phil White and his lawyer were facing them.

Back off. You're losing him, Turner told himself.

"Do you like the two sisters?" he asked, and White settled into his chair.

Nice, Turner thought. It was easy to get the young man back on track.

White admitted he liked the sisters a lot. They were nice to him too and sometimes paid him when he had nothing to do. Who did he like best of all of them? He thought he liked Crystal. She was sexy and dressed nice. Turner remembered the see-through dress in the closet and thought maybe White wasn't as simple as he seemed. Did he ever see anyone hurt Crystal? No. Did he ever see anyone hurt Alexandra? The young man clenched his fists and then leaned forward, as if he had a stomachache, before answering.

"Another lady hit her," he finally said.

Turner carefully maneuvered him through the scenario, in which a woman had come to the bungalow about two weeks before while Crystal was gone. She got into an argument with Alexandra. The two women yelled at each other, and the taller woman hit Alexandra's face several times with her open hand. She went away and left Alexandra crying outside the front door. White claimed he couldn't understand what they were saying because he was working near the main house and trying to stay out of sight so the women wouldn't think he was spying on them.

White volunteered the information that he didn't see or hear anything on the night Alexandra and Crystal disappeared. He hadn't seen the roommates for several days. From the way the young man was talking, Turner realized White either didn't know or was pretending not to know that Alexandra was dead. He decided not to mention the murder.

"Tell me more about Crystal," Turner said.

54

White said he thought Crystal slept most of the day. She would yell at him if he tried to mow the lawn before late afternoon. When Alexandra came back from work, they would go out together at night sometimes.

"How do you know that, Phil?" he asked.

He explained how he stayed late one night to help the sisters and saw Crystal and Alexandra leave together. They were dressed in short sexy dresses. He shifted in his chair and took a quick look at Chernack.

"Did you ever hurt Alexandra?" Turner softened his voice a little.

White stared dumbly at him. Why would he do that? he asked. Chernack started to object, but Turner quickly changed the subject. Had White seen the mound of dirt by the back door of Alexandra's bungalow?

"Yes," he said. "I made it."

Turner was surprised by the response and the lack of interference by Chernack. He sat back and asked White to explain. He said he found a knife in the middle of some thick shrubbery behind the bungalow. He was afraid of knives, so he buried it.

"Were you wearing gloves?" Turner asked.

"I always wear my work gloves."

Chernack stood and leaned against the wall. "Maybe we should stop here, sergeant," he said. He was hesitant, as if he didn't want to be confrontational. "Could we go outside a minute before my client continues?"

"I only have one or two more questions," Turner said. "It might be best to just finish."

"I don't think so," Chernack said, a little more forcefully.

"Then let's take a break," he said, not trying to hide his sarcasm. "You need anything, Phil?" he asked, touching the younger man's shoulder.

"You got a bathroom?"

Turner called for one of the detectives to take White to the men's room.

When his client was out of sight, Chernack turned to Turner. "I'm sorry, but you seem to be heading in a direction that suggests some culpability on my client's part."

Turner stared at the mirror, but he knew Montgomery and Stevenson wouldn't intercede now. It was his play.

"Mr. Chernack."

"Terry," he said.

"Terry, I don't know what Phil's involvement was. I don't believe he's capable of killing anyone, or I would've Mirandized him. But he may have seen things that'll help us put the pieces together. I won't try to hold him, but I've got to talk to him, have him available to me."

The lawyer seemed to know that he was in over his head. He asked to continue the interview the next day. He said his client wouldn't invoke his rights, but he needed time to confer with a criminal attorney. Turner tried to persuade him to stay and allow White to answer a few harmless questions, but the young lawyer stood his ground.

"I have enough to book him for tampering with evidence," Turner said, challenging him.

Chernack's smile faded. Even through the glass, Turner could imagine Montgomery's jaw tightening, and he knew immediately that although the guy might be inexperienced in criminal law, he wasn't a pushover. Turner looked at the two-way mirror and mouthed the words, "Show's over." He winked and waited until Montgomery and Stevenson walked around to the interview room.

"Mr. Chernack," Montgomery said, shaking his hand, "thank you for your cooperation. We'll be in touch with you tomorrow."

Chernack looked confused for a second until he realized that the mirror must've been used to spy on them. He stopped White before he entered the interview room again and pushed him toward the front desk.

"Come on, Phil. You're going home."

White tried to say goodbye, but the attorney pulled him away, warning his client not to say anything else.

For a few minutes, Turner, Montgomery, and Stevenson waited quietly in the cramped interview room until they were certain Chernack was out of hearing distance.

"Sorry, Monty, I guessed I pushed too hard," Turner said, looking to Stevenson, who nodded in agreement.

"The second you told Chernack we could arrest that kid, his attorney instincts kicked in, but don't sweat it," Montgomery said. "You did a great job. We got more than we had this morning." He ran his hand over his shaved head. "Besides, even if we could do it, I don't want him in custody yet."

"You thinking he's a suspect?" Turner asked. White didn't seem capable of remembering to tie his shoelaces. From what Turner had seen, committing such a terrible crime was way out of White's league.

"No, but I think he knows more than he's telling."

"We need to get his gloves," Turner said, thinking out loud. "We've got a home address now. Maybe we can stop by tomorrow and ask for them."

"He's got a lawyer. Let's do it right," Montgomery said. "Call Chernack first."

As they filed out of the interview room, Stevenson told them to come into his office. The captain's office was a cramped room located near the front desk. Stevenson could've commandeered better accommodations, but RHD was so crowded that he said he preferred to leave the bigger space for working detectives.

Katy O'Neal had just returned from West L.A. station and was waiting for them. She had information on Alexandra's partner the night she'd arrested Catherine Moody. O'Neal sat glumly on a beat-up sofa under the only window and waited until everyone found somewhere to sit in the crowded space. Turner wondered if she was ever out of her bad mood. He had never seen her smile. Then without any discussion, she began reading from a spiral notebook, dryly reciting the facts. Maria Perez had been Alexandra's partner the night they arrested Moody. Perez was generally thought to be another lesbian officer, but a good cop. That's why she'd been selected for several special assignments, including the hype unit. She had been promoted to sergeant and was now working Internal Affairs in the West Bureau field office.

Turner knew that the fact that Perez worked in the same division where the car containing Alexandra's body had come from wouldn't escape Stevenson's notice, but the captain never glanced up from his desk as O'Neal read from her notes.

"Nobody I talked to at West L.A. thought they were anything but partners," O'Neal said.

"Because?" Montgomery asked.

"Our victim preferred the less-obvious-looking lesbos. Even with the booking photo, Perez couldn't remember the Moody arrest. She claims they took down three or four hypes a night for a year."

"You know that West Bureau IA office moved to McGann's headquarters building a few months ago?" Turner asked Stevenson.

"No, I thought they were still on Hollywood or Sunset."

"McGann had extra space, and the city was only too happy to let that lease on Sunset go away."

"Yeah, well, a big so what, Turner," O'Neal said. "She works in the same building as McGann. I'm gonna guess they never had a sexual thing." She threw a color photo of a stocky Mexican woman in an LAPD uniform on Turner's lap. The woman in the picture had short-cropped hair and a plain unsmiling face. He was annoyed with O'Neal's attitude, but before he could respond, Stevenson stood up and took the photo out of Turner's hands.

"We don't stop thinking, Detective O'Neal, just because the piece doesn't fit," Stevenson said, staring at her. "Until we get something solid, everything's on the table."

She seemed surprised at his harsh tone and sat up. "Sorry, boss," she said. "My mouth is always a step ahead of my brain."

"We know," Stevenson and Montgomery said at the same time, and Turner relaxed.

"It's been a long day. You and Turner still want to interview McGann tonight?" Stevenson asked Montgomery.

"Absolutely," Turner answered, knowing Montgomery wouldn't object.

"Okay, it's set for 1900 hours. That's seven o'clock, O'Neal." Stevenson grinned at the sulking detective.

"I said I was sorry. Give me a break."

"Connelly wants to be there, Turner," Stevenson said, giving the groaning O'Neal a dirty look. She smiled at him and shrugged. This time Turner had to agree with her. His captain wasn't needed and usually just took up space.

"We need to get a tail on the handyman and pick up Catherine Moody," Turner said.

"I agree," Montgomery added. "But what about McGann? Can we get IA's internal surveillance detail to set up on him?"

"Martin will never go for that," Stevenson said, pacing behind his desk. "This isn't some patrol cop buying a bag of weed."

Montgomery stood in front of Stevenson's desk and crossed his arms. "Did I miss something, boss? This guy is a suspect in a homicide, and we can't use ISD to watch him?" His voice was strained. He obviously didn't enjoy disagreeing with Stevenson.

Stevenson wiped his palms on his pant legs. "I didn't say we shouldn't do it. I'm saying he's a goddamn deputy chief, and it's going to be a hard sell."

Turner agreed with Montgomery but was quiet. He had already figured out that this captain didn't like to be pushed. Stevenson was the kind of boss who supported his people. He would most likely take their request to the chief of police. The internal surveillance detail was the perfect choice to keep an eye on McGann.

"What's ISD?" O'Neal asked.

"You got to be kidding," Montgomery said. "You don't know about ISD?"

"If I knew, asshole, I wouldn't have asked."

"They're a bunch of detective supervisors and sergeants who make cases on dirty cops," Turner said before Stevenson could snap at O'Neal again. "They follow them until they catch them committing crimes."

"Best surveillance team in the department," Montgomery added.

Turner knew that if ISD followed McGann, they could gather intelligence, and if nothing came of the surveillance, nobody would ever need to know that the deputy chief had been followed.

"I'll talk to Connelly after the interview tonight," Stevenson said wearily. "But she's not the problem. Martin knows better than to let IA get an up-close-and-personal look at most of his staff guys, especially McGann."

Turner knew Stevenson was right. According to what Paula had told him, most of Martin's staff, with a few exceptions such as Jacob Bell, wouldn't survive any real scrutiny. That would be embarrassing for the department and, more important, for Martin.

"We'll get a couple of detectives to set up on Phil White tonight if that's okay, boss," Montgomery said, but didn't wait for an answer. "Katy's going to ride with Hollywood Vice and try to find Moody or Crystal or whatever she's calling herself. Turner and I will do the interview on McGann and backtrack on the IA car. It was a West Bureau IA ride, but according to the check-out sheets, it hadn't been driven for a month. All the keys are missing, including the garage set."

"You need some more help on this?" Stevenson asked.

"Not yet," Montgomery said. He looked at Turner, who didn't agree but again deferred to Montgomery's judgment.

"SID's been all over that crime scene two or three times. There's not a print except McGann's on the car, plus an abundance of hairs and fibers," Turner said, wanting to change the subject before he was forced to admit he would welcome all the help he could get. "Her lifestyle is the only thing we've got to go on right now," he added.

"The knife was wiped off pretty good, but we've got enough blood smears to make a match if it's Alexandra's. No prints, of course," Turner said.

"Did we send the lab guys through that backyard behind the bungalow?" Stevenson asked.

"They did it this morning, Captain, right after we dug up the knife," Montgomery said. "There was nothing. Sprinklers go on every night. It's like a jungle in there. If White hadn't seen it, nobody would've ever found it."

"When you get the gloves tomorrow, have White show you exactly where he says he found the knife," Stevenson said. "Let's grab some chow before the interview," he said, shifting uncomfortably behind his desk. "It'll be in Jacob Bell's office."

"No way," Turner said too loudly. When he realized everyone was staring at him, he tried to control himself. "Sorry, but you've got to be joking. Bring him down here to an interrogation room. We can't interview him in his backyard."

"The chief of police says he gets interviewed in the chief of staff's office. So he gets interviewed in the chief of staff's office," Stevenson said deliberately.

Turner stood and leaned over the desk. "Does he get to write the questions, too?" he asked.

"Don't be a fucking smart ass, Turner. That's the way it's going to be. Live with it." Stevenson's face was burgundy. Even O'Neal knew enough to keep her mouth shut when Stevenson's face turned that shade of red.

Turner and the detectives quietly left the captain's office. It was only six o'clock, and he figured Paula would still be in her office. He needed something to get his mind off how disappointed he was about how this interview with McGann was being manipulated. He called Paula and asked her to meet him. She was actually finished for the evening and, as usual, starving. They decided to grab a quick bite at a sushi bar in Little Tokyo down the street from Parker Center. He really needed a quiet hour with her. Actually, a couple of sakes would be better, and then some long passionate lovemaking before they fell asleep in each other's arms, but that wasn't going to happen that night.

They talked about the case as they walked across the street to San Pedro and then through the Little Tokyo mall to their favorite restaurant, Omasa. She wanted to know everything. She was familiar with Maria Perez. She knew Perez had been fired during her eighteen-month probation period as a new cop because it was discovered that her father was involved in drug dealing. The department could never prove that Maria was aware of it, so the courts eventually reinstated her, and she got her job back. By reputation, she'd become a good cop and supervisor. She was openly a lesbian, but it was never an issue in West L.A., where a number of gays had migrated.

Paula also agreed with Stevenson that Martin would never allow ISD to follow McGann or any other staff officer.

"Let's talk about something else for a few minutes," Turner finally said. "I'm tired of thinking about Alexandra Williams and her sordid little life."

Paula looked hurt. "Sorry," she said. "This is such an interesting case. It fascinates me. Guess I need to get out of that office and back to real life again."

"No, it's me, honey," he said as apologetically as he could. He wasn't trying to be disagreeable. Her curiosity made him wonder if another investigator would be doing a better job. "I'm too old for this game. I'm trying, but my heart isn't in it anymore. I used to laugh at the bullshit. Now it just disgusts me. I want to grab McGann by his collar and slap him. I hate that he and his buddies are incompetent, arrogant assholes and they're running the store. A few years ago that never would've bothered me. I just did my job. But now . . ." He stopped and realized he was whining like those cops who always blamed management for all their problems. "Don't mind me. I'm frustrated with this mess," he said.

Paula touched his face. "I think you're tired, lover."

"You're right," he lied and smiled, hoping she would just let it go.

They finished their meal and headed back toward Parker Center. She slid her arm around his, and they walked without talking. He liked her company and enjoyed the short stroll back. She snuggled close to him, and he could smell the sweet fragrance of herbal shampoo. It was nice for a few minutes to concentrate on the insignificant joys of living.

Montgomery and Stevenson were waiting in the outer office of the chief of staff when they arrived. Captain Connelly was sitting at Paula's desk. She nodded at Turner without smiling. The president of the Command Officers Association was also in the room with a woman whom Turner didn't recognize, but Paula whispered that she was the COA attorney.

There were way too many people to sit in on an IA interview, but Turner had interrogated hundreds of criminals and wasn't intimidated. He knew McGann wasn't as clever as he thought he was, but Connelly was squeamish, and the COA wouldn't want to set any precedent by allowing IA to probe too deeply into a staff officer's life.

"Don't worry, Turner. I've reserved the auditorium if we run out of room," Montgomery whispered, grinning at him.

Connelly reluctantly got up and allowed Paula to sit at her own desk. Turner guessed that the hierarchy protocol probably dictated that Paula decline to take a seat from a captain, but she didn't. He knew Paula resented how Connelly treated him. She would pretend to have work just to keep Connelly standing.

At about 7:30 P.M., the door to Bell's office opened, and he stepped out with a confident McGann by his side.

"Okay, folks, let's get this thing done. Bring in some chairs," Bell said, waving them into his larger office.

Bell stood and allowed McGann to sit behind his desk. McGann settled into Bell's comfortable leather chair. Turner half expected him to put his feet on the desk. Connelly and the others all stood behind McGann.

"Sorry, sir, that's not going to work. I need to get you over here closer to the tape recorder," Turner said, avoiding Stevenson's stare. "Maybe we can all sit around this table." He put the machine on a round table that Bell used for paperwork.

"Can't you bring that thing over here and put it on the desk?" McGann asked, sitting up and looking at his lawyer.

"No outlets and, stupid me, I didn't bring the right extension." Montgomery did his best poor black country-boy imitation.

Turner swallowed a laugh and placed his hand over the bulging extension cord in his jacket pocket. "I apologize, sir," he said, pointing to the secretary's swivel chair he'd moved from behind Rose's desk. "Could you, please?"

McGann reluctantly stood and looked at the attorney. The little COA lawyer probably thought the situation was just fine as she slipped into the leather chair. Everyone found a place to sit around the small table. The tape recorder sat in the middle while Turner explained to McGann what was going to happen.

"We haven't initiated a formal complaint yet," Turner said. Connelly nodded as he spoke. "The purpose of this investigation is to determine whether or not you had an inappropriate relationship with a subordinate, and if so, whether that relationship reflected badly on you or the department."

"No one really believes you did anything wrong, but you know this has to be done," Connelly said, trying to minimize the process. She attempted to explain what she meant and began to ramble, losing track of her point. Everyone around the table stared at her in silence until she finally stopped mid-sentence and nodded for Turner to continue. Turner thought it was too bad they had closed the outer office door. Paula would've enjoyed this moment.

McGann tried to balance his tall frame on the skimpy secretary's chair as he waived all of his rights, both criminal and administrative. He claimed he wanted to talk about his relationship with Alexandra Williams. He preferred to tell his story and then answer any questions Turner or Montgomery might have. Montgomery said Turner would ask all the questions.

McGann looked over at the COA lawyer. She sat in the leather chair with her arms folded. The COA president was studying the carpet, and Bell stared at him from across the table. He started his story from about a year before.

"It was at the West L.A. Christmas party. She was barely off probation, but she had the spunk to introduce herself. She kept telling me what a great guy I was. I told her she was beautiful and smart. We were both a little drunk."

"Was your wife there?" Turner asked.

McGann glared at him. "No, she preferred to stay home with the twins. Patricia is smart enough to avoid the craziness that goes with these parties, but it was one of my divisions. I had to go."

"Sorry, please go on," Turner said. He thought McGann sounded too rehearsed. He wanted to shake him up a little.

"We talked and danced and had a good time. I liked her." McGann hesitated as if he had unintentionally admitted something. "We were at the Sheraton, and she had a room for the night. A lot of the officers did it so they could drink and not have to worry about driving home."

"So somehow you ended up in her room," Turner said. This story was getting too long.

"She shared it with another cop, a short, sort of homely Mexican woman who left as soon as we got there. I slept with Alexandra. "

"You had sex," Turner said.

"I was drunk. I can't remember most of the night, except I woke up about 3:30 A.M., naked and in bed with her. I got dressed and drove to my brother's house. My brother lied for me and told Patricia I'd been there all night after the party."

"When did you see her again?"

"We had sex maybe twice after that, but I hadn't talked to her for months before she was killed. Nobody ever saw us together, and I never did anything good or bad for her career. It was just sex, nothing else, and nobody knew." He stopped and looked around the room. His expression said, "That's it; can I go now?"

Turner scribbled a few notes and continued to look down. He waited until the silence was uncomfortable, and he enjoyed watching McGann twist nervously in the chair. He took a picture of Maria Perez and put it on the table in front of McGann.

"Do you recognize her?" Turner asked.

"I believe she was Alex's roommate in the hotel room. Is she involved in the murder?"

Turner ignored the question. "When did you have sex with Alexandra the next time after the Christmas party?"

McGann hesitated and looked at the lawyer again. She scratched her head and leaned back in the chair. "I'd advise you to answer the question," she said.

"We met both times in a parking lot near the Hollywood Bowl."

"Whose idea was it to meet there?" Turner tried to imagine this lanky, pretentious deputy chief rolling around in the back seat of a police car with the pretty lesbian.

"Hers. I'd park, and she would come and drive me to some secluded spot." McGann avoided looking at Bell. "It was always off-duty and in her private vehicle. I stopped after the second time. It was over in less than a month." McGann's voice was strained. "Look, I'm not proud of what I did. The whole thing made me uncomfortable."

No shit, Turner thought and bit his lip, trying not to say it out loud. This guy was a pro. McGann carefully worked to insulate himself from misconduct charges better than anyone Turner had ever interviewed.

Turner knew his next question was doomed before he asked, but he had a hunch and had to try. "Would you describe the kind of sex you had with Alexandra?"

"Wait a minute," Bell objected.

At the same time Connelly shouted, "Sergeant Turner."

Turner ignored them. "She's been described as a lesbian. Would you say your sex was, in your experience, normal?"

"It was just regular intercourse. I don't know what's normal. Nothing kinky, if that's what you're asking." McGann answered matter of factly before anyone could object again.

Turner continued with a series of questions and found that McGann had never been to Alexandra's home. He had never met any of her friends except Perez. He did not see her the night she was murdered and had no idea how her body found itself in front of his home in the trunk of a police car. Alexandra had never threatened him, and no one ever talked to him about her. They never had an argument. He never struck her. Frankly, he'd nearly forgotten about Alexandra Williams until her body appeared practically on his doorstep.

McGann had the perfect alibi for the night of the murder. He was working. Half of West Bureau's personnel saw him in the building until nearly 10 P.M. Patricia would say he was home by 10:30 P.M. and in bed asleep by 11. But, Turner wondered, did he stay in bed or slip out when she and the twins were asleep?

The deputy chief was admitting to minor misconduct. He'd had a relationship with a subordinate but had carefully kept it away from work and could prove that Williams was neither helped nor hindered by his intervention. Turner knew that on prior occasions the chief of police had shown reluctance to punish his staff for this kind of indiscretion. The West Bureau job was bottom of the barrel for a deputy chief, so what could Sam Martin do to him? McGann probably knew Martin didn't like him, but it didn't matter. The chief of police always protected his staff.

Stevenson got up and began pacing behind Bell's desk. Turner wondered if the RHD captain had something he wanted to ask, but Stevenson turned his back to the room and looked out the window.

"Why do you think the car was parked outside your house?" Turner asked. He wanted McGann to do some speculating, hoped he would talk too much.

"I've been asking myself that question a thousand times a day. It wasn't there when I got home that night. I'm positive. I saw it before I started my run in the morning. I felt something wasn't right. I rushed breakfast at Judy's."

"Who's Judy?" Turner asked, wondering how many women this guy had had.

"Judy Taylor's café, where I stop for breakfast every morning," McGann said, deliberately curling his upper lip in an ugly smirk, as if he knew what Turner and everyone else in the room were thinking. "I kept wondering about that car, but Judy always wants to talk." He stopped and slapped his forehead. "Goddamn it," he said, jumping up. "I was so upset I forgot." He looked around the room as if everyone should've known what he was talking about.

"Forgot what?" Turner finally asked.

"Judy Taylor at the café. She told me two plainclothes cops were in her place that night. The café's on Beechwood just down the hill from my place. They were acting crazy like they were under the influence. I was so upset I forgot to give it to IA." He took a sheet of paper off the table and wrote the address of the restaurant and Judy Taylor's name. "You need to talk to her. Find out who they are."

Turner took the paper and shoved it in the back of his notebook. From McGann's smug look, he guessed the deputy chief figured he'd just solved the crime, so the dead woman should be just another mini bump on his career path.

"It's probably nothing, but I'll check it out," Turner said and saw McGann slump a little in his chair.

"Are we finished?" McGann asked tersely. He wasn't accustomed to having his ideas dismissed so easily.

"Not quite," Turner said.

"I think we are. Aren't we?" McGann stared at the attorney, but before she could respond, the COA president interrupted.

"Perhaps you could submit the remainder of your questions in writing, Sergeant," he said.

Turner looked at Montgomery, who seemed ready to call it a night, but he had one more question and decided to risk McGann's wrath and ask it.

"Can you take us to the spot Alexandra took you to when you parked at the Hollywood Bowl?" Turner asked as McGann was about to walk out of the office.

"No, I can't," McGann said without stopping or turning around, and he was out the door before Turner could ask another question. Connelly tagged behind him, almost tripping on her chair to leave as quickly as possible.

The attorney groaned as she pushed herself out of the leather chair. She bent over slightly, stretching her back while handing Turner her business card. "I'd like a copy of the tape at your convenience," she said, shaking her head. He generally didn't care much for lawyers, but he liked her. Maybe it was the disgusted look on her face when McGann had described his encounters with Alexandra.

Paula was waiting for Turner in the outer office, and they watched from the doorway as Connelly huddled with McGann down the hallway near the elevators. Their animated conversation stopped when they realized they were being observed. After a few minutes, they stepped onto the elevator and were gone.

Stevenson and Montgomery joined them in the outer office, where they waited for Bell to finish a phone call. Turner assumed he was briefing the chief of police about the interview.

"Nice job, Turner," Stevenson said. "Nothing like pissing off the guy who controls your life." From the sarcastic tone in Stevenson's voice, Turner guessed he'd done all right. They'd had a good interview for the personnel investigation, but it didn't do much for Montgomery's murder case.

"What's the plan now as far as your homicide investigation?" Bell asked when he'd completed his call. Before Montgomery could answer, Bell closed the door to the hallway and locked it. "What I say stays in this room," Bell said, looking at Turner, who nodded. "We can all agree McGann's a sleazebag, but I still don't see him hurting that girl. Do you, Sergeant?"

Turner didn't answer for a few seconds and wouldn't look at Paula. "I'm not sure," he finally said. "At this moment, he's the best suspect we've got."

"Jacob," Stevenson said, "I've got to ask you something. I've already spoken to Connelly tonight, and she didn't like the idea but agreed to support me on this. I want to use ISD to tail McGann." He rushed the last few words, and it took Bell a second to realize what was being asked.

Bell laughed, folded his arms and shook his head several times. "You can't honestly believe the chief of police would allow that?"

"Not if I asked him, but he might if you did it," Stevenson said and added quickly, "It's the smart thing. You heard that interview. The man is telling us just enough to slap him on the hand."

"What I heard or didn't hear is immaterial. Sam Martin will never let you do surveillance on one of his deputy chiefs, period. So don't even think about it. I'll give you your answer now—absolutely, unequivocally, no." Stevenson started to argue, but Bell turned his back and stepped into his office. "Don't waste your breath, Stevenson. Find another way," Bell said, closing the door.

They sat quietly staring at the door to Bell's office until it opened and he came out, carrying his briefcase and jacket. He locked his office door and slipped the jacket on. Still, no one said anything. He paused in the hallway and glanced back at them.

"I know how hard you're working on this, but find another way," Bell said before turning and walking away, his heavy foot-steps echoing in the empty corridor.

"It's late," Stevenson said. "Let's get the hell out of here. I need a drink."

"Wanna go to the Freeway?" Montgomery asked, looking at Turner and Paula.

"What are you talking about?" Turner asked.

"It's a shitty little bar on Figueroa. Freeway is a nickname the guys at RHD gave it because it's the last place to grab a drink before you get on the Harbor or Hollywood freeway to go home."

"No, thanks," Turner said. "I've got notes to review. I want to think about this thing with a clear head."

"I always find it easier to think by myself with a good scotch in my hand," Stevenson said. He didn't bother to say goodnight and was gone before Turner could pick up his papers.

EIGHT

I t was nearly midnight, and Turner couldn't believe Montgomery had talked him into riding with Katy and these Hollywood Vice cops. Montgomery had promised his wife that he wouldn't work all night, again, but he didn't want his partner working alone. Turner hoped Paula would be more forgiving.

They'd finished their third roundup of street prostitutes in less than four hours. These guys never stopped making arrests. Everyone needs at least a coffee break, he thought. They already had twenty girls in custody sitting on the booking bench at Hollywood station, but they kept going back to the streets for more. Unfortunately, none of those arrestees was Catherine Moody.

Katy told him they'd need to take a different approach if they were going to find Alexandra's roommate. Earlier in the evening, she'd queried the vice computer and retrieved all of Moody's arrest reports, finding some prior addresses and names of crime buddies and pimps. When she was a young police officer, Katy had worked for the detective in charge of the Hollywood narcotics squad. He was a bloodhound and could locate practically anyone in this area. She convinced Turner to abandon the vice cops who were sorting out their hookers and walk with her across Wilcox, where a rundown brick building camouflaged the division's gas pumps. All of West Bureau Hollywood narcotics operations were housed in that building, sharing space with an assortment of cockroaches and mice. It was a hand-me-down condemned structure that had gone to the department when no other city agency would live in it. The detectives found that it suited their needs perfectly, and no one except the criminals knew it was a police facility.

Detective Mark Sullivan was sitting at his desk in the grimy back room of the narcotics office. He was alone, staring at a computer, struggling to do the supervisor's paperwork that always confounded him. He'd worked for LAPD for thirty-five years, twenty-eight of which had been in the Narcotics Division. He was overweight, had gray hair, and his beard was white stubble. Sullivan worked only in high gear. The crooks respected and feared him only a little more than his own people did.

Katy leaned against the door frame until he looked up. "Katy, how's my darling girl?" he asked, almost smiling. "Come back to do some real police work?"

"Aren't you ever going to retire, old man?" Turner asked.

"And give up all of this?" he asked, pointing to the piles of debris around him before shaking hands with Turner. "How are you, Mike? It's been awhile."

Turner started to explain why they were there, but Katy interrupted and began telling Sullivan everything she knew about the Alexandra Williams murder investigation. She showed him copies of the arrest reports she'd taken from the vice computer. Turner knew that Sullivan was a smart cop, a bear of a man, who never gave up the hunt. His Achilles heel was paperwork, but he had keen instincts.

"We have to find her, Sully, but Katy and I don't think we're going to do it tagging along with the vice guys," Turner said.

"No shit, not if she's got a half a brain and stays out of their radar. You check these prior addresses?" Sullivan asked.

"Nobody knew her or had seen her. Big surprise. She could've been staying with Williams for as long as a year. Can your people try to bed her down for us?" Katy asked.

Sullivan pushed away from the computer and took a brown-stained cup from his desk. He poured coffee from an equally dirty-looking pot.

"I gotta couple of guys that don't have anything going. Maybe they've got a snitch that wants to earn a few bucks."

"I've got to warn you there might be a cop or two involved in this one, Sully," Turner said, watching for Sullivan's reaction. There wasn't any, so he added, "Apparently, the street name she used was Crystal."

"Speeder?"

"Coke and Meth."

"Dope is always involved somehow. This pimp Dean, he's a Meth dealer," Sullivan said, pointing to an arrestee on one of Crystal's most recent reports. "I know where he stays. If you want, we could go right now, maybe catch him on the street."

Turner agreed and asked Katy to call the lieutenant at Hollywood Vice and give him her cell phone number in case his officers picked up Crystal.

"Business must be good," Katy said, sliding into the back seat of a new Dodge Integra. "I can remember when your cars were so old you took spare parts on search warrants because you knew at least one of them would fall apart before you got back."

Sullivan grinned. "Praise the Lord and asset forfeiture." He keyed his radio and asked one of his detectives to meet him at the northwest corner of Hollywood Blvd. and Western. A voice immediately responded. When they arrived at that location, the detective and his partner were already backed into a parking space behind a taco stand on the corner. Not bothering with introductions, Sullivan told the detectives they were looking for Jimmy Dean. Both men knew Dean and said they'd seen him earlier in the week. He hung around the Carlton Street Hotel, half a block from where they were on Hollywood Blvd.

Turner asked if there was a place where they could watch the Carlton. He didn't want to talk to Dean yet, hoping either Crystal would meet with him or they could see him make a dope deal. He knew Dean didn't have a reason to tell them anything unless they had a case on him. If they caught him selling Meth, he wouldn't stop talking.

The narcotics detectives pointed to the roof of the arcade across the boulevard and said it was the best place to see the front of the Carlton. Turner could stay on the roof with Sullivan and Katy, and the detectives agreed to remain close as a chase unit just in case they got lucky and Crystal actually showed.

When Turner got to the roof of the arcade, he had some second thoughts about being up there. He was wearing clean Levis and an expensive leather jacket. The roof was filthy. He could smell the human waste and urine and carefully avoided walking close to the corners, where they were likely to step in it. The tar on the floor was still sticky from the heat earlier in the day and stuck to his favorite boots. Garbage and used hypodermic needles were thrown everywhere, and he knew enough not to rest his hand on the wall.

"Don't you miss all this, Katy?" Sullivan asked, taking a deep breath and smiling at her.

"About as much as you miss sitting in front of that computer."

They settled in at the roof's edge behind a small retaining wall where they had a clear view of the Carlton's front door and most of Hollywood Blvd. from Western to about three blocks west. It was nearly 2 A.M., but the boulevard was crowded with working girls, drug dealers, and most of those otherworldly characters who appear only late at night in places like Hollywood. Sullivan tested his radio reception, and his detectives could hear him. Turner knew how these narcotic detectives worked. They'd labor all night and be ready to serve a search warrant at first light. They wouldn't stop unless someone sent them home or they had to go to court. He'd come to the right place. He wanted to find Crystal and would be willing to stay all night to do it.

He saw several girls and drug dealers easily locate buyers and wondered what kind of customer stayed out this late and wandered around the streets. He was usually in bed by 11 P.M. with a glass of wine in one hand and a channel changer in the other.

When the gay bar down the street closed at 3 A.M., the scenery changed dramatically. Transvestites and transsexuals in gaudy short skirts and transparent blouses showed off their hormone-induced breasts to anyone who wanted to look. Business picked up considerably. There were movie stars he recognized but whose names he didn't know, and men in business suits who stopped their expensive cars and offered the front seat to anyone in a red wig and high heels. Drug dealers were doing a booming business. A little speed made illicit sex so much better.

Turner watched men in every imaginable position in the alley or in the back seat of a parked car derive some kind of pleasure from another man dressed like an ugly woman. He noticed Katy seemed fascinated, but she wouldn't look at him or say anything. Turner saw what he thought at first was a pretty young Mexican girl relieving herself in the alley. Eventually he realized there were too many moving parts.

"How do you do this every day? These people are pathetic," Katy said when the nastiness finally overwhelmed her.

Sullivan placed the binoculars on the ledge. "Maybe," he said, leaning against an air conditioning unit. "But not as sick as the bastard that butchered that cop."

"Why don't you get away from all this crap? If I could, I'd retire. I'd be out the door so fast." She turned away from the street and looked at Sullivan. "Don't you want to be around normal people?"

"So what's normal, Katy? Those guys down there are doctors and lawyers. Some kid's third-grade teacher just drove up the street to have hairy-legged Lola suck his dick."

"Okay, so maybe I'd rather not look at it. Sorry, Sully. I'm better with killers than I am with perverts."

"You're still young. Lots of time to learn."

She laughed in spite of her disgust. She was obviously crazy about Sullivan. He was a rare breed of old-timer who'd seen everything and done everything and knew human nature better than most psychiatrists. Turner wondered what LAPD would be like when all the Mark Sullivans were gone.

Radio static brought their attention back to the front of the hotel. "Sully, wake up. Your man is on the street," one of the detectives said.

Sullivan picked up the binoculars and found Dean quickly. He was standing in front of the Carlton, wearing his best pinstriped pimp outfit, inspecting the wigs and costumes worn by his girls.

"Don't see your girl," Sullivan said. "Want to give him some space and see if she shows?"

"I think we should watch until he deals or maybe we get one of your undercover guys to buy from him. We've got to give him a reason to talk," Turner said.

"Wait a minute. What's this?" Sullivan leaned his elbows on the wall and adjusted the binoculars. He described a clean-cut-looking male Caucasian who'd just stopped his Ford Bronco in front of the hotel. The man wore a light jacket and jeans, but Sullivan said he could see the familiar bulge at the waistband. The guy was packing a gun. He walked up to Dean, and they shook hands like old friends. Sullivan read the license number on the back of the Bronco, and Katy wrote it on her palm. Sullivan watched Dean's hands. He focused on those hands and waited. Finally, it came—the quick motion to his pocket and the handshake with the Bronco man. Both men put their right hands in their jacket pockets.

"Gotcha," Sullivan whispered. "This is your case. You want my guys to stop this guy? He's probably an off-duty cop. Dean passed something to him and got something back."

"Dope?" Turner asked, looking at Sullivan and wanting him to say yes.

"Don't know, but that's a good guess. We can stop him far enough away from here so Dean won't see anything."

"I'm not sure he has anything to do with our case, but make it look like they're working and just saw him. If he's got Meth, we take down Dean, too."

Sullivan radioed his chase unit to stop the Bronco when it got a few blocks from the Carlton. He warned them the driver might be an armed off-duty cop. As Sullivan finished his transmission, the Bronco driver began to move away from Dean. He avoided the groping hands of the drag queens and climbed back into his four-wheel drive. Sullivan gave the Bronco's direction as it pulled away from the curb and repeated the order to let it travel at least a quarter of a mile before stopping it. He put the radio on the ledge and then picked it up and keyed it again.

"Wear your raid jackets," he said. "I don't want this guy thinking he's being ripped off. Let him see you're the police."

About an hour later, business on the boulevard was slowing down when Sullivan's detectives finally checked in and asked to meet him somewhere. He told them to go to the office and wait.

"We're not alone, Sully. You sure you want us to go there?" The detective's voice sounded strained. Turner shrugged, and Sullivan told him again to go to the office.

"You ready to shut this down?" Sullivan asked. "I don't think your girl is going to show. Dean's wasted, and it doesn't sound like my guys got any dope."

Turner took the binoculars and focused on the skinny pimp. He was sitting on the top steps of the Carlton with his head propped against the wall and his mouth open. The drugs and alcohol had done their job.

"I'm beat," Katy said, standing and stretching. "Can you put a team on him for a couple of nights, see if Crystal shows?"

"If she doesn't, I'll send a guy to buy from him. We'll put a case on Mr. Dean, and he'll be begging to help you."

Turner was too tired to come up with a better plan. He knew the next step would be to pay a couple of snitches. Money was a great incentive for a tweaker. But at this moment, he was anxious to hear what the detectives had found in the Bronco.

"Maybe we should pick up Dean," Turner said, thinking out loud. "Before he disappears, too."

"No way," Katy said. "We've got nothing. Let's wait and see what Sully's guys have."

"It's your homicide," Turner said.

"Leave him," she said.

They worked their way down from the roof of the arcade, maneuvering around smelly bums sleeping in the alley. Cardboard tents had sprung up overnight. Hollywood's street people were tucked in the corners of every unsecured parking lot. Shopping carts piled with dirty rags and assorted junk were parked near the makeshift lodgings. Those who couldn't find cardboard were wrapped in layers of filthy clothes, huddled close to the buildings or each other for warmth.

Katy insisted they stop at Starbucks for some low-fat muffins and coffee, but when they arrived at the Narcotics office, they found a pot of strong coffee and a dozen greasy donuts sitting on Sullivan's desk.

"Nothing has changed around here," Katy said as she took a napkin and dabbed at the grease seeping out of the donut box onto the unfinished reports on the supervisor's desk.

Sullivan ignored the healthy muffins and grabbed a crème-filled heart attack. "What did you find?" he asked with his mouth full.

Charlie, the younger-looking detective, started the story while his partner seemed content to listen.

"We stopped the Bronco, and the guy identified himself right away. He gave me his license and police ID and admits knowing Dean. Says Alexandra Williams introduced him to Dean a few months ago."

"Did he have any Meth on him?" Sullivan asked.

"No, just a piece of paper with a phone number that he says Dean gave him tonight."

"Bullshit," Katy said. "Search the car again."

Charlie glared at her but didn't respond. He turned to Sullivan and finished the story. "This guy says Dean introduces guys to girls, not those street whores but classy chicks. He gives you a phone number and a list of parties, and the rest is up to you. This cop claims it was nothing illegal, just some kind of dating service."

Sullivan interrupted. "How much did he give Dean tonight for the phone number?"

"Hundred bucks," Charlie said, smiling.

"This kid works Devonshire," the older detective said. He had finished his second donut. "Wait 'til you see him . . . the new LAPD."

Charlie picked up the story again. "He claims a bunch of coppers use the service, mostly for the parties. He denies using drugs and is willing to pee for us. We showed him a booking photo of Crystal. He'd been to Alexandra's house and had seen Crystal there."

"Where is he?" Turner asked.

"He's across the street. His captain and the IA team are on their way out here."

"Who called them? We need to talk to him first." He stood and dialed Montgomery's home number on his cell phone. Turner woke him. It was only 5 A.M., and the Freeway bar had done its magic. He was sleeping soundly but cleared his head quickly when he heard Turner's story. He asked Turner to put the officer in an interview room and not let him talk to anyone before he got there. Turner hung up and told Charlie to bring the Devonshire officer back and lock him in the interview room. A few minutes later the confused young man was taken from the captain's office across the street back to the narcotics office.

"What else did he tell you?" Katy asked the older detective.

"Not much. Alexandra was the one who introduced him to Dean at a party. Of course, he didn't know the names of any other guys who used the service, but a lot of guys did it. He claims he only met one woman, a schoolteacher. They had a few dates, went to a few more parties, then decided they weren't right for each other. He says it wasn't all sex. It was just a way to meet pretty women and have a good time."

"Sully, do we snatch Dean?" she asked.

"Yes," Turner said.

"My gut reaction is, not yet," Sullivan said, ignoring Turner. "Let's wait for Montgomery. He's the lead detective. Dean is obviously in the middle of this mess, but it's not my call."

"Crystal's got to be the link." Katy rubbed her temples. Her head was throbbing from lack of sleep. "Shit, I don't know. I'm too tired to think straight." She pointed at the young detective. "Who knows you brought him over here?"

Charlie grinned. "I told the watch commander, but he's a friend of mine. I told him to tell the Devonshire captain we took his guy to breakfast."

76

Katy dropped into a chair and reached for the last cup of Starbucks. "Did you run the number through Criss-Cross?"

Charlie gave her the piece of paper with the phone number that they had taken from the Devonshire officer. "Not listed," he said. "I called it, but no answer, so we'll have to go through the phone company, and you know how helpful they are."

"Did Dean tell him who he was calling?" Katy asked.

The older detective shook his head. "He says no. I believe him. He still can't figure out what all the fuss is about. Dean told him to call the number tonight and there would be a list of parties and the name of a woman, some kind of model."

"For dog food commercials, if Dean knows her," Sullivan said. He was staring out the window at Hollywood station. "Montgomery better move his ass. That IA woman and the Devonshire captain just walked in the front door of Hollywood."

Charlie assured them the watch commander had promised to stall at least an hour from the time the captains entered the station. Half an hour later, Montgomery pulled into the parking lot near the gas pumps.

The Devonshire officer had been stashed in a storage room converted to an interview room packed with stored files. Charlie told him to sit at a cramped little table and write a statement. No one had asked for a written statement, but Charlie figured it would keep the young officer busy and give him an opportunity to get his story together.

"Long time since that task force," Montgomery said, shaking hands with Sullivan.

"Don't miss CRASH these days," Sullivan said, looking at Turner. "Since that asshole Perez, you can't raise your voice around gangbangers without some IA turd wanting your badge. You, Turner, wouldn't survive a week in a gang detail these days."

"Mickey Turner?" Charlie asked, jumping up to shake Turner's hand.

"The IA turd," Turner said.

"What the hell are you doing in IA?" Charlie asked.

"Shamelessly trying to promote for a bigger pension," Montgomery said. "Like the rest of us."

"Anybody want to talk to this guy before his captain comes over here and demands his rights?" Katy said. She had their attention and quickly recounted the evening's events.

"Are you guys awake enough to pick up Dean?" Turner asked, looking at Charlie and his partner. "Is that okay with you, Monty?" Montgomery agreed, and Turner caught the scowl on Sullivan's face when he started giving orders to the narcotics detectives. He wanted Sullivan on his side and hadn't meant to usurp the supervisor's authority. When something needed to be done, he couldn't help himself. He just did it, and Dean needed to be picked up.

Sullivan shrugged. "We're still on the clock," he said, nodding at his detectives, who gathered their gear and were gone. "Anything else?"

"No, let's talk to the kid," Turner said. From Sullivan's tone, he knew he'd pissed off the veteran supervisor, but there wasn't time to unruffle feathers now.

Katy grabbed Montgomery's arm before he could move toward the interview room.

"Let's think about this a minute," she said, stepping in front of him. Turner stopped and waited for Montgomery. "His rep and boss are probably across the street waiting for him. If we interview him without a rep or at least offering him one, we could lose everything at a board of rights."

"I don't really give a fuck about the board of rights," Montgomery said. "This is a homicide investigation first, and IA's not going to screw it up. Sorry, Turner."

"Sure you are," Turner said, standing outside the interview room with his hand on the doorknob.

Katy stared at the floor. She seemed to sense that any further discussion was a waste of time.

"I'm not going to be the one who tries to explain this kidnapping and fucked-up decision to Captain Stevenson," she said and then pleaded, "Come on. You know he's going to blame me. He always thinks every screwed-up thing is my fault." She looked from Montgomery to Turner. "Forget it. I don't mind being a detective for the next thirty years." She sat on Sullivan's desk and took a bite out of the biggest donut left in the box.

When Turner pushed open the door, a startled Officer John "JD" Carter jumped up, nearly knocking over the table. He was twenty-two years old, with dyed blond hair and most of his baby fat. He was tall and carried himself like a cop, but unlike most of his peers who were barely out of the police academy, he seemed flabby and out of shape. Turner also noted the tiny diamond stud in his left ear. Montgomery introduced himself and explained to JD that he might be a witness in a homicide investigation.

"Do I need a rep?" JD asked.

"Don't worry about that for now," Turner said. "Did you know Alexandra Williams?" he asked before JD could pursue the rep issue.

"I been to her house once with this girl that worked Devonshire with me," he said, not yet fully grasping the seriousness of his situation.

"What girl?" Montgomery asked.

"She was Alex's classmate. Alex owed her money since the academy and called one day out of the blue to come pick it up. She needed a ride, so I took her."

"How much money?" Turner asked.

"Two hundred dollars."

"Then what happened?" Turner couldn't believe how easily this kid answered their questions.

"Alex invited us to an underground party, one of those RAVE deals at a warehouse downtown, but her classmate wouldn't go. She didn't like Alex."

"Is that where you met Dean?"

"Yeah, he told me for a hundred bucks he'd put me on a list for all the parties."

"So you paid him." Turner kept waiting for the little red light to go off in this kid's brain, but it didn't look like it was going to happen anytime soon.

"Sure, why not? The guy was sort of sleazy, but most of these underground party people are that way. The parties are great. That's where I met the schoolteacher. We hit it off, and Dean let us go to another party for free."

"When did you see Alexandra again?" Montgomery asked.

"Didn't. After me and the teacher broke up, about a week ago, I went to her house, but Alex wasn't home. Crystal was there. She's the one told me where to find Dean at the Carlton. It was stupid to go there, but I like parties and pretty girls, so I gave him another hundred bucks."

"You ever buy drugs from Dean?" Turner asked.

"No way, man," JD said too loudly just as he stood up. "You can test me. Like I told the other guy, I'll pee without a rep."

Turner calmed him down again, and JD told them that he didn't see anyone else at Alexandra's house and that he never talked to her again. He repeated gossip he'd heard that Alexandra was a party girl who went both ways and that a lot of her class-mates and partners attended those parties.

"What about Crystal? Did you have a relationship with Crystal?" Turner asked.

"Hell, no. I never even seen her again." JD was fidgeting. He scratched his arm and pulled at the ends of his hair. Turner knew the young officer was beginning to wonder if he'd talked too much. They probably wouldn't get a lot more from him.

"Where were these parties?"

"Different places. You know underground parties move every night, mostly in Hollywood. What's going to happen to me?"

"As soon as your captain gets here, you can go," Turner said, avoiding Montgomery's stare.

"Did Dean and Alexandra go to those parties?"

"Don't know. I didn't look for them."

"Crystal?"

"I told you I only saw her once." His voice was strained, and he made eye contact with Turner for the first time.

Turner sat back, glanced at Montgomery, and then asked, "What do you think was going on with Dean and Alexandra, JD?"

The young officer stared blankly at Turner. "Whadda you mean? I don't know nothing about them. I partied, that's all. I didn't do nothing wrong." He hesitated, then added, "Did I?"

The buzzer on the intercom prevented Turner from saying something he probably would've regretted later. Katy told them Devonshire's captain, Captain Connelly, and a lawyer from the protective league were walking across the street toward the nar-cotics office. Turner figured the watch commander had finally succumbed to the pressure.

Several of the narcotics detectives dressed in business suits were trickling into the office to prepare for court. They were gathered around Katy, trying to pull as much information as they could from her about the officer stashed in their storage room. Katy smiled and flirted and coyly avoided telling them anything. She met the two captains and the lawyer at the door and tried to keep them distracted until Turner and Montgomery were finished.

She led them outside to the parking lot, where they could talk away from the nosy detectives. She recounted very slowly and methodically every unimportant detail of what had happened during the night. She took time to apologize more than once about misplacing JD. Finally, when the conversation was beginning to sound a little stupid, even to her, she saw Turner standing in the doorway.

He shook hands with the Devonshire captain, who yawned and tried to look concerned. "Your officer's in the interview room," Turner said, ignoring Captain Connelly.

"Have you already interviewed him, Sergeant?" Connelly asked.

"Yes, I have," Turner responded quickly, looking at his captain.

"You know a department employee still has certain rights," the lawyer said, pushing in front of Connelly. Gil Martinez introduced himself as the protective league's attorney. Turner knew him and believed Martinez was a second-rate ambulance chaser who'd gotten the job with the league because he came cheap and couldn't get a job anywhere else.

"This is a murder investigation. We have a dead cop. Saving this guy's job is the least of our concerns," Montgomery said. He was standing behind Martinez, and the lawyer looked as if a sniper had attacked him.

"Well, it's my concern, and it should be yours, Sergeant Turner," Connelly said, turning to the Devonshire captain for support, but he had walked down the hall toward the interview room. She hurried to catch up with him.

"Yes, sir," Turner whispered, grinning at Montgomery.

"Well, it's my concern, and it should be yours," Katy said, mimicking Connelly when the door to the interview room closed. Turner laughed at the little detective's total disrespect for rank.

"Wait until Stevenson hears what you've done," Turner said to her, barely avoiding her sweeping kick.

They found Sullivan hunched over listening to the base radio when they returned to the front office. Charlie was on the air, telling his supervisor they'd found Dean.

"It's not good news," Sullivan said, clicking off the microphone. "Dean's dead."

Turner had a sick feeling. "Did they have to?"

Before he could finish, Sullivan interrupted, "He was dead when they got there. It took a while to find him. Let's go. Hollywood homicide is already out there."

"We can't get a break," Montgomery said, looking at Katy, who was pale and seemed shaken. "What's wrong with you?" he asked as Turner guided her to a chair, where she sat and folded her arms.

"I'm stupid," she said. "I should've listened to Turner and picked him up right away."

"Just bad luck," Turner said, wishing they had picked him up right away.

"You're just tired. Why don't you get a couple of hours' sleep? Turner and I can go to the Carlton," Montgomery said, rubbing her shoulder. She nodded, picked up her bag, and left quietly.

"O'Neal," Turner shouted at her as she crossed the parking lot, "you did a good job last night."

She turned and waved over her shoulder as if she knew she hadn't.

Sullivan drove Turner and Montgomery to the Carlton Street Hotel, where a sizable crowd had already gathered. It didn't take long on the street for news of a killing to spread, and then the victim's worldly possessions disappeared faster than rigor mortis. Uniformed officers guarded the front door and kept the street people and news media out of the hotel. Reporters had picked up police radio chatter and knew there was a dead body somewhere inside the seedy Carlton. Addicts and pimps died there all the time, but this was different. The cops seemed to care about this one. Sullivan found a place to park on the sidewalk off the boulevard, and Charlie met them before they reached the steps.

"Sorry, boss. Got here about fifteen minutes too late, according to the wits," Charlie said, leading them through the lobby, which reeked of dried urine and mold, then past the steel cage that housed the front desk and the manager's office. Turner remembered when the steel bars had been installed after an angry dope dealer didn't get paid on time and stabbed the night manager. The Carlton was home for parolees, Section 8 vouchers, and illegals who knew rent was required only when the manager needed money for gambling or narcotics. The rooms and hallways were filthy and had the permanent stench of human body odor. The only pattern on the carpet and walls was a splattering of vomit or bloodstains or worse. None of the rooms had hot water, and the police had kicked in every door at least once. No one ever complained. It was a place to stay with no prying questions and no last month's rent.

Charlie led them out the back door and into an alcove that housed the fire escape. Staring at them, sprawled at the bottom of the ladder, was James Hargrove Dean in his finest silk bathrobe. The homicide scene was hidden behind the tall brick wall of the office next door. Turner glanced up from the body and saw that the fire escape steps zigzagged along the side of the hotel to the top of the ten-story building.

"Ninth floor," Charlie said before he could ask. "Fell and hit his head on that piece of steel that secures the ladder," he added, pointing to an iron rod that had a slight bend. He motioned up. "The open window to the left of the ladder is his room. Wits heard him scream as he went out the window and all the way until he hit bottom."

Charlie's partner leaned out the window and looked down at them. He shouted that the homicide detectives were in the room if anyone wanted to talk to them.

"If you're done with my guys, I'm gonna cut them loose," Sullivan said, looking from Montgomery to Turner. "My lieutenant's gonna kill me if I run up any more overtime." Charlie stared at the ground. Turner understood. No good cop wanted to leave in the middle of unfinished business.

"Thanks for all your help, Sully. We'll catch a ride with the homicide guys," Montgomery said. The narcotics detectives were leaving as the Hollywood homicide detectives stepped into the alcove.

"I thought you were assigned to us full time. Who's watching Phil White if you're here?" Montgomery asked the detectives, not trying to hide his displeasure.

"Nobody's watching Phil White," the younger one said. "Because nobody knows where the fuck Phil White is."

"We never found him, and no one, including Daddy, seems able to locate him," the other one added. "We talked to Katy, and she told us about this guy's connection to Alexandra. She thought we might as well do something useful until we get a lead on White."

"That's my Katy, always thinking," Montgomery said, smiling at Turner.

"Don't thank us, Monty. We wanted to do it," the younger one said sarcastically.

"Thanks. Now tell me what killed this turd."

"I'd say that piece of steel," he said, pointing at the bent metal protruding from the ladder. "But if you want to know who tried to teach him to fly, that may take a little longer."

"You know he got pushed?" Turner asked.

"Suicide and accidental are not options here," the detective said. "Fought pretty good for a junkie. The room's trashed, and we got witnesses that heard his screams. Nobody tried to help him, of course, but Sullivan's guys almost walked in on it."

"Great. We finally get a halfway decent lead, and somebody wastes him practically under our noses," Turner said, and he was immediately relieved that Katy wasn't there to hear him. He didn't want to hurt her feelings, but it would've been so easy for her and Sullivan to pick up Dean the night before.

"Anybody in the hotel see anything, ID anybody?" Montgomery asked.

"They survive in this toilet by not seeing all the crap that floats by," Turner said as he leaned over Dean's crumpled body.

Turner and Montgomery left the Hollywood detectives at the crime scene. It would take most of the day to finish their investigation, but they agreed that if White surfaced, they'd pass the homicide case to another team and pick up the surveillance again. The consensus was that Dean's killing was too much of a coincidence not to be connected to Alexandra Williams. Although Dean probably had any number of people who wanted him dead, the timing of his death was interesting.

Turner suggested they get a car and drive to Internal Affairs at West Bureau. He was exhausted but wanted to talk to Maria Perez. As Alexandra's partner, maybe she knew more about this business arrangement Alexandra and Dean had developed.

He left a message on Katy's voice mail to track down the Devonshire classmate and find out why Alexandra owed her the two hundred dollars and why she thought Alexandra had decided to pay it back after a year. Turner thought about JD and his bleached hair and diamond stud. The guy walked and talked like a cop but looked like something out of a punk rock band. Turner knew he was out of step with the younger people who worked this job. They were different. They saw LAPD as a job, not essential to their lives. If somebody had told Turner twenty years ago, during the worst times, that he could no longer be an LA cop, his life would've been over. He still loved it after all these years.

They drove surface streets from Hollywood to the bureau offices in the Wilshire area. It was a few miles, but it gave them a chance to talk. Young officers like JD didn't always understand how little of their lives stayed private when they joined this police department. Some of the same pleasures their civilian friends enjoyed could get a cop fired in a heartbeat.

"Bottom line is, they're paying for girls, Monty. It's prostitution, no matter how you look at it."

"I called Stevenson before we left narcotics. He wants us to interview everybody at West L.A. and Devonshire."

"Great. Are they going to give us a dozen more people?" Turner asked. He knew there were details that weren't getting done now because they didn't have the resources to spare.

"Don't think so, but Katy can do it. This is her kind of thing."

Turner sighed and stared out the passenger window at the cheap furniture stacked in front of the stores along La Brea. He'd been told Armenians controlled this section of Hollywood, and they cluttered the sidewalks and alleys with overpriced junk. "We don't need everybody. We just need one of these space cadets to tell us why anybody would want to kill her."

"How does McGann fit into all of this?" Montgomery asked, not listening to Turner. "He and JD don't exactly travel in the same social circles."

"McGann's a lying sack of shit. We'll never get a straight answer from him."

They were quiet for several minutes until Montgomery said, "You know Katy's interviews will be a total waste of time. Not all these kids are as brain dead as JD. They learn how to say 'Where's my rep?' before they know how to make an arrest." He made the turn into the regional facility that housed the offices of McGann's West Bureau and circled several times before he could find any space in the crowded parking lot.

The Bureau and IA offices were in the newer part of the facility, away from the Wilshire Division, with an outdoor walkway connecting the two buildings. Wilshire Division looked like most of the geographic stations. It was old, not very well maintained, and too small for the number of officers and detectives who worked that busy part of the city. Deputy Chief McGann's bureau offices were state-of-the-art—big, open spaces with conference rooms, plenty of new furniture, and computers.

The IA offices were on the second floor of the Bureau building. The receptionist glanced at their ID cards and pointed to a room behind her where several investigators were working. Turner immediately recognized Maria Perez. He was surprised to find that unlike her picture, Perez was a pleasant-looking, friendly woman. Her dark hair had grown to shoulder length, and she wore it loose around her face, creating a softer appearance. She smiled when they introduced themselves and immediately agreed to talk to them. Her pantsuit looked expensive and stylish, but Turner noticed she wore a man's watch, was nearly as tall as he was and had broader shoulders than most women. She'd obviously logged some hours in the weight room. She also had an outspoken honesty that he liked immediately.

She led them to the empty break room down the hall from her office and poured each of them a cup of coffee before sitting at the table. She crossed her legs like a man, but seemed to think better of it and put both feet on the floor.

"I loved Alexandra," she said sadly. "In my heart, I knew something bad would happen to her one day."

"Why? What was she doing, Maria?" Montgomery asked as he pulled his chair closer to the scratched Formica-top table.

"She tried everything. She was beautiful, and life came too easy. Most straight women on the job hated her because she was a good cop, too." She paused, obviously trying to control her emotions.

"You okay?" Turner asked. He couldn't believe it would be this easy. They had a witness who actually knew something and was willing to talk.

She smiled at him and seemed surprised by his concern. "I'm fine. Sorry. It was such a waste. Like I told your partner . . . O'Neal, right?" she asked, and Turner nodded, "Alex wasn't interested in me. She liked prettier women and occasionally pretty men like McGann."

"Did you know Catherine Moody, aka Crystal?" Montgomery asked.

"I met her. I arrested her, I guess. I don't remember that bust, but she was with Alex one day when she showed up at my place. Crystal looked like a hooker. Later I told Alex to dump her." Perez stopped and seemed to be remembering something. "I knew she wouldn't. Alex liked playing with fire. They partied. Alex said there weren't any drugs, but she lost a bunch of weight." She hesitated again as if she were uncertain how much she should say.

"Did she use drugs?" Turner asked.

"I hoped she didn't."

"You worked the hype car, Maria," he said. "Don't tell me you can't recognize a junkie."

"Her pupils were dilated—cocaine, maybe speed. Alex denied it. I never saw any dope, so there wasn't much I could do. I told her to keep Crystal away from me, and she did."

"Did you know Jimmy Dean, tall black pimp in Hollywood?" Turner asked.

"Don't know that name. We didn't talk much after I made sergeant."

"Why?" Montgomery asked.

"This job is a career for me. None of it mattered to Alex," she said. "She'd sleep with guys and then never talk to them again just to piss them off."

"What do you remember about her and McGann at the Christmas party last year?" Montgomery asked.

She smiled and pushed her hair away from her face, leaning back in the folding chair and crossing her legs again.

"Alex and I were sharing a room. She drags him up there after the party and tells me to find another place to sleep. So I did. In the morning, I come back to get my stuff and she's sitting in bed, half naked, laughing her ass off telling me what she made him do." She stopped, her mouth partly open, as if she were suddenly speechless.

"And?" Turner finally said.

"He was still there in the room," she whispered.

"What did she make him do?"

"I don't remember all of it. S and M stuff, you know—crawling, begging, spanking, that kind of thing. She didn't go into details."

"Was he angry?"

"More embarrassed, I'd say. Alex told him he could call her that night, and he went away like he'd just conquered the world."

"Do you know if they met again?" Montgomery asked.

"Don't know."

"Were there others?"

"Oh, yeah," she laughed. "Guys, lesbians, and a female lieutenant, but I don't know which one. A couple of them are lesbians."

"Who?" Turner blurted out. He was embarrassed and felt stupid that Paula's face had jumped into his head.

Perez hesitated a few seconds and then said, "Brenda Todd and Sara McKnight in the chief's office. I'm not outing them. Everybody knows they're lesbians, but I'm pretty sure neither one of them had a thing with Alex. They're kinda into each other. Alex told me there was a female lieutenant she slept with and liked a lot, but she wouldn't tell me who it was, which makes me think whoever it was hadn't come out yet. That was unusual for Alex."

"What was?" Turner asked again.

"That she cared for someone. Her lovemaking usually didn't involve much love."

"Did Alex ever talk about making anyone pay for sex or arranging partners for other cops?" Montgomery asked.

"God, no. Was she doing that, too?" They didn't answer, and she sighed. "I heard through the grapevine that she had lots of money the last few months. She said it was overtime and off-duty jobs, but that was a lie."

"Why? There was overtime money available."

"Alex hated to work a minute more than she had to, and as far as I knew, she never had an off-duty job."

Turner stood and walked over to the coffeepot. His mind was a little fuzzy from lack of sleep. He poured himself a cup and was trying to decide whether or not he should try a bluff. He brought the pot to the table and slowly poured a little into Perez's cup.

"Why did you give Alexandra the keys to that IA vehicle?" Turner asked.

She ran both hands through her hair several times. "I didn't. I know everyone thinks I did, but I didn't. I swear on my mother's grave. Alex was smart. She knew where the keys were kept. That car was never driven. She could use it anytime she wanted." She looked from Turner to Montgomery. "Shit, why would I do that? Why would she do it? She drove a BMW."

Turner put the coffeepot back on the burner. For the first time in the interview, he didn't believe Perez.

"Okay," Turner said. "Is there anything else—friends, enemies, anyone who might want Alexandra dead?"

"Crystal is your best bet," she said quickly. "Have you talked to her?"

"Not yet," Turner said, reluctant to admit they couldn't find her.

Montgomery closed his notebook and stood to shake hands with Perez just as McGann entered the break room with his coffee mug. He wasn't paying any attention to them and dropped a couple of quarters into a can on the counter. He glanced up after pouring his coffee to see Montgomery, Turner, and Perez staring at him. Turner thought he caught McGann blushing.

There was an awkward silence until Perez said, "Good afternoon, Chief. How are you?"

McGann nodded at her. She shook hands with Montgomery and Turner and agreed to call if she remembered anything. She grinned sheepishly at them while her back was to McGann but managed to look serious as she left the room.

When she was out of sight, McGann edged closer to Montgomery and Turner. He didn't mention Perez or ask what she had said, but he thanked them for keeping him informed on the status of the Williams case. They glanced at each other just long enough to know it had to be Captain Stevenson who had passed on the information, demonstrating how well he knew the chain-of-command game.

"No problem, sir," Montgomery said without the slightest hesitation.

"Is there anything you need from my bureau?" McGann asked. "I believe Stevenson said he could use additional detectives for interviews. I'll give you some from West L.A.," he said. His demeanor was cold and formal.

"That would help," Montgomery said, shuffling papers into his notebook.

"Is this Dean our killer?" McGann asked.

Turner couldn't believe that McGann already had that information. They had just told Stevenson about Dean a few hours ago. "You know he's dead?" Turner asked.

"Yes, but that could be totally unrelated. People in his line of work don't live long." McGann smirked. He liked this theory.

"Too soon to say," Montgomery said. He looked annoyed, like he really didn't want to have this conversation.

"Have you talked to Judy Taylor at the café?" McGann asked. He had a back-up theory.

"We have an appointment with her tomorrow. I'm sure you'll get the progress report," Montgomery said and grimaced at Turner, knowing he had crossed the sarcasm line.

McGann turned his back on them and dumped his coffee in the sink. Turner waited for the explosion, but the deputy chief walked past them without a word. He stopped in the doorway and without turning around said, "Sergeant Turner."

"Yes, sir," Turner said, knowing that his promotion was going up in flames.

"When can I get a copy of my statement? I'm anxious to have this personnel investigation finished as soon as possible."

"I'm working on it every chance I get, sir." Turner wasn't about to tell him he hadn't written a word and had no intention of doing anything until the homicide investigation was over.

"Finish it," McGann ordered as he left.

Turner poured himself another cup of coffee. Montgomery took an oversized Baby Ruth bar from a box on the counter and left a dollar bill for some kid's Girl Scout troop. He broke off half and gave it to Turner.

"Here, have lunch," he said. "You look like shit."

"Thanks. The guy is such an arrogant asshole. Did you see the look on his face when he saw us talking to Maria?"

"I guess he remembers the evening, too," Montgomery said, laughing. "I wonder exactly what it was Alex made him do."

"I don't know, but I hope it was really humiliating," Turner said, stopping abruptly when he saw Patricia McGann and the twins standing in the doorway behind Montgomery.

Montgomery noticed his expression and turned. "Patty," he said, jumping up. "Come over here." He gave her a warm hug. She had gotten close to Montgomery on the morning of the homicide, and he'd called her for several days afterward to ask how she and the twins were doing. Turner noticed she had lost weight and seemed nervous and fidgety. The twins started pestering him immediately. They leaned on the table and tried to engage him in conversation.

"They aren't usually this friendly. Sorry if they're bothering you," Patricia said, trying to pull the girls away from him.

"No, it's okay. I wish I could get the bigger ones to take to me that way," he said. Turner pulled out a chair for Patricia, but she shook her head.

"I brought them down so we could have dinner with Jim. He's really good with the twins, and they miss him. I was on my way to his office," she said, but made no attempt to leave.

"You and the girls okay?" Montgomery asked.

"Yes, I'm staying with my sister. I'll probably go back to work as soon as school starts. We're selling the house."

"So it's over?" Montgomery asked, as if he hoped the answer was yes, and it was. She'd had enough of Jim McGann. There was no reconciliation this time.

The twins climbed on and off Turner's lap and were chattering about school and their auntie's house and her dogs as they drew pictures on Montgomery's notebook. Patricia was reluctant to say too much because she said the girls heard everything. She tugged on Montgomery's arm, and they moved away from the table and closer to the windows. The girls were busy talking and drawing and weren't interested in their mother's conversation, but the room was small, and Turner heard everything.

"I should've left years ago, Monty. He can make you believe him and love him and forget all the indiscretions, but Alexandra was just one too many," she said, then hesitated. "I wouldn't be surprised if he did cause that poor girl's death."

"What do you mean?" Montgomery asked.

"Not directly, of course, but the man has no soul. He's just a big clumsy bull bumping into people's lives, never caring about the damage he's done. If he wasn't their father, I'd never see him again."

"I'm glad you're coming back to work." Montgomery hugged her again and became serious. "Can I ask you something personal?" he asked, and she nodded. "Do you think he was seeing anybody else at the same time he was with Alexandra?"

She laughed loud enough that the girls looked up from their scribbling. "What do you think? Alexandra was a brief, unsatisfying experience for Jim, which means there was someone else. There was always someone else." She paused for a few seconds. "My guess would be that goofy woman who works at Operations."

"Sally Wolinski?" Montgomery asked. He sounded surprised.

"She did everything but move in with us before Alexandra died."

Turner saw the dark circles under Patricia McGann's eyes and noticed her heavily chewed fingernails as she walked over to him and captured the twins.

"Thanks, Patty. I'll keep in touch," Montgomery said.

She smiled at Turner and pushed the girls out of the break room into the hallway as they screamed goodbye to him.

"Well, that was interesting," Turner said.

"Nothing we didn't know already. McGann's a sleaze, and Wolinski couldn't care less as long as it gets her a good job."

"Stevenson could've seen a lover's spat in the chief's conference room."

"Probably, but so what?" Montgomery asked, shrugging. "None of these little pieces fit together in a way that's helping us find a killer."

Turner had been thinking about something all morning and decided the time was right to talk about it. He pushed Montgomery back toward the window and away from the door and hallway.

"Monty, I'd like to try something," he said. Montgomery looked worried. "The chief said we couldn't use ISD to follow McGann. Did he say you and I couldn't follow him?" Montgomery didn't answer. "You know I'm right. We need to follow him. I'm betting his lifestyle will tell us how fucked up this guy really is."

Montgomery frowned. Looking down at the standard LAPD worn-to-the-tar-paper linoleum floor, he said softly, "I can't believe you're a fuckin' IA sergeant. Don't you know a move like that could negatively impact your career?" Turner could see that Montgomery was struggling not to smile, so he folded his arms and watched his partner's performance. "This case isn't important. The truth isn't important. What the hell is wrong with you? Are you trying to solve this homicide?" Montgomery grabbed Turner's head with both hands and kissed his forehead. "I think I love you, man," Montgomery said, pretending to be overwrought.

"Hey," Turner said, pushing him away and nearly falling over the table.

"How the hell did you sneak into Internal Affairs?" Montgomery picked up his notebook, giving Turner a dirty look when he saw the twins' artwork scratched all over the cover. He dropped a stack of reports into Turner's arms and grinned. "Does the chief of police actually know where you work?"

NINE

Paula tried to keep her mind on her work, but couldn't stop staring at Sylvia Diaz. The little civilian police commissioner sat in front of Rose's desk, snapping and unsnapping the latch on the briefcase in her lap. Diaz had just come from the chief's office and wanted to talk to Bell. Paula's boss was out of the office, a situation that seemed to further agitate the already disconcerted woman. Diaz, a wealthy businesswoman, wasn't accustomed to idle time. She fussed with her short, freshly styled hair and checked her manicured nails. Other than a large diamond wedding ring and diamond earrings, she didn't wear any jewelry. She didn't look like a woman in her late sixties—partly a good gene pool, partly a good plastic surgeon.

Paula tried to keep her entertained with small talk, but she was obviously annoyed and wanted to speak with Bell.

"Lieutenant Toscano, you'll be a captain soon. Won't you?" Diaz asked.

"Not for a few weeks," Paula said and then thought maybe the commissioner had heard something. "Have you been with the chief?" she asked, trying not to sound like she was fishing for information.

"I will not allow him to protect this McGann," Diaz said, not even attempting to answer Paula. "Internal Affairs has refused to share information with Elaine Miller." She looked up at Paula. "What do you think of that, refusing to cooperate with the inspector general?" It was as if she couldn't contain her emotions any longer. A little teapot boiling over was the first image that came to Paula's mind. "The Christopher Commission was clear on that point. Wasn't it?" Diaz asked but didn't wait for an answer. "The IG gets everything she wants. Doesn't she?"

Paula waited, not certain Diaz wanted an answer this time. She glanced at Rose who was looking down at her desk shaking her head.

"What do you think of Elaine Miller?" Diaz asked. This time she was staring at Paula and obviously expected some response.

Paula hesitated and avoided looking at Rose. The secretary's message was silent but clear. Paula had heard it a thousand times. "Girl, you do not get in the middle of pissed-off elephants 'cuz your puny little insignificant ass is the only one that's gonna get stomped."

"Elaine's an intelligent, competent woman who wants to do what's right," Paula heard herself say in a nervous voice she didn't like. "She's doing the best she can in a position that by its very nature creates hostility. I respect her and like her." Paula thought she should have felt better about speaking the truth, but now she wished she had tempered her support a little.

"Not a very popular opinion on this floor, I would imagine," Diaz said. "What do you think, Rose?"

"I don't think nothing. But thanks for asking," Rose said, turning on her computer.

"Thank you, Paula, for being so candid. Tell Jacob I couldn't wait, but I'll call him tonight," she said, using Rose's desk to help support her weight as she stood.

When they were alone Paula leaned back in her chair and waited for the secretary's tirade.

Rose looked up at her. "Don't stare at me, girl. I'm not going to say nothing. You're hopeless, so why should I waste my breath?" she asked, continuing to type as she talked.

"The woman asked for my opinion."

"She asked me, too. You don't see me giving my opinion, did you?"

"No, but it's different. Elaine is my friend."

Rose exhaled loudly and glared at her. "In this place, the only friend you got is the one you see in the mirror every morning."

"You're wrong. I don't believe that. The department has lots of decent people. Some are just weaker than others."

"Yeah, I'd say there's plenty a that weak shit going around." Before Rose could finish, they were interrupted by Lieutenant Wolinski, who walked past them into Bell's office. They stopped talking and watched her. Wolinski didn't acknowledge their presence until she had thoroughly checked Bell's office and was certain he wasn't there.

Unlike Paula, Wolinski hardly ever wore her uniform. She had an expensive wardrobe that looked great on her tall slender figure. She was pretty, and her thick blond hair moved like it belonged in shampoo commercials. Paula had to admit to a twinge of envy as well as annoyance every time she saw the woman.

"Where is he?" she asked Rose curtly, ignoring Paula.

"We're fine. How are you, Lieutenant?" Rose answered.

"He's at city council," Paula said, trying to accommodate Wolinski and get rid of her as quickly as possible.

Wolinski fidgeted in place for a few seconds and suddenly transformed into Miss Congeniality. She giggled and waved her papers in the air, talking about how some new sergeant in her office couldn't keep his eyes off her. She bantered on about where she'd bought her shoes, what she was doing that night. Eventually the silliness disappeared when she reached the moment of telling them why she was there.

"My boss wants Bell to review a few organizational changes in Operations. Ask him to take a look at these if he gets a chance," she said, giving a folder to Paula. "I put most of it together this morning, so it may not be perfect."

Paula glanced at a few pages and was amazed at the quality of the work Wolinski could produce. She knew Wolinski was smart, and she could never understand why she needed to perform her dumb blond routine. It had to be more gratifying to do work like this than sleep with some of these guys, or maybe not. Paula had never known anyone like Wolinski, who could go from irritatingly rude to world-class dingbat in sixty seconds. That was the extent of her two-dimensional personality.

"This looks great. I'll leave it for him," Paula said, hoping their business was done, but Wolinski didn't leave. She moved a chair closer to Paula's desk and sat with her back to Rose.

She leaned in so close Paula could smell the onions she must've eaten for lunch. Paula inched back a little, trying to reclaim her personal space.

"Does Turner have a suspect in the Williams case?" Wolinski whispered, loudly enough for Rose to hear.

"I don't know, Sally," Paula said, looking at Rose, who was shaking her head again. "Mike is doing the IA stuff. He doesn't talk about it," she lied unconvincingly, knowing McGann was probably the reason for Wolinski's curiosity. He might've even put her up to pumping Paula for information.

"He must have some idea by now. I'm sure he tells you at least that much," she insisted, staring into Paula's eyes for a hint of the truth.

"I told you he doesn't talk to me about it. Frankly, I don't want to know," Paula said, thinking Wolinski was struggling with whatever it was she really wanted to ask.

Wolinski smiled and tossed her pretty blond hair away from her face with a quick jerk of her head, a gesture that always irritated Paula.

"Just curious," she said. Suddenly her face looked drawn and tired. Her shoulders slumped slightly.

"What's wrong?" Paula asked. The change was so dramatic that Paula asked without considering how little she cared about Wolinski's well-being.

Before Wolinski could answer, Bell came back into the office and stood in front of Rose's desk, collecting a stack of messages. Rose told him about the police commissioner's visit. When he finally noticed Wolinski and greeted her, she instantly became Mrs. Hyde. She giggled and twirled out of the office in a flurry of one-liners and sexual innuendos that made Bell smile and Paula gape in amazement. Bell had frequently told Paula he liked Wolinski and believed that in spite of her insecurities, she was a talented, intelligent woman. Paula didn't like her and thought she made Sybil's multiple personalities look normal.

Bell didn't stay long. He had another meeting and wouldn't return to the office for the rest of the day. Paula saw it as a rare opportunity to leave early. Mike wouldn't be done for a while, so there was no reason to hurry home to an empty apartment. She decided to spend some time with Brenda and catch up on gossip.

She found Brenda in her office with Sara. They were sitting on the couch, engaged in an intense conversation when Paula peeked around the corner. She wasn't trying to surprise them, but Brenda seemed startled.

"Sorry, am I interrupting something?" Paula asked, sitting in the chair behind Brenda's desk.

"Yes, I believe you are," Brenda said. "But I'm grateful. We were about to have an argument."

"We never argue," Sara said. "Brenda just badgers me until she gets her way." She slumped on the couch. Sara was in her uniform. Unlike many of the department's lesbians, she was slender and pretty. Her red hair was in a French braid and looked very professional. Although she was smarter than Brenda, Sara always allowed her lover to have her way. She wasn't ambitious, and she hated any kind of disruption or unpleasantness in her life. She usually welcomed Brenda's bossiness, and it was unusual for Paula to see them disagree.

"Can I tell her?" Brenda asked Sara.

"I'm going home. I don't care. Come home early. I'm making dinner." Sara kissed Brenda on the cheek and tousled Paula's hair on her way out.

"She's angry with me," Brenda said.

"What did you do this time?"

"Told her the truth. She won't stand up for herself. Wolinski is pushing her out of the chief's office, and Sara won't talk to Martin."

"What do you mean pushing her out? How can she do that?"

"The same way Sally does everything. She knows how to work the system to get what she wants, and right now she wants to be in the chief's office. She's politicking for a switch between her and Sara."

"Does Sara care? She's been there a long time, and the pay's the same. Maybe she's ready for a change." Paula knew Sara didn't have any ego involved in where she worked.

"That's not the point, Toscano. It's the way Wolinski's doing it."

"It's the way she does everything. If Sara doesn't care, why do you?"

"Because I like having a snitch in the chief's office. Besides, Sally irritates me. I know she irritates everybody, but doesn't it drive you crazy that she does this shit to nice people like Sara and gets away with it?"

Brenda pushed herself off the couch and paced in front of her desk. Her office was not the normal LAPD drab gray. She had come in on a weekend and painted it forest green with dark brown trim. She found an antique walnut desk, matching bookshelves, and a Persian throw rug, transforming the room into an English study. She had decorated the walls with family pictures but none of the awards, certificates, plaques, or other vanities usually found in these Parker Center offices. It wasn't institutional enough for most of the staff officers, but every female officer who happened to glance in the room had to smile.

"Aren't you curious why Wolinski wants to leave Operations? Dougherty lets her run the place. He's a great guy to work for; Martin's not. Martin lets him call all the shots in Operations," Paula said.

"Sally wouldn't do it unless she got something out of it," Brenda said.

"Maybe it has to do with the Williams thing," Paula said.

Brenda stopped moving. "What has Sally got to do with the Williams murder?"

Paula explained what she'd seen during the chief's meeting. "Sally's treating McGann like a leper now."

"Who isn't?"

"No, it's different, like a lover's spat. She was pumping me for information. Being in the chief's office can't hurt if you want the inside scoop."

"I pump you for information, Sherlock."

One of the detectives shouted from the outer office that the inspector general was on line one. Brenda picked up the phone and listened for several minutes. She agreed to meet Elaine Miller and asked if Paula could join them. Paula tried to signal that she didn't want to go, but Brenda ignored her and hung up.

"I'm going home," Paula said. She didn't want another night with the girls. She wanted to make a late dinner and have it waiting for Mike when he got home. She wanted wine and lovemaking, not more bitching and shop talk.

"Too bad. You have to come. Elaine and my favorite commissioner want to meet us at Corky's." Paula groaned. She hated Corky's. It was a crowded, windowless little restaurant and bar with cheap leather booths that smelled of Neetsfoot oil. It was near the courthouse and a favorite of the older lawyers and judges in downtown Los Angeles. Sylvia Diaz was part owner and liked having power meetings in her private booth.

"I'm sure they don't want me there," Paula pleaded.

"The president of your police commission says otherwise," Brenda said, putting her hands together as if praying. "Please don't make me meet with Diaz by myself. I swear she's the Godfather in drag."

"All right, but only for an hour. Then I leave, no argument." Paula did want to be at that meeting despite her protests. Becoming a department insider and policy maker was something she'd always wanted. She would stay until the meeting was over. She tried to tell herself that none of this political bullshit mattered and that it wasn't as important as her personal life, but she knew that was a lie. She thrived on department intrigue. When she was honest with herself, she knew she wanted to participate in every important decision—to have those in power come to her, confide in her, and rely on her. When she was honest, she saw a little bit of Sally Wolinski in herself.

"Sylvia never wants a meeting at night unless she's really pissed off," Brenda said, snatching her briefcase. Paula promised to meet her at Corky's, but she needed to change her clothes. She didn't like wearing her police uniform in a place that was known primarily for its happy hour.

She called Turner from the locker room. He was still at RHD and told her he couldn't leave for at least a couple of hours. She asked a few questions about his day and finally told him she was going to Corky's with Brenda to meet with IG Elaine Miller and Diaz. He didn't ask why and said he would get something to eat on his own. For a brief moment, she almost told him to leave everything until the next day, and she'd meet him at home with dinner and more. But she didn't. She told him she loved him and missed him and would see him later. They hung up. She dressed quickly, and as she drove to Corky's, she had a familiar empty feeling that she knew wasn't hunger.

When Paula arrived, Brenda and Elaine were already settled in the commissioner's booth. It was at the back of the restaurant away from the bar and most of the noisier customers. The décor was 1940s, since most of the interior hadn't been touched since the Second World War. Charcoal sketches covered the walls, the product of a political cartoonist who'd spent most of his day drinking and drawing at Corky's polished-brass-and-marble bar during the Korean War. He paid his tab with caricatures of politicians. The drawings were behind glass. Many had been signed by the subjects of the artist's wit.

Paula slid into the booth beside Elaine. Brenda poured her a glass of Chardonnay from a half-empty bottle. Elaine nibbled on a variety of appetizers—tiny meatballs, chicken wings, cheese and crackers, fried shrimp, olives—enough to feed them for days.

"So where's Grandma Diaz?" Paula asked, snatching the last crab cake.

"Called. She's running late," Elaine said, pouring herself another full glass of wine. Judging from the IG's glassy stare, Paula guessed that Elaine had consumed most of what was missing from the bottle. Paula narrowed her eyes and stared at Brenda, who shrugged as if to say it wasn't their business how much Elaine drank.

"You okay?" Paula asked, moving the bottle away from Elaine's reach.

"You're going to be a captain soon, right?" Elaine asked, pointing her finger at Paula and slurring her words a little. Paula nodded. "Then tell me. Do they send you out and install some damn microchip that makes you people incapable of having an independent thought before they allow you in that command officers' association?"

Paula laughed. "Why do you ask?"

"Because I can't get a single captain or higher to cooperate or work with me in this fuckin' department."

"Maybe they just don't like you," Brenda said, filling Elaine's glass again. Paula tried to stop her, but Brenda slapped her hand.

Elaine took a sip of wine and tried to concentrate. "That's possible. God knows I can't tolerate most of them." She laughed by herself. "But I still think there's some sort of implant. They can't actually support that police chief. Some of them are pretty smart."

"They support the man in the corner pocket," Brenda said. She was serious. "They respect the office and the power, not the man. You're fighting a losing battle, missy. They're like a clan. They protect the head of the family at all costs. You're an outsider. You're expendable. They'll close ranks on you."

Elaine sat up and pushed her glass away. "What about you? Are you part of this inbreeding?"

Paula looked at Brenda, who finally said what they were both thinking. "I'll talk about the man, laugh at him behind his back about his phony Mexican heritage, complain about the way he does his job, but I won't betray him. Not as long as he has those four stars on his collar. I'd be surprised if you could find anybody on this department who thinks differently."

"Maybe the protective league," Paula said, shrugging.

"I'm talking about working members of the department."

For the first time, Elaine looked sober. "It's good for me to know you think that way," she said. "I'm wasting my time. If I can't count on people like you, he's won."

"It's not a question of winning or losing," Paula said. "We need you to keep him honest, to keep all of us on track."

"Let me guess who you are talking about," Sylvia Diaz the little commissioner said, suddenly appearing behind Paula. Brenda moved over, and Diaz came around and slid in the booth beside her. She was dressed in a black brocade evening suit with a blue sapphire pin on the lapel. It was a swan with ruby eyes. She looked elegant. The moment she sat at their table, every employee in the room worked as if what he or she did really mattered now. "Our chief of police, correct?" Diaz asked with a smirk.

"It seems Chief Martin has the complete loyalty of his department managers," Elaine said sarcastically.

"Good, I would expect nothing less," Diaz said, glaring at Elaine. "I have spoken to the chief about the McGann investigation. He has promised to cooperate with you."

Elaine shook her head. "You know he won't honor that promise."

"You are the inspector general. This is not a personal quarrel. He will not defy your office." Diaz wasn't a patient woman. "Demand respect," she said too loudly. Then she leaned closer to Elaine and whispered, "I will tell you this. The Police Commission will support the inspector general, but you cannot make this a battle between Sam Martin and Elaine Miller. Frankly, you will lose."

Elaine laughed. "So I've been told more than once tonight." She stood, steadied herself, and carefully climbed over Paula as she threw twenty dollars on the table. "Got to go. See you tomorrow, Sylvia," she said softly. Looking at Paula and Brenda, she shook her head. She wasn't angry but seemed disappointed. She walked toward the door with a steady, sober stride.

Diaz sighed as she watched Elaine leave. She motioned for one of the waiters to bring another bottle of wine, a better one. They drank quietly for a while.

"Tough business we're in," Brenda finally said.

"If only you knew," Diaz said wryly. She described her meeting with the chief earlier that day.

"He'll sacrifice Nancy Connelly. She'll end up taking the heat for the department dragging its feet," Brenda said.

Paula knew that Connelly would fall on her sword for Martin, but she didn't say anything to Diaz. The clan didn't feel any kinship with Diaz, either. You wore a gun and carried a badge or you didn't. It was that simple.

The three women had a pleasant time after they stopped talking about business and started enjoying each other's company. Diaz, like all self-made individuals, was interesting and knew how to make other people feel comfortable around her. They talked, ate, and drank as the commissioner's guests for another hour. Shortly after 11 P.M., Paula excused herself and reluctantly left the restaurant. She liked the old woman's stories about the who's who of Los Angeles politics. Diaz had financed many elections in the city and had seen the dirty laundry of some pretty influential people, including the current mayor.

The old woman seemed to enjoy telling stories, saying she was fascinated by human nature and what motivated and sometimes destroyed people.

"I have lived long enough to learn that people keep repeating their mistakes," Diaz said, winking at Paula. "I make certain I am there at the right time to take advantage of that. I do not judge or condemn. I marvel at individual strength and become rich off weakness."

As Paula walked to her car, she thought about the crafty woman and worried that Elaine may have crossed a line with her. The wine was making her sleepy. She didn't feel like she'd drunk too much, but she drove carefully. She didn't need a DUI arrest before her name came up on the captain's list. She called the apartment on her cell phone. Mike wasn't home yet. She parked on the street in front of the building and moved quickly up the dark sidewalk to their front door. She switched on the porch light as she entered and then walked through the rooms, turning on the lights. She hated dark places, but lights left on in empty rooms drove Mike crazy. Their electric bill was huge every month. She played back the message on the answer machine. It was Mike telling her he was on his way home. He'd recorded it about five minutes before she arrived.

Paula checked the mini-bar. There was plenty of brandy. She went to the bedroom, undressed, and threw her clothes on the bed. After a quick shower and shampoo, she put on her favorite if shabby robe and went back to the kitchen, where she sliced some

cheese, cut up an apple and a pear, and arranged them on a plat-
ter with a few crackers. She was pouring two glasses of brandy
when Turner opened the door.

Mike Turner was tired, exhausted. He found Paula in the kitchen
in her bathrobe with wet curly hair, sipping on brandy and holding a plate of cheese and fruit. He knew she'd been out with the
girls and expected to find her passed out on top of the bed. He
felt a jolt of energy when she smiled at him.

"What's the occasion, Toscano?" he asked, taking a piece of
cheese.

"I needed some time with somebody I love. I picked you."

"Lucky me." He kissed her and took a sip from the glass of
brandy sitting on the counter. "Who were the other choices,
I wonder?" He kissed her again on the back of her neck and
grabbed a handful of apple slices. "I'm gonna take a shower," he
said, leaving her in the kitchen.

The warm water seemed to revive him. Sex had been the last
thing on his mind as he'd dragged himself home, but seeing Paula
in that ugly robe in her bare feet with wet hair had excited him.
He wanted her. He put on his short terrycloth robe and combed
his hair straight back. She liked it that way. He lowered the living
room lights and put on her favorite blues CD. She was sitting on
the couch with her head resting on the back.

"Who in her right mind would choose drinks with the girls
over this?" she asked.

"You didn't. I just got home, remember?"

"It doesn't make any sense. But you know if it happens again,
I can't help myself. I'll probably do it."

"I have no idea what you're talking about, Toscano," he said,
sitting on the couch beside her. He picked up the brandy glasses
and handed one to her, kissing her gently before leaning back.
"You have no idea how much I need this," he said, rubbing
against her shoulder.

"Me, too. I've missed you. I got spoiled knowing you'd be
here every night. Our quiet, organized life has disappeared."

"Boredom is highly underrated, Toscano. I feel like I've aged
twenty years in the last few weeks."

"You look tired," she said, touching his face.

"I am, and disgusted."

"With the investigation? Sorry, I promised myself I wouldn't talk about work tonight. Do you want to?"

He didn't, but he started talking about Alexandra's strange life before he realized what he was doing. He told her how he thought McGann knew more than he was revealing. He worried that everyone, especially McGann, would walk away from this investigation with no more than a slap on the wrist.

"McGann's a deputy chief. He saw how self-destructive Alexandra was and took advantage of her. He had some responsibility as her boss. He failed, and now the department will protect him," Turner said. He finished the brandy and poured another. He couldn't remember being this worked up over anything in a very long time.

"We both knew nothing was going to happen to him, lover," Paula said. "And you can't change that. It's like Brenda told Elaine. If McGann goes down, the organization suffers, and no one's going to let it happen."

"We'll see. This is a long way from being over."

Paula shifted a little on the couch. "I understand protecting the department, even if it means McGann walks," she said, looking away from him.

"Not if I have anything to say about it."

She picked at her well-chewed nails. "They can still pass over you on the lieutenant's list. You know that."

"Maybe I should move out until they promote you," he said. He was serious and thought he saw her blink and look away for just a second.

Paula pushed away from him and stiffened her back. "You'd better be joking," she said. "You don't really believe I'd kick you out just to make captain." She forced a laugh and added, "Besides, they've got to make me. Sally and I are the only females on the list."

She snuggled up close to him again. He put his arm around her but felt somehow that he'd failed the loyalty test. He asked about her get-together with the girls, trying to steer the conversation in another direction.

"I think Elaine might resign," Paula said.

"Doesn't Sylvia support her anymore?"

"Sylvia wants a stronger IG who'll challenge Martin."

"Maybe Elaine isn't into empty gestures," he said, immediately regretting the comment. He didn't want to discuss departmental hypocrisy again.

"Maybe Elaine doesn't use her influence effectively."

Turner could sense Paula shifting into argument mode. Instead of saying the wrong thing, he touched the back of her neck, rubbing gently.

"Maybe we shouldn't talk anymore," he said, and he could feel her body relaxing.

He kissed her and slid the bathrobe off her shoulders. He didn't care about Elaine or Sylvia or some poor misguided dead woman. He loved Paula and wanted her. They made love on the couch and fell asleep with her on top of him. Sometime during the night, Turner got a blanket from the bedroom and covered them. He lay there and held her close, believing his love for Paula was the one certainty in his life. Finally, too tired to think, his mind and body exhausted, he slept.

TEN

He was cold, and the couch wasn't long enough for his six-foot frame, but the persistent ringing was what finally woke him from a deep sleep. He fumbled for the mobile phone and found it under the coffee table. He was alone on the couch and afraid to look at the clock over the fireplace. Paula was gone, so he was probably late for work.

The caller was Nancy Connelly's adjutant, who wanted to know if Turner was planning on coming to Parker Center. When Turner could focus on the clock, he saw it was only 7 A.M. He remembered that the adjutant liked to start early so he could read the paper without any interruptions and end his workday before the afternoon rush.

"Why do you want to know, Myron?" Turner hated to wake up this way and was thinking of ways to make Myron's life miserable.

"Captain Connelly wants to see you this morning." Myron's voice sounded high and testy. Turner knew Myron preferred his middle name, Bill, but Turner didn't care.

"I'll be there at eight," he said and pushed the off button. He stretched and sat up. He could smell Paula's perfume in the air. She must've just left for work. He pulled the blanket off the floor, wrapped it around his shoulders, and shuffled barefoot into the kitchen. The Pergo floors were cold. Still clutching the phone, he dialed Montgomery's home number while he started the coffee. The answer machine picked up, so Turner tried Montgomery's cell phone, and he answered on the second ring. The detective was on his way to Hollywood station to borrow a lease car from the narcotics squad.

"Sully's gonna let me pick one. Since you and me are going to spend a lot of time in that car, I want one that'll fit your big old ass."

Turner laughed. "I'd worry more about your long skinny chicken legs if I were you."

They agreed to meet at RHD before lunch. He was feeling guilty about not having written anything on the personnel investigation. He needed some time to work on the computer and might get a few pages started after his meeting with Connelly.

Montgomery hung up, and Turner poured a mug of coffee, which he took to the bathroom. He showered, dressed, and packed a change of clothes—Levi's and a sweater—for their surveillance later that night. A few more gulps of coffee and he loaded his briefcase and clothes in the truck. He drove north to Beverly and decided to take surface streets downtown.

Hollywood looked cleaner than he'd seen it in years, but as he drove farther east through the Rampart area, it was business as usual. The illegal day laborers had taken over several street corners, and the street vendors opened their carts for business in front of many legitimate storefronts where the owners who paid business taxes and had expensive licenses didn't even bother to complain any more. The Los Angeles city council had made it clear—legal status didn't matter. Graffiti was spattered in every alley and on every wall. The gangs in this neighborhood took their names from hometowns in Mexico and Central America. The city fathers south of the border must have been ecstatic watching the little hoodlums steal across the border. There was a time when all of this would've bothered him, but these days Turner was just glad he didn't have to work the streets and deal with the idiotic rules that kept him from dragging busloads of these losers back to Mexico.

He laughed to himself, thinking how quickly he'd probably get fired if he were patrolling in a black-and-white police car right then. They ought to give these young coppers medals for going to work every day.

The north end of the city was all business—courts, city halls, federal and state buildings, and Parker Center. Even the new cathedral a little farther west looked like some kind of government building—no stained glass windows or ornate architecture for L.A. The building was an ugly fortress of block walls. Drop below Fourth Street and east of Los Angeles Street, and you were in the transient zone of cardboard condos and city-procured, crime-infested outdoor toilets. He loved this disconnected city.

He parked in the erector set behind Parker Center and crossed San Pedro to the back door of the police building. The basement was crowded, so he took the freight elevator to the fifth floor, where Nancy Connelly's office was located. It was exactly

8 A.M. when he stood before Sergeant Myron "Bill" Nichols. Myron sat behind an enormous, immaculately clean desk and stared at Turner without speaking as he entered the office. The thick glass covering the desktop was spotless and had obviously been polished that morning. Turner thought about his cramped space in the investigators' room at IA, which was cluttered with papers, reference books, and half-filled Styrofoam coffee cups.

"Is she in, Myron?" Turner asked and saw the sergeant's jaw tighten at the use of his first name. "Sorry, Bill." Turner grinned.

"Not important," Myron lied. "She's in there with Lieutenant Wolinski."

Turner sat in the chair near Myron's desk. Myron stared out into the hallway. There was nothing on his desk to work on and nothing he wanted to discuss with an aging, unpredictable cop who was everything Myron disliked and feared.

"Will you be on the transfer next week?" Turner asked, trying to pass the time.

The timid sergeant straightened a little. This was a subject he cherished. He'd been with the department for five years and was a Sergeant II and about to be a lieutenant in record time. Getting promoted was the one thing Myron Nichols had found he could do better than anyone else on LAPD. As a recruit he'd barely made probation, but Myron's tactical skills didn't matter because guys like Myron never worked the field. He hadn't made an arrest in five years. He found jobs at every rank that kept him safely in Parker Center, which suited just about everyone. The thought of Myron in the field, directing officers and making decisions, scared Turner.

"I'll be the day watch commander at the Harbor," Myron said, dusting the single hash mark on his sleeve, one mark for every five years. Most lieutenants had three or four. If Turner made lieutenant this year, he'd have five. Turner stood quickly and Myron flinched.

"Sorry," Turner said, laughing. "Just wanted to grab a cup here." He pointed to the coffeepot behind Myron, who blushed. Turner had known the captain at the Harbor division and pitied the poor guy. He'd have his hands full trying to make this one a leader of men.

The door to Captain Connelly's office opened, and Lieutenant Wolinski stepped out, slamming the door behind her. Her cheeks were crimson, and her body language screamed rage. She seemed startled to see Turner and stopped for a second to regain her composure, pushing her blonde hair away from her face. Her Mona Lisa smile made him want to put his arms around her and protect her from whatever had upset her so badly, but he knew better. You can't comfort the Mad Hatter. She nodded at him and calmly left the office. As Turner watched the little drama, he knew that Connelly was more than capable of driving people to distraction, but this was more.

"Don't you think you should check on your boss?" Turner asked the stunned adjutant.

Myron hesitated. He didn't like confrontation and didn't deal well with emotionally spent people. Finally he got out of his chair, slowly opened the captain's office door, and peeked inside.

Turner heard Connelly tell him to leave the door open. In a shaky voice Myron told tell her that Sergeant Turner was waiting. She called him in.

Connelly was standing by the window that overlooked First Street. Unlike Wolinski, she seemed calm, unflustered. She was wearing her uniform without the Sam Browne utility belt. She was a middle-aged full-figured woman in a tight, unflattering costume.

"Good morning," she said as if Sally Wolinski had never been there. She didn't turn around, so Turner sat in one of the chairs positioned in front of her desk. After several seconds, she sat down behind the cluttered desk, the only piece of furniture in the room that offered a clue that this place was an office. She'd filled the large space with antique tables, chairs, and benches. The bookcase shelves and the window ledge that ran the length of one full wall were filled with knickknacks, porcelain figurines, and pictures of her grandchildren. She had placed a handmade throw rug in the middle of the room. Turner always thought it looked like his grandmother's sewing room. It was clear to him that Connelly wasn't the best person to be running IA.

"What can I do for you, boss?" he asked when she didn't say anything.

She looked up at him. Her face was drawn but determined. "I need the McGann investigation finished by next week—no excuses, no extensions." He started to speak, but she held up her hand, and he waited. "The chief is getting pressure from the commission, and he wants to give them something at their meeting next week."

"I can have the interviews done by then." He hesitated and then figured he might as well put everything on the table. "This personnel matter isn't going to be over until the homicide investigation is finished. McGann's involvement in Williams's murder is critical to adjudicating the internal complaint."

She wouldn't look at him. "The chief doesn't see it that way. He wants us to only deal with the relationship between Williams and McGann." She cleared her throat. "He sees the homicide as a different and separate issue."

"So why am I sitting over at RHD?" He shifted uncomfortably in the delicate birch colonial chair.

"You're not. I'm bringing you back. You'll work on the internal investigation full time; confine your efforts to the relationship between them." She managed to say it without that nervous break in her voice and seemed pleased with herself.

Turner was angry and disappointed, but those feelings surprised him, since this was what he'd wanted. He was out of it, but for some reason he felt as if a thief had just picked his pocket.

"Does Captain Stevenson know I've been taken off the homicide?"

"Let me worry about that," she said, smiling nervously. She stood, and that was his cue to leave. Turner guessed she wanted the discussion to end before he reached the point of challenging her. She wasn't clever enough to defend something she was told to do. She opened the door and stood in front of Myron's desk. "Because this is so sensitive, Sergeant Nichols has prepared a place for you to work in private." She pointed at the tiny office across from hers. Myron grinned at him.

Turner was a good soldier, the perfect policeman. He knew how to follow orders, and he'd make it happen, even if he didn't always agree. Ignoring Myron, he walked across the room to his new temporary office and closed the door, spoiling the adjutant's curiosity.

The office was small but had a large desk, two empty file cabinets, a phone, and one of the department's new Dell computers. None of the investigators in IA had these yet, but one sat unused in this empty office. He took the pages of interview notes, tapes, and witness statements out of his briefcase and carefully arranged them on the desk. He was happy to see that the room had another door to the hallway, so he wouldn't be forced to deal with Myron every morning. The keys to both doors were in the middle desk drawer. He locked the door that led to Myron's office and pulled one of the file cabinets in front of it. He felt better.

He called RHD. Montgomery hadn't returned with the borrowed car, but Katy was there, and he asked her to come up to the office. She took the stairwell and located the hallway door after she and Myron discovered, to his annoyance and dismay, that his easy access was blocked.

"This is bullshit," Katy said after Turner told her what had happened. "A cop is dead, for Christ's sake. We don't have enough people as it is." She was pacing as her anger grew. She pointed in the direction of Connelly's office. "The woman is a menace. She shouldn't have any say in this."

Turner watched until she stopped. "Do me a favor," he said when she was sufficiently worked up. "Tell Stevenson what happened."

She stared at him. "He doesn't know?"

He smiled and shook his head. "Nope."

Katy grinned back at him. Wearing Levis, with her long brown hair hanging loose, she looked like a delinquent teenager. "This is gonna be so good," she said as she left the office and ran down the two flights of stairs to the third floor.

It was Captain Connelly's good fortune to be out of Parker Center when Carl Stevenson heard from his irritating little detective that he had lost one of his investigators on a critical case, without any discussion or input from him. He calmly sent Katy out to interview restaurant owner Judy Taylor and then closed the door to his office. Katy didn't need to be there to know what was going to happen next. She'd seen that look on Stevenson's face on many prior occasions. It usually meant trouble for somebody. She was relieved it wasn't her this time.

Stevenson needed to think. He had successfully survived many years as a maverick in this tightly controlled environment because he carefully planned every one of his spontaneous emotional outbursts. He wouldn't argue with Connelly. The best argument wouldn't persuade someone who didn't have the power or gumption to change a decision. He would talk to Jacob Bell, a reasonably principled man and the only one who could occasionally convince Sam Martin to do the right thing.

He took the elevator up to the sixth floor, carefully rehearsing in his mind how he would approach Bell. You couldn't bullshit him. Stevenson knew he could pretend to be indignant about the way Connelly had taken back her sergeant without any discussion or notice. It wasn't the way things were done in the LAPD. If she'd talked to him first, Connelly could've done whatever she wanted. She'd made a protocol blunder, but shabby etiquette wouldn't be enough reason for Bell to overrule her. Stevenson decided to tell the truth. He needed Turner and his expertise to complete this homicide investigation. They'd all look foolish if the personnel investigation prematurely whitewashed McGann's behavior but he was ultimately found to be involved in the killing.

Bell's office door was open. He was at his conference table reviewing correspondence and stacks of projects with Paula Toscano. Rose looked up from her computer and motioned for Stevenson to enter Bell's office. He hesitated until Paula stood and picked up an armful of folders.

"He's all yours, Captain," Paula said as she slid by him and gently closed the door as she left.

Stevenson sat across the table from the older man and methodically recounted the status of the Williams investigation. He intentionally noted every lead they'd uncovered and every step they'd taken, hoping the complexity and volume of work would persuade Bell to keep the veteran Turner on the case.

"I think she made the right decision," Bell finally said.

"How can you say that, Jake? IA's investigation is RHD's investigation. It makes sense not to duplicate efforts or prematurely clear this guy if he's involved."

After forty-five minutes, the best deal Bell would offer him was the assurance that Turner could act as a liaison between IA and RHD. He'd report to IA every day and could work with RHD as an ancillary duty. Bell also agreed to talk to Connelly and explain to her how he'd slightly revised Turner's status.

"He's an IA investigator, Carl, not an RHD detective. As long as you treat him that way, you're welcome to take advantage of his expertise."

Stevenson could feel his face getting redder. "I get it."

"Don't bother to give me your 'Whatever happened to police helping police?' speech. Connelly has a division to run, too."

"I have a dead cop, and finding her killer is a priority, isn't it?" he said, glaring at Bell. He knew he was challenging the decent old man and for a second almost felt ashamed.

"Everyone wants to solve this homicide. The department can't stop functioning to do it."

"Efficiency is a wonderful thing, Jake, but sometimes you've got to make some tough choices."

Bell sat back and smiled. "I've known you a long time, Carl. I know what you're trying to do. I've seen you work your magic and get your way. But I believe whoever made this decision, Connelly or Martin, is right this time. Turner needs to finish this IA thing. The decision stands."

After a few more attempts, Stevenson realized he'd salvaged all he was going to get. He and Bell both knew he'd liberally interpret Bell's invitation to "take advantage of Turner's expertise."

Paula stopped him when he left Bell's office. She confided in him that she was surprised at how disappointed Turner had been to return to IA, and how relieved she was that they could go back to their old routine.

"I kind of like the guy who knew what he wanted and didn't need the adrenaline highs," she said. "This reawakening makes me a little uncomfortable."

Stevenson had known a lot of good cops like Turner who'd burned out and thought the game was over for them. Then one day they catch the scent again, and it draws them back into the hunt. Maybe Paula had never seen this side of the man, and it was upsetting the tranquility she loved in him, but Stevenson guessed this driven, edgy man was the real Turner, and she'd better get used to him. He had tasted blood again and would never be happy back in the cage. Stevenson knew Turner would remain part of the investigation one way or another, but he decided to let Turner tell her that.

He walked down the flight of stairs to Connelly's office in Internal Affairs. When he got there, he was breathing heavily, and his face was damp with perspiration. Connelly was out, and Myron was at his desk picking at a bean sprout sandwich his wife had prepared.

"Where's Turner?" Stevenson demanded, still a little short of breath.

Myron sighed and stood up. Without a word, he walked to the hallway and pointed to the next door. "There." He smiled weakly at the overweight captain and returned to his desk.

Stevenson knocked on the door and entered the office without waiting for an invitation. Turner looked up from his paperwork and then stood quickly.

"Captain, did Katy tell you?" he asked innocently.

"You know damn well she told me." He sat in the one extra chair in the room and motioned for Turner to sit. As Stevenson described the meeting with Bell, Turner couldn't hide his disappointment. He'd hoped for more. "You'll continue to work on my homicide," Stevenson said. "Report to this office every morning, check in, and get the hell out. Finish this IA crap on your own time, but finish it. If Connelly wants you to do anything, you do it, then get the hell out of here. If somebody questions you, send him to me, and I'll explain that I'm taking advantage of your expertise." He took a deep breath. "You got that, Sergeant?"

"It works for me," Turner said calmly. He felt like jumping up and down and screaming for joy but didn't move. He knew better than to thank Stevenson and waited for the grouchy captain to say something else. Stevenson glowered at him as if he were responsible for causing him all this turmoil, put his hands on his knees, and lifted his large body off the chair.

He opened the door and stopped for a second before turning around again. "I'm not going to ask why you and Montgomery needed to borrow a car from narcotics division. Just try not to do anything to embarrass RHD, or the two of you will find yourselves working morning watch in the Harbor . . . for Myron."

He was gone, and Turner sank back in his chair. It wasn't all that he'd hoped for, but he wasn't cut off from the investigation. Clearly, nobody really wanted this to be an in-depth personnel complaint on McGann, and Turner could easily accommodate them. He'd finish this worthless complaint as soon as possible and work with Monty to find the truth another way.

Turner decided to work on transcribing his interviews until Monty contacted him. He put a disk in the computer and started with McGann. He pulled a small tape recorder out of his briefcase and put in the first tape. He would paraphrase McGann's statement but didn't want to do it just from his notes. After a few minutes, he turned off the recorder and sat back. He thought about the strange scene between Wolinski and Connelly that morning, and the link between Wolinski and McGann, and McGann and Alexandra, Alexandra and Dean, Alexandra and Crystal. Monty was right—bits and pieces and no real connections. He believed Maria Perez had given Alexandra the IA car, but why? Perez was a company lady, a career cop, not likely to risk her job for the likes of Alexandra. Wolinski's face kept popping into his thoughts, the silky blond hair and clear complexion and that smile, so out of sync with the out-of-control anger she'd displayed earlier.

He slid his chair back and stretched a long luxurious stretch. His neck was sore from sleeping on the couch. A twinge of pain made him feel guilty, as if in his thoughts he had just cheated on Paula. He needed to concentrate on the investigation. He picked up Alexandra's personnel package. He had read her background. There was nothing unusual, but the Personnel Division didn't always do a thorough job on the backgrounds for police candidates. When the department went through a hiring binge, some interesting selections were made. The mistakes or disqualifiers usually didn't get discovered until that person reverted to his or her normal lifestyle after making probation.

He wondered if that was what had happened with Alexandra. He'd copied the names and addresses of her mother and an aunt that she'd provided on her application. They were the only family she claimed. Her references were all out of state and conveniently dead ends. He and Monty needed to find the mother and aunt and interview them. This was the only way Turner knew how to do police work—look under every rock until you find something worth keeping.

His phone rang and startled him. It was Stevenson's secretary. She told him Stevenson wanted to see him in his office, now. Turner hung his jacket on the hook behind the door and spread his paperwork around the desk. He left the computer on but locked the disk, tapes, and any significant witness statements in the top file cabinet drawer. He opened his briefcase and left it on the extra chair. He wasn't worried about anyone reading his notes. He was one of the few detectives who could take Gregg shorthand, and most of the city's civil service secretaries couldn't take or read shorthand anymore. He looked around. It definitely appeared to be a working IA investigator's office, an investigator who'd just stepped out for a minute or two.

He grabbed his bag with the change of clothes and left his office door unlocked for Myron's bed check. Myron would leave in about an hour, and Turner could lie about how much time he'd spent in the office that afternoon. He ran down the stairwell to the third floor.

When Turner arrived, Stevenson was in his office with Montgomery. They were discussing the Dean homicide. The Hollywood detectives had just called from the autopsy and reported that Dean had died from the fall. He'd broken his neck hitting the steel bar at the bottom of the fire escape. Although he had more than a recommended dose of heroin in his system, the drug didn't kill him. About a dozen witnesses had heard him screaming and heard the struggle in his room. No one had seen anyone in or around it. If the detectives were to believe the witnesses, Jimmy Hargrove Dean had never interacted with another human being the entire time he'd lived at the Carlton Street Hotel.

"They searched his room and didn't find much more than a filthy needle and a piece of damp cotton in a spoon," Stevenson said.

"Hepatitis starter kit," Turner said.

"It was just like Alexandra's place—no paperwork, no address books, nothing to tie him to another person," Stevenson added, ignoring Turner. "Your basic crash pad. Nothing to cook on, and one of those small refrigerators full of beer and candy bars."

Montgomery shook his head for a few seconds and then said, "This guy had $400 suits in his closet, over $500 in his wallet and was wearing enough gold to get a small country out of debt. Why would he live there?"

"Maybe he didn't," Stevenson said. "Maybe the Carlton was his place of business."

"If one of the locals pushed him out that window, we would've found him butt naked, no money, no jewelry, nothing," Turner said.

Montgomery groaned. "You're all giving me a headache with your maybes. Let's work with what we know."

"We know somebody pushed him out the window. Why?" Stevenson asked.

"Alexandra," Turner said. "Dean worked with her. She's killed. A few days later, he's killed. It's connected."

"What's the connection?" Stevenson asked. "I don't see any damn connection that would get them killed."

"We've got to find Crystal," Turner said, adding, "if she's still alive." He knew he was right. The Hollywood whore was the link between Dean and Alexandra and probably knew why they were dead. "Sully's still looking for her, but I think we need to get a team to sit on that bungalow in West L.A. That was her home. I'm guessing she'll come back."

Stevenson agreed to find a couple of detectives to baby-sit the empty bungalow behind the sisters' house in West L.A.

Katy called from the café in Hollywood. She'd interviewed Judy Taylor but didn't get much more than a good lunch for her efforts. Taylor couldn't give a solid description of the two cops she believed were under the influence of drugs. She described a black guy and a white guy, both wearing shoulder holsters and carrying handcuffs on their belts. She didn't see badges or the make or color of their car, but she was certain she could identify the men if she saw them again.

"The woman's paramount concern," Katy said sarcastically, "was that this inquiry not cause any hardship for Jimmy McGann. I almost lost that great lunch."

Stevenson told her to come back to the office and work with Montgomery for the time being. Turner shot a quick glance at Montgomery. He hadn't intended dragging Katy into their conspiracy, but explaining the surveillance to Stevenson at this point would be more problematic than stuffing Katy in the back seat all night.

"Turner," Stevenson called to him as he was leaving the office, "if you happen to be out with Monty and Katy tonight and something goes down, you decided to join them at the last minute as a ride-along."

Turner nodded. "Got it, boss."

"Let's at least try to make this look like I'm not an insubordinate son of a bitch."

Most of the other detectives had gone for the day as Turner and Montgomery huddled in a corner of the detective bay to plan their strategy. They would watch McGann every night for a week or two, following him home from work each day. If nothing happened, then they might watch him during working hours. Staff officers were pretty much on their own during the day. He could be doing anything he wanted on company time, but the odds were better that he'd be more comfortable doing illicit stuff on his own time.

By the time Katy returned from Hollywood, Turner had changed clothes and checked out radios and spare batteries from RHD's kit room. Montgomery borrowed a camera that one of the detectives from Robbery Special had forgotten to lock up.

Katy wasn't happy about being thrown in a car with no explanation, but she'd worked with Montgomery long enough to know he wouldn't talk about where they were going and why until he was ready to explain.

"I had plans tonight," she said, tossing her workbag on the back seat. "Your silence is irritating."

As soon as they drove away from Parker Center, Turner explained where they were going and apologized for getting her involved.

"If something goes sideways, I'll keep you out of it," he said.

She curled up in a corner of the back seat and closed her eyes. "I appreciate the gesture," she said calmly. "But don't bother. I'm cursed anyway."

"Good. Then you keep the logs." Montgomery grinned at Turner, who was trying not to laugh.

"There's some kind of fate that's determined to fuck up my career, so I figure I might as well go with the flow and enjoy my slide into obscurity."

"Quit whining. Your life is no worse than anybody's. You're a good detective, and someday you'll get promoted," Montgomery said, grinning in the rearview mirror at her. "Until then, quit screwing up."

She playfully slapped the back of Montgomery's bald head. "What is it the two of you expect to see by creeping around after this high-ranking degenerate?"

"Don't know," Turner admitted.

As he drove toward the west side, Montgomery told them why he was so familiar with the area around Wilshire station and the Bureau offices. His grandmother had lived on a side street off Venice Boulevard and across from the old police station when he was growing up. He spent most summers at her house and dreamed about the day he would drive a black-and-white and wear that uniform. One of the older sergeants at the station caught him hanging around the parking lot and brought him into the police explorer program. Later on he helped Montgomery study for the police academy.

"He was a fat white guy with emphysema but treated me better than my old man ever did. He's dead, but I can't come back here without thinking of him."

Montgomery parked the Taurus under the big oak tree in front of his grandmother's house. Turner could see the front of the station and the parking lot driveway from there.

"This is a great point," he said. "Your misspent youth has been helpful."

"It's gonna be tough with just one car," Montgomery said, sliding down a little in the seat.

"If it gets too hairy where he might make the tail, just let him go. I've got his current address," Turner said. He didn't want McGann to know they were following him, or it would mean both their heads.

"How do you know he's even here?" Katy asked

Turner borrowed Montgomery's cell phone and dialed the number to McGann's office. He identified himself and asked to speak with the deputy chief. McGann's adjutant put him on hold, and when he came back on line after several minutes, he told Turner that McGann was in a meeting and asked if he could help. Turner declined and asked if McGann would be available later. The adjutant said McGann would be leaving soon and would call Turner in the morning. Turner flipped the phone to Montgomery.

"The rabbit's in his hole. Now we wait."

Katy lay down on the back seat, using her bag as a pillow. She'd participated in several surveillances and knew you had to take advantage of down time. In a few minutes, she was snoring loudly. Turner pushed his seat back and stretched his legs. It was dark; if they didn't do anything stupid, McGann shouldn't see them. Headlights in a rearview mirror all look alike to the average driver, and the IA surveillance guys told him that most cops never pay attention to what's around them when they leave work.

119

McGann's new apartment was in the Marina, so Turner told Montgomery they'd probably need to make a U-turn to go west when McGann left the station.

After an hour and a half, Turner wondered if the adjutant had lied to him. Lying for your boss was a big part of an adjutant's workload. Driving through the parking lot to see whether McGann's car was still there wasn't an option, so he looked over the seat at Katy and gently shook her. When she was clear-headed, Turner told her to take a radio and walk across the street to see whether McGann's car was in the lot. If McGann left while she was in the lot, they'd leave her there, and she could catch a ride downtown with a black-and-white patrol car. She mumbled something about being expendable and took the bulb out of the overhead light before opening the door.

Turner watched as she crossed Venice Boulevard, pulling on her jacket as she ran. Fifteen minutes later, she came back across the street and jumped into the back seat.

"He's there," she said. "He's in his office, and his car's parked in the stall." She took a napkin out of her pocket and unwrapped half a dozen chocolate cookies. She took one and gave the rest to Montgomery. "Everybody's gone except him, the commander, and his adjutant. I heard them talking."

"Good work, girl. Where'd these come from?" Montgomery asked with a mouthful of chocolate.

"McGann's office. They looked good, and I was hungry. Sorry, no milk, and the coffeepot was empty."

As Turner took one of the cookies from Montgomery, he caught headlights turning out of the driveway. It was a big Crown Victoria. "It's our man," he said, hitting Montgomery on the shoulder. With the binoculars, he could barely make out the driver's silhouette in the headlights from passing traffic, but it was McGann's car.

Montgomery started the engine and slowly moved forward without turning on his lights. When the traffic had cleared, McGann drove through the break in the island and went east-bound past their street. The car was out of sight, and Montgomery drove quickly to the corner. They could see McGann's car stopped at the next light and waited at the corner. When the light changed, McGann made a quick U-turn and went back west-bound on Venice. Montgomery hadn't moved, and he waited at the corner with his lights off. McGann made a right turn at La

Brea, and Montgomery cut through the island and made a cautious turn onto La Brea. The car was two blocks ahead. Montgomery slowed and allowed more traffic to filter in between them.

"Is he looking for a tail or just indecisive, I wonder?" Katy whispered to Turner.

"We'll give him lots of room, so it won't matter," Montgomery said.

McGann drove north on La Brea until he reached Melrose, where he turned west into heavy traffic. Montgomery groaned as he got caught in the turn lane on a red light. He was first up, and Turner told him not to worry because he could see that McGann wasn't making much progress, either. Before the green arrow allowed them to turn, Turner had lost sight of the Crown Victoria but quickly picked it up again waiting at a red light before La Cienega. After McGann drove through the intersection, he made a quick right turn at the next street and parked his car in a red zone just past the corner. He had a city placard that he took out of the glove compartment and placed in the front window.

Montgomery hadn't expected him to park so quickly and was forced to drive past his car. Fortunately, McGann was intent on looking at himself in the rearview mirror and didn't pay any attention to them. Montgomery drove around the block and came back on Melrose in time for Turner to see McGann cross La Cienega and enter a small club, The Spot, on Melrose. When McGann was inside, Montgomery drove by the building. The usual Melrose Avenue crowd was standing outside, drinking and smoking and dressed in shabby-looking jeans that probably cost more than Turner's entire wardrobe. Montgomery parked down the street on the other side of Melrose, where he could see the front door from his side-view mirror.

Katy removed her jacket, brushed her shoulder-length hair, and put on some fresh makeup. She opened her utility bag and found a box with costume jewelry. She replaced her conservative diamond studs with a pair of dangling earrings. She pulled off her tennis shoes, put on a pair of black boots, and stuffed the tennis shoes back into her bag. She tucked her black sweater into her tight Levi's and suddenly looked all dressed up. Turner watched, staring at her over the car seat, amazed at the transformation. She was an attractive woman.

"Do you want to go in?" she asked him. He shook his head but didn't speak. She stared back at him. "What? Yes, I do have a life away from LAPD. I go out. I've been in this club."

"You look great," Turner finally said, and Montgomery nodded in agreement.

"If he comes out, do not leave without me," she said, getting out of the car. She went around the back of the car and leaned into Montgomery's window. "However, if I get lucky and pick up some stud, feel free to disappear."

She walked across the street and talked to the doorman, an overweight Samoan giant in a colorful polyester shirt who guarded the front entrance. He laughed at whatever she said, hugged her and opened the door.

"Maybe we should've gone with her," Montgomery said almost to himself. He looked up at Turner. "I'm not worried. I'm jealous."

Katy knew the layout of the club. She'd been here once on a less-than-memorable date. She'd hoped it would be crowded, and it was. She didn't want to bump into McGann, who may or may not remember her. She maneuvered around groups hovering at the bar and located the stairs to the balcony. Anyone standing up there couldn't be seen by the patrons downstairs. Since most people came to The Spot to be seen, the second floor was nearly empty. Katy stood back from the railing, studying the faces below her. It was elbow to elbow on the dance floor, and they were three deep at the bar. Pretty young girls wearing as little as possible were generally too thin, and they all had long silky hair like hers. The men were a mix of the older, richer business types in stylish suits and young boyish-looking guys in baggy wash-and-wear with flat stomachs and hair tied back in ponytails. She slid along the rail to the other side, surveying the club from that angle. It was twenty minutes before she recognized McGann's lanky frame and handsome face poking out of the horde. He was talking to someone at the bar, but Katy couldn't see who it was. She leaned over the railing, but the person sitting on the barstool was hidden behind a wall of backs and shoulders. Katy was about to go downstairs and risk discovery when a small table opened and McGann snatched the drinks and moved to claim it.

A short Hispanic woman sat across the table from McGann. She wore a tight skirt and tank top. Although she was a little better-looking all dressed up, Maria Perez couldn't alter her appearance very much, and Katy recognized her immediately. McGann's conversation seemed to be more intense than the usual empty chatter found in these places. He leaned on the table and listened intently to hear what Perez was saying. His expression never changed until his head jerked back. He was obviously upset with what she was saying.

Katy decided to move closer and hide among the barflies. She got to the bottom of the stairs and froze as McGann stood and went to the bar. In a few seconds, he returned to the table with two fresh drinks. Katy was just a few feet away from them by then, but they'd stopped talking. He gulped his drink and said something to Perez that Katy couldn't hear. Perez pushed her drink away and gave him a sickly smile. He stood again, moved behind her chair, and kissed Perez gently on the cheek. He was sucked into the sea of bodies, and Katy watched the top of McGann's head move closer to the front door. Before she could follow him, Katy saw a young pretty woman who was standing beside her move to the chair near Perez. The woman put her arm around Perez. Katy stepped back behind an Asian couple and watched the two women, trying to remember every detail about the new player. When she glanced back toward the door, McGann was nowhere in sight. She weaved her way through the room until she stood near the open door and watched McGann walk away from the club the same way he'd come. She slipped out and went in the opposite direction toward the Taurus. She didn't look at him and hoped Montgomery had picked him up in the side-view mirror. As she got closer to their car, she heard the engine start. She calculated that McGann must've made the turn onto the side street and was approaching his car. She ran the rest of the way and jumped into the rear seat.

Montgomery eased the car back into traffic and drove around the block to catch McGann's car as it came northbound. As if on cue, the big Crown Victoria drove by them on the side street. Montgomery bet that McGann would take surface streets to the Marina and avoid the freeways if he'd been drinking. McGann followed the script and stayed in his own backyard away from the chippies who enjoyed catching LAPD drunks. As they drove, Katy briefed Turner on the meeting between Perez and McGann and described Perez's mystery girlfriend.

"Sorry, didn't have time to get her girlfriend's name."

"Don't be," Turner said, giving her arm a gentle squeeze. "You proved this guy is in this mess up to his silver stars. We'll question Perez again, and if she's smart, she'll give up her girlfriend and tell us what she and McGann had to talk about."

"Alexandra is still the common denominator," Montgomery said. "I think Perez and McGann were both doing her."

Turner sat back and was quiet until they saw McGann drive into a security building in the marina. They were able to park in a lot that faced his apartment, and they soon saw the light go on in his kitchen. The apartment was on the bottom floor and had a balcony that faced the water. They watched McGann go from room to room until the apartment was dark again. Only a small flashing light came from one of the rooms, and Turner guessed it was the television.

Turner got out of the car and threw his pager and cellular phone on the seat. He walked as close as he could to the apartment window. He ducked into the bushes and hoped Monty was watching for good citizens walking their dogs who might interfere with his peeping-tom activity. He stood on a planter and peeked into the bedroom, where he saw McGann lying on top of the bedspread. McGann was naked except for the drink in his hand, and he was watching a movie. Turner stepped down and carefully slipped out of the shrubbery.

He returned to the car and leaned into the passenger window. "It's a wrap," he said, taking his cell phone off the seat. "Let me call Paula before we take off." Turner walked away from the car again without waiting for a reply. He stood a few yards away and dialed his home number. She was asleep. He felt bad for waking her, but he wanted to talk to her. He always wanted to talk with Paula when things were going well. She tried to sound interested, but he could hear she wasn't quite awake. He told her he'd be home in about an hour and they could talk in the morning. Turner never understood why it was so important that he share everything with Paula. It was almost as if it hadn't happened unless she knew about it, experienced it with him. He said he loved her and hung up. He was certain she'd be asleep before her head hit the pillow again and wouldn't remember their conversation the next day.

Montgomery drove them back to Parker Center. Turner watched Katy get into her car and waited until she'd driven away from the parking structure behind Parker Center. He walked across the street and in the back door of the building. He needed to lock his door and rearrange his office for Myron's inspection in the morning. He took his jacket and briefcase, locked the office door, and left. He planned to get a few hours' sleep, then come back early in the morning to work on the personnel investigation.

Paula was curled up in a corner of the bed when he got home. She didn't stir as he dropped his clothes on the floor and slid between the sheets. He moved closer and slipped his arm over her hip. She relaxed and molded to his body. Her warmth and rhythmic breathing drew him into the darkest part of the night, where he couldn't see Alexandra's face or that of his dead partner—a welcome, peaceful sleep.

ELEVEN

When Paula woke the next morning, Turner was already gone. His side of the bed looked as if it had been slept in, but she couldn't remember seeing him the night before. She found two chocolate cookies on the kitchen table with a note that read, "Toscano's breakfast. Sorry I had to leave early. I'll call. Love you, your roommate." She smiled and thought, "Leave early? When were you here?" She was disappointed because she'd planned to have a serious talk with him. The McGann investigation was impacting their relationship. She thought he'd have welcomed an opportunity to back away from it, but he'd manipulated Stevenson into keeping him at least part time in RHD. They hardly ever saw each other or talked anymore. She felt as if she were living with a hyperactive street cop instead of a supervisor who was about to make lieutenant any day.

She loved him but didn't like this reversion. They should be discussing department policy and long-term objectives, not autopsies and search warrants. She liked the adrenaline high too and missed it, but at this stage in their careers, they should be managing cases, not sitting up all night doing the grunt work. She was beyond the nuts and bolts of police work and thought he was, too. He'd told her he was. She knew this business was like a narcotic. Turner had gotten a taste and was hooked again. She'd enjoyed it when she'd been a working cop, but at the present she wanted to call the shots, not do the bookings. He was slipping back into that other world. It was a small crack that in a few more days might become a canyon unless he walked away right then. Her real fear was that he didn't want the life she wanted for him and would never really accept it. He had so much to offer and was capable of so much more. She felt as if he was settling for the easy, familiar road of his past and throwing away his future. She'd rehearsed saying all these things, making such a good argument, and then he hadn't come home, at least not while she was conscious.

The phone rang just as she stepped out of the shower. It was Turner. They chatted about what had occurred the night before with McGann. He was excited and encouraged by the progress they'd made. She half listened, trying to decide whether to broach the subject of her disappointment. Instead, she told him not to get his hopes up.

"Unless McGann killed Alexandra Williams, Sam Martin and Connelly will protect him despite his indiscretions. They'll protect the organization," she said, trying to deflate his enthusiasm and bring him back to reality.

"I understand that, but knowing it's bullshit doesn't make it smell any better."

She could hear the frustration in his voice but wanted to make him think like a lieutenant. "Martin has other ways he can deal with one of his deputy chiefs. Ways that won't destroy the department."

Turner was quiet for a few seconds, as if he could hear the agitation and knew her well enough to know it had nothing to do with McGann.

"You mad at me?" he asked.

"No, I just think you need to start looking at the world with a little broader perspective."

"Sorry, kiddo, my perspective is never going to be that broad."

She changed the subject and told him she'd better get dressed or she'd be late for work. They both knew she had plenty of time. He told her he'd call her at the office and would be working late again that night.

When Paula hung up the phone, she looked in the mirror. "Coward," she said to her image. She knew what she should've said: "Stop playing homicide detective, finish your personnel investigation, act like a lieutenant, and come home at night." She could say it to the mirror, but Turner's voice was strong and honest. Suddenly she felt like a weakling for offering a compromise, but reasoned that's what managers are supposed to do. They make things work for the organization. She tapped her head against the mirror. What kind of captain was she going to be? She stared deeply into her eyes. Leaders should believe in something, have principles and strong values. Here she was, quoting the gospel according to Sam Martin. She was relieved she hadn't said more to Turner.

She wiped the remaining condensation off the mirror and applied her makeup. She tried to think about something else. She'd always wanted to be a captain, a commanding officer of her own division. She was just realizing what achieving that goal might mean to her sense of who Paula Toscano really was.

Turner knew Paula was probably right. He didn't like it but understood how the department worked. Sam Martin was not a man who would allow his department or himself to look foolish. If necessary, he would give McGann every menial task he could find or invent but never give the man his trust or confidence again. However, he would never let the public know that one of his personally selected staff had been anything less than perfect. Knowing all of that, Turner still wasn't about to quit.

By the time Myron peeked into his office, Turner had finished typing McGann's interview and was starting on the Perez tape. He waved at the startled adjutant, who was surprised to see anyone in the office earlier than he was. As soon as Myron left, Turner called Montgomery and woke him. He told the sleepy detective that whenever he dragged himself into the office, they would go out to Alexandra's mother's house and possibly the aunt's, if they could find her. Montgomery told him that the Hollywood detectives didn't have any luck at the bungalow in West L.A., but they were there again this morning, watching for Crystal or Phil White to return.

Turner didn't know how much help Alexandra's mother would be, but he didn't expect much. He was curious about this dead woman and was desperate for some intimate details and insights into her life and personality. Alexandra was beautiful and talented and apparently had impacted a number of lives in a short period of time. Someone hated her enough to mutilate that gorgeous body and dump her into a car trunk like an old tire. There were so many unanswered questions, and he calculated he had about a week to unravel the mystery before Connelly demanded his report and assigned him to something else.

The picture in this puzzle was hidden from him, and he didn't know if he had the time or ability to find it. He was working with some good detectives, but the general rule was that if you didn't solve a murder in the first few days, you probably weren't going to solve it.

He had slept well the night before, but not long enough. Most of the formatting for the complaint had been done, so he took out the disk and turned off the computer. He needed coffee but wasn't in the mood to deal with Myron. The canteen on the first floor was another option, but he had to stand in line with family and friends of arrestees who were being processed for release. He preferred their company to Myron's. He bought his coffee and a candy bar and squeezed through the crowd in the lobby, working his way back to the elevator. In this old building, it took some stamina to wait for one of the cars to come back down, but he sipped on his coffee and tried to relax. As the door finally opened, someone tapped him on the shoulder, and he turned to see Elaine Miller behind him. She introduced herself, but Turner remembered her. Paula had introduced them at a Christmas party the year before. Miller made small talk about Paula and her pending promotion to captain. Turner didn't mention his own promotion. These days he was hoping he could sneak into a lieutenant position before anyone noticed or objected.

At the third floor, everyone except the two of them got off the elevator.

"Were you told not to give me copies of the McGann personnel investigation?" she asked quickly when they were alone.

"No." He waited for her to ask, but she hesitated as if she were afraid his answer would be "but you can't have them." Instead, he said, "You're welcome to everything I have," and he could see her relax. She was prepared for another battle. "Don't get your hopes up. The most I've got is an inappropriate relationship. Maybe."

The elevator stopped on the fifth floor, and she held the button to keep the door closed.

"Are you finished with it?"

"Guess I am. The chief wants it next week."

"Are you still working on the homicide?" she asked, and he nodded. "I take it we've bifurcated that investigation from this one. Never mind. I know we have. When can I get copies of what you have?"

"Got a minute? Come to my office. I'll give you a copy now."

She allowed the door to open. "Don't you need to check with someone?"

"Probably, but then someone might say no." He smiled at her and opened his office door. She stood in the middle of the room and looked around.

"This is all yours? It's bigger than mine, and I've got two assistants."

"They don't want anyone looking over my shoulder. And besides, nobody likes you." He laughed, mostly at the surprised look on her face. "I'm sure that thought never crossed your mind," he said, and then she laughed.

"But the chief keeps telling everyone how critical I am to keeping his department corruption-free," she said innocently.

They looked at each other. "Lying?" he asked. She responded, "Lying."

Turner took the disk out of his desk drawer and loaded it into the computer. He checked the printer and made a single copy of everything he'd done.

"I'll have it finished next week and bring you the rest then. Okay?"

"Better than okay. Somebody's actually cooperating with me, willingly."

He stepped closer to her and whispered, "If he's involved in Williams's murder, this isn't the investigation you want. Do you understand what I'm saying?"

She nodded and took the copies from him. "Keep me in the loop and I'll help you. No one has to know where I get my information."

"Nobody can know, or we're both fucked," he said.

Miller bumped into Montgomery as she stepped into the hallway. He started to apologize, but she hurried away without acknowledging him.

"Come on in, Monty," Turner said, pulling him inside and closing the door.

Montgomery looked around the room and examined the case notes scattered over the desktop. He put his arm around Turner's shoulder.

"If you made some kind of deal with her, it better include your partner."

"No deal. Just bought us some job insurance."

"Did somebody see us last night?" Montgomery asked, looking worried.

"Relax. Nobody saw anything. It can't hurt to have the IG in our corner. I only gave her the personnel stuff, but we should feed her some of the criminal case, too."

"Maybe. Let's think about that. Stevenson will forgive the surveillance, but a leak on the homicide investigation might be a harder sell."

Turner didn't say anything. He had already decided that when the time came, he'd do it and wouldn't ask anyone's permission. While Montgomery waited, he arranged his office to look like he'd been working and had just stepped away. He locked the important papers in the file cabinet and strategically placed his briefcase and jacket. "Good night, Myron," he whispered as he closed the unlocked door.

Katy was waiting for them at the back door of Parker Center. Montgomery led them to the Taurus in the jail parking lot. She tossed her workbag in the back seat and crawled in, pushing their bags onto the floor. She had a Thomas Guide and directed them through the heavy rush-hour traffic. She told Montgomery to get off the eastbound San Bernardino Freeway at Valley Boulevard, and she guided them on surface streets to Santa Anita Street in El Monte and the Kingsdale trailer park.

They managed to win favor with the security guard at the main gate by identifying themselves as police officers and listening to every theory he had on ridding the world of scumbags. The guy was middle-aged, and his breath smelled of beer. His uniform was too big and sorely in need of washing and ironing. The snap-on tie had tiny cigarette burns and grease stains. He was a police wannabe and told them about every junior college criminology class he had taken in the last ten years before he finally raised the wooden arm and allowed them to drive onto the property. He offered to lead them to Mrs. Williams's trailer space, but Turner declined, telling him he had a duty to stay at his post and protect the park. The guard tapped the cellular phone attached to his belt in a manner reminiscent of television's bumbling cop Barney Fife and told them to give a shout if they had trouble and needed an assist.

Katy buried her head in her bag. Turner knew she wanted to say something. She always had a smart-aleck remark popping into her head and immediately out of her mouth, but his stern look had warned her to shut up.

Montgomery waved and drove forward away from the guard shack and onto the newly paved road that circled the park. The place wasn't what Turner had expected. His idea of a mobile home park was the sleazy rundown image portrayed by Hollywood. It was a refuge for the poor losers who had nowhere else to go. These trailers looked like clean well-constructed little cottages. Each space had a well-kept front yard, and sunrooms were attached to many of the larger units.

On one of the older streets in a back corner, they finally found Mrs. Williams's space. Her mobile home was small and very neat on the outside, but it had been there a while. Mature trees and shrubbery surrounded it, their roots anchored to the foundation. Katy pointed to the name Williams on the mailbox, and Montgomery parked on the gravel near the driveway. There was a BMW partially covered in the back near a patio. Turner guessed it was Alexandra's.

Before they could ring the doorbell, the front door opened, and the screen door was unlatched. A well-dressed woman in a dark-blue business suit stood in the doorway. Turner introduced himself and the others. The woman extended her hand to each of them and invited them into her home. It was clean and attractive inside. The furniture wasn't trendy or expensive, but she had a good eye for color and design. The small space looked comfortable and functional. She offered coffee that she produced immediately, and they sat in the dining area.

Mrs. Williams was a tall handsome woman in her mid-fifties. Her hair was auburn, with streaks of gray. She had it cut short and combed straight back away from her face. She wore a knee-length skirt and unfashionable spiked heels. The tight sweater under her jacket revealed a figure any woman half her age would envy. The first thing Turner noticed was the similarity of her eyes to Alexandra's big blue eyes. She reminded him that, as she had explained during their phone conversation, she didn't have much time. She was a receptionist for a small accounting firm, and they expected her back at work that afternoon.

"We want you to know how sorry we are for your loss," Turner said. "We're hoping you might be able to help us find her killer. Did she ever tell you about anyone she was afraid of or someone who might have . . . anything?" He stopped. Suddenly he felt as if he were intruding.

Mrs. Williams's expression didn't change. It was passive, cold.

"Alex didn't confide in me, Sergeant. We hardly spoke." Her voice was raspy and low. "This is a two-bedroom trailer, and I had three kids. The three of them slept in one room. I raised them alone." She couldn't wait any longer and took a cigarette from the kitchen counter. "You mind?" she asked. They all did, but everyone said no. "They wanted out of here first chance they got. You blame them? This park wasn't this nice when they were growing up. My old man left when Alex was five." She coughed. "I kicked the bastard out."

She was quiet and looked down at the floor. Turner started to ask her something but thought better of it. Montgomery and Katy turned to him, and he shook his head just enough for them to see. They waited. She looked at Turner. "I caught him touching the older girl. I figured he must've been doing it to all of them. Alex was practically a baby. The boy was only a coupla years older. Even Cathy was only ten. Cathy was his, but it was like she was my own. Her real mother overdosed right after she was born. I was the only mom she knew."

She stood and went into the living room, returning with an ashtray. "They all got sick, got infections and stuff, so I knew I was right. The boy is dead now, too." She stopped but didn't show any emotion. She leaned back in her chair and blew the cigarette smoke over her shoulder. "His father really messed up the kid's head. He got arrested selling his butt for drugs or whatever. Got killed two years ago over a $50 dope thing." She hesitated. "Is this the stuff you want to know?"

"Yes, please, Mrs. Williams, if it's not too difficult for you," Turner said.

"Hell, it can't hurt to talk about it. I've lost them all now. Nobody left to cry for."

"Cathy, too?" Montgomery asked.

"Might as well be dead. Haven't seen her since she was sixteen. She hates me, blames me for letting him hurt her and the other kids." She pounded the cigarette into the ashtray. "Maybe I did kinda know in my heart. But who wants to believe a father would do that? He's fucking me every night. What the hell did he need?" She ground the cigarette until there was nothing but ashes, then lit another. "Cathy got arrested for drugs and prostitution just like her brother. She stopped calling after I refused to send bail money any more." She sighed and crossed her arms. "I thought Alex had made it. I thought she was the one . . ." Her voice trailed off.

"Did Alex ever bring her friends here or talk about them?" Turner asked after she didn't speak for several minutes.

"Not hardly," she said, laughing dryly. "After high school, Alex didn't have much to say to me. She always worked and made her own money. She could do anything, smarter than the other two. Liked men too much. Had to lock her in her room. She was pretty, don't you think?" Turner nodded.

"Did she like being a cop?" he asked.

"Bragged about how much better she was than the other women she worked with. Said they were all jealous of her. I went to her graduation. She looked so good in that uniform." Tears ran down her cheeks, but she didn't seem to notice. Then she looked up at Turner. "Who could've done that to her?"

Turner offered her a handkerchief, but she pushed his hand away and went to the kitchen, where she pulled a paper towel from the roll and blew her nose. She took another clean towel and sat at the table again.

"Do you want to stop?" he asked.

"I always thought you guys had those gaudy funerals and were a big family, but nobody from the police station ever came to see me, didn't say sorry or tough luck or nothing. I buried her in that uniform. Nobody but me was there." She folded her hands in her lap and looked around at them. Turner glanced at Montgomery. The department did have big funerals for officers killed in the line of duty, but Alexandra's death was different. There was something tawdry, unseemly about the way she lived and died. He didn't want to explain that to her mother.

"Did she ever mention the name Crystal or Dean? Did she talk about anybody in the department?" Turner could see she was emotionally exhausted, but he wanted to change the subject and realized he might not get another chance to talk to her.

"Never heard those names, hon. She had friends, but they never came here. She was generous with her money, didn't believe in saving for tomorrow. See that car in my driveway? That's hers." She laughed. "I don't know how to drive. Might as well be a flowerpot."

Mrs. Williams was a chain smoker, and Turner noticed that Katy seemed bothered by the nicotine cloud that hovered above the table. The little detective coughed a few times and eventually stood, as if she were stretching her legs, and went into the living room area. She stopped in front of Alexandra's graduation picture from the police academy. It was hanging on a wall with a number of family pictures.

"This is a great picture of Alexandra," Katy said when she saw Mrs. Williams staring at her. "Nice-looking kids," she said, examining the family photos. She stopped in front of a picture of a blond, smiling little boy and next to that another one of a tattooed, sullen teenager. "Turner, come here a second," she said. He looked up, and she said more loudly, "Come here."

He smiled at Mrs. Williams and went into the living room. "What?" he whispered when he was beside Katy. He was annoyed but didn't want to argue with her right there. She pointed at the picture of a pretty girl who looked to be about thirteen years old. It wasn't Alexandra. Her hair was brown and curly. She had big brown eyes and a delicate nose. Turner shrugged and repeated, "What?"

Katy searched the wall for other pictures of the girl and found one where she was a few years older.

"Mrs. Williams, is this Cathy?" she asked, pointing at the picture. Turner looked but didn't know what Katy was doing. Mrs. Williams stood in front of the picture and touched the glass.

"Yes, that's her, years ago."

"Did Cathy use your last name?" Katy asked, and she sounded as if the answer wasn't really important, but Turner saw her start to fidget like a bird dog with the scent.

"No, she hated her father. She always used my maiden name, Moody. Catherine Ann Moody."

Katy turned her back to Mrs. Williams and mouthed "yes" to Turner, who moved closer to look at the photo again. Montgomery jumped up and went to the wall. It was there in her eyes. The hair was a different color from the one in the booking photo, but it was Crystal. Turner shook his head. How could they be so stupid? He asked Mrs. Williams to sit on the couch in the living room. She did, but she seemed nervous, maybe sensing their excitement.

"Do you know where Cathy is?" Turner asked, sitting beside her.

"No, I told you she won't talk to me. What do you want with Cathy?" Her voice was testy.

"We think she might know who killed her sister," Turner said. "The killer might be looking for her. We want to find her first." He wanted to scare her, but Mrs. Williams just looked at her watch.

"I have to go back to work. My bus will be at the gate in a few minutes," she said.

"Will you call us if she contacts you?" Turner asked, handing her a card with his and Monty's number.

She took the card. "I have to go," she said.

Montgomery offered to drive her to work, but she refused. They left the trailer, with Mrs. Williams locking the door behind them. She walked past their car toward the front gate. They watched her stride confidently to the waiting bus. Her gait was steady and firm. From a distance her figure appeared much younger.

"Nice obs, O'Neal," Montgomery said as they watched the bus pull away from the front gate.

"No shit," she agreed. "Who woulda thought?"

"How did all that family crap get past the background check?" Turner asked no one in particular. "There were only about a dozen reasons to keep her out of the department. Who did her investigation, the Braille Institute?"

"It's a numbers game," Montgomery said, starting the car. "You pick one from column A, one from column B. My guess is they had a class coming up that needed more women. Welcome to LAPD, Miss Williams."

The security guard opened the gate and waved them through. He saluted Montgomery and pretended to be talking on his walkie-talkie. Montgomery returned the salute and maneuvered the Taurus into traffic.

"I'm surprised he hasn't been recruited by the department," Montgomery said. "Looks like lieutenant material to me."

Turner grinned and ignored him. "That explains the Alex and Crystal living arrangement. Do you think Mom knows where she is?"

"She's not a warm and fuzzy mommy, someone who'd keep in touch," Katy said. "Let's face it; that trailer's not exactly Walton's Mountain, either."

"Where would she go, then?" Turner asked. "She can't have that many options."

"Where she's comfortable—Hollywood's streets," Montgomery added.

"Then why hasn't Sully's crew found her? They've been out there every day looking for her, and they're good." Katy fell back against the seat. "I hate to say this, but I got a gut feeling she's dead, too."

"If she's not dead, somebody's hiding her." Montgomery said. "Let's get off McGann and look for her and White. They disappeared at the same time."

"Let the Hollywood guys find them. McGann's the key to this case," Turner argued. He didn't think McGann killed Alexandra but believed the answers would come from somewhere in McGann's world.

"I vote for switching," Katy said.

"Your vote doesn't count," Turner said.

"It counts more than somebody from IA."

"Nobody gets a vote but me," Montgomery said. "It's my case, and I agree with Katy. We'll leave the Hollywood detectives watching the bungalow and try to track down White. If it's a dead end, we'll jump back on the McGann surveillance."

Turner was frustrated. McGann had lied. Perez had lied, and yet they were going to waste time hunting down a mental case who couldn't remember where he lived. He was upset, but this was Montgomery's homicide investigation, and he'd made up his mind, so Turner sat quietly as Katy found an address and telephone number for Phil White's father in Brentwood. She called, and he agreed to meet with them, even giving them directions to the secluded home.

The traffic was always terrible in the West L.A. area, especially in the late afternoons. There were no shortcuts. Turner noticed that, unlike himself, Montgomery was a patient driver who didn't let turmoil affect him. Montgomery was a black man in a predominantly white man's profession. He had survived his early years, unlike a number of blacks who had left the department bitter and disillusioned. He had endured, but not by howling at the wind. Like his driving, Montgomery's career stayed a steady course, slow and deliberate, until he got what he wanted. He had a wife and little girl. Police work took a back seat to his life at home, and Turner respected him for that. He worked hard but definitely knew what was important. Turner felt his anger dissipating.

The White residence was the last house on a very narrow street in Brentwood that backed up against a fire road. There weren't any sidewalks, and parking wasn't allowed without a permit.

When Montgomery turned the Taurus into the driveway, the front gate rolled open. An older bald man wearing sweat pants and a tank top that revealed bony arms with loose tanned skin motioned for them to move forward. The man closed the gate and gestured to Montgomery to lower the driver's window. Phil White, Sr. introduced himself and welcomed them to his home. He opened the car door before Montgomery could get out and shook his hand vigorously. He then rushed to the back door to help Katy. She laughed and awkwardly allowed him to hold her hand while she climbed out.

They followed him into a pale-yellow three-story modern structure with lots of windows and steel framing. Turner thought White looked to be about sixty years old. He was taller than his son but much thinner. His clothes looked several sizes too large for him.

"Please come in, come in," he said, taking Katy by the arm and escorting her into an enormous living room that looked out onto an even larger balcony. When he reached the center of the room, White stopped and waited. Attorney Terry Chernack entered, as if on cue from the balcony.

Chernack introduced himself to Katy and shook hands with Montgomery and Turner.

"Mr. White has asked me to sit in on your interview, if there's no objection," Chernack said in a tone that told everyone it didn't matter if they objected. He was staying.

"No problem," Montgomery said, sitting as far from the attorney as he could.

Katy stared at the handsome young attorney with dark thinning hair and brown puppy eyes. Turner guessed that Katy was wondering why everyone but her knew him, a situation he was certain she'd remedy as soon as possible.

Turner explained that they didn't want to interview the senior Phil White but were hoping he might assist them in finding his son. He tried to downplay the son's involvement in the crime and emphasized that they really needed to find a girl who might be staying with Junior.

White listened intently while staring at Katy. Finally he asked her, "Did Philip tell you I was a musician?" He didn't wait for an answer, instead rattling off the names of several obscure movies for which he had written the musical scores. Her expression was vacant, but White continued, telling her that most of the movies were old and not very well received when they were released, keeping his genius hidden from the world. Currently he taught music at a private college, but he might have to retire because his hearing problem was getting worse. He took a breath, and Turner was able to change the subject back to the son.

"Was Phil Jr. a musician?" he asked.

"Lord, no, my son is not mentally sound but was a brilliant student before the sickness. His mother had the same condition, I'm afraid. Their minds are very fragile."

"How does he live? Are you supporting him?" Turner asked.

White and the lawyer briefly exchanged glances. "Terry makes certain he has money for food, clothing, and a place to live."

"Have you spoken to him?"

"The boy calls me every day," the old man said, taking a tray with cakes and coffee from a little Mexican woman who crept into the room. He put the tray on a glass-covered table in front of the couch and poured coffee for everyone except Chernack. "Most days it's gibberish. Don't know what he's going on about."

"Do you know where he is, Chernack?" Turner asked impatiently.

"Yes." Chernack looked at White, who nodded.

"Is he with a woman?" Montgomery showed him Crystal's booking photo again. "This woman."

Chernack didn't look at the photo. "She's with him," he said.

White snatched the photo from Montgomery's hand. "If we take you to her, you get her out of my son's life," he ordered.

"We don't have any reason to arrest her," Turner lied. "But she may be a witness in a police officer's murder." That wasn't the answer the old man wanted. Turner knew they could charge Crystal with the cocaine found in her room. It was a weak case no self-respecting DA would ever file, but it would keep her in custody for a few days. At minimum, the threat of prosecution could be a bargaining tool if Crystal thought it was enough to send her back to jail. He wasn't certain he wanted to share all that information with White's attorney sitting in the room.

"I don't want that woman living with my son," White said. His face was rigid, his eyes nearly closed. "I'm a very wealthy man who would give every penny of my fortune if I could make my son understand the beauty of Vivaldi's adagios or the tragedy of *Hamlet*. I know he never will, but I will not allow him to be a victim. He's a simpleton who can't recognize evil."

"Mr. White will use every legal means to separate his son from that woman," Chernack said. He was visibly uncomfortable with the old man's growing anger.

"Why didn't you give her up the day we told you about her criminal record? You knew we were looking for her," Turner said.

"Phil had formed an attachment." Chernack hesitated. "The time's come to sever the bond permanently . . . one way or another." He turned to the balcony view. "It would be best if you took her away."

The old man's face was a blank canvas. He wasn't angry any longer, just determined. Turner guessed it didn't matter to him whether what they did was legal or not. He was giving the police a chance to step in and handle the situation before he did it his way. Chernack was all business and as composed as any high-priced criminal lawyer. Turner also supposed that Chernack had faked his lack of experience during the younger White's initial interview. As soon as the attorney recognized the booking photo of Crystal, he most likely realized that his boy was in over his head, so he removed him from the interrogation. Chernack's innocent civil-lawyer act had lulled them into thinking he couldn't be devious. Turner wouldn't make that mistake again.

"How do you want to handle this?" Montgomery asked. "If they know we're coming, she'll disappear and take your son with her."

"I deliver money to them once a week. They expect me tomorrow morning," Chernack said. He smiled. "She's always there for the money."

"What's the address?" Katy asked.

Chernack took a business card out of his wallet and wrote an address and telephone number on the back. He gave it to Katy.

"What time do you usually leave the money?" Montgomery asked.

"Why don't you meet me for breakfast at the Roosevelt Hotel on Hollywood Blvd. at 9 A.M.? It's a short drive from there to the motel."

140

"I know this dump," Katy said, holding up the business card. "It's two blocks from Hollywood station."

Turner shook hands with White and was ready to leave, but the old man insisted that he show them the rest of the house. He was grateful for their help and wanted to express his appreciation by allowing them to drool over his possessions. The tour took about an hour. The music room alone was bigger than Turner's apartment. Awards covered the walls for musical scores Turner had never heard or couldn't remember. As soon as he stopped worrying about his son, White was a warm and charming man. Chernack treated him more like a father than a client. The two men had a comfortable rapport, and Turner suspected that White might be the lawyer's only source of income.

White hugged everyone several times, not allowing them to say goodbye. Finally he looked tired and excused himself to rest before dinner, so they were able to make their escape. Chernack escorted them to their car and opened the gate. As they drove away, Turner noticed that the lawyer was back in the house before the gate had closed again.

"They're staying at the Tower Gardens on Schrader," Katy said, flipping the business card over the seat to Turner. "It's a dive. We should get Sully's people to go with us."

"Good idea," Montgomery said. "You set it up and make the game plan. I hate to hurt that old man, but we've got to take Crystal and Junior."

"Don't feel too bad," Turner said. "Chernack will have him out in about five minutes."

Katy leaned over the seat between them. "Didn't you guys see that old man's face when he talked about his kid? I think he's tired of dealing with the demented son and plans to have the lawyer lock him away where he can't cause any more trouble."

"I don't care as long as I can find him when I want him," Turner said.

When they returned to RHD, it was nearly 9 P.M., but Stevenson was still in his office. Montgomery and Turner briefed him on what they'd learned about the Williams family and the imminent recovery of Crystal and Phil White. Stevenson was pleased with how the case was going but asked Turner if he'd mind staying a minute as Katy and Montgomery were getting ready to leave. The detective bay was empty, but Stevenson got up and closed his office door when they were alone.

Turner tried to remember what he'd done lately that could've gotten back to Stevenson and upset him.

"You had a meeting with the IG today," Stevenson said.

Turner breathed a little easier. "I met with her and gave her copies of the personnel investigation, as much as I've finished."

"Who told you to do that?"

He sat up a little. "No one had to tell me. Miller's the IG, and she asked for them."

"Captain Connelly has a different opinion on that subject."

"Meaning?"

"Meaning that as your commanding officer, she'd like all such requests to go through her office. Therefore, from now on you shall not give anything to the IG or anyone else who has not been approved by Connelly. Clear enough?"

He could feel his face flush. "I understand," he said, starting to get up, but he changed his mind and sat again. "No, I don't understand. We're supposed to cooperate with the woman."

"No, the department is supposed to cooperate with her. Captain Connelly *is* the department as far as you're concerned."

"With all due respect, sir, that's bullshit. You know Connelly's been stonewalling her."

"Maybe, but if you want to stay on this case, you'll do what you're told." Stevenson didn't blink. He stared at Turner and gave no indication whether he agreed with the order. Turner understood him well enough not to argue. He got up to leave before he said something he'd regret.

"Mike," Stevenson said before he was out the door. "You're doing a good job. Don't do anything stupid. I'd hate to lose you. You'll make a good lieutenant, so don't screw up your promotion."

Turner nodded and disappeared into the dark, deserted detective room.

Stevenson wanted to say more but didn't. He thought Connelly was justifiably irate. He had calmed her down a little, but Turner shouldn't have given Elaine Miller a very sensitive personnel investigation before the IA captain or the chief of police had

had an opportunity to review it. Although he didn't think much of Connelly or Chief Martin, Stevenson believed in the chain of command.

He rubbed his eyes. He was almost too tired to get up and drive home. Why was Connelly so upset? Everyone knew that McGann's personnel investigation was practically worthless without the homicide data. He groaned out loud, suddenly contemplating the possibility that Turner had given the IG material related to Williams' death. No, Turner was too smart for that. How did Connelly find out about the IG? It had to be Myron. That little larva didn't miss anything. He had nothing to do all day but spy and kiss butt. What a disaster Myron would be as a lieutenant. Stevenson would pay to see Myron at his first command post. The whole thing would be over before Myron had made a decision. Turner, on the other hand, had plenty of challenges in his career—gotten bloody, dirty, and knocked down—but he had survived and was a stronger man for it.

This is a strange organization, Stevenson thought; it rewards the weak and destroys the strong. He removed his jacket from a hook on the wall and locked his office door. He was sorry he'd gotten down on Turner. He respected the guy. Turner was a man of courage. He'd proved his worth years ago, but he'd probably have a difficult time being promoted to lieutenant. Nobody wants the garbage man in the club.

"Strange organization," he whispered to those kindred spirits who roamed the halls of the sixth floor, and he imagined that Bill Parker would wipe his name off the building if he had a way to do it.

TWELVE

When the chief's entourage, which now included Sally Wolinski, arrived on the first floor, his security officers walked in front of and behind him as they moved slowly toward the hearing room at the end of the long corridor. Martin stopped to talk with anyone who'd listen. Friend and foe alike welcomed an opportunity to make small talk with the chief of police. He always wore his class-A uniform with four stars perfectly arranged on his collar, but even the dark-blue uniform couldn't hide the beginnings of a bulging waistline just over the Sam Browne.

Paula waited near the Police Commission hearing room with Bell. She saw Brenda step out of her office as the chief approached. Martin stopped and greeted Brenda. She was in charge of commission investigations so he couldn't avoid interacting with her. He did it quickly with as little conversation as possible, which probably suited Brenda fine.

As they walked, Sally handed Martin a notebook with what looked like a collection of reports. She whispered in his ear with her hand touching his arm. Martin was smiling and was obviously pleased with whatever Sally was telling him. They passed Paula without acknowledging her. Bell fell in line behind them as they entered the hearing room.

Paula waited for Brenda, who trailed behind the chief. She smiled at her friend, but Brenda was upset and angry.

"Did you see that?" she said, pulling Paula away from the door and the tiny crowd of people who'd congregated there. "Wolinski's strutting by the chief's side like she earned that position. She stabbed Sara in the back to get that job. I'm furious."

"It's just a job," Paula said, worried about her friend's wild stare. "Someday Sally will be old and ugly and the manipulating won't work anymore."

Brenda rolled her eyes and pushed her way into the hearing room. "I hate that woman," she said to no one in particular.

When she got inside, Paula saw Martin standing up front with two of the police commissioners, and Bell sat in the first row of spectator seats directly across from the chief. Sally sat beside Bell, which gave Paula a momentary jolt of jealousy. She knew they'd be the chief's primary support, but she was Bell's adjutant and belonged at his side. It was stupid, but Sally had a way of bringing out the worst in her. She sat across the aisle with Brenda, who had her own report to give the commission. Brenda said she came early to hear Martin "make a fool of himself."

The room was full, and several community people and department members stood in the back, struggling with the media for elbow room. Martin looked confident, smiling for the cameras. He slid his comb through his thick black hair and heavy mustache. Maybe he couldn't speak Spanish, but he certainly looked Hispanic. Paula knew the media had figured out that Martin was a play Mexican. They tolerated the subterfuge because it made an otherwise dull chief a little interesting. His wife had bought him a large pencil drawing of an old Mexican sheriff with a bandoleer across his chest and a smoking shotgun in his hand. He hung the drawing over his desk and showed it to every visitor. It was his favorite, maybe because Sylvia Diaz hated it.

The five commissioners were ready to begin the meeting at exactly 10 A.M. Diaz was so short she sat on pillows that kept her from disappearing behind the table. Brenda had covered the front of the table to hide the old woman's legs. She told Paula that when Diaz got angry and pounded the gavel on the table, her tiny legs dangled from the chair, and with her perfect white hair, she looked like a deranged grandmother elf.

After finishing an agenda filled with permit changes and other monotonous business, Diaz told the audience to clear the room. The commission would go into executive session on a matter that involved a criminal investigation and personnel matter. Only the chief, his associates, and the city attorney were permitted to stay. Martin didn't look at her. He joked with the sergeant-at-arms, who stood behind them. Diaz announced there would be a fifteen-minute break while the room cleared.

The chief's demeanor told everyone that he had prepared well for this meeting. He smiled and laughed with the other commissioners until Elaine Miller entered and walked to the front of the room. His smile faded, and he slumped sullenly as he watched her sit behind Paula and Brenda. Elaine grinned at Paula as she glanced over her shoulder. Nancy Connelly, who was sitting in the back, took the opportunity to move closer to the front of the room and sit beside Sally. Sally looked up at the IA captain but didn't speak or change her expression. Connelly greeted the chief, then concentrated on her paperwork.

When the meeting resumed exactly fifteen minutes later, it was less formal. Without the public and media scrutiny, everyone could relax. Diaz tried to keep a sense of order and decorum, but the other board members liked Martin and enjoyed his sharp humor. The chief joked with them and made crude, irreverent remarks that could be laughed at without crossing the political-correctness line. Three of the members were lawyers, and Martin always had a collection of new attorney jokes. When he finished his summary of the Williams case and the McGann investigation, the four male members of the board congratulated him. Diaz tried to challenge him on the lack of real progress in the McGann investigation, but the other commissioners supported the chief. Even Elaine Miller had to admit that she was finally receiving regular updates on the personnel matter, thanks to Sergeant Turner. Paula saw Connelly blush at the mention of Turner's name instead of his captain's—an intentional slight.

Martin told the board that the McGann report would be on his desk by the end of the week and that he would come to them with a recommendation at their next meeting. Paula looked for another reaction from Connelly, but there wasn't one. Mike didn't sound like he was that close to finishing his investigation the last time she'd talked to him about it.

"And, don't bet me I can't," the chief said, pointing at the black lawyer sitting across from him, "Remember that wager on the eighteenth hole?"

"You have enough of my money. I'm betting on you this time," the commissioner said, laughing.

Brenda leaned closer to Paula and whispered, "Didn't I tell you all their real business was done on the golf course or standing in a row in front of the urinals holding their favorite body part?"

Paula was trying not to laugh. Elaine rested her arm on the back of Paula's chair and whispered to Brenda loud enough for Paula to hear.

"You can't play golf, Brenda. I've seen your backswing," Elaine said. "But I'm sure they'll let you hold the body part if you want to be one of the boys."

Brenda snorted, but no one paid any attention to her. Paula knew Brenda was right. Diaz was intelligent and honest and did most of the work on this commission, but it was Martin who knew how to work the boys.

When the executive session ended, the public and media came back into the room. The remainder of the meeting went quickly. Brenda's report took a few minutes. Chief Martin held court behind his chair with officers and community people for the remainder of the meeting. Paula thought his behavior was rude, but Diaz never reprimanded him and seemed almost relieved that she could continue without his input. When it was over, Diaz stared at the chief as she gathered her papers and slid them into her bulging briefcase. Paula watched him, too, and was always amazed by how little people expected from the man. Everyone liked his humor, and he had the ability to converse with the devil. He was natural and just as comfortable with the mayor as he was with the homeless woman who slept outside the back door of Parker Center. The chief always had something to say, a question or comment to show he was interested. The perfect politician, Paula thought, and frowned. That's the problem. He knows too much about keeping his job and too little about doing it.

Paula took Diaz's briefcase as the older woman stepped down from the platform.

"You were so much better today. I liked your confidence," Diaz said to Elaine.

Elaine smiled and handed Diaz an envelope.

"It's my resignation," she said.

Paula was stunned. She couldn't think of anything to say that didn't sound stupid. She heard Brenda's angry "oh, fuck" under her breath and watched Diaz staring at the envelope as if it were a pornographic movie.

"But I thought it was better," Diaz mumbled, holding the envelope in front of Elaine's face.

"Better isn't good enough. I know how this job needs to be done, and that's never going to happen. I'll go back to my old firm. My dad's a partner there. They can hardly turn me away," she said with a nervous laugh.

"When?" Diaz asked. She was visibly angry now.

"Ninety days. That gives the mayor and the commission plenty of time to find my replacement."

Diaz's face flushed as she stuffed the envelope into the side pocket of her briefcase. Paula thought Elaine looked calmer than she'd been in a very long time. She was very matter-of-fact and seemed almost relieved when the envelope was out of her hands and in Diaz's possession. Connelly stood across the room, quietly observing them for a few minutes, and then walked over to Elaine and offered her hand.

"I'm sorry you've decided to leave. You've had a very difficult job. It's not easy to be a pioneer," Connelly said as if she'd memorized the speech.

Paula glanced at Brenda. They'd heard Connelly's clichés so often they could almost predict what she'd say next. She didn't have a chance to finish this time because Elaine interrupted her and excused herself. She claimed to have a business lunch that couldn't be missed.

Diaz tucked her briefcase under her arm and marched out behind Elaine without another word. Everyone had gone except Brenda, Connelly, and Paula.

Paula dropped into the nearest chair.

"The media are going to have a field day with this one," she said.

"It's probably for the best," Connelly said, glancing around the room to be certain they were alone. "She really never fit in here."

"It's not easy to be a pioneer," Brenda mimicked perfectly, right down to Connelly's annoying stutter. "You're such a phony, Nancy. The reason Elaine had such a difficult job is because you treated her like shit. I don't blame her for being frustrated."

"As usual, you don't know what you're talking about," Connelly said. She retrieved her notebook and purse from her chair and headed toward the door.

"I know she couldn't pry a personnel complaint out of your hands until Sam Martin told you to let go," Brenda said, and when Connelly paused at the door, she added, "I know a deputy chief is getting a free ride on some serious misconduct, and so does our ex-IG, who shortly will have no reason to keep her well-founded suspicions to herself."

Connelly's riveting stare at Paula said everything: Mike Turner is talking to you, and you're talking to Brenda. Paula got the message loud and clear. She wanted to jump up and deny everything but didn't. She knew that Connelly would take it out on Turner, but she wasn't going to fight his battles. Mike was a big boy. Besides, Connelly didn't know anything. What could she do? She could talk to Martin, keep Paula from making captain right away. Paula told herself she didn't care, but she couldn't deny feeling just a twinge of fear.

"Why did she give you a dirty look?" Brenda asked when they were alone and she was straightening up the hearing room.

"She thinks I'm leaking information to you. I wish I knew something to leak. Mike and I hardly ever talk anymore."

"Sorry. The woman knows how to push my buttons. She and Wolinski are everything I hate about women on this job."

"Well, they're the ruling class for now, so you've got to figure a way to live with them, or they'll find a way to live without you," Paula warned her best friend. She was suddenly very weary, but she waited until Brenda locked up the hearing room before leaving.

On her way back to Bell's office, Paula remembered the conversation with Elaine Miller at Sylvia's restaurant. At that time, Brenda had pledged her loyalty to the man who sat in the corner pocket, but each day Paula noticed that Brenda seemed less inclined to support Sam Martin. The chief's ego was creating a subtle pollution of mediocrity and mistrust. Maybe, Mike was right, and eventually the department, all of them, would pay for the man's lack of integrity. Maybe, Alexandra Williams already had.

THIRTEEN

Turner stared at the pictures of steamy cups painted on the front of the machine on the second-floor mezzanine of Parker Center. He'd decided that coffee from a vending machine was an evil invention conjured up by someone who hated the precious brown bean. The hot liquid dispensed from those contraptions wasn't coffee, and no real aficionado would be fooled by the color or the aroma. Nevertheless, he'd left the apartment before 4 A.M. and needed caffeine. He looked at the loose change in his hand. It was enough, but this stuff wouldn't do. Connelly wanted the investigation, and he'd have it for her by 8 A.M., but not until he made a run to the bagel shop across the street, where they served bucket-sized Starbucks.

As soon as he gave Connelly the McGann investigation, Turner would find Montgomery so they could ride to the Roosevelt together. Connelly was scheduled to be preoccupied with the police commission most of the morning, and Turner intended to have Crystal and Phil White in custody long before that meeting was over.

He walked down another flight of stairs to the first floor and into the lobby. It was deserted at this time of the morning. The desk officer read the sports section of the L.A. Times while his partner slept curled up in her chair behind the counter. The day watch would relieve them in a couple of minutes, so they'd lost all interest in their job. Turner pictured change of watch as the perfect time for neighborhood terrorists to strike any station. He greeted the overweight grey-haired officer, who peered briefly over his newspaper. The man grunted back, but Turner didn't take it personally. The man treated everyone the same . . . badly.

As Turner crossed Los Angeles Street, the emptiness of the city at dawn reminded him of the many satisfying nights he'd spent in a patrol car. He enjoyed the deserted downtown. At this hour, no one was out there but the cops and the bad guys. Patrol was special for him. Riding in a black-and-white eight hours a night, he knew his partner better than the guy's wife knew him.

They heard each other's fantasies and complaints, listened but didn't judge. Occasionally they did stupid things, but it always stayed between them. Finding the right partner, a perfect match—someone you knew would watch your back and be your friend for the rest of your life—didn't happen to everyone. Turner knew he'd never be as close to another human being as he had been to Tim Andrews.

It was always at dawn, with the smell of wet asphalt, that he thought about Andy. They had depended on each other to stay safe and alive. He had failed his friend. When Andy was killed, a part of Turner died, too. It had been over twenty years, but it hurt as if it were this morning. For a long time he'd catch himself saying, "I gotta tell Andy" or "Wait till Andy sees this." Turner had missed him so much that for years he was angry and mean all the time, taking his rage out on his friends as well as the bad guys. Paula was the first person he was able to talk to about the loneliness and guilt he felt because he was still breathing and Andy wasn't.

The quiet streets, the smells, brought it all back—the muzzle flashes in the dark, Andy's last labored breaths and his widow's unmistakable, accusatory black stare at the funeral. "I hate you," her eyes said. "He had me and the kids. We needed him. It should've been you."

He walked faster, trying not to think, and in fifteen minutes he was back at Parker Center with his coffee, a bag of bagels, and the start of a migraine. He hadn't had one for years, but thinking about Andy was stirring up some painful memories. He was relieved to get back to his office, where he could close the curtains and swallow half a dozen Advil. The department psychiatrist had shown him how to relax in a darkened room and stop the headache before it really got started. It worked, and in half an hour he was ready to begin writing again until he got a whiff of the Polo cologne that Myron poured on himself every morning. The sickening odor always hung in the air for hours. Turner grabbed the bag of bagels and went into Connelly's outer office. Myron looked up at him and nodded. Turner offered him one of the bagels.

"This your last day, Myron?" Turner asked, waiting for the smug expression to grow on the sergeant's face as he stuffed his mouth with an onion bagel. "Get your badge and bars and be sitting in the watch commander's chair at the Harbor," Turner said. Myron nodded. "Well, that's great, Myron," Turner said as he turned to leave and then added, "if it keeps your scrawny ass out of my office."

Myron had taken a big bite and was in the process of swallowing when he tried to say something. Instead, he spit pieces of bagel on his desk and nearly choked as he managed an unintelligible squeak at Turner's disappearing back.

"I'm sure I'll pay for that someday," Turner said to himself as he returned to his office. "But, damn, it was worth it."

The personnel investigation was done an hour before Captain Connelly got to work. Turner had had an opportunity to double-check the format and compose a note to the IA captain. He summarized each of the statements and suggested findings on the counts of misconduct alleged against McGann. Normally, the investigating sergeant wouldn't do that, but he knew Connelly needed this. Besides, there was little doubt about the outcome of this one. She'd told him to write the complaint with two allegations. McGann had had an improper relationship with a subordinate, and he had failed to notify the department, which at his rank was the chief of police. It had become a simple investigation. Both allegations would be sustained, and McGann would receive a slap on the wrist, probably five suspension days. It was a cheap price tag to put on honor and accountability.

Connelly thanked him several times as she thumbed through the investigation.

"This is wonderful," she said. "You've done a very thorough job in a short time. I'd like to take you with me to the commission meeting in case they have any questions."

Turner swallowed hard. "This summary sheet should be all you really need," he said, giving her a list of questions the commission might ask, and all the responses. "You know this case better than me," he lied, but he knew she wouldn't want to share the praise with anyone if the commissioners were pleased.

"I don't know."

"If you don't feel comfortable, I could easily make the presentation." He spoke carefully, implying that possibly she couldn't handle it. It worked; she straightened her back and assured him she was more than capable of doing it herself.

He took a deep breath. Too close, he thought. He didn't want to miss the operation at the Tower Gardens Hotel or the look on Crystal's face when she saw the police standing at her door. Luckily, Connelly didn't ask what he would be doing that morning.

Turner was ready to go when Montgomery arrived.

"What's gonna happen now?" Montgomery asked. "Will they give you another case? More importantly, will they let you keep that great office?"

"She didn't say anything. I don't want to get pulled off this."

"Stevenson will find a way to keep you. We still got a lot of department people on the fringes of this case."

Turner worried that Stevenson wouldn't have much chance of keeping him now that McGann was officially out of it. He wondered how much fallout there would be if anyone ever found out about the surveillance. He and Monty had promised each other that if it became a problem, they'd take full responsibility to protect Stevenson and Katy. It was their gamble. Win or lose, they would take the heat.

Traffic was light, so Montgomery reached the Roosevelt Hotel on Hollywood Boulevard in a few minutes. Turner didn't talk during the trip. He was thinking about the McGann investigation and feeling a little ashamed of the whitewash package he'd delivered that morning.

Katy was waiting on the sidewalk on Orange Avenue near the side entrance to the hotel. Montgomery parked in the empty space marked for "tour buses only," ignoring the parking attendant who was pointing frantically at the wording. Montgomery took a placard from the glove compartment and put it in the front window. It had a city seal, and "Official Business" was written across the front. The attendant scowled but didn't say anything. Turner guessed the guy wasn't making enough money to argue with the police, and most likely he didn't have a green card in his wallet.

"Chernack's already inside," Katy said. "He's waiting for us in the restaurant." She led them through the parking lot into the back door of the hotel. As they stepped into the lobby, Turner felt the presence of resident ghosts from a more glamorous Hollywood era.

"What a great place," he said, examining the refurbished Spanish tile and wool carpets. He passed the restaurant and stood in a larger elegant lobby where tourists wandered around the perimeter staring at pictures of the old Hollywood and those celebrities who had spent part of their lives in this wonderful building. He peeked inside a large banquet room with giant chandeliers. A bronze plaque on the wall said the room had housed the first Academy Awards. Turner wasn't a stargazer, but this place had a magic about it. He almost expected to turn around and see Tyrone Power sitting in one of the plush leather chairs talking to Humphrey Bogart. L.A. didn't bother much with historical sites, and frankly there weren't many worth remembering, but old Hollywood was unique.

He and Montgomery wandered toward the front entrance facing Hollywood Boulevard, silently perusing the faded photographs that decorated every wall until Katy stepped in front of them. She snapped her fingers several times under their noses.

"Come back from fantasyland, guys. Reality check. We got work to do," she said, nudging them back toward the restaurant.

"The woman has no soul. This place is great," Montgomery whined.

Turner took one last long look at the lobby and fell in behind them. He made a promise to himself to take Paula there for dinner. She'd think he was crazy and give him a hard time. To Paula, Hollywood meant weirdos, prostitutes, drug dealers, and t-shirt shops. She was right, but not in here. This was special.

Chernack was eating breakfast when Turner and Montgomery arrived. He had ordered for the late arrivals. The attorney was dressed casually and looked like a college kid as he stood to shake hands.

"Sit down and eat," Chernack said. "You've got time. They don't expect me until ten." He added with a grin, "They're both there."

"How do you know that?" Turner asked. He was afraid Chernack might've been too eager to be helpful and tipped their hand.

"I was talking to Phil, and she got on the line to tell me they needed more money. Seems she can't make ends meet on the paltry $1,000 I give them every week."

Katy finished the last forkful of her scrambled eggs while staring at Chernack. They smiled at each other. Obviously, Katy had recently made a new friend.

"Sully's guys are sitting on the hotel. They're not going anywhere," she said, still chewing.

"Can they see them in the room?" Turner asked.

"Miss Crystal isn't one to pull the shades down," Katy said. "Not easy for a whore to change old habits." She turned to Chernack, adding, "Sorry."

"Don't be. I know what Catherine Moody is. That's why I'm helping you."

Katy removed a diagram of the Tower Gardens Hotel from her jacket pocket.

At the bottom of the page was a drawing of Phil White's room. She told them where to park their cars, how they would approach the hotel without being seen, and where each of Sullivan's detectives was stationed.

Montgomery took over and told Chernack that he'd go to the front door with Turner and Katy. Chernack would knock on the door, but as soon as it opened, he would step aside, and the detectives would take Phil and Crystal into custody. Turner caught Chernack's grimace and dreaded the next few seconds.

"Detective . . ." Chernack began to protest.

"It's a precaution, Terry." Montgomery was calm, as if he'd anticipated this conversation. "Until we have everything under control, both of them will be in custody. I won't arrest Phil, but you have to do something for me."

The lawyer's features stiffened. He wasn't a college kid any longer. He was a high-priced attorney in a three-piece suit with a cold hard stare.

"Tell me what you want," he said in a tone that conceded he was about to get screwed.

"Put Phil someplace where he can't disappear again, a place where we can talk to him."

Chernack seemed to relax.

"I intended to put Phil somewhere. His behavior is detrimental to his father, but I pick the place, and you don't talk to him without me."

"Of course," Montgomery said.

Chernack sat back in his chair and folded his arms. Turner admired the guy's tenacity and loyalty to Phil's father. He'd underestimated the attorney at first and now suspected that under the preppy exterior was a heavyweight street fighter.

When everyone knew what they were supposed to do, they paid for breakfast and agreed on a meeting location near the hotel. Although the Hollywood police station was two blocks away, Montgomery thought it best not to use any uniformed officers. They didn't know how many young officers had taken advantage of Alexandra's services or if they knew Crystal and might warn her.

They drove eastbound on Hollywood Boulevard, maneuvering around the tourists who seemed to believe that being on vacation allowed them to walk anywhere they wanted.

A stocky middle-aged man in baggy white shorts and long black stockings stood in the left turn lane taking digital pictures of Mann's Chinese Theater. He seemed oblivious to the symphony of horns and the obscenities shouted at him. Montgomery stopped his car beside the man and rolled down his window. He called the man over to his car, showed his badge, and told him he couldn't stand in the street. The guy, who obviously didn't understand a word of English, nodded, smiled, and took a step away from the car. He took several pictures of Montgomery and then tried to get the detective to take pictures of him and his wife standing in front of the theater. Montgomery refused to take the camera, rolled up his window, and drove away, leaving the man in the street.

He glanced up at his rearview mirror and smiled at Turner.

"No time to save the really dumb ones this morning," he said.

At the corner of Hollywood and Schrader, they made the turn southbound and parked a block away from the hotel.

Turner slipped his vest and raid jacket on. Everyone else was ready to go. They followed Katy as she jogged down the sidewalk. Turner was the last one and was breathing hard. He was working too many hours and was out of shape. Lately, Paula nagged him constantly about his unhealthy lifestyle. He was impressed with how easily Chernack ran. He was agile and stayed low. Turner guessed the lawyer had had some military training at some time in his life.

When they reached the front door of the Tower Gardens, a female narcotics detective held the door open for them. She motioned to the left side of the hallway and gently slapped the west wall, holding up four fingers. Turner counted four doors, and when they stopped, Chernack was positioned in front of the door, looking directly at the peephole. He looked as if he had just strolled in from the street. His breathing was normal, and not a hair was out of place as he waited for Montgomery's thumbs-up signal. Everyone but Chernack was hugging the wall on either side of the door, close enough to make entry when the door was opened.

Chernack knocked and said in a calm voice, "It's me, Phil. Open up."

Turner heard a deadbolt open and a chain being removed. The door opened slowly and then all the way. As he was told, Chernack walked inside the room, keeping the door open. He stood between the door and the threshold, leaving a gaping hole and making it impossible for Phil to close the door again. With guns drawn, the detectives entered the room quickly and grabbed Phil before he had an opportunity to resist. They gently laid him down on the floor and handcuffed him, then moved from room to room clearing the small apartment.

The bathroom door was locked when Turner and Katy got there. She jumped and tried to kick the door at the lock but bounced harmlessly away. Turner didn't know why, but the sight of the little detective springing off the door was funny, and he laughed. She glared at him and tried the kick again, with the same result. Then they both laughed until he braced his back against the hallway wall and kicked once at the door. It sprang open.

Crystal, dressed only in a bra and panties, ignored them and was frantically attempting to stuff plastic baggies down the toilet. She had succeeded in backing up the plumbing, and water flooded the room. In her panic, she had tried to flush two plastic bags of money and blocked the pipes. Before Turner could catch her, Crystal scrambled into the bathtub and was halfway out a small window before she spotted one of Sullivan's detectives standing outside, so she slid back into the bathroom. Turner stared at the red and yellow tattoo of a snake that started on her shoulder and covered her spine down to her waist. He tried to help her out of the tub, but she shoved Turner's hands away and stepped out, raising her arms submissively. She stared at the toilet and shook her head in disgust when she saw a bag of money float to the top of the bowl.

"My life is so fucked up," she mumbled as Katy grasped her wrist and led her out of the bathroom. Katy took her to the bedroom, where she found a relatively clean pair of jeans and a cropped sweater under a pile of dirty clothes. Crystal dressed and took a pair of stained socks out of her tennis shoes and put those

157

on before Katy handcuffed her and brought her back into the living room. Katy motioned for her to sit on the sofa beside Phil. Crystal was docile and seemed resigned to the idea that she'd been caught. She started to sit beside Phil but caught the hard stare of Chernack standing behind his client's son and moved to a chair across the room.

Unlike Crystal, Phil was trembling. He gazed down at the soiled worn carpet and rocked slowly back and forth until Chernack gripped his shoulders, forcing him to stop. Phil sat back and for the first time seemed to notice Crystal. He smiled at her. She tilted her head slightly and smiled back. Her long brown hair was still wet, combed straight back. Without makeup she looked like a teenager. She was tall and too thin, unlike her mother and sister, with big brown eyes and olive skin. Turner watched the interaction between her and Phil and wondered if she had some real affection for the strange young man or just had a financial attachment. In any case, Crystal's smile seemed to calm him.

Montgomery stood in front of Crystal and explained why they'd come to the apartment.

"Phil's father was worried about his son's safety, and we want to question you about the murders of Alexandra Williams and Jimmy Hargrove Dean."

When Montgomery mentioned Dean's name, Crystal's head snapped up. She didn't know he was dead. Her eyes narrowed; she glared at Montgomery, studying his face to try to decipher whether he was telling the truth. She knew cops lied for all kinds of reasons.

Montgomery didn't blink, and it seemed to register with Crystal that Dean was really dead.

"Will you cooperate?" Turner asked.

"You gonna arrest me?"

"We found you trying to flush dope and money. What do you think?" he asked.

"I'm supposed to help you put my ass on death row for a little coke and a few dollars?"

"Did you kill anybody?" Montgomery asked.

"I didn't kill nobody, and that stuff's not mine. Jimmy asked me to keep it and never came back. It's his."

"It's convenient he's dead and can't deny it."

"Don't you think if it was mine, I would've spent all that money? Ask that guy," she said, nodding at Chernack. "He'll tell you I spend lots of money. I won't spend Jimmy's goddamn money or touch his stash 'cuz he'd kill me."

"Jimmy's not the one who was trying to flush it," Turner said. "So as of ten minutes ago, it was officially yours."

Crystal sank back into her chair. She and Turner both knew dope and money together meant a sales beef, and she was screwed. "Can we make some kinda deal?" she said softly, not looking at anyone.

"Maybe," Turner said. "Can I talk to you a minute?" he asked, motioning for Chernack to come with him into the bedroom. Katy was collecting the evidence and had soggy baggies piled on the bed. Turner shut the door. "I want you to take Phil away from here," he said to the attorney.

Chernack paced in front of the bed. "What do you intend to do with her?"

"What do you care? Your client's rid of her."

"She needs a lawyer," Chernack said, ignoring the groans from Katy. "Sorry if that offends you, but she is a suspect in a criminal case. She needs an attorney."

"Wonderful. Would you care to be her lawyer?" Turner said sarcastically.

Chernack exhaled and said, "No, but I will if she wants me."

Montgomery stepped into the room and closed the door behind him.

"What's up?" he asked, looking at Turner.

"I want Phil out of here."

Chernack took a slip of paper out of his pocket and held it out to Katy. "Can you drop Phil at this address? It's all arranged," he asked.

"Will he go with her?" Turner asked.

"He'll do whatever I tell him to do. Besides, he likes Katy, so it'll be less traumatic."

"Katy, take one of Sully's detectives and get him out of here," Montgomery said. "Turner and I can finish up. Get me on my cell when you're done."

Katy tossed her half-filled evidence envelope on the floor. "I really hate baby-sitting this guy," she said, snatching the piece of paper from Chernack's hand.

"You going to talk to him first?" she asked Chernack as she followed him into the living room.

Chernack stood in front of the young man and told him to stand up. Phil hesitated for a second and then did as he was told. He looked down at the attorney, who was several inches shorter. In a stern voice, Chernack told him he would go with the lady detective and obey her.

"I want to stay with Cathy," Phil whispered, loud enough for everyone in the room to hear.

In a calm voice, Chernack repeated that Phil would go with the detective. The color drained from Phil's already pale face. He bit his lower lip, and tears ran down his face as he stared at Chernack.

"Philip," Crystal said. "Go with them. It's all right."

He tried to wipe his nose on his shoulder but couldn't quite reach it with his hands behind his back. Katy took hold of his bony arm. "Can we go now?" she asked, pulling him toward the door.

"Guess that's a yes," she said as he shuffled forward.

Montgomery finished collecting the evidence, and Sullivan offered to have his detectives book it. Turner suggested they take Crystal back to the Hollywood narcotics office to talk to her. She seemed puzzled when Turner presented Chernack's offer to represent her but agreed as soon as the lawyer told her there wouldn't be any cost.

Before they left the apartment, Chernack looked around for anything of value belonging to his clients. He found a picture of Phil and his father stuck to the frame of the bedroom mirror. Father and son stood side by side, not smiling, not touching. Phil appeared to be a teenager in a school uniform, tall and skinny with stringy blond hair. The only other picture on the mirror was of Phil and Crystal taken at the L.A. Zoo. Chernack removed both photos and put them in his pocket. He asked Crystal if there was anything else she wanted to take. She laughed.

"Just lock up. We're paid to the end of the month."

At the small narcotics office behind the Hollywood Division's gas pumps, Crystal wasn't hampered by her handcuffs as she slid easily out of the back seat. She walked directly to the unmarked door and waited for someone to open it for her.

"No stranger to these parts," Montgomery said, leaning closer to Turner, who had made the same observation.

Chernack paused a few yards from the door, watching a plain-clothes officer drag a shirtless young man with a shaved head and rings piercing every part of his body inside the building. The kid looked emaciated and smelled like a garbage can. He was heavily tattooed on his arms and chest and tried to spit at Chernack in one last speed-induced act of defiance. He missed his target, and the detective apologized as he yanked him away. In the dilapidated lobby, Chernack was greeted by a pretty black woman. She smiled and pointed to the room behind her, where Turner waited with Montgomery. Sullivan was in the corner, standing over a table of soggy money.

Turner unlocked Crystal's handcuffs and told her to sit. She mumbled something as she rubbed her wrists and slowly complied. The tattooed arrestee's screams and curses echoed from the other end of a long hallway. Chernack stared in that direction and seemed uneasy, distracted by the clamor.

"Sorry about the noise," Sullivan said. "I told my guys to take him to the thirteenth floor and book him." Chernack looked puzzled, and Sullivan explained they were taking him to the county hospital's jail ward. "Once they're out of here, we should be alone for a couple of hours."

Chernack appeared to relax and sat as far as he could from Crystal. He'd spent his career wearing expensive suits and sitting in luxurious office suites dealing with other men in expensive suits. He was getting a front-row seat with a view into a forbidden world, and he seemed to be enjoying it.

Turner offered Crystal a can of Diet Pepsi and sat across the table from her. "Why did you run?" he asked before she took her first sip.

"Sorry, Sergeant Turner," Chernack said. "Did you intend to give her Miranda?"

"I'm not going to ask her about the narcotics. But if makes you feel better, I can do that," Turner said, thinking to himself, "you pain in the ass."

"Please." Chernack glanced at Crystal and sat back with a smug expression.

"Don't try to impress me. I ain't paying you," she said to him. Then to Turner she added, "I know my rights. I don't want to be silent."

Turner looked at Chernack. "Let's do it anyway."

"Fuck him. It's my fucking life and . . ." Her tirade was cut off by Turner reading her rights to her. She quickly waived them. "I ran because I was fucking scared. Don't," she ordered, pointing at Chernack, who had started to say something.

Chernack sat back and folded his arms. "Don't let sound legal advice distract you."

"Like you give a fuck what happens to me."

"I don't care what happens to you. I'm hoping they lock you up forever if it keeps you away from Philip, but it offends me when someone's rights aren't protected."

Her eyes narrowed, and she turned her back on the lawyer. "Alex was asking for it," she blurted out. "Running around with Jimmy, taking money from cops to set them up with hookers."

"You saw her take money from other cops?" Turner asked, glancing at the tape recorder to be certain it was running.

"Hell, yes. They give her $100. She gives them a number to call, and I seen them at the parties."

"Tell me about the parties, Crystal," Montgomery said. He was trying to control his excitement. It was a better rush than alcohol or sex when a case came together.

"Don't fucking call me Crystal. My name's Cathy." She looked from Turner to Chernack and back to Turner. "Jimmy set up the underground parties at different dives in Hollywood." She snorted a laugh. "Couple of times, Alex splits just before vice busts the party. Stupid cops meet some working girl and fall in love. Alex gives them one freebie; next one they pay for. She made so much fucking money."

"You know how many cops?" Turner asked, starting to feel a little edgy.

"Some come back more than once. A few cheap bastards only took the freebies. Alex was the one that knew them. I did a couple myself early on, but don't ask me to do no fucking lineup. I don't remember faces."

"Why did Alex have the police car?" The car was a loose end that had bothered Turner from the beginning.

162

Crystal laughed and shook her head. "She used the cop car to move the girls around, drop 'em off, pick 'em up. She only had it a coupla weeks. She'd put on the radio to know where vice was working. She and Jimmy drove all over the city in that fucking car. Jimmy called it his bitch mobile. It was cool."

"Where'd they keep it?" Montgomery asked.

"At the police station when they weren't hustling."

"How did they pick the young cops to hit on?" Turner was having a difficult time believing this woman because her story was exactly the one he didn't want to hear.

"Don't know. You guys got e-mail? Alex talked to them on the computer at work."

Turner groaned and turned away. She recruited over the department computer. LAN was a closed network that every employee could access, including the chief of police. He was convinced now that the dead woman had bigger balls than he'd ever have.

"Who killed her, Cathy?" he asked, not expecting an answer.

Crystal sighed and drew her legs up close to her chest, resting her head on her knees.

"Cathy?" he repeated.

"I don't fucking know. That's why I ran. Another pimp . . . a cop she blackmailed." She hesitated. "Maybe Jimmy. He was a crazy motherfucker . . . her macho girlfriend, maybe. Phil says they fought all the time."

"How did you find out she was dead?" Montgomery asked. He was pacing around the table now.

"I got a personal fucking message," she said, wiping away tears with the sleeve of her sweater. She sat up and waited a few seconds. "That night Alex got killed, I get home about two in the morning. There's this bloody knife sitting on the fucking kitchen counter. You got some Kleenex or something?" she asked, rubbing her nose with the back of her hand. Suddenly she couldn't manage the emotion growing inside her, and she sobbed uncontrollably. Sullivan reached into his desk drawer, retrieved a roll of toilet paper, and handed it to her. She cried softly for a few more seconds and then blew her nose. "My sister's chain and locket were wrapped around the knife." She reached under her sweater and pulled out a chain from around her neck. She opened the tiny gold locket and showed them baby pictures Turner guessed were of her and her sister. "Alex never took it off, even in the shower. I ain't stupid. Some psycho left that for me. I ran."

Turner sat back and listened as Crystal answered every question she was asked. Her voice droned on as if she'd carefully rehearsed each answer. Phil, she said, buried the knife at her direction. "Dumb fucker didn't know better. He puts it right by the door." Jimmy gave her the drugs and money the next day because he figured some cop killed Alex, so he was going to play it cool for a week or so.

"Why a cop?" Montgomery asked.

"Who's got the most to lose if Alex blabs?" Crystal said, looking at him as if he were stupid.

Montgomery shrugged. "Depends on what she's got to say."

"Alex liked pissing people off . . . treat 'em like dirt, then give 'em the best fuck of their lives. She screwed with people's heads, too."

Turner reached into his briefcase, removed a color photo of McGann, and put it on the table in front of her. "Did she fuck him?" he asked.

Crystal laughed. "Pathetic creep." She twisted in the chair as if trying to get comfortable. "He didn't kill her." She looked up, and everyone was staring at her. "What? I'm telling you he didn't kill her."

"How do you know that?" Turner finally asked. "He's got a lot to lose."

"You guys ain't real bright for cops. Alex took care of him. He liked having the crap knocked out of him, and she liked doing it. It was the only way he could get off." She looked at their puzzled expressions and shook her head. "Spankings, doggie collars—you know, leather masks and shit like that."

"We know what it is," Turner said. "What we don't understand is why you're so certain he didn't kill her."

"The freak needs her," she said. She got smug telling them about McGann's fetish, as if his weakness tainted all of them. McGann had given Alex a couple of hundred dollars once or twice a week to debase him. Her sister even let Crystal and Jimmy watch a few times. McGann wore a hood and didn't know they were there.

"If his face was covered, how'd you know it was him?" Turner asked, hoping for some reason not to believe her.

"It was him. She didn't do that with nobody else, and they was at the place that belonged to some fag friend, whose name I don't know," she said, grinning at them.

"Take us there," Turner demanded.

She wiggled and stared at the dirty floor. "If I can remember," she said coyly. "I'm pretty sure I can." Crystal was too savvy to give away everything for free.

Turner figured McGann was smart enough to have cleaned out the house. Any evidence was long gone, but it was still worth a look.

"That creep needed Alex. He ain't about to kill her."

"How long were they doing this?" Turner asked.

"Six months I knew about. Ask that little toad Perez. She's Alex's bun boy. Set up their dates. How pathetic is that shit?" She turned to watch the shirtless tattooed boy being dragged by one of the detectives through the office and out the back door. "Fucking loser," Crystal said.

Crystal told them how Sergeant Maria Perez would do anything Alex asked.

"She'd kiss Alex's butt for a pat on the head. Sometimes she got sex with Alex, but not much. She's one ugly bitch."

Turner took a deep breath and asked the one question he and Montgomery were avoiding. Did she know anyone else in the police department who worked with Alex and Jimmy?

She thought a minute, shook her head and then, counting on her fingers, said, "About ten or twelve guys paid for girls. There's that head job with the whips and Perez. That's it."

"Who was the woman lover?" Turner asked, wishing they could stop before it got worse.

"Some fucking Amazon that hit her pretty good a coupla times. Didn't see that one. Phil told me. Alex wouldn't talk about it, said she liked the woman, said most of the time the woman was smart and fun. That was freaky. Alex don't like nobody. Don't think the Amazon's a cop."

"Did Phil describe her?" Chernack asked.

"Fuck, no, he can't hardly remember what day it is."

"What is Phil to you, Crystal, just an easy way to make a buck without taking off your panties?" Chernack asked. He was visibly annoyed. He knew he could hurt her with words, so he did.

165

His unexpected attack surprised her, and it took a second for her anger to surface. It was as if this perfect gentleman had reached over and slapped her, but to everyone's surprise, she didn't respond immediately.

"It's not like that," she finally said.

"What is it, Crystal, love?" Chernack persisted.

"Fuck you. I'm not Crystal."

"Chernack, you mind?" Turner asked. He was as surprised as Crystal. The mild-mannered attorney had shown signs of warm blood, but he was interfering with the interrogation.

"I mind. I'll protect her rights, but I don't have to like her. Changing your name doesn't change what you are." Chernack never raised his voice, but he was clearly irritated.

She jumped up and shouted at the lawyer, "What the fuck do you know, you asshole? Like you ain't no fucking parasite."

"Shut up, both of you," Turner said and pointed at Crystal. "You sit the fuck down." She did and turned her chair to sit with her back to Chernack. The lawyer was quiet.

"Do me a favor, man. Don't ever volunteer to be my attorney," Montgomery said, grinning at Chernack, who ignored him.

Turner tried to get Crystal back on track, but she was upset and wouldn't offer any more information. He and Montgomery exchanged looks; they knew the interview was over. Turner explained to Crystal that they had to book her, but they'd make certain the district attorney rejected any filing on the narcotics if she continued to work with them. Technically, they couldn't promise the case would be dropped, but they knew that any judge or D.A. would go along with them on this one. Trading a narcotics case for a couple of homicides was always a good deal.

Crystal was on probation, so the narcotics found in her apartment could send her back to jail for a violation of that probation. She didn't care about finishing her time for the old conviction but didn't want a new charge, especially one for sales. When Montgomery turned off the tape recorder, she readily admitted that she felt safer in jail for a while after what had happened to her sister and Jimmy. Turner and Montgomery knew that if she was locked up for the next few months, at least they could find her. If they couldn't solve these homicides in three or four months, the investigation would most likely fall into the black hole of unsolved cases with the hundreds of others that LAPD detectives had pretty much abandoned.

Before Crystal was taken to the Van Nuys jail, Turner gave her his pager number and reminded her that unless she cooperated fully, their deal was off, and she'd be charged with possession of methamphetamine for sale.

"I ain't stupid," she said matter-of-factly, and didn't seem interested any longer. She never looked at Chernack and seemed lost in her own thoughts as she was cuffed.

As soon as she was gone, Turner gathered his notes and put the tapes in a box. He played a portion of one of the tapes just to reassure himself that the recorder had worked.

Chernack was quiet until they heard the car leave the parking lot. Then he apologized to Turner for his behavior during the interrogation.

"Send me a copy of the paperwork on her probation violation and the D.A. reject when you get it," he said after Turner told him not to worry about his outburst.

"You're still representing her?" Montgomery asked.

"I didn't hear her say she wanted to replace me," Chernack said, adding, "Can you give me a ride back to my car at the Roosevelt?"

They left the attorney standing next to his new silver SL 500 Mercedes convertible.

"The little turd is rich, too," Montgomery mumbled as he drove away from the hotel parking lot.

"Little conflict of interest, you think?" Turner asked, laughing.

"Why? Because he hates his client and wants to see her rot in prison?"

They laughed. Turner felt good and really didn't care what happened to Crystal as long as it didn't affect their case. He decided that a good systems analyst was essential at this point to backtrack on Alexandra's computer messages and responses.

"I don't think anybody's going to take me off this case now," Turner said. "I'm thinking that for the internal stuff we need more IA guys.

"We've got to talk to McGann again," Montgomery said. "When he knows we found Crystal, he might tell more of the truth."

"Except the kinky sex stuff, which he'll deny. He'll deny he paid for it and play stupid about the love cottage."

"He doesn't know Crystal was there and saw him. If she can find it again, we might have something. Otherwise it's pretty much his word against hers."

"Whores don't carry much weight at a board of rights," Turner said.

Montgomery stopped at a red light and stretched his neck, trying to work out a kink. It had been a long morning. "Let's take her out and see if she can find the house. Maybe we can locate a neighbor or the owner who remembers seeing him and Alexandra."

"That's great for the internal investigation, but what about the homicides? Do we grab Perez again?" Turner asked. He felt like a kid in a candy shop. Suddenly there were too many directions to choose from. Slow down, he told himself. What's most important? "McGann is still our prime suspect in both homicides," he said, thinking out loud.

Montgomery nodded. "He's certainly got motive. Maybe she threatened to reveal their love sessions or, worse yet, had pictures or something . . . wife, kids, career gone."

They were quiet for the remainder of the trip back to Parker Center. Pieces of the puzzle were on the table. The hard part was making them fit and getting a picture that made sense.

Stevenson and Connelly were waiting with Jacob Bell when they arrived at RHD. Bell was sitting at Stevenson's desk. He wore a grim expression and didn't bother to greet them. The cold welcome didn't bother Turner. He didn't want to waste time with small talk, either. He closed the door, placed the tape recorder on the desk in front of Bell, and proceeded to summarize what Crystal had told them. Finally, he switched on the recorder and let Crystal tell her story. Turner watched Bell's jaw tighten as he listened to the description of McGann's coarse activities. He thought there was something resembling fear in Bell's eyes as he waited for her assessment of the extent of the department's corruption. He seemed relieved that she could put a finite number on the damage. A dozen was too many, but it could've been worse.

"Of course we'll re-interview Jim McGann," Connelly said defensively. "This woman could be lying. We owe him the benefit of the doubt until we have more than a prostitute's word."

"Nobody's going to argue with that, Nancy. On the other hand, what reason does she have to lie?" Stevenson asked.

Connelly snorted and looked at Stevenson as if he were stupid. "We've offered her quite a deal up front. The better the lie, the better the deal," she said.

"I think she's telling the truth," Turner said, talking directly to Bell. He didn't feel obligated to include Connelly any longer. Certainly Bell would call the shots. "We need a computer expert and a couple more IA investigators. We can all work out of the office I've been using. We've got to start now before these guys figure we're on to them and start hitting the delete button."

"Just a minute," was all Connelly could say before Bell stood and interrupted her.

"I agree with Sergeant Turner," Bell said, talking over her protestations. "Nancy, you decide what you can afford to give. Carl, your homicides are probably tied to the internal investigation, so Turner stays with you." He looked directly at Connelly.

"I really think we should discuss alternatives before we jump into this," she said. Her voice trailed off. Bell's stern expression left no room for discussion.

"What about the internal surveillance detail?" Turner asked. "Can we use them?"

Bell didn't hesitate. "Use them. They report to you. You report to me," he said, pointing at Stevenson.

Connelly's face flushed. She was angry and on the verge of tears.

"Sorry, Nancy," Bell said. "This belongs to the chief's office now." Bell knew he was stepping on toes, but he didn't have time for the subtleties now. Someone needed to take charge, and the tone of his voice made it clear it was going to be him.

Bell excused himself. He wanted to brief Chief Martin before the rumor mill started spewing versions of the truth around Parker Center. He held up his hand as Connelly started to say something.

"There's nothing more to discuss," he said firmly. "Just do as I ask. If you can't, I'll find someone who can." He left, leaving the door open behind him. Connelly slipped out behind him. She didn't dare approach him again but probably had little desire to remain in the room with these men who had witnessed her embarrassing rebuke.

Stevenson gently shut the door. "Call the surveillance team," he said to Turner.

Turner felt a surge of energy. He was certain they were doing the right thing, but they couldn't make mistakes, either. This wasn't some sappy policeman smoking a joint behind his apartment building. This was one of the highest-ranking officers in the department. They had to do it right. He called the squad leader he knew and trusted. His team was working another case, and he explained that Captain Connelly would need to okay the change. Turner assured him that it wouldn't be a problem, and then he and Montgomery waited in the empty RHD squad room for the surveillance team's arrival.

Turner sank into one of the detective's chairs and put his feet up on the squad table. "Finally," he said, taking a deep breath and crossing his arms over his chest.

FOURTEEN

Paula Toscano was finishing the last of her paperwork when Bell was called to Stevenson's office. She'd tried to call RHD, but no one would answer the phone. Mike was her only hope for discovering what had put that very worried and sick expression on Bell's face.

When Bell returned to his office, he didn't say anything as he closed his door. She saw the phone light up almost immediately. It was probably Martin. The chief of police was one of the few numbers Bell dialed himself.

She tried again to reach Turner. This time he answered on the first ring, but he sounded disappointed. He explained that he was waiting for the surveillance supervisor to call, and what Crystal had revealed.

"I feel a little jealous not being part of this," she said. "Sorry my call wasn't your surveillance guy."

"I'm not," he said.

"I miss you."

"Can you come down for a while? I can't leave right now, but we could have a cup of coffee and a few minutes together."

"Let me see if Bell needs anything when he gets off the phone," she said. "A few minutes in the break room are better than nothing."

A few seconds after the light went out on the phone line, Bell opened the door and asked Paula to step into his office. He told her everything. She acted surprised, even though Turner had just finished telling her the same story. She felt proud that Bell trusted her. He said he respected her common sense and judgment and needed an intelligent, discreet sounding board. She supported his decision on the surveillance detail, which made him smile.

"Given your association with Turner, I wouldn't have expected you to disagree with that one."

"Do you need me anymore?" she asked. "If not, I think I'll go to RHD for a few minutes."

Bell smiled. "No, I'm so tired I might sleep on my desk. No more work will be done in this office tonight."

Paula thought he did seem very tired, and she offered to drive him home.

"Just kidding, dear," he said. "I'm more than capable of going home. Maggie has seen me walk through our front door every night for thirty years. I'm too old and well trained to stop now."

Everyone was in Stevenson's office when Paula arrived. Montgomery seemed uncomfortable until Paula explained that Bell had filled her in on the investigation. She dragged the secretary's chair into the room and sat next to Turner. Katy was discussing the computer work that needed to be done. She was competent on computers but didn't know much about the department's internal closed computer system. She was willing to oversee the work but wanted an expert to do the search. Choosing that person was critical. The wrong choice meant that by the next morning, rumors would be flying around the department. Some might even be close to the truth. With Alexandra and Jimmy dead, the computer search was the only way they'd find Alexandra's police contacts.

There were several computer nerds in the department, but it was impossible to know whether any of them had contacted Alexandra. Paula wasn't anxious to get in the middle of their discussion, but she knew that Rose, Bell's secretary, had her degree in computer science. She was honest and would do anything Bell asked. Stevenson jumped on her suggestion. He'd worked with Rose and immediately knew the no-nonsense black woman was the answer to their dilemma.

As soon as the computer expert was decided on, Turner managed to get Paula out of Stevenson's office and into the dark break room. When they were alone, he put his arm around her waist, kissed her for a very long time, and then held her quietly. Paula gently pushed back a little and reached over his shoulder to flip on the light switch.

"I need to spend more time down here," she said, kissing him again. He stroked her curly hair.

"We need to spend more time, period." He led her to a table in the corner and pointed to a full pot of coffee. "Hungry? I've got three kinds of Girl Scout cookies."

"Not that hungry. Sorry I butted in on your meeting."

"Don't be. Rose is perfect. Did you hear?" he asked suddenly, remembering what Stevenson had told him before her arrival. "The ranking on my lieutenant's band comes out tomorrow." She looked away from him for just a second, but he caught it. "I don't expect to be number one, but I should be high enough to make it. What's wrong? Did you hear some bad news about my ranking?"

She smiled, but he could see it was forced. "No, of course not . . . you should do well. I'll try to get a copy of the list tomorrow."

"I'm not a kid," he insisted. "You can tell me the truth." She wasn't a good liar, and he hated being the last one to know bad news.

"I'm not hiding anything," she said, hesitating. "It's just that you're such an innocent about how promotions happen in this department."

"I've got more time and experience than most of those other guys."

"Think Alice in Wonderland. Queen of Hearts?" She closed her eyes and sighed. "Just because you're the most qualified doesn't mean you'll get promoted. There's diversity, grudges, pay-backs. Oh, hell, forget it. I'm sure you'll do fine."

He didn't want to think about it anymore. He was getting angry because he knew she was right. He'd worked hard for this promotion, but it didn't matter. He was a guy with a questionable past. Myron was their poster boy, so fuck them. Turner could've worked himself into a really disagreeable mood, but Stevenson interrupted them to say the surveillance sergeant had arrived. In a few seconds, everyone gathered in the break room. No one asked Paula to leave, so she sat quietly in a corner

The sergeant in charge and his female assistant squad leader were the two representatives from the internal surveillance detail. They wore jeans and casual clothes and didn't look like on-duty police officers. The sergeant had on a pair of worn cowboy boots and a San Francisco Giants baseball cap. His long stringy hair was in a ponytail. His assistant's hair was cut in a short punk style. She had three earrings on each ear, which for some reason Turner thought was very attractive on her.

Finally Stevenson told them to grab a cup of coffee and sit down so he could begin the briefing. He introduced everyone, and then the RHD captain went through every detail of the investigation. Turner was surprised that nothing had been kept back, but Stevenson explained that he wouldn't put a surveillance team on the street without letting them know everything he knew.

"Can't remember a case we've done with a staff officer," the sergeant said when Stevenson had finished. "There's been plenty of allegations, but nobody ever seemed interested in knowing if they were true."

"This isn't your run-of-the-mill cocaine-sniffing cop," Stevenson said. "We know you can do those. This one, you can't make a mistake. There's one rule. Don't get caught." He explained that whatever they found would be found again another way. He told the sergeant that Turner would be his contact person. "If McGann robs a bank, call uniformed officers to make the arrest. He can't know you're following him."

"We like being invisible," the female said, smiling.

"Don't feel like you have to do something," Montgomery said. "Just follow him. Tell us where he goes and who he sees."

They decided that the surveillance would begin that night as soon as they could get their squad together. When the sergeant left with his assistant, Turner began to feel anxious. All his concerns about being promoted didn't matter right then. He wanted this to work. If McGann found out they'd picked up Crystal, he might hide in his Marina apartment until the storm passed.

"I think Bell is going to be pleased with the way surveillance is approaching this," Paula said, wiping crumbs from a peanut butter cookie off her uniform. "This sergeant has a lot of confidence, but I think he'll do it your way."

"He'd better do it my way," Stevenson said. He reached over Paula and picked up the phone. The light had been blinking for a few seconds. He listened for a while, grunted once, groaned and said, "What a fucking mess." Everyone was watching and listening to his side of the conversation. When he hung up, they waited for him to say something.

"Are you going to tell us or what?" Montgomery finally asked.

"It was Connelly. The duty room just called her at home. West Hollywood sheriffs responded to an assault call at Maria Perez's duplex. She threatened her neighbor with a gun. Connelly thought we might want to talk to Perez before IA got her."

"Connelly's trying to help us?" Katy asked. "What's wrong with this picture?"

Turner knew. Bell had made it clear he expected Connelly to cooperate with RHD. She was so accustomed to unquestioned obedience that it never would've occurred to her not to call Stevenson.

"You want to come?" Stevenson asked Paula. She looked at Turner, who had his jacket on and was ready to leave.

"It's up to you," Turner said. "You could wait with the captains in the hanging-around corner while we do all the work." He avoided Stevenson's glare and winked at Paula. She agreed to come and generally stay out of the way. Turner was glad. He knew Connelly would put her own spin on what happened. He wanted Paula to see everything in case Bell asked.

Maria's duplex was on a quiet street off Beverly Boulevard in West Hollywood. The homes in that area had an early California look of white stucco and red tile roofs. The duplex stood beside its twin, front porches nearly touching, separated only by a sidewalk. A sheriff's deputy sat on the porch railing. The front door was open, and another deputy stood there with his back to the porch. Four patrol cars surrounded the house, so the RHD cars had to be parked across the street. Motion lights flooded the sidewalk as Turner and the others approached the front door.

The deputy slid off the railing and greeted them with a nod as he shouted for his lieutenant. A short balding man in a dark suit came out of the house and introduced himself to Stevenson. He gave Stevenson Maria's holstered weapon. Stevenson led the lieutenant to the other end of the porch. They spoke softly for a few minutes before returning to where Turner and the others waited.

"They have a signed crime report. Neighbor says Maria brandished the gun, pointed it at her," Stevenson said, looking at the lieutenant, who nodded in agreement.

"What does Maria say?" Turner asked. He hated having only one side of the story.

"She says she kept it in the holster by her side," the little bald man said clearly, not believing it.

"Wits?" Katy asked.

"Nope," the lieutenant said quickly.

"Neighbor's a chronic caller, kind of the local screwball. She can't describe the gun. We won't get a filing," the deputy said, sitting back on the railing. He shrugged at the lieutenant, who glared at him.

Stevenson thanked the deputies and told them that if they were through with Perez, his people would take it from there. Their lieutenant looked at his watch and left quickly. West Hollywood wasn't exactly a hotbed of criminal activity, so the deputies weren't as anxious as their boss to get away from this boring call. They joked and exchanged stories with Katy, who kept them occupied on the front porch.

Perez was familiar with Turner and Montgomery, so they'd conduct the interview. Stevenson said he and Paula would keep everyone outside, including Connelly, whenever she showed up, until they were finished.

When he entered the small living room, Turner saw Maria Perez sitting to his right in a breakfast area. She quietly watched them as they approached her. She shook her head and looked at the brick-colored linoleum floor as they sat at the table on either side of her.

"This is embarrassing," she said, trying to smile and taking a quick sip from a large glass of water in front of her. She was dressed in sweatpants and a baggy sweater. She wore tennis shoes without socks. "Do you want something to drink?" she asked, pointing at the glass.

"No," Montgomery said. He wasn't smiling. "We want to talk to you. This time we want the truth."

"That old woman is crazy. Why would I point a gun at her?"

"We don't give a shit about the old woman," Turner said. "We have Crystal."

She leaned her head back and closed her eyes. "Fuck," she whispered.

This was a different woman, not the one they'd seen in West Bureau. In that first interview she was confident and in control. Tonight Turner could feel it. She was vulnerable. It was late. The encounter with the sheriff's deputies and the prospect of facing Connelly had her on edge. The mention of Crystal's name was the final blow. Turner could see the fear on her tired face, in her eyes. He could smell it and knew how to use it. He took out a small recorder and put it on the table in front of her.

"She told us everything." Turner sat back and waited.

Maria stared at him and then down at the table.

Turner decided to take a chance. He thought he understood her pride.

176

"You want a rep?" he asked with a tone that said, "Are you the kind of scumbag that needs a union rep before you can talk?"

"I said I didn't need one before, and I still don't need one."

"Okay," he said, trying to put just a touch of fake admiration in his voice. "I want the truth about Alexandra." She closed her eyes and was silent. Turner picked up the recorder and put it back in his pocket. "It's late," he said. "I guess we go with what Crystal told us." He stood and walked behind her chair.

"I want to talk to you," she said. "It can't get any worse, can it?" she asked, looking over her shoulder at Turner, who didn't answer, and leaned against the wall. "I guess you know Crystal was Alexandra's stepsister?" she asked, and Montgomery nodded. "Alex didn't even like her, but she let Crystal stay at the bungalow because she thought it was funny, you know, living with a hooker."

"Did Crystal introduce Alexandra and Dean?" Turner asked, placing the recorder back on the table.

"Crystal worked for Dean when she worked. Mostly, she slept all day and partied all night. It got bad when Alex met Dean. She got worse . . . nothing mattered anymore—the job, her life, friends." Her voice drifted. She looked up at Montgomery. "I loved Alex. I would've done anything for her. She was sick. Me, too, I guess." She laughed nervously.

"What did you do for her?" Montgomery asked.

"I got the car and took all the keys from IA so nobody else could use it." She stared at the tape recorder. Turner was pacing behind her, but she didn't seem aware of anything except the slow-turning wheels of the recorder. "I never knew what they were doing, why she wanted it. She asked and I did it," she said softly to the small box.

"What else?" Turner asked.

"Carried messages between her and McGann. Sold my soul and my pride to be with her once or twice a month. I'm sure Crystal thought that was hysterical," she said, twisting in the chair to find Turner.

"What messages?" he asked, coming around the table again.

"When they could meet."

"Were they written, verbal? Where did they meet?"

"She told me. I told him. Alex decided when, and they always met at the house."

"Where's the house?" Montgomery said.

She studied Montgomery's face and then Turner's. She appeared puzzled, as if she wondered whether they were testing her or maybe didn't know about the house.

"Either you tell us, or Crystal takes us there tomorrow. We'll be in the house one way or another. Just depends how many brownie points you want to chalk up."

Maria wasn't clever, and the dark lines under her eyes told Turner she was exhausted. She sighed.

"It's in the Hollywood Hills. I can take you, but I don't know the address. Now if you want."

"Did you ever see what was going on in that house?" Turner asked.

Her expression changed, as if she had swallowed something rotten. "No," she whined. "I dropped her off a couple of times. I've never even been inside."

"Do you know what was going on in there?" Montgomery asked.

"Sex, I guess."

"Alex never talked about it, described it to you?" Turner asked.

Maria was emphatic. "Why would she do that?"

"What else?" Turner was impatient. He was certain she was still holding back.

"Nothing. I took the car and did her errands."

"Who killed her?" Turner said too loudly. He was pacing again. "Did you kill her? She treated you like shit. Maybe you got tired of her crap, cut her throat, and dumped her in front of her lover's house." He didn't believe that, but her attitude was so frustrating.

She shook her head slowly, covered her face with both hands for a few seconds and then looked up at Turner. Her eyes were bloodshot, but there wasn't a single tear.

"I didn't kill her. I couldn't even find the courage to say no to her. Crystal and Dean, they were her kind. Maybe the pack turned on her."

"Did you see her the day she died?" Montgomery asked.

"A couple of times in the morning," she said, then stopped for a second as if trying to remember. "She came to get the car at the bureau. Later I drove to her house in West L.A. to tell her McGann wasn't coming that night."

"What time was that?"

"About 8 P.M., but I only stayed a minute. Crystal and Dean were there, and Dean was teasing that poor handyman . . . fondling Crystal in front of him. It made me sick, so I left."

"Phil White was there?" Turner asked.

"He was always hanging around Crystal until she made him go home. He's harmless."

"What time was McGann supposed to meet Alex?"

"Eleven."

"What did Alex say when he cancelled?"

"Nothing. She just shrugged and went into her room and shut the door. It didn't matter. Nothing mattered to her."

"Was that unusual for McGann not to go?"

"That was the first time I knew about."

"Did you see her again that night or know if she met anyone?" Montgomery and Turner were shooting questions at her. She twisted from one to the other as if she were watching a tennis match.

"No, I've told you everything I know."

"Why did you meet McGann at The Spot this week?" Turner asked, almost talking over her answer. He wanted to surprise her, and he did. Her expression was confused and then angry. How did they know about that? Her eyes narrowed, and she swallowed hard.

"He asked to meet me," she said finally.

"Why?" he asked and then sighed. "Don't make me drag this out of you."

"He wanted to know what I said to you. He was really angry that I told you about that night after the party. He said he wished he'd met with Alex the night she got killed because maybe he could've done something." She hesitated. "He promised to keep me out of the investigation."

"Who was the girl you were with?" Turner asked.

"She's nobody, a friend. She's not a cop."

"Give me a name," Turner insisted.

"Nicky Harden." Maria was angry.

"Why was she there?" Turner didn't feel any need to be sensitive.

"I asked her to come. I didn't want to be alone with him. I'm afraid of him. I know he lied to you. Nicky doesn't know about any of this. She never even knew Alex," Maria pleaded.

"Has McGann threatened you?" Turner asked.

"No, but I'm not stupid. He's got a lot to lose, and two people are already dead."

Turner got up and tapped Montgomery on the shoulder, motioning for him to come back out onto the porch. Stevenson, Paula, and Katy were huddled with Nancy Connelly, who had just arrived. They were talking quietly in a corner of the porch. They discussed what Maria had just told them, and Stevenson decided they should have Maria show them the location of the house in the morning. Katy argued they should take her out right then, find the house, and leave someone to watch it until morning, when they could have a search warrant ready. Turner was tired and wanted to go home with Paula, but he knew Katy was right. By morning, Maria could have a change of heart, and he didn't want to rely on Crystal.

"I'd better go," he whispered to Paula as they stepped away from the others. "Monty will take you back to your car, and I'll be home in a few hours."

"Why not let Monty do it? It doesn't take two of them to write the warrant."

"Because he's got a wife who's threatening to take their daughter back to North Carolina if he doesn't stop his string of all-nighters. He needs to go home."

"So do you, lover. You look terrible."

He kissed her quickly on the cheek. He was exhausted, but leaving wasn't an option.

Perez sat alone at the dining room table. Turner watched her, but she didn't seem to have noticed the meeting on her front porch. Her expression told Turner she was most likely calculating the odds of keeping her job. He wondered if in retrospect she thought her behavior with Alexandra Williams was foolish, or whether she still had feelings for the dead woman. Tomorrow would be a bad time for her. It would be like waking from a nightmare, and she'd realize that her career was over. She couldn't be trusted. She'll survive, Turner thought. It was possible to lose everything and still survive. He knew that to be true.

Stevenson drove, and Connelly sat in the back seat with Perez. Turner sat up front. He didn't feel much like talking, so he listened to Connelly explain to Perez how the sheriffs would get a reject on the crime report they'd taken. They were whispering, but he could hear everything.

"Doesn't matter," Perez said. "I'm resigning."

"That's a little drastic," Connelly said.

"Don't want to be a cop anymore," Perez said, staring out the car window. She spoke only to give Stevenson directions and ignored Connelly's attempts to start a conversation.

Connelly was quiet, too, and then after a few seconds said, "It's stupid to throw away your career. I can't understand just giving up."

"Don't worry about it," Perez said.

"I sacrificed my first marriage and precious time with my children to survive in this department, to make it easier for your generation. The job always came first. When I was a patrol captain, I left my son's wedding to go to a shooting scene. One of my officers shot a woman who'd threatened him with a knife. He was upset. I comforted him, told him he did the right thing. I was dressed in my mother-of-the-groom gown, and all I could think about was dancing with my handsome son on his wedding day, but I stayed there."

Turner looked at Stevenson, who didn't seem to be listening. Perez was still staring out the window. He'd been a patrol sergeant at the time and remembered the shooting Connelly was talking about. He recalled that she'd left the shooting scene in less than an hour and returned to her son's wedding, leaving a lieutenant in charge. Her officers criticized her for not waiting until the shaky officer had been interviewed by the shooting team. The bureau chief at the time gave her a commendation for her dedication to duty. Two weeks later, that same bureau chief, who happened to be Jim McGann, recommended her for the coveted Internal Affairs job. Connelly had figured out the key to success in LAPD. It wasn't what you did or what your subordinates thought. It was how you looked to the guys in charge.

Perez tapped Stevenson on the shoulder and told him to make the next turn onto a barely visible narrow road and park in front of the second house. There wasn't much lighting, and Turner couldn't make out the street sign. Even officers who worked this division their entire careers didn't know all of these hidden side streets in the Hollywood Hills.

Perez pointed to the house across the street. There wasn't any front yard. It was the only one on the street without a security light over the front door. Stevenson removed a flashlight from under the front seat and gave it to Turner.

"Try not to trip on anything," Stevenson said.

Turner walked across the street and was surprised he didn't hear any dogs barking. He wouldn't live in this secluded neighborhood without some kind of nasty, noisy animal. The Maglite gave him plenty of light, and he jotted the house numbers on his hand. Even at night, he could see the bright white stucco and tile roof. He had what they needed for the search warrant but wanted to make certain there weren't any animals in the backyard. He slid along the side of the house in a narrow space near the block wall and reached over the gate to lift the latch. There was nothing but a hot tub in the cramped backyard. He stepped into what he thought was a flowerbed and squeezed between a row of bushes to look into a window. It was too dark inside to see anything. He was wearing a new light-brown suit that Paula had bought for his birthday. As he pulled out of the hedge, he was pissed because the jacket was probably filthy. She was convinced he didn't like the suit and would think he ruined it on purpose. He didn't like it but wouldn't be that obvious. When he came back to the front of the house, Turner saw Stevenson shuffling through some junk mail he'd pulled out of the slot.

Everything was addressed to Occupant, but Turner knew he could run utilities and find out who paid the bills. He glanced into the back seat of Stevenson's car. Connelly and Perez were still sitting beside each other, staring out opposite windows. Turner didn't care much or have much respect for Connelly, who was in way over her head, but thought she had to be one lonely woman. He was smiling as he opened the door and sat in the passenger seat. Stevenson asked him what the joke was. He shook his head. He'd been thinking Connelly would be made a commander before she retired, but he would probably never make lieutenant. For a second, the whole upside-down system seemed kind of funny.

They waited outside the house until a couple of RHD investigators arrived and agreed to watch the place until they served the search warrant the next morning. After depositing Connelly at her car and Perez on her front porch, Stevenson tried to convince Turner to go with him to the Freeway bar. Turner declined, and Stevenson muttered something about apron strings before taking him to his truck in the parking structure behind PAB. Turner knew a lot of cops like Stevenson. He'd go home and sit in front of his television, watching bad movies and drinking cheap booze until he passed out.

Turner called Katy at RHD at about 2 A.M. as he pulled into his driveway. He gave her the information for the search warrant and told her to go home. They could get the warrant signed in the morning. The house was secure.

"I'm about done," she said. "There are some advantages to not having anybody who gives a damn what time you get home."

"Sometimes I think you're the smart one," he said, thinking about how upset Paula would be.

"Yeah, I smell because I haven't had a shower for two days. My skin looks dead. My hair is dry and hasn't been styled for months. I'm tired of all these nights of dead bodies and 2 A.M. callouts. End of this year, I'm out of homicides so I can get a life."

"Good for you," Turner said.

"I mean it," she insisted.

"Like I said, good for you. Go home." He closed the phone and put it into his pocket. He also knew a lot of cops like Katy. There wasn't a chance in hell she'd leave RHD unless they threw her out.

FIFTEEN

Turner's truck was temperamental the next morning. He sat patiently as it coughed and sputtered, trying to achieve that primo gas-guzzling, eight-cylinder Chevrolet roar that he loved. He opened his briefcase while the engine idled. Something had been bothering him for days . . . those two plainclothes officers who'd been seen by the café owner at the bottom of McGann's street the night Alexandra was murdered. He knew it was too much of a coincidence that they'd been there on that particular night.

Were they in the café while Alexandra was alive? Did anyone see their car? Judy Taylor hadn't seen badges. Maybe they weren't even cops, maybe security or some other agency. He wanted to show Taylor some of the players in this homicide to see if she recognized anyone besides McGann. Maybe he should wait until they found some of Alexandra's clients on the department computer.

It was Friday, and normally that wasn't the day to find a judge in court. They don't like to work on their getaway day. Montgomery knew a black judge who usually worked on Fridays. She'd grown up in the Crenshaw area of Los Angeles, had had to work harder than everyone else to get a break and, most important, hated criminals. She loved cops as long as they didn't lie to her. With any luck, Montgomery would already have the warrant signed, and they could search the house before lunch.

Traffic on surface streets was Friday-morning light. Judges weren't the only ones in Los Angeles who liked the three-day weekend. Montgomery paged him before he reached Parker Center to tell him the warrant had been signed. When he arrived at RHD, Katy was already there, looking fresh and rested. He envied her. He could remember those days when he could work all night and be ready to go before sunrise. His body wasn't willing to do that anymore.

Bell's secretary, Rose, was in Stevenson's office. Montgomery told Turner that Rose had put up quite a battle before agreeing to assist them with the computer search.

"I ain't got no time, no talent, and no desire to get in the middle of this nasty business," Montgomery said, imitating Rose.

"So how'd he get her to do it?" Turner asked.

"Bribed her, got one of the other secretaries to do her regular work until she finished the computer search."

Stevenson left Rose in his office. They saw her sitting in his chair in front of his computer.

"You already gave her the serial numbers and names we had?" Montgomery asked when Stevenson joined them.

"She's going to use my office and lock everything in my desk if she leaves before we get back. I've seen her work. If Alexandra left a trail, Rose will find it."

Montgomery briefed them on the search warrant. Katy had found a phone number listed in Alexandra's name at that address, and they'd call before making entry. Nobody expected anyone to be inside.

Turner was feeling anxious. Things were starting to happen, and this was the time good detectives made great moves to solve a case, or bad ones let it slip away. Instincts and experience should kick in if they had any. They're such unique creatures, he thought. A witness cries at the wrong time, tells the story slightly differently the second time, and their shit meters register like a seismic disturbance. He didn't know if he could ever be a good detective. He didn't have the patience or mind for detail, but he did admire the breed.

Turner, Katy, and Montgomery rode with Stevenson, and two uniformed officers followed in a black-and-white as they caravanned up the street to the small house in the Hollywood Hills. They parked around the corner out of sight in the unlikely case anyone was watching from Alexandra's house. Katy tried calling the number, but no one answered. Turner led the small group around the corner to the place he'd visited the night before. Junk mail was piled up on the doorstep. In the daylight, he could see that the outside was in need of new paint and stucco. It was chipped and streaked with water stains from the tile roof. One of the uniformed officers squeezed along the side of the house and entered the backyard. Turner knocked loudly on the front door, announcing that he had a search warrant and demanding that the door be opened. They waited, but there was no answer.

Montgomery took a screwdriver and slid it into the track near the door lock. He punched the tool hard into the lock and pushed up. The door popped open. The young uniformed officer standing beside him with his weapon drawn peered over his sunglasses at the tall nerdy-looking detective.

"Not a lot of youth programs when I was growing up," Montgomery said, shoving open the door.

With the uniformed officer trailing, Turner and Montgomery walked slowly through the rooms. As they expected, it was empty. Turner called for Stevenson, Katy, and the second uniformed officer to come in through the sliding glass door.

There was a stale musty odor throughout the small house. The living room was sparsely furnished—one couch with a cheap slipcover, an upholstered chair that looked like it could've come from the trailer where Alexandra's mother lived. Turner pulled back the heavy, dusty drapes and opened the front windows. The smell made him lightheaded. Everyone except Stevenson pulled on a pair of the standard latex gloves. It was the captain's way of telling them he had no intention of doing anything other than observing.

Montgomery thanked the uniformed officers and sent them back to patrol. For a few minutes, everyone else wandered around quietly, not touching or moving anything. It was a two-bedroom, two-bath home with a large kitchen. The living room was small, and the second bedroom was set up like an office with bookshelves and a desk. A closet-sized bathroom was inside the master bedroom, and the second bathroom was in a short hallway facing the living room. Katy took dozens of digital pictures in each room. Turner followed Montgomery into the master bedroom. A mattress without sheets was on the laminate floor, with a stained white blanket tucked around it. A shabby cardboard box that at one time had held a Sony television sat under the window. Turner pulled back the curtains and found wooden shutters covering the windows. He opened the shutters to let in some light and looked out on a brick wall. He kicked at the box and heard something rattle inside. He unfolded the flaps and saw a pile of chains and leather straps inside. A thin piece of wire that looked to be about ten feet long was rolled up on top of the pile. Montgomery, who was standing beside him, picked up the wire and then carefully removed each of the items as Katy took pictures. There were two sets of chains with leather straps and a leather mask. While she took pictures from different angles, Montgomery opened the closet and told Turner to come and see. There was a variety of outfits; some were definitely Crystal's taste, but most seemed expensive and classy-looking. Katy checked the labels and confirmed that they were very pricey. Purses, shoes, and boots were piled carelessly on the floor of the closet.

Suddenly Montgomery went back to the cardboard box, picked up the wire, and stood by the window. He examined it for several minutes and then carefully laid it back on the floor. He knelt down and then, with his nose inches from the floor, stared at the laminated wood. He crawled around the mattress, examining the floor. Katy shrugged at Turner. Neither of them spoke, but they watched Montgomery as he ran his finger along the seams of the floorboard. After he'd made a circle around the mattress, Montgomery stood and looked up at a large hook in the ceiling. The wall behind the mattress was covered with a sheet of mirror. Montgomery examined the edges of the mirror. He pulled the blanket off the mattress. It was clean. He lifted one corner, and Turner helped him flip it onto the other side. That side was clean, too.

"Okay, Holmes, you want to tell us what's going on?" Turner asked.

Montgomery ignored him and turned to Katy. "Call SID. Tell them I want them here now." She didn't move, as if waiting for some explanation. "I think our victim died in this room," he said almost to himself. He pushed the mattress away from the wall and used his pocketknife to lift one of the floorboards that butted against the mirrored wall. Taking the flashlight sticking out of Turner's back pants pocket, Montgomery looked closely between the wall and the board. After several seconds, he gently released the board and stood. Turner and Katy were staring at him. None of them noticed Stevenson standing in the doorway until he coughed and held up a knife that was a duplicate of the one found buried at the West L.A. bungalow.

"There's four more of these in the kitchen drawer," Stevenson said. "The murder weapon makes a setting for six."

Montgomery nodded as Katy moved outside to get better reception on her cell phone.

"What's going on in here?" Stevenson asked.

"Katy's getting SID. Alex was killed here. I'm certain. There's blood everywhere," Montgomery said, picking up the wire again.

Turner glanced around the room and noticed Stevenson doing the same. The room was cleaner than his apartment.

"You got infrared vision, partner? Where's the blood?"

Montgomery motioned them to come closer to the window and held up the wire.

"See that dried brown gunk between the weave? I think it's blood." He went to the mirror, and they followed him. Barely visible with the flashlight was a strip of something brownish along the edge of the mirror. As the stream of light moved down to the floor, Turner saw something caked between the floor and the wall. "Somebody tried to clean up, but you can't. Our killer did a pretty good job, but there's always too much blood," Montgomery said. "Check the washer and dryer and the garbage for rags or towels . . . plastic for the mattress. It's too clean. She had it covered."

"Makes sense, given her lifestyle," Turner said. He was impressed and could tell Stevenson was, too. The guy was a good detective, and Turner could almost see his mind, taking inventory in the room.

"The killer might've wrapped everything in the plastic, including the body, to take it to the car. We need to find out if the garbage has been picked up since that night." Montgomery was talking and moving toward the kitchen. The washer and dryer were on a service porch outside the back door. He pulled sheets and towels out of the dryer, pointing to some discoloration as he handed them to Turner.

"The killer used them to clean up the room. Smell them. It's like he poured a whole bottle of bleach in there." Montgomery went into the backyard as he talked and opened the garbage can. It was empty. He paced around the yard as Turner stood in the doorway, holding the towels and watching. Finally he stopped and leaned against the above-ground hot tub. He jumped when the motor automatically kicked on the filtering system. He started to walk back to the house but stopped and returned to the hot tub. Lifting the cover, he peeked in and then shoved the cover with both hands until it slid to the ground.

He motioned for Turner, who was still holding the towels, to come outside. Turner stood beside him and peered into the bubbling water. It rolled like seaweed in the murky ocean—a large piece of clear plastic. Montgomery reached down and turned off the pump, and the water was still. They stared at the death shroud washed clean by warm water and chlorine.

"Leave it," Montgomery said, pulling the cover up onto the spa. "SID might still get prints."

It was late afternoon before everyone was notified and the print geeks were swarming all over Alexandra's perverted love nest, tainted now by violence and death. Turner was fascinated by the activity. He had never been part of a big homicide investigation and watched as Montgomery hovered over the technicians as they painstakingly examined the bedroom inch by inch. They bagged and tagged anything that could be tested for blood or other body fluids. The evidence was there. Someone had tried to wipe it clean but missed those places that Montgomery seemed to know were always missed.

"With this kind of violence, the way she was attacked, blood was flung everywhere," Montgomery explained as he pointed to a tiny smudge on the bedroom wall. "It drips and clings. A killer cleans what he sees, which is nothing compared to what he leaves behind."

One of the technicians was scraping the rim of the washing machine. Blood had seeped under the rubber gasket that lined the lid when the killer shoved the bloody towels into the machine.

"Maybe we'll get lucky and find some of his blood. From her wounds, it looked like Alexandra fought," Montgomery said.

"No bloody clothes," Katy said, standing between him and Turner as they watched the man work on the washer.

"She wasn't wearing any. The slip wasn't damaged, and it was too clean. It was put on after she died. My guess is, the wire made the throat wound. It cut right through her neck," Montgomery said, thinking out loud.

Katy looked up at him. "Garroted?" she asked. Her mouth twisted in disgust when she said it.

"Just guessing. Military guy with the right background would know how. It would explain the weird pattern around the neck wound." Montgomery moved away from them and looked at the wire he'd placed on the mattress with the other paraphernalia from the box. "Can you imagine," he said softly, glancing back at Turner.

SIXTEEN

Sitting on Alexandra's patio in the darkness listening to the stillness of the chilly night, Turner couldn't hear traffic or televisions or the neighbor's family dispute. The canyons absorbed those random sounds you heard in any other city neighborhood. He'd pulled a kitchen chair out to the narrow patio between the house and the hot tub. One of the lab guys made a coffee run. Sipping from the cup gave Turner an excuse to get out of those oppressive rooms and away from the search for a few minutes.

They had already uncovered hundreds of dried blood spots that had been overlooked by the killer or someone who had tried to clean up the murder scene. Turner's back and neck were sore from examining every possible place blood could've been left. He'd logged too many hours sitting in a patrol car, and it had left him with a fragile back.

Montgomery was a master. From what was left of the blood patterns, he had re-created that awful night. He surmised that the wire had cut her throat while she fought off the knife attack. Maybe there were two assailants. At first Montgomery thought Alexandra might've been hanged somehow from the hook in the ceiling, but he'd changed his mind because of the blood around the mirror. The wire was thin and sharp. It could easily have been pulled over the corner of the massive mirror and hooked behind it onto one of the bolts. He guessed that as she slumped forward from her other wounds, her body weight tightened the wire and cut her throat. It wasn't meant to kill her, just restrain her.

A chill ran through Turner's body as he pictured the scene. Pretty diabolical, he thought. Alexandra could watch herself dying in the same mirror she'd used to give pleasure. As he sat comforted by the serenity of the night, he knew he was too old to be exposed this late in life to such extremes of human cruelty. He'd already had enough bad experiences during his years on the job to keep him up at night. This would certainly add to those sleepless hours.

The technicians were packing up their work kits. He could hear Montgomery giving them last-minute instructions. He should probably go back inside but didn't want to move. The house smelled sour. Death had claimed it like an animal marking its territory. Turner decided he needed some time to recharge before heading back to the office. The front door closed, and he could hear Montgomery and Katy talking. They were looking for him. He shouted for them to come to the backyard. In a few seconds, he could sense them standing behind him at the sliding glass door.

"Grab some coffee on the kitchen counter and come out for a few minutes," Turner said without turning to look at them.

Montgomery pulled another chair outside and sat beside Turner. Katy sat on the hot-tub cover and sipped from a can of diet soda.

"Nice," Montgomery said, staring at the sky. "We're ready to wrap up."

"Where's Stevenson?" Turner asked.

"He left an hour ago to check on Rose," Katy answered. "We need to get back, too. I think that computer will give us our suspect."

"I'm tired," Turner admitted. For some reason, knowing how the pretty woman had died had taken all the energy out of him. "Mind if I call it a night?" Before Montgomery could answer, Turner's cell phone rang. It was the surveillance supervisor. His team had followed McGann to Parker Center, where he'd met with the chief. Afterward he'd stopped for several drinks at a Marina club and then gone home alone in the middle of the day. They'd leave a squad watching him all night and stay with him twenty-four hours a day.

"Looks like the chief sent McGann home. Crystal's tape must have been too much," Turner said, putting his phone in his pocket.

"You think McGann could've done something like this?" Katy asked, thinking out loud.

"Don't know, but I don't think he's stupid enough to dump her at his front door. He didn't know she was in the trunk, but that doesn't mean he didn't kill her here and somebody else made the surprise delivery," Montgomery said.

"But who?" Katy asked.

"How the hell should I know? I'm making all this up. Let's wait and see whose prints we get and go from there."

"We got prints?" Turner asked.

"We got a few, maybe Alexandra's. We'll see." Montgomery stood and picked up his chair. "Let's get out of here," he said to Turner, who didn't move. "You got that newbie homicide detective look, partner. Most people don't want to believe anyone could do that to another human being. It's overwhelming. It's fatiguing." He put his hand out to Turner, who hesitated, then grasped it and allowed the skinny detective to help him out of the chair.

Montgomery offered to take Turner home and pick him up in the morning. Turner didn't argue. He was weary, and Montgomery's death scenario kept playing in his head.

"If it's not McGann, who are the best suspects?" Turner asked as they drove away from the house. He hoped talking would keep him from thinking about the crime scene.

"The rest of the world," Montgomery said.

"It isn't random, right?" Turner would force him to share his thoughts. "List of possibilities?" he asked, and Montgomery nodded. "Crystal?" Turner asked. "She's not my first choice."

"Low possibility . . . not strong enough, and Alexandra's her sister," Montgomery said.

"Phil White?" Turner asked. "He's a dark horse."

"High possibility . . . strong, demented . . . would've done it for somebody else . . . like Crystal."

"McGann?"

"Possible . . . wouldn't dump that close to home . . . alibi is soft."

"Dean?"

"Low possibility . . . she was his money tree, and he's dead, too."

"Maria Perez?"

"High possibility . . . jilted, strong, and knew McGann wouldn't be there."

"Patty McGann?" Turner asked. Montgomery glanced at him before answering.

"Not possible . . . she was ready to leave McGann anyway . . . too classy."

"One of her lesbian girlfriends?"

"High possibility . . . volatile, unstable lifestyle, easily pissed off, and Alex loved to piss off everybody."

Turner laughed. "So much for political correctness."

192

"I know what I know. Who else?"

"That's everyone I'd put into the suspect category. You got more?"

"We've still got to identify the mystery woman Alex fought with at the bungalow."

"Lesbian girlfriend category," Turner said.

"Two guys at Judy Taylor's café?" Montgomery asked as he parked in front of Turner's apartment.

"Convenient red herring for McGann to throw out, but in the neighborhood so we can't completely ignore them."

"Maybe," Montgomery said. "See you in the morning."

"Come in for a beer, no shoptalk. Quick drink and you're on your way."

"I'm exhausted, but I really want a beer. I got a little homicide fatigue myself."

Turner knocked before going inside. He didn't want to surprise Paula, who might be waiting naked on the couch with another one of her welcome-home surprises. She answered the door in her sweats.

"Forget your key?" she asked, kissing him and then seeing Montgomery. She laughed. "I get it."

They sat in the living room, and Paula brought out some toasted Italian bread with basil, tomato, and cheese. She opened a bottle of Chianti and insisted they'd like it better than the beer. Nobody argued.

"Do you know if Rose had any luck?" Turner asked Paula as he took the bottle of wine and poured three glasses.

"I didn't stay long, but she found stuff. They'd deleted everything, but Rose had some "techie" geek guy give her access to the backup servers. Turns out nothing is ever really deleted . . . from anywhere."

"I bet Katy's already back at the office doing background on those names," Montgomery said between sips of wine. "She never sleeps. The woman's a zombie."

After a few minutes, both men took off their jackets, and it wasn't long before they'd eaten nearly a whole loaf of bread. Montgomery didn't finish his wine. He said he wanted to drink more, but getting the city car home without an accident was a priority. Detectives with DUIs didn't stay in Robbery Homicide.

193

There was still plenty of drinking and driving. Most of the older detectives had a local garage that would fix minor auto damage for a small fee or a good bottle of whiskey. Guardrails and stop signs suffered a high mortality rate around their favorite drinking holes.

"I figure it's easier and cheaper not to drink too much," Montgomery said.

"Besides, he drinks like a girl. One glass of beer and he's ready for a nap," Turner said.

"How does Stevenson do it?" Montgomery asked, shaking his head. "How does he function with the amount of alcohol he consumes?"

"He's a good man, but his liver is going to blow up one of these days," Turner said.

"Isn't he the one who got drunk and drove to Las Vegas in his police car during the last riots?" Paula asked.

Montgomery looked surprised. "How did you know about that?"

"Brenda Todd. Brenda knows everything. She has spies everywhere . . . except the chief's office now."

"What happened to Sarah?" Paula had forgotten to tell Turner about the switch. She explained Sally Wolinski's latest move. Turner shook his head. "Wolinski knows what she wants. She's a female McGann with balls."

"She's smarter than McGann. Patty said she called his house and stalked the guy until he got tainted with this scandal. Then she backs away from him like he's got the plague," Montgomery said. He snatched the last piece of bread before Turner could reach it.

Turner poured himself another glass of wine. "Why did Stevenson go to Las Vegas?" he asked, holding the glass under Montgomery's nose.

"He was going home. When he woke up, he was parked in the sand on the center divider of the I-15. He saw the casinos. He was hungry, so he drove down the strip, got breakfast, and was back in the office before lunch. He called it an extradition for the early-bird special. The guy has nine lives."

"The one or two lives he has left have high blood pressure and heart disease," Turner said. He liked Stevenson but knew he was self-destructing. As long as the man could get up every morning and do his job, he'd survive, with or without his liver. The detectives in RHD protected Stevenson, looked the other way at his indiscretions.

Montgomery put on his jacket. He thanked Paula for the food and drink and her pleasant company. He had to get home and explain to his wife why he'd missed dinner again. He swore that his daughter had started calling the gardener daddy.

"Her mother and I are both black, and the gardener is Japanese. You can understand why I'm beginning to worry."

As Montgomery drove away, Turner and Paula sat on the retaining wall outside their apartment. They stayed there for several minutes in silence.

Finally Turner had to ask, "How bad was it?"

"What?"

"The list."

"Three from the bottom . . . you'll make lieutenant, but it's going to be a while."

"That sucks. I figured it was ugly when you didn't say anything in front of Monty."

"Sorry," she whispered, leaning over to kiss him on the cheek.

"I sort of expected it." He tried to laugh, but it sounded like a grunt. "How long before I make it?"

"Beginning of the year, when the retirements hit."

"That's a long time to be good and not kill anybody."

She put her arm around him. "You can do it. Actually, the timing might be perfect."

"How do you figure that?" He was always impressed by how well she understood the workings of the department. There was some strange logic to all the political manipulation of the insiders. He'd never get it, but Paula thrived on the intrigue.

"This case will take at least until next year to wrap up, so they can't use it against you, no matter how it turns out. Did they tell you McGann wants to be interviewed again?"

"It figured after what Crystal told us. I'm surprised Martin's going to let him do that."

"He wants the lying charge to go away, so he doesn't have to deal with it."

"So the prick walks away without a scratch."

"You think he killed her?" Paula asked.

"Don't know. Everything points to him, but it doesn't feel right. I don't think he did it." He surprised himself when he said it out loud, but he'd pretty much eliminated McGann.

"The computer names might give you some new leads."

He slid off the wall and helped her to the sidewalk. "Come on, Lieutenant," he said, holding her hand. "Let's go to bed and make wild passionate love. If I can't be one, at least I can play with one."

SEVENTEEN

The next morning, Turner arrived at Robbery Homicide about the same time as Paula's phone call telling him she'd make captain in the next two weeks. Bell had told her the good news when she got to work. Most of her day had been spent accepting congratulations from the hordes of jealous adjutants on the sixth floor.

She told Turner she was feeling guilty after his bad news the day before about the lieutenant's list. He assured her he was happy for her but was puzzled. He never saw Paula as competition and wondered if that was how she viewed him. He genuinely cared for her and wanted to see good things happen in her life.

"Rose and Bell have mixed feelings. They don't want to train a new adjutant."

"Where are they sending you?" he asked, trying to sound as enthused as she did.

"South end, most likely 77th, and you won't believe this," she said, but didn't wait for him to ask what. "Wolinski won't get promoted. She has to wait, and she's pissed. She has more time as a lieutenant than me, and she's been pushing to make it first. Nobody can believe the chief skipped her for me." She was quiet for a second. "Are you sure you're okay with this?" she asked.

"We'll celebrate tonight. Monty's waiting, so I've got to go," he said, hanging up. Any other time, he was certain she'd object to his hasty departure, but she had plenty of attention right then and was probably happy to get off the phone. He felt a twinge of guilt. Maybe he was a little jealous. He was a good cop, better than she was, but he loved her and wanted her to be happy. She could do the paperwork and pass the promotion tests, but she'd never really been tested in the field. He'd put his ass on the line for years, had bruises and broken bones, and had been shot at and seen his best friend bleed to death in the gutter. He'd earned a promotion. It was easy to have a clean package if you never got your hands dirty. He told himself it didn't matter, but it did.

"You sick?" Rose asked. She'd been standing there staring at him. "You look like shit."

"Thanks, I'm just tired," Turner said.

She handed him a paper with five names. "Captain Stevenson said to give these to you or Montgomery. They tried to delete their e-mails to Officer Alexandra Williams. If there's more, I'll find them."

As Turner was reading the list, Montgomery came in, and Rose gave him another copy. Connelly had created a mini IA task force for them, so Turner would assign each team one or two of the officers to interview. He knew one of these officers might be their killer, but he doubted it. Whoever killed Alexandra hated her. It wasn't a business deal gone badly. It was personal. One team would interview McGann. It was a formality, and Turner didn't want to waste his time doing it.

Katy called Montgomery from Latent Prints and told him not to leave because she was on her way back to RHD with a present.

"We got a good match on a partial print from the Dean homicide," she said, grinning at them when she got there an hour later. "Did you know they print you when you're committed to a mental institution?"

"Phil's print was in Dean's apartment?" Montgomery asked.

"Some sharp technician dusted under the window ledge and found the partial along with Dean's prints. It looks like Dean hooked his fingers under the ledge to keep from being propelled out the window. Phil left his print trying to pry Dean loose," Katy explained.

"We'll meet you at the institution, but call Terry Chernack and give him the option to meet us there, too," Montgomery said.

Turner doubted that Chernack would allow Phil White to talk to them now that they had evidence that linked him to a murder scene. He and Montgomery arrived at the Levin Institute in Van Nuys a few minutes before the attorney. They met in the parking lot and walked silently into the lobby. Katy was already inside filling out the visitor paperwork.

The Levin Institute was one of the oldest structures in the state. It had been built at the turn of the twentieth century and used as a private women's university until the '50s. A rich widow had left an endowment in her will and intended that it remain the best women's college in the nation. What she couldn't have foreseen was the sexual revolution and the fact that few women wanted to spend their four years of higher learning surrounded by other women. Her descendants gradually allowed the property to be used for the wealthy mentally ill—a serene, albeit costly, alternative to the state's indifference.

It was well funded and, unlike the few state-run facilities, spacious, clean, and fully staffed with the best doctors and nurses. In the lobby, Turner wandered around looking at the expensive furniture. Original oil paintings decorated every wall. He examined the commendations and awards behind the front desk. A pamphlet on the counter showed that the facility had several residence halls and that each room resembled those in a four-star hotel. There was a restaurant with real food, a fully equipped gym, an Olympic-sized swimming pool, and an enormous library, a university holdover.

They didn't want to talk in the lobby, so the receptionist suggested they use one of the family rooms on the second floor. Chernack led them to a large parlor with leather chairs and a fireplace. He told them there were drinks behind a carved mahogany bar if they wanted them. A fifty-inch plasma television was mounted over the bar.

Montgomery opened the drapes covering a huge picture window that looked out on a landscaped estate complete with a mermaid water fountain. He sighed and sank into one of the leather chairs.

"Almost adds a new dimension to being committed," he said.

"Not if you can't leave," Chernack said.

"I don't know. I think you could leave me here a long time before I felt the need to travel," Katy said, glancing around the room.

"Why are we here?" Chernack asked Montgomery.

Montgomery told the attorney what they'd found.

"I'll let him talk to you," Chernack said quickly, as if he had expected this moment to come.

Turner waited for the caveat. There had to be one. "But," he said, and it came.

"He stays here, not in jail, supervised and locked in—but here regardless of what he says or admits. He's incompetent and institutionalized. Unless a court sends him somewhere else, he stays here. Agreed?"

"Not a problem for us," Montgomery said. "The DA's office might not feel compelled to honor our promises."

"Let me worry about the district attorney. He's elected. The only real danger for Phil is sitting in this room. He's a child in a man's body. I won't let him go to jail."

"We don't need to book your client," Turner said, interrupting Chernack. "We need to solve two homicides. If he confesses, it doesn't matter if he's incarcerated at the Beverly Hills Hilton." Just being Phil White is probably punishment enough, Turner thought.

"Phil can be difficult," Chernack said to no one in particular. "But he couldn't kill anyone. He isn't capable of that kind of violence."

"Let's go talk to him," Turner said, standing in the doorway.

"He's different since the last time you saw him," Chernack warned. "He's deteriorated. He doesn't talk and is moody and angry most of the time. He wants to be with that woman and blames everyone, especially me."

Chernack directed them along a pathway through manicured lawns and gardens, twenty-five acres backed up against the hills—a little piece of paranoid schizophrenic heaven.

Phil's security building was set away from the other residences. A fourteen-foot wire fence surrounded the structure, and an armed guard stood at the gate. He recognized Chernack and opened the gate. He ran a metal detector over Chernack's clothing, and the three officers immediately displayed their badges. He asked them to place their weapons in small lockers near the front door. After they did, they were buzzed through the glass doors. Turner saw security cameras mounted in every corner turn as they walked down the hallway. This building had the same stylish, expensive décor as the main building, but even dressed up, a jail is still a jail.

They stepped into an elevator operated by a uniformed guard who used a key to access different floors. Phil's room was on the third floor. The hallway was well lighted, and its walls were also covered with oil paintings. The door to every room had a small window at eye level.

Chernack told them to wait while he went to the reception desk. He whispered with a young-looking man in a white smock who accompanied them to White's room. Chernack introduced him as Dr. French. Dr. French explained that Phil had behaved very well in the last few days, and they were considering moving him to a lower-security residence. He looked at Chernack and said he understood that Phil White would remain in this security building indefinitely, but he wanted them to know Phil was not a threat. However, he did say he was afraid that meeting with the officers would initiate a setback for his patient.

They stopped at the last door at the end of the corridor. The doctor looked through the small window before opening the door and allowing them to enter.

Phil was sitting in what looked like a wooden lawn chair. He turned and didn't seem to know or care who'd entered his room. He was unshaven and had lost some weight. His thinning blond hair was long and matted. He wore a pink hospital gown and had a bandage on his arm over the vein.

Turner thought he didn't look like a sane man and for the first time looked damaged. He couldn't stop staring at Phil, whose glassy eyes gazed back. There was no sign of life or thought behind those dead eyes. The doctor tried to disappear into a corner of the room. He obviously wanted no part of this encounter.

"Philip, look at me," Chernack demanded, standing in front of the young man's chair. Phil did look up slowly and touched Chernack's hand, as if to be certain the image was real. "We need to talk to you."

"All right," Phil said in a clear, steady voice that surprised Turner. He looked around the room at each of the police officers. "What do you want?"

Montgomery dragged another lawn chair closer to Phil. "Do you know where you are?" he asked.

"No."

"Do you know what day it is?"

"No," he answered, twisting in his chair toward the doctor.

"Do you remember Crystal?" Turner decided to try a different approach.

"Yes," he said and stopped squirming. Turner had his full attention. "Where is Cathy?" he asked.

"Where are you?" Turner asked.

"Levin . . . I can't leave. It's Wednesday."

201

"Better," Montgomery said. He explained Phil's rights to him. He asked the same questions, and this time Phil answered quickly and coherently.

Montgomery asked Phil if he knew Dean.

"Dean was a pimp. Where's Cathy?"

"Cathy's in jail. She's safe," Turner said.

"Why did you go to Dean's room the morning he was killed?" Montgomery asked.

Phil looked at Terry Chernack, but the attorney didn't say anything. He turned to the doctor, who was examining the wall.

"He was hurting Cathy. He gave her drugs, made her have sex for money." Phil nervously wrapped the corner of his hospital gown around the arm of the chair. "I could take care of her."

"What happened to Dean that morning?" Montgomery asked.

"Nothing," he said louder.

"Was Cathy there?"

"No. She said not to go. We had his money. We could run away as soon as Terry stopped bringing my dad's money." He avoided looking at Chernack.

"Did you push Dean out the window?" Turner asked, feeling as if he were fanning a burning stick of dynamite. White continued the repetitive motion of twisting the hem of his hospital gown around the arm of the chair. His gown was damp under the arms, and a saucer-sized spot of sweat appeared on his chest.

"He was alone," Phil whispered. "He stuck that needle in his arm. It made him mean. He slapped me, said bad things to me, said I was like one of his girls, said maybe he should treat me like one. I pushed him, told him to leave Cathy alone." The room was chilly, but perspiration trickled down the sides of Phil's face. Strands of hair were stuck to his forehead.

"What did you do?" Turner demanded.

"He said Cathy was his. I was her . . ." He hesitated. "I was her idiot playmate." Phil let go of his gown and sat up. "I dragged him to the window. He laughed at me until he saw I wanted to push him out." He giggled nervously. "He screamed like a little girl, begged me not to hurt him."

"Did you push him out the window?" Turner asked.

Phil took the hem of his gown and wiped the sweat off his face and neck. "Uh-huh. I wanted to scare him good." He looked at Chernack again. "I looked down and saw him in the alley. He wasn't moving, just staring at me. I ran back to the apartment."

"Did Cathy know? Did she tell you to kill him so the two of you could keep his money?"

"No," he whined. "I was afraid to tell her. She might get mad at me . . . leave me. I didn't mean to kill him." For the first time, Chernack looked up with just a hint of interest.

"Did you hurt Alexandra?" Turner had to ask.

"No," he shouted. "Alex was my friend."

Turner believed him. It took a special kind of hate to kill that way, not as impersonal as tossing someone out a window.

"Would you recognize that woman you told us hit Alex? Do you remember telling us that?" Montgomery asked.

"She was tall and had brown hair and a loud voice. That's all I know." He reached over and clutched Montgomery's arm. "Is Cathy okay?"

Montgomery peeled White's hand off his arm. "She's in a place where nobody can hurt her and she can get healthy again."

Phil glanced around the room. He looked dazed or maybe drugged. He laughed at the doctor in the corner, and then he was crying. He wiped his eyes with his sleeve and stripped the bandages off his arm. He touched the needle punctures along the vein and said, "I'm getting better, too." He closed his eyes, and his body slumped as if he were falling asleep, retreating into his private world. Chernack herded everyone out of the room.

There was no need to discuss it any further. They'd heard the confession. Montgomery would get a court order to keep Phil White in custody at Levin Institute. Chernack said he'd make certain a judge was available to sign it.

Hollywood detectives could clear at least one of the homicides with the physical evidence and Phil's confession. They'd come back and get more details and a formal confession when Phil was lucid again.

On the drive back to Parker Center, Turner and Montgomery debated whether or not Phil, despite his mental illness, was capable of killing Alexandra. He'd admitted burying the knife, but was he the one who'd left it for Cathy to find? They finally agreed it was too complicated. The logistics of cleaning up, putting her in the trunk, and driving her to McGann's house would've been too difficult for him.

The one thing that kept nagging at Turner was why the body had been left at McGann's house. It was a message from the killer to McGann. Who hated him enough to want to ruin him? Who knew that Alexandra's body being there would open a Pandora's Box for him?

Turner did know it would've been easier and a lot less stressful to his career and life if they could've ended this investigation with one deranged killer. But it didn't fit. Whoever killed Alexandra Williams was still out there, and they were no closer to finding the killer.

EIGHTEEN

Being gracious and humble wasn't easy for Paula. She was excited about her promotion and knew she was the best choice. She tried not to exhibit too much confidence and exuberance, or it might be perceived as arrogance; but behaving like a captain was exhausting. Toward the end of the day, she simply resorted to thanking well-wishers and changing the subject. Not having Rose in the office was unfortunate. Bell's secretary had a way of putting things in perspective. Every compliment would've been countered with a dose of Rose's reality.

Later in the day, Rose did stop by for a few minutes. She had to take her son to a karate lesson, and she scrambled to clean off her desk. She told Paula that she'd finished her assignment at RHD. In less than forty-eight hours, she'd uncovered fourteen officers who'd contacted Alexandra. Most had tried to delete their messages, but failed. Alexandra had made no effort to hide her contacts, so she'd left an easy trail. The officers were all young men with three to four years on the job. Some had already come forward and told their commanding officers about their involvement with Alexandra.

"It's a shame," Rose said, shaking her head. "That little girl might've ruined some promising careers."

Paula snickered at the idea. "Come on. Nobody forced them to pay for sex."

"They're young and horny, and she took advantage."

"They're cops. They should know better."

Rose leaned against the wall and stared at her. "You got a lot to learn, honey. They're flesh-and-blood men who happen to wear uniforms. They got the same parts and vices other men got. Temptation can be a bitch."

"If they give in to it, they can be bank tellers, because they can't be cops anymore."

"Whew, you is one unforgiving lady," Rose said, laughing. She stuffed her sweater into her handbag. "You'll learn. It's like raising children. Gotta let 'em make mistakes, teach them. Don't preach, don't pretend they're perfect, because if you force them to hide every mistake, one day you wake up and you got a full-grown cheating, lying monster on your hands. Then everybody's gonna say that Captain Toscano, she's one tough mama, but none of her kids seem to like or respect her." Rose pulled her bag over her shoulder and leaned over the desk to gently touch Paula's cheek. "I'm proud of you, honey. You've got a good head and a good heart. You'll do fine."

When Rose was gone, Paula stayed at her desk. Maybe I will, she thought, but her confidence was slipping. She didn't agree with Rose but didn't really know what she believed any more. She'd seen so many likable, intelligent people take that captain's job and not make anybody happy, including themselves. Power is an elusive beast. Just when you think you know how to wield it, the brute turns on you. Paula's biggest fear was being perceived like Connelly, a nice-enough woman who looked lost at anything more complicated than a preplanned staff meeting. The other side of the coin was McGann. He was always so certain he was right, but his decision-making process was a series of miscues and ulterior motives that everyone saw through.

She wondered if there was a leader in this organization whom she could look to as a role model. It was so simple for Mike to take charge, but what had it gotten him besides suspensions and the bottom of the promotion list? He did the right thing and supported the department. He honored the traditions, but what good did it do him? Paula knew that Sam Martin expected her loyalty and that she would support him, but could she be honorable and support the chief? Her head was aching. In another couple of weeks, she'd have herself talked out of this promotion or be a raving lunatic.

Bell wouldn't be back that night, and Paula was cleaning off her desk to go home when Brenda called. She reminded Paula to stop by the Police Commission meeting room before she left. Paula tried to make an excuse because of her growing headache, but Brenda insisted that she couldn't miss a Mafia meeting.

Paula knew Mike wouldn't be home for a while. He'd called to tell her about Phil White's confession and said he'd be working late. She wasn't looking forward to being alone at the apartment after the excitement all day. She was still on a bit of a high, and it would be nice to share a few minutes with her friends.

She'd been sitting in the same spot nearly all day. Her back and legs were stiff when she stood, and her side was sore where the ammo pouches on her Sam Browne poked into her side. This is what she had in her future: sitting at a desk ten to twelve hours a day babysitting cops. What a life! She sighed and decided to stop doing whatever it was she was doing to herself. There would be plenty of people to mentally torture her once she actually had the job.

Elaine Miller stopped Paula outside the door to the commission room. The IG hugged the taller woman and congratulated her. Paula was surprised. Elaine was usually the least demonstrative woman she knew.

"I'm one of them now, Elaine," Paula joked. "The Paula you knew will soon be replaced by a command pod."

Elaine pushed open the door for her. "Hardly. There are still signs of intelligent life on your planet."

Inside, they were greeted by Brenda, who had arranged cookies and a small cake on the board table. "Congratulations, Captain Paula" was written on the top with blue frosting. A small Styrofoam ice chest had sodas that Paula guessed came from the commissioners' private refrigerator. Nancy Connelly came in late with paper plates and plastic forks.

"How did you put this together so fast?" Paula asked as she opened a can of Pepsi. Nancy Connelly hugged her and gave her a small wrapped package.

"Now we have ten female captains," Connelly said. The statistic was more important to Connelly than it was to Paula, who never really thought of herself as a female anything. Connelly was still consumed by the inequities of the past. Paula saw diversity as inevitable, while Connelly expected it as retribution. Paula unwrapped the package and found a set of captain's bars.

"Those belonged to Harry Sims. He heard you were being promoted and asked me to deliver them with his good wishes," Connelly said.

Everyone crowded around to see what Paula held. They were the same silver bars that every captain on the department wore, but these were Harry's. He'd retired the year before with exactly twenty years. Everyone respected him and hoped that one day he'd be chief of police. He'd retired early because he couldn't work for Sam Martin.

Paula held the small pieces of shiny metal in her hand. Harry Sims was her mentor but not a close friend. She understood his message, and her head was starting to ache again.

"Where's Harry when you really need him?" Elaine asked, smiling at her.

"Harry did what was right for him." Paula didn't want to get into the Harry Sims saga again. It always led to an argument. Her personal philosophy was, if it's not right, fix it. You don't walk away. Elaine always argued that the chief set policy, so how long do you do what he wants if you think he's morally and ethically corrupt? You can't fire your boss, and Harry would never sabotage him. His choices were limited, Elaine would insist.

Paula had participated in the argument a hundred times. Elaine wanted to make Harry a martyr and declare Sam Martin evil. It would support Elaine's decision to resign. Paula wasn't certain that Martin was the devil and that every choice was a moral dilemma. She put the captain's bars in her pocket, determined not to have that discussion again right then.

In less than an hour, most of LAPD's female lieutenants and captains had found their way to the hearing room. The department's self-proclaimed Mafia had convened to celebrate the promotion of one of their own. Even Diaz stopped by to offer her good wishes and unsolicited advice. The only lieutenant conspicuously absent was Sally Wolinski. Brenda joked that Wolinski never came unless the party was for her.

Paula had to admit she enjoyed the gathering. By 10 P.M. everyone except Brenda, Elaine, Connelly, and Paula had gone. The four women cleaned the room and sat around the table.

Brenda offered a toast. "Here's to the next woman chief of police."

"You have to have one before you can have a next one," Paula laughed.

"Be a good captain, and maybe the first one will be you," Brenda said, then blushed and avoided looking at Connelly, who always told them she was entitled to become the first female chief. Brenda routinely dismissed Connelly as a lightweight, and it never occurred to her that she could or would be promoted again.

"Better figure out this job before you start applying for the next one," Elaine said.

"Why should I be different from everyone else? Myron Nichols bought his captain's bars the same day he got his lieutenant's," Paula said.

"There's a great example for you to follow," Brenda said. "They put a live chicken in his locker at the harbor and glued his boots to the floor. Don't be holding that man up as a model."

"The captain at the harbor said anyone who accidentally discharged a weapon that hit Myron would automatically be considered suspect," Elaine said. Brenda stared at her, trying to decide if what she said was true.

"She's joking, Brenda," Paula said.

"No, I'm not," Elaine said, and when Paula's eyes widened, she laughed and added, "Gotcha."

"Was Sally disappointed that she didn't make captain?" Brenda asked Connelly.

"No, why should she be? She'll make it."

"You don't think Martin is hesitating because of her relationship with McGann, do you?" Brenda tried to sound concerned.

"Hardly. She stopped seeing him long before this Williams thing."

Paula looked up at Connelly. Why would she say that? Connelly must've seen Patty McGann's statement. Turner told Paula that Wolinski was calling the McGann house up to the time of the killing. Paula kept quiet because she wasn't sure how much she was supposed to know.

"Is McGann still a suspect?" Elaine asked.

"I'm not involved in that investigation," Connelly said.

"But you still have your people working with RHD, don't you?" Elaine persisted.

Connelly was visibly upset. "The chief gave Mike Turner to RHD. He doesn't report to me." Paula wanted to change the subject.

"Is he still working on the personnel investigation?" Elaine asked.

"You know he is," Connelly said sharply. "There won't be much left to do."

"Really," Elaine said with a touch of hostility. "I understood we have two witnesses who've corroborated some serious misconduct." Connelly stood. She was angry, but before she could say anything, Elaine added, "My source isn't anyone in this room."

Paula could feel dampness under her arms. Her wool uniform felt like a down comforter in the middle of summer.

"Then who?" Connelly demanded.

"I have information I'm entitled to have. My source is immaterial. It should've been you," Elaine said. Connelly was quiet, so Elaine continued. "The commission will want to know why the chief or Internal Affairs didn't provide the IG with that information."

"You know this is tied to a criminal case. We can't give you everything. Frankly, the information you have is not within your purview." Connelly had calmed down and sounded condescending.

Paula and Brenda sat watching the two women like they were opponents at a tennis match.

"I disagree," Elaine said. "The commission will disagree, and, frankly, the city council will disagree. Because of the magnitude of police-officer misconduct connected to this crime, I insist that I'm entitled to everything."

Connelly blushed. "We'll see about that, won't we?" She calmly tossed her empty cup in the trash. "Goodnight, everyone," she said as she left the room.

The room was quiet for several seconds, and then Elaine said, "Don't ask."

"You've got a snitch," Brenda said. "Paula, you told me you didn't know anything."

"I told you it wasn't anyone in this room," Elaine said. "I'm finally earning my paycheck. I know everything Martin knows," she added smugly.

Paula had an uneasy feeling about who was giving Elaine Miller a blow-by-blow description of the investigation. She knew Turner had given Elaine information in the past, and only a few people knew about the additional officers implicated in the case. Martin would be furious. This would be a major betrayal, in the chief's eyes.

If she'd suspected Turner, then Martin would, too. Why would Mike jeopardize his career to help the inspector general?

"I need a real drink," Paula said. "Let's go to Corky's."

"Sylvia's place?" Elaine asked and then added, "Good choice."

"Maybe we'll get some free drinks," Brenda said, turning out the lights and holding open the door.

By the time Paula arrived at Corky's, Brenda was sitting in one of the booths and had finished half a bottle of ZD Chardonnay. She slid in beside Brenda and grabbed a handful of fried calamari.

"Where's Elaine?" she asked with a mouthful of tentacles.

"In the back office with Sylvia," Brenda said, pouring her a glass of wine.

"Sylvia was here?"

"She owns the place. She's always here when she's not at Parker Center torturing me." Brenda said.

They drank and ate, and Paula nearly forgot about the problems that would greet her when the sun came up. It wouldn't do any good to ask Mike if he was the source. He wouldn't tell her. He was stubborn, and if he thought he was right, he wouldn't argue about it and wouldn't defend himself. As much as Paula hated to admit the sad truth, if McGann was going to get what was coming to him, leaking information to the IG was probably the only way it would happen, but Elaine should've found another way. Turner shouldn't have to sacrifice his career to get McGann.

When Elaine and Sylvia emerged from the back office around midnight, they were somber. Elaine refused a drink and said goodnight without any further conversation. Sylvia sat in the booth with the three women and ordered another bottle of wine.

"I am an old lady," she said. "Why do I do this job?" No one said anything. "I love my restaurant," she continued. "And your Police Commission is nothing but a headache. So why do I do it?" Again, no one responded. She nodded as if coming to some agreement with herself. "Someday I will stay home and play with my grandchildren, but not tonight. Tonight I woke up Sam Martin and told him how to run his department. He does what I say because he needs my money and influence."

Paula exchanged a quick look with Brenda. Being in Sylvia's inner circle wasn't something she wanted. She figured the old woman had had too much to drink and hoped she wouldn't remember what she'd said or whom she said it to in the morning.

"What happened with Elaine?" Brenda asked.

"Miss Miller wants to introduce a memorandum that has punitive measures if the department does not cooperate with the inspector general. It will emasculate him and every chief after him because he is too stubborn to do what he should do."

"Can you get the commission to stop it?" Paula asked.

"Maybe, if he does what he should do. I told him, 'Throw some bones to the wolf so it doesn't come back and eat your children.'" She filled their glasses again. Paula tried to refuse, but Sylvia pushed her hand away. "Drink. You should celebrate."

Paula didn't feel like celebrating. All she could think about was Elaine's source. She knew Martin would be thinking about it, too.

"Did the chief say anything about who talked to Elaine?" Brenda asked, glancing at Paula.

"He says he'll give Wolinski the task of uncovering the mole. He says she is intelligent and compulsive and won't give up until she finds the traitor." Sylvia laughed. "He says to me, 'Sylvia, I want to find whoever talked to that woman, but I need proof. This is a death penalty case. I don't want to make a mistake when I lop off somebody's head.'"

Paula felt her stomach turn. A good day had suddenly turned very bad.

NINETEEN

Mike Turner's office was an island in a sea of Internal Affairs investigators. He sat at his desk and examined the walls covered with flow charts and evidence links. Homicide books and stacks of reports covered every surface.

He'd moved two more tables and several chairs into his office and managed to confiscate another computer . . . one computer for McGann's personnel investigation and the other for the Williams homicide.

Most of the IA sergeants who wandered into the space were confused by the methodical nature of Turner's work. Real, intuitive police work frightened them. They came to IA as a necessary step toward promotion, and as a by-product it fulfilled another goal—keeping them off the dangerous streets. They openly resented and avoided supervisors like Turner, closet cops who had somehow intruded on their administrative world.

The surveillance team viewed Turner's office as a haven. The internal surveillance detail was assigned to IA, but they never considered themselves part of the division. The office had become operations central for the Williams homicide, too. Even Captain Stevenson spent part of his day sitting in Turner's office with his feet on the desk, waiting for his updates.

Since Myron had been promoted and left, Turner was pretty much ignored, so he started wearing Levi's and t-shirts. He found that it was easier than changing clothes every time he wanted to jump in the car and work with one of the surveillance guys. The detail was following McGann every day, twenty-four hours a day. He wasn't a good suspect, but at the moment he was their only one.

It had taken Turner nearly all day to review the statements of the fourteen officers who had exchanged e-mails with Alexandra. Katy had participated in all of the interviews and as usual did a quick and thorough job. As he read each statement, it became clear to Turner that none of these young men had been close to the homicide victim. She introduced them to Dean, and then the pimp did all the work. Bell gave Connelly the job of adjudicating the complaints, and she had a reputation for heavy-handed discipline. He'd talk to Bell and make certain the punishment was appropriate . . . another nail in his promotion coffin.

Every one of the officers had a solid alibi for the night of Alexandra's murder. The only shaky alibi belonged to McGann. He could have gone out while his wife slept. His sex habits were a target-rich environment for blackmail and a good motive for murder. He was looking better all the time, mostly because there wasn't anybody else. The one thing that didn't fit was the car left in front of his house.

Turner threw the interviews on his desk and looked at his watch. The surveillance supervisor should already have been there with his update. Maybe he should call Paula. She'd been acting very weird the night before. He expected her to be happy, but she'd gotten back from drinking with the girls and gone to sleep without talking to him. He put the phone down. It would be better to wait and talk to her at home that night. He'd try to get home early and make dinner like he had before this case began. He felt a little guilty, but for the first time in years he was enjoying the job again. Police work was fun, but he didn't want his relationship with Paula to be a casualty of the job. It was easy for this work to consume you. He had done it before, but he was determined not to lose her.

Somebody was banging on his door. He yelled for whoever it was to come in, but the kicking continued. He got up and opened the door. Montgomery was standing there holding a tray of coffee cups. He had a bag of donuts in his mouth. Turner cleared a space on one of the tables and took the tray. Montgomery spit the bag out of his mouth.

"Thanks, partner," he said. "The surveillance guys are on their way up. They look beat."

"Maybe they saw something useful last night," Turner said. He needed a break.

"Don't know. They didn't say. Can you work tonight? They want to show us something." Montgomery was devouring a donut as he spoke. Turner was staring at him, and the skinny detective laughed. "Nervous energy makes me hungry."

The surveillance supervisor and his female assistant came in looking tired and hungry. Their clothes looked as if they had slept in them. Their eyes were bloodshot and glassy. They concentrated on drinking their coffee.

"This guy never sleeps," the supervisor finally said. "He travels all night."

"Where's he go?" Montgomery asked.

"The guy's a fucking tour guide for every adult bookstore and porno movie house in the city and most neighboring cities."

"Last night we followed him the entire length of Figueroa Boulevard from Harbor City to the Valley, the longest street in the country," the female said. She took one of the donuts and another cup of coffee. "It's the first time since I've been in the squad that I ran out of gas and never left the city . . . practically never left Figueroa," she added.

"He stopped at every adult video store and bookstore and in between stops checked out a variety of street whores," the supervisor said.

"Did he talk to anybody?" Turner asked.

"Hell, no, and I think the guy's some kinda psych case."

Turner was disappointed. It was damaging but not fatal. If McGann were a patrol officer, the chief would fire him as a liability, but there were different rules for the guys who wore those brass stars. They needed to catch him doing something illegal.

"Write it up," Turner said, noting that the two surveillance officers were looking at each other a little sheepishly. "What's wrong?"

"McGann has a visitor before he starts his little trip every night. Wolinski spends a couple of hours there." The supervisor said it as if the information were something he'd rather not talk about.

The information didn't surprise Turner. He expected McGann to have someone in his bed. He thought Wolinski had better survival instincts but knew that sexual attraction was rarely an intellectual process. "How does that work if he's out wandering the streets every night?"

"She doesn't spend the night, but they're definitely sleeping together. As soon as Wolinski's out the door, he's in his car, and we're off to the races."

"I'm not asking this for any prurient interest," Montgomery said, and Turner could almost see his black skin blushing. "What kind of sex is it? Is it the Alexandra S&M thing?"

Turner was trying to visualize Wolinski in black leather.

"Not even close," the female answered. "Makes Ozzie and Harriet look exciting. He's a missionary-position lover with Wolinski, and that's it."

"You guys saw all that? You are good." He hesitated a second. "None of this is in your logs, right?"

They grinned, looked at him as if he were a child, and didn't answer. "They argue a lot. She can get nasty and mean when he pisses her off, but the real question is how much our pretty lieutenant is telling McGann. Everything we get is going to the chief's office, so he might know he's being watched."

"I don't think that's a problem. If she knew you were watching McGann, she wouldn't get within a mile of him," Montgomery said. "I'll ask Bell, but my guess is he's hand-delivering your logs to the chief."

"Why did you want us with you tonight?" Turner asked. He was thinking about his earlier plan to go home early.

"Thought you guys might want to see this for yourselves. I'm not a shrink, but my guess is he's looking for an Alexandra Williams replacement. You're the expert, Monty. Don't these guys who kill for sex usually do it more than once?"

"If you believe that FBI profiling crap, they do. I'm still not sure this killing is about sex . . . maybe greed, maybe hate. There was a lot of anger at that killing scene."

"What do we do if we see him pick up some sweet young thing? If we let him go, maybe he kills her in some hotel room. If we take him down, picking up a whore is a low-grade misdemeanor. Case's over. Martin gives him absolution. Two trips to the department shrink and he's back at work."

"If he tries to kill her, you take him down, but he'd better have a knife at her throat, or we're all fucked," Turner said. He was serious because he knew how quickly the chief would back away from their investigation unless they uncovered something more serious than prostitution.

"This is a waste of time," the supervisor moaned. He was tired and not in the mood for subtleties.

"No, this is strictly a hunt for a killer. I want you to find out if McGann's our killer. If you can do that, you've done your job. Blowing this surveillance on anything less is unthinkable. None of us will survive the fallout, especially Stevenson. It doesn't matter where the approval came from; accountability won't go any higher than him."

The female, who was politically more astute than her boss, got the message. She stood. "No problem, guys. I'll explain the sixth floor to my boss on our way home. I'm beat. Give us a call if anyone wants to come out and play tonight." She took another cup of coffee for the road and gently pulled at the supervisor's ponytail.

"I get it," he said. "I just don't like it. They got us chasing policemen without work permits, and this guy gets a pass unless he's killing someone." He stuffed a donut in his briefcase and followed his assistant.

When they were gone, Montgomery said to Turner, "What do you think? Do we need to see this for ourselves?"

Turner thought about Paula. "No," he said without any further explanation. They hadn't had a chance to talk about the surveillance before Stevenson made his daily visit, with Katy right on his heels. She was excited and told them she'd met with Judy Taylor at the Hollywood Hills restaurant that morning. Taylor had called asking for the meeting. She had the California section of the *Times* and showed Katy a picture of Dean that had run with the story about his death. It was one of his better booking photos and was right next to the high school yearbook photo of Phil White, Jr. The story detailed how White, the son of a prominent philanthropist, was a suspect in the murder of the pimp. The story wouldn't have been worth a nickel of newsprint if Phil Sr. hadn't been his namesake's daddy.

"Taylor recognized him from the photo as one of those guys in her restaurant the night Alexandra was killed," Katy explained.

"Phil White?" Montgomery asked.

"No, Dean. She said Dean was high and acting stupid. He was wearing a stainless-steel piece and had handcuffs. She saw him driving the police car that Alexandra took from IA."

"But when Taylor saw the two men, it was well before Alexandra was killed." Turner was thinking out loud.

"There goes the rogue cop theory," Stevenson said. "Thank God."

"Dean had the car, but he's got no reason to kill her," Montgomery said.

"She's his meal ticket, and how does he know where McGann lives? A guy like Dean, if he kills a cop, he runs. He disappears.

217

He wasn't acting like a pimp that just hacked up a cop. You saw him, Katy. He was out there doing business as usual the night before he died," Turner said.

Stevenson wasn't as eager to eliminate Dean as a suspect. "He's running around in one of our cars. Maybe he killed her and maybe he didn't, but he was up to something that night."

"Crystal said he used the car to transport his whores and dope. Besides, we can't put him in the car after she's dead." Katy didn't mind challenging her boss. She smiled, knowing it annoyed Stevenson.

"He was high and driving her car. He looks good to me," Stevenson said, staring at Katy.

"He was sleazy, boss, but killing wasn't his style. He didn't have any violent crime on his rap sheet." Turner didn't want to argue, but Katy was right this time.

Stevenson's face got a little redder. "He was with somebody at that restaurant. Dig up his associates. Talk to Crystal again. There might be a live body out there who can tell us what happened."

Katy had a detailed description of the second mystery man at the café that she'd gotten from Judy Taylor. She was already having a composite made that they could show Crystal. Even a tweaker like Crystal should recognize Dean's partner. Montgomery called the county jail to set up an appointment to interview Crystal and found out that they'd released her two days before on probation.

Katy groaned. "We'll never find her again."

"We have the address she gave her probation officer," Montgomery said. He ripped the page off the notepad and gave it to Turner.

Turner looked at the slip of paper and laughed. "You've got to be kidding. Don't you recognize this address? It's Phil White's father."

"The old goat took her home?" Katy asked.

"I've got to find out what Bell wants to do about Wolinski's choice of lovers. Let me know what happens with Crystal," Stevenson said. Katy followed him out. She wanted to pick up her composite sketch at SID before they left.

Turner called Phil White's father, who confirmed that Crystal was staying at his house in Brentwood. He reluctantly agreed to allow them to meet with his house guest.

When Turner, Montgomery, and Katy arrived, the gate opened again, but their host didn't greet them in the driveway. A somber Mexican woman waited by the open front door and welcomed everyone in broken English. She herded them into the living room, where Phil senior was waiting.

The elder White wasn't the same elfish man who'd entertained them on their first visit. The sweatshirt and tennis shoes had been replaced with dress pants and an expensive cashmere sweater. He looked older and frailer, but his hospitality hadn't changed. He was warm and friendly, despite the fact that they had incarcerated his son. He ordered the Mexican woman to bring refreshments.

"I know you're curious about Miss Moody," White said and, not waiting for a response, added, "I've agreed to pay all her expenses, buy her a new car, and give her a considerable allowance, and for those insignificant things she promises to keep my son alive."

"I don't understand," Turner said.

"He wants to die. She makes him want to live. To keep her money, she must visit him every day. If he gets violent or incoherent or in any other way is unable to interact with her, she'll get a sizable settlement. She'll get more money when she's thirty, and I've changed my will to give her a small inheritance. She can leave anytime, but if she does, she forfeits the money, and the agreement is dissolved."

"You know she only cares about the money," Montgomery said.

"I didn't get this rich by being stupid. My son doesn't know, and he wants her." The old man sat on the couch beside Turner. He put his bony hand on Turner's arm. Turner didn't move. White's touch was like a dead leaf rubbing against his skin, dry and hard. His eyes were watery and bloodshot. He was a tired, worried old man. "My son was dying," he said in a raspy whisper. "He tried to kill himself. I took her to him, and it was like a miracle. He's talking and laughing again."

"You've let a very bad person into your life," Turner said. "It might be dangerous for you."

"I don't care. She's keeping my son alive." White got up to help the Mexican woman with the tray. "Tell Miss Moody to join us, Elena."

In a few minutes, Catherine Moody came into the living room wearing a sharp-looking pantsuit. Her hair and nails looked as if they'd been done professionally, and someone had explained how to apply expensive perfume without a hose. She was well groomed and looked almost classy. Turner smiled because he couldn't help knowing that the illusion would disappear as soon as she opened her mouth.

Catherine kicked off her shoes and sat in an overstuffed chair with her feet tucked under her. "So what can I do for you?" she said, not trying to hide her disdain.

"You look good," Turner said, hoping to break the ice.

"No thanks to you. I'd still be in county waiting for my fucking get-out-of-jail-free card you promised me if it hadn't been for Mr. White." Her face flushed. White sat on the arm of her chair, and she calmed down.

Turner sat back and relaxed. Under the million-dollar makeover still beat the heart of a hooker. He noticed Terry Chernack slip quietly into the room. Katy saw him, too, and waved.

"Hi, Terry," Katy said sheepishly.

"Great, the shyster's back," Catherine said, turning away from him.

Chernack ignored her and chatted briefly with Katy. Montgomery updated him on the status of charges against the younger White. The court would most likely postpone any hearing until White was mentally able to participate. His lawyer assured them that would never happen.

Catherine was getting restless. She demanded to know what they wanted and why they were bothering her. Katy took the composite out of her briefcase. She explained that Dean had been seen at a Hollywood Hills café with another man hours before her sister's killing. They wanted her to identify the man.

"Give it to me," Catherine ordered.

Katy held the drawing in front of her. "Look familiar?"

"Looks just like the stupid fuck." She sat back and smirked.

"Does the stupid fuck have a name?" Turner finally asked after waiting several seconds for her to speak again.

"He has a name," she said, and she seemed to be calculating what the information might be worth to her—another marker she could cash in sometime in the future.

"Let me explain something to you, Crystal." Turner deliberately used her street name and saw her back stiffen. "You got out of jail to provide a service to Mr. White. All this," he said indicating around him. "I can take it away. You're on probation. I'll violate you quicker than you can spend this nice old guy's money. Don't fuck with me, or it's midnight and you're back sitting in the fucking county pumpkin."

Catherine stared at the floor and then at White. "You'd better tell them," he said. "I can't interfere."

She rubbed her freshly manicured nails as if trying to decide whether or not the new life she had was worth it. Turner knew that the old Crystal would tell them where to stick their composite, but she had something to lose now.

"Fuck him," she said. "It's Monkey . . . Sonny Fuentes. Everybody knows him. Sullivan's guys arrest him about every ninety days." In a fatherly gesture, White patted her shoulder. "The guy's a hype, loves tar, the Mexican junk . . . got a bad habit, not one of those Hollywood needle freaks," she continued. "He was Jimmy's connection but always chipped some for hisself."

"He was with Dean the night Alex was killed." Montgomery said.

"Probably. They were always together, identical pieces of shit."

"Did you see them together?" Katy asked.

"No."

"Did Alexandra know Fuentes or work with him?" Turner asked.

Crystal laughed. "No way. He wouldn't go near Alex. She threatened to kick his ass and bury him alive if he got close enough for her to see his face. The freak is a real loser. Alex hated losers."

"Does he carry a piece?" Turner asked.

"Hell, yes. Everybody wants to kick his ass. He's been shot twice trying to rip off dealers. The weirdo is real stupid, too."

"This is your keep-out-of-jail question. How do we find him?" Turner didn't want her to have any second thoughts.

She didn't hesitate. "Same as Jimmy, the Carlton. If he ain't there, he's busted." She grinned. "Did I mention Monkey's a dragon? Can't miss him, the ugliest bitch on the boulevard." It was common knowledge that cops hated dealing with drag queens, hysterical women with the strength of men who are always big and always want to fight.

"More good news," Katy said sarcastically.

Chernack walked them back to their car. He assured Turner that Catherine Moody would make herself available whenever they needed her. She had tried to undermine him when she first arrived but hadn't counted on the lawyer's influence with the senior White. She learned quickly that her skill in manipulating men wasn't good enough to affect their long-standing relationship. Chernack said he made it clear that White considered him another son who would control the family fortune when the father died and that he could make her money disappear without a trace unless she did exactly what she was told.

"I detest that woman," Chernack said when they were away from the house. "Phil had cut his wrists and wasn't eating. She saved his life, but she's such a pile of trash."

"You probably didn't put any loopholes in that agreement she signed, did you?" Montgomery asked.

The attorney answered stoically. "Houdini would marvel at the number of escape clauses in that piece of paper. If she tries to screw the old man, she'll wish I'd left her in jail."

"There you are. I wondered where the real Terry Chernack had gone for a minute," Turner said. "How good is Phil Jr. now?"

"Better, mostly coherent. Why?"

"Can he give us a better description of the woman who fought with Alexandra?"

"Probably not, but I'll ask."

Katy waited while Turner and Montgomery got into the car. She talked with Chernack a few minutes behind the car. When she got in, she was smiling but wouldn't tell them what they'd talked about.

"Not an attorney, Katy," Montgomery said, kidding her as he drove away from the estate. "A car salesman is better."

"Shut up, Monty." She wasn't going to talk about it, so Turner figured it must be serious. He called Sullivan at Hollywood Narcotics and told him not to go home before they got there. He offered to take the detective to dinner, so Sullivan said he'd wait.

Sullivan had already pulled the arrest books off the shelf and had them sitting on his desk when they arrived. The name Sonny Fuentes with the alias Monkey was listed several times. Crystal was right. He got arrested about every ninety days. Sullivan wrote down the booking number for the latest arrest and took that package out of the file cabinet. He had been arrested a month before for being under the influence of heroin. The case hadn't been filed because the police lab lost his urine sample, and the city attorney wouldn't file without it. So Fuentes got a free pass.

A computer check showed that he wasn't currently in custody for any other charge under any of his aliases. Sullivan retrieved a large notebook from under one of the detective tables. Inside he found a rap sheet and picture of Sonny Fuentes. Actually there were several pictures of Sonny—as a man and as a female.

"He makes one scary woman," Sullivan said. "This is the squad's hype book. Make copies and put it back. Take what you need, but bring it back so my guys can work."

"Does anyone who isn't blind and desperate ever hit on this guy?" Montgomery asked as he held up a picture of the female version of Sonny.

"You'd be surprised. We catch some rich good-looking guys paying for sex with these dragons. Straight sex doesn't give them what they need."

"What's that, Sully," Katy asked, "AIDS and lice?" She handed the photo back to Montgomery. "Let's eat before we look for this Monkey person."

Sullivan took them to a Greek restaurant on Ivar a few blocks from the station. The owner was an immigrant who really liked the police. He led them to a large booth in the back of the room. It was a small family-owned business, and nearly every table was occupied. Turner thought it was some of the best Greek food he'd ever tasted. It was such a comfortable place that they stayed longer than they'd intended. The owner kept bringing samples of his favorite dishes and tried to convince them the meal would taste so much better with a little Retsina. Turner suspected that Sullivan didn't turn down the wine on his regular visits. When Turner asked for the bill, the owner insisted that the meal was his treat. Turner knew why a lot of restaurants didn't charge or charged less for police officers. They always had a detective or uniformed officer sitting in their establishments. It was cheap protection, but he could never make himself take a discounted or free meal. He didn't argue with the owner. He checked the price of his meal on the menu, added on the tip, and left the cash on the table.

When Sullivan saw how much money Turner had left, he shook his head. "These IA guys," he said. "Refuse a free meal but sleep like a baby after they screw some poor cop."

"Turning down a few free meals will save you from that triple bypass before you're fifty, old man," Turner said, patting Sullivan's bulging stomach. Sullivan grunted and walked away.

They had the room number where Fuentes stayed at the Carlton, and Sullivan agreed to go with them as additional backup. Fuentes's room was on the fifth floor. Agreeing that being trapped in the Carlton elevator was a bad idea, they walked up the stairs. The noxious smell of urine and stale vomit saturated the stairwell. Katy covered her nose with her coat sleeve as they climbed. The red 1940s carpet hadn't been cleaned for decades. The brown pattern on a deep red background made it the ideal choice for a place like the Carlton.

When they reached the fifth floor, they stopped so Sullivan could catch his breath. Several of the doors had heavy outdoor security screens. They belonged to either the families with small children who didn't want drunks or drug addicts kicking in their doors in the middle of the night, or to drug dealers who felt the same way about the police. Sullivan pointed to several twisted doors without locks that his squad's steel ram had removed from the hinges during the service of search warrants.

Room 512 had a wooden door. It didn't matter, because they didn't have a warrant and couldn't force entry. Turner was hoping that Fuentes would open the door, but one way or another they would get inside. He motioned for Katy to stand in front of the peephole and knock on the door. These guys always opened the door to a woman.

She did, and when someone inside the room asked who she was, she identified herself and asked him to open the door. To his surprise, Turner heard the chains being removed from inside the door, and it opened slowly. The strong smell of incense made Katy cough and take a step back. Turner moved in front of her and pushed open the door so he and the others could enter.

A short bald man wearing a pair of French-cut briefs stood in front of them. He had rings attached to nearly every part of his body. It wasn't Sonny. He was Caucasian and looked to be in his late fifties. A very large black man wearing a long Dolly Parton wig and a polyester kimono bathrobe sat on a shabby couch drinking what looked like red wine from a water glass.

"We don't have narcotics, honey," the black man said. "But please look around."

Turner asked if there was anyone else in the apartment. The bald man led him and Montgomery to the back bedroom. It was dark except for a small lamp with a dim blue light on a nightstand near the bed, giving the room a hazy out-of-focus look. The walls were painted a dark color, and strips of chiffon were nailed to the center of the ceiling, draping down the walls. On the bed, on top of a shiny greenish comforter, was Sonny Fuentes. He was sprawled naked and pretending to be asleep.

"Poor girl," the bald man said. "Do I really have to wake her? She didn't sleep a wink last night."

Turner stared at the human hybrid. The top half was a well-endowed woman, but below the waist there were definitely male parts. Montgomery finally answered, explaining that they really needed to talk to "her."

The bald man gently shook the sleeping man, tugged at the comforter, and said, "Cover yourself, dear. We have company."

The drowsy man-woman sat up in bed. "Why are the police here?" The raspy question came from under the comforter that Fuentes had pulled up to his nose. Even half awake, he could smell the police a block away. The bald man removed a woman's cotton robe from the closet and gave it to Fuentes, who slipped it on under the blanket.

Fuentes's hair was shoulder length and dyed orange-red. He tied his hair back with a rubber band he found on the floor. Fuentes groaned with every movement and allowed the bald man to assist him in walking to the living room.

"Are you injured?" Montgomery asked, as they watched Fuentes grimace after every step.

"He's been beat up," the bald man offered. "Punks, Nazi punks. You should see the bruises on his chest and legs."

"No, that's okay. I believe you," Montgomery said quickly. Apparently, he had seen more than enough of Monkey for one night. "Do you need an ambulance?" he asked.

"Just let me sit somewhere," Fuentes whispered dramatically. The bald man gestured for the black man to move over, and Fuentes slowly sank onto the couch.

Turner knew enough not to sit on anything in the cluttered apartment. He had collected more than his share of lice and other assorted vermin from crash pads like this one. The incense and cheap perfume were an attempt to mask the body odor and dirty-clothes smell that permeated the small room, but they failed badly. When everybody was safely positioned in the living room, Katy volunteered to help Sullivan guard the hallway. Turner guessed she'd go to the fire escape and try to get some fresh air, but these smells stayed in your hair and clothes until you washed them.

The bald man seemed to be the dominant one in this little group. He chattered away while Fuentes's fidgeting became more pronounced as his drug-induced sleep wore off.

Finally he got up and stood behind Fuentes, rubbing the skinny man's shoulders and neck. "I could talk to you officers all night. You're all so fascinating, but it's getting late."

"Actually, Sonny is the one we came to see," Turner said. He really wanted to get this over with and get out of there.

Fuentes looked up and whined, "Why? What did I do?" He pulled the robe more tightly around his throat and tried to sink into the couch. "I was the one attacked."

"We're not saying you did anything." Montgomery tried to calm him by talking to him like a child. "We want to ask you about a friend of yours. It's important you be completely truthful with us. Do you understand?"

Fuentes nodded. As soon as Turner mentioned Dean's name, the drag queen relaxed. He could say anything he wanted about the pimp. A dead man couldn't hurt him, and besides, he said, "I never really liked that nasty man." He crossed his legs and let the robe open to the top of his thigh. He instantly became the female version of himself.

"Tell them everything, honey," the bald man said. "I never liked him either. He made her work the streets and kept the money."

"You and Dean were together a lot," Montgomery said.

"He bought me things and was mostly nice to me," Fuentes said in a raspy voice. "He liked me." Fuentes smiled coyly at Turner as he answered. He was flirting.

"The night the woman cop was killed, you were with Dean," Turner said. Fuentes started to deny it, but Turner interrupted him. "You were seen at a Hollywood Hills café and in her police car."

"We were wasted," Fuentes giggled. "Speedballs," he added, shrugging at the bald man. "What a rush! We had fun."

Turner interrupted him again, trying to keep the man on track. "Tell me what you and Dean did that night, everything from the time you got together until you left him."

"Let's see. I dressed in my man clothes. We had to take his girls to a party. It was at a place in the hills. We had speedballs and lots of drinks there before they made us leave." He giggled again. "We got a little out of control."

"Is that when you went to the café?" Turner asked.

"I guess. We had the cop car, so nobody stopped us. They'd see us and wave. It was fun."

"Why did you go to the café?"

"I was hungry. The lady thought we were cops, and she got mad at us for being too loud. Jimmy thought she might call the station to complain, so we split before they came and found out we weren't really cops."

"What did you do then?"

Fuentes rolled his eyes back, trying to retrieve something from the back of his head. "Drove around, then took the car back," he said as if he were answering a pop quiz. He let the robe slip off one shoulder, giving Turner a glimpse of his hormone-enlarged breasts. Turner looked away and thought he was about to lose his Greek entrée.

"Just when was that?" Montgomery asked, trying not to look at the half-naked drag queen.

"Midnight-ish, I guess. The way Jimmy was sneaking around, it was pretty clear to me his little cop friend didn't know he had the car."

"What do you mean?" Turner asked, wishing the little freak could tell a straight story.

"He drives back to her house in the hills and tries to sneak the car keys back in her purse. She comes from the bedroom wearing that great little outfit. I, of course, can't go in, or the bitch would kill me. So I'm sitting on the hot tub watching."

"You can't see the bedroom from outside," Turner said.

"That's right, but little miss Law and Order comes into the living room in her best leathers. Jimmy is panting and following her around, trying to get some cash out of the bitch, but she's laughing at him. I can't hear it all, but Jimmy's definitely begging for money and trying to explain why he needed the car. She was mad."

"Was anyone else in the house?" Turner asked. His heart was pounding.

"What do you think? The woman's dressed in her best leather." Fuentes laughed at his own joke.

Turner wanted to reach over and grab his skinny neck but instead said, "Concentrate, Sonny. This is important."

"Jimmy pretty much gave up anyway, but this Amazon thing with wild brown hair comes out of the bedroom. She says something to him. Jimmy's a rat on a wheel trying to get out of there . . . crawls out the back door . . . steals money from one of their purses on the way out." Fuentes pouted and examined his black porcelain nails. "We get back in Jimmy's wreck. He drives me to the boulevard and dumps me. End of story."

"Tell me more about the big woman," Turner said.

"What's to tell? She's in a bathrobe, with that Janis Joplin hair and attitude."

"Did you see her face? Would you recognize her?"

"Sorry, I saw a lot of hair. She was big like a man." Fuentes looked from Turner to Montgomery.

"That's all she had on, a bathrobe? How big was she?" Montgomery asked.

"She was barefoot. It looked like the games were about to start and Jimmy was in the way. She was much bigger than the little cop bitch . . . as big as you maybe," Fuentes said, indicating Turner. "Tall but not so fat," Fuentes giggled, putting his hand over his mouth. "Sorry, but you could lose a few pounds."

Turner smirked. "No problem," he said, thinking to himself that criticism from a confused sonofabitch like Fuentes really didn't bother him. "You can't identify her is what you're saying?" he asked.

Fuentes shook his head. "Sorry."

"Think about the woman for a few days, and call if anything else about her comes to mind," Turner said, handing Fuentes a business card.

"Of course, officer," Fuentes said in his sweetest female voice. He demurely closed his robe, which had nearly fallen off during the course of the interview.

"And don't go anywhere. You're a witness now. If I can't find you, you become my number-one murder suspect, comprende?" Montgomery said.

Fuentes looked hurt. He straightened his robe over his lap and said, "Yes." He pulled the rubber band off his hair and shook his head until the orange spikes were pointing in all directions.

The bald man maneuvered behind the couch and rubbed Fuentes's shoulders again. "Is there anything else, officers? She really needs to get her beauty sleep," he said, helping Fuentes to his feet and pointing him in the direction of the bedroom. The black man had fallen asleep sitting up. Turner figured he was on heroin and nodding off. He tried to calculate how much sleep would be required to make Fuentes anything but ugly.

"Thank you for your cooperation," Montgomery said, shaking hands with the bald man, who continued chatting nonstop about nothing in particular. He waved from his doorway until they were on the next landing and out of his sight. Turner heard the apartment door close a few seconds later.

All the way back to the narcotics office, Katy complained about the amount of time it had taken to question Fuentes. She wanted to take a shower and get the smell of the drag queens out of her hair and clothes. Sullivan laughed about her dash to the fire escape for fresh air as soon as she got out of the apartment. She sulked silently in a corner of the back seat until they reached the station.

Montgomery told Sullivan and Katy the details of their interview with Fuentes and described the mysterious Amazon woman.

"You don't think Fuentes and Dean could've killed her?" Sullivan asked.

"No, the big woman either killed her or knows who killed her," Turner said. "Fuentes and Dean were petty thieves. Fuentes is telling the truth, or as close as he ever gets to the truth. If he wanted to lie, he had an opportunity to lay the whole thing on Dean, but he didn't."

"Alexandra died between 0130 and 0200 hours. The other woman was there at the right time."

"We're so close, Monty. I can almost smell it," Turner said.

"That's me," Katy mumbled from the back seat.

TWENTY

Turner knew nearly every cop bar in the city and a few in the neighboring jurisdictions, so finding a bar that was close and not frequented by cops was easy. He chose one in San Pedro. Even if a cop wandered in, the guys in the Harbor Division were out of touch with the rest of the department and not likely to have contacts in the chief's office.

Tony's Shack wasn't too seedy. The liquor was good, and Turner could watch the water and fishing boats until she arrived. He looked at the glass of scotch in his hand. I drink too much, he thought. When this case is over, I'll quit.

If he were smart, he'd retire. There was a little town near Springfield, Oregon, where one of his old partners had moved after retirement. It had plenty of fishing and lots of land, no freeways or rap music. It was old-people country. Young people didn't go there because there was nothing to do. His buddy described sitting at the breakfast table and watching deer graze in his backyard. Nobody locked his door or wanted to interfere in your life.

Lose a few pounds, stop drinking, and live in God's country. Not a chance, he thought. He was bored just thinking about it. He still needed the adrenaline rush. He looked at the package on the table. He might not have a choice once he delivered this. Probably the worst that could happen was that he wouldn't get promoted. No, the worst that could happen was that Paula would give up on him and leave, but he knew he should have done this a long time ago. The department needed a major overhaul. Martin rewarded all the wrong behavior and put his own interests above the good of an organization to which Turner had given most of his adult life. He'd sacrificed his marriage and at least one good friend to LAPD, and he wasn't about to see it dragged into the mud by the likes of McGann and Martin . . . the wrong people making the wrong decisions for the wrong reasons.

He wasn't certain that Elaine Miller could fix it. Maybe it had gone too far for any inspector general to fix, but he knew he had to try. With McGann's investigation and the information on

Alexandra's activities, Elaine would have the ammunition to try to change what Martin was doing. Turner believed that the least it might do is bring some equity to an out-of-control discipline system and force accountability from Martin and his staff officers, who lacked the integrity and ability to lead.

With few exceptions such as Jacob Bell, McGann was the prototype of a Martin staff officer. Turner sipped his scotch. He hoped that his judgment hadn't been clouded by his disappointment in not being promoted as quickly as he thought he should have been. He didn't think so, but he knew that's what other people would think if they could prove he was the leak. Fuck them, he thought. He knew why he was doing it.

His investigation showed how differently McGann was treated compared to the other officers involved in the case. It was clear that Martin was engineering the investigation to give McGann a slap on the hand and allow him to come back. It wasn't the sex that bothered Turner. These were adults. They were going to pair up. That was natural and expected, but McGann had seen a young woman on a downward slide, taken advantage of her weakness, and preyed on her willingness to engage in self-destructive behavior as long as it pleasured him. He had a duty to Alexandra—if not as a deputy chief, then as a human being—to try to help her. The selfish prick hadn't even had the decency to admit his involvement with her after she was dead.

When he'd finished his drink, the panic hit him. What would Stevenson think about him? There wasn't enough liquor in this bar to make him feel better. He felt guilty when he didn't speak out, and he felt sick to his stomach at the thought of betraying his chief. He knew why these young cops were hesitant to say anything when they saw their fellow officers do something wrong. They didn't condone misconduct, but it wasn't easy for one cop to point a finger at another one. It was like giving up your brother to strangers who couldn't understand the pressures. If you didn't live this life, you couldn't understand the thought process. He wasn't certain he understood it. He just knew he was doing the right thing, and it made him feel bad.

Every head at the bar turned toward the front door, so Turner figured a woman must have entered. He caught Elaine's image in the mirror behind the bartender. She was squinting, searching for him in the low light and hazy cigarette smoke. Nobody tried to enforce the no-smoking law in this dive. It would've been as pointless as a dress code. He waved and called her name. She saw him and smiled at a toothless bum wrapped in several layers of dirty clothes who tried to get spare change from her as she slid past his barstool.

"Great location, Mike, thanks," she said, staring suspiciously at the stool before she sat down. "I'm being sarcastic, but, you know, all of a sudden I'm really thirsty."

Turner laughed. "It's the ambience."

"Right, early American dumpster." She motioned for the muscular bartender with acne and ordered a gin and tonic. She took a twenty-dollar bill from her wallet but just as quickly put it back. "You're paying. It's the least you can do for dragging me to San Pedro."

"It's probably better. If you pay, I'll really feel like a snitch."

She stopped smiling and began to study his face. "If you've had some second thoughts, don't do this," she said. She took the envelope off the bar and put it on his lap. "I'll get the information another way." She gulped her drink. "Shit, all I need is to pick up the L.A. Times and see you blew your brains out because you felt remorse. Don't I have enough problems?" She held up her glass and shrugged at the boy bartender, who took the glass and gave her another.

Turner put the envelope in front of her. "With that decent attitude, how did you ever get to be an attorney? Don't worry about my mental state. I intend to live long enough to aggravate the brass for at least another couple of years and then stick it to the city for at least another thirty retirement years."

She started to say something, but Turner held up his hand. "Just take the damn stuff, Elaine. I don't like what I'm doing. I don't like myself very much right now, and nothing you can say will change that. It's the right thing to do, but I'm a shit for doing it. I'm just not smart enough to get Martin any other way."

Finishing her second drink, Elaine stuffed the package into her large shoulder bag. "Did you ever think the next guy might be just as bad as or worse than Martin?" she asked him, motioning for the bartender.

"It's practically a sure thing with the department's incestuous promotion system," he said, grinning at her surprised expression.

"Then why?"

"McGann, he won't get away with it. Over the years, I've watched so many of these staff and command guys beat their wives, molest women and children, harass their officers, and sleep their way through the ranks. They get a pass with the chief's blessing while a real cop makes an honest mistake and his career is ruined."

"But why now?"

"McGann could have helped Alexandra Williams, probably had an obligation to help her. Instead he used her. It's simple. I don't want him to get away with it." He ordered them two more drinks.

"Powerful guys who can't lose get beat . . . the Seven Samurai," she said, nodding.

Turner pushed a fresh drink in front of her. "What about the Seven Samurai?"

"What about them?" she asked, grabbing a handful of stale peanuts.

"Maybe you've had enough to drink."

"I'm pretty sure I've had enough. This is one of those places where you feel obliged to drink too much."

He ordered two cups of black coffee and returned the nearly empty glass of her fourth gin and tonic to the bartender.

"I'm so sorry I got you into this," she said, and started digging in her purse for the envelope.

He put his hand over her purse and said, "Remember, I'm the one who contacted you. My only condition is you don't tell them it's me unless they accuse Stevenson or one of the other investigators. Stevenson's about to retire. I don't want anybody screwing with him or his pension."

Elaine hugged her shoulder bag and drank the coffee. When she'd finished, she set the cup down and leaned on her elbow. He looked up and saw her staring at him.

"Feeling okay?" he asked.

"Dandy. How about you?"

"I've been better."

"I hate this job," she said, touching his arm. "I can't wait to get back to defending murderers and rapists, people who have an appreciation for evil. At least they don't pretend to like the people they hurt." She slapped the top of the bar, startling the toothless man, who had fallen asleep beside her. "This place is so fucked up. Good people hiding in filthy bars . . . no offense," she said to the

233

bartender, who shrugged and walked away. "Whispering about the way it ought to be while McGann and Martin strut around for the entire world to see, taking care of business like decent men." Turner could see she was struggling to get her thoughts organized in a gin-soaked brain. "But that's not the worst of it," she said too loudly. "You all have this perverted sense of loyalty to people you don't respect." She twisted on the barstool toward the toothless man, who watched her with childlike fascination. "What the hell is that all about?" she asked the bum. He grinned at her with a vacant stare, wiped his nose on the sleeve of his sweater, slid off the stool, and left without a word.

They were quiet as they watched the man disappear into the night.

"I think I might've scared him," she said timidly.

"I was getting a little frightened there myself," Turner said. He had to laugh. She looked sober but more miserable than he felt. He threw fifty dollars on the bar, straightened his jacket, and said, "Come on. I'll walk you back to your car." She turned away, embarrassed, and wiped tears from her face with the back of her hand. He leaned over and kissed the surprised woman on the cheek. "You're a good woman, Elaine. Try not to fuck this up and ruin my life."

TWENTY-ONE

It was 4 A.M. when Turner finally gave up trying to sleep. Paula had been asleep when he got home, so he didn't have to lie to her about where he had been and why. He crawled out of bed, gently placing the blanket around Paula. She slept so peacefully, like a child, curled on her side with her chin resting on her hands. She looked as if she were praying. Turner smiled. It had to be to some pagan police god. Police work was her only religion.

He liked to watch her sleep. It relaxed him. He couldn't imagine his life without her. He knew she loved him, too, but it was different for her. She would go on with her life undaunted, no matter what happened between them. He wouldn't.

He picked his robe off the floor and tiptoed out of the bedroom. Her gentle purring continued as he pulled the door shut. He switched on the kitchen light and took a bottle of brandy from the cupboard over the refrigerator. He poured himself a larger-than-usual amount and sat on the living room sofa. This Williams investigation was robbing him of some well-deserved rest. His mind refused to shut down and stop thinking about all the little details. He'd used most of the trip home from the bar concocting a story to convince Paula he wasn't Elaine Miller's source. She was afraid that the possibility he was the snitch might ruin his chances to make lieutenant. He cared less about the promotion than solving the murder and making certain McGann didn't escape some punishment, but he couldn't tell her that, either. He didn't need to lie, because Paula got tired of waiting for him and fell asleep. It was better that way. In the morning, she'd be too concerned about her own business to worry about him. Sometime during the day, he'd probably get another call at work when she started obsessing about his future again.

He was thinking about reverting to his detective rank. Stevenson had already offered him a position in RHD, but that offer might disappear if Stevenson found out about him and Elaine. The RHD captain would see his actions as a betrayal. Turner hoped that would never happen, because the last few weeks had rekindled the fire in his belly. He liked police work again. He liked being a detective. He wanted to be a lieutenant, but if it didn't happen, he could survive in RHD.

Turner dumped the contents of his briefcase on the coffee table. If he couldn't sleep, he might as well look at the investigation. Flow charts, copies of statements—he'd gone through them so many times without finding the critical piece of information that might help him find a killer. Dean probably knew the big woman with the wild brown hair. If the pimp knew her, then Crystal most likely knew her. With her street savvy, Crystal was certain to keep a little information in her piggy bank for a rainy day. What a family they were—Crystal, Alex, and their suicidal brother. Mrs. Williams's perverted husband would spend a long and painful time in hell explaining himself.

The interviews from Alexandra's co-workers described her as an intelligent, hardworking cop. She was friendly but distant. The men thought she was a lesbian because she wouldn't date them. Turner shook his head. Typical male cops, he thought. If you don't want me, you must be gay. Most of the women officers didn't like her. They felt she was conceited and arrogant. They claimed that she flirted and used her beauty for favors. No specifics were given.

An interesting comment came from two of her male partners, who said that on several occasions, they had to stop Alexandra from using excessive force. She got heavy-handed with male suspects. One drunken domestic-violence suspect lost his voice and most of his teeth when she hit him in the throat and face with baton blows. He was six foot three and weighed two hundred thirty pounds, so everyone but her partner, who knew the guy was incapacitated, thought she was justified. She was a martial arts expert and could generate the power of a weight lifter. Eventually she found partners like Maria Perez who quietly covered for her.

Alexandra was one messed-up lady, but Turner wondered whether she'd met her match in the big mystery woman. She had to know and trust the woman, believe something pleasurable was about to happen, or she'd never have allowed herself to be that vulnerable. He guessed that such intimacy with a man wasn't likely. It was that woman. He was certain. The next day he would call Chernack and have him bring Crystal downtown. She was going to tell him the woman's name, or she was going back to jail.

He stretched out on the couch and shuffled through pictures of the crime scene in front of McGann's house. There was a little blood smear on the inside of the car, very little, like someone had rubbed something across the seat. The blood drops on the ground were curious, too. It was her blood, but how did it get outside the car if she was delivered in the trunk? There should've been more or none. Turner sat up. "Fuck," he said. It was like cookie crumbs leading to the trunk. The killer wanted the body found there before the car got towed.

The little drama had been designed to play out in McGann's front yard. Someone targeted him. Maybe none of this was really about Alexandra, and McGann was the mark all along. Leaving the body in front of McGann's house wasn't an afterthought. Alexandra was killed so her body could be dumped there. Turner laughed. We've been looking in the wrong place, he thought. Some devious mind would've had to work overtime on this one. But if that was the plan, it worked. McGann's life and reputation were in shambles.

Who hated him, maybe loved him enough to kill that way? Patty couldn't pull it off. She was too small and was looking for a reason to leave her husband anyway. Nancy Connelly seemed to have feelings for McGann, but she was too old and not big enough, either. There was only one McGann woman left, Wolinski. Not exactly a wild, brown-haired Amazon, but big enough and smart enough to pull if off. She was sleeping with him, which was out of character for the career-minded lieutenant and showed that reason alone wasn't controlling her actions. She had to be genuinely attracted to the guy. Love . . . lust made people do stupid things. Turner found SID's pictures of Alexandra's body in the car trunk and lying on the coroner's gurney. No rational person could do that to another human being . . . but an out-of-control, jealous lover?

He stacked the pictures on the coffee table and finished the brandy. It was nearly 6 A.M., and he wasn't sleepy. He made a pot of coffee and started breakfast. The alarm couldn't rouse Paula, but the smell of coffee and sautéed onions did it every time. He decided to make his special omelet with bacon, onions, and pepper cheese. He liked to cook. It calmed him, cleared his mind. The alarm stopped buzzing, and a few seconds later, Paula shuffled into the kitchen wearing her Miss Piggy slippers and granny shirt. She kissed him on her way to the coffeepot and poured herself a big cup. She sat at the table and watched him cook for a few seconds until the caffeine reached her brain cells.

He set the plate of toast and eggs in front of her. She gazed up at him and smiled.

"Is it Sunday?" she asked, still not quite awake.

"Couldn't sleep. Thought I might as well make us breakfast."

She nodded with a mouthful of omelet, took a gulp of coffee, and asked, "Did your briefcase explode all over the living room, or were you working all night?"

He could feel the "are you the snitch" conversation coming up, so he needed to distract her.

"I think I know who killed her," he said as matter-of-factly as he could. "Is the omelet good?"

"It's always good. Who?" she asked, putting her fork down.

"I need to do a few things before I can say for certain."

"I don't need beyond a reasonable doubt. Your guess is good enough."

He took a bite of his eggs. "I don't want to tell you yet. I'll tell you tonight."

"You don't trust me?"

"Of course, but I could be wrong. Let me check some stuff, and then I'll tell you."

She sat back. "You make me breakfast but won't confide in me." He started to say something, but she interrupted. "No, it's too late. Now I don't want to know."

"Okay," he said, grinning at her.

"If you don't tell me tonight, you're in big trouble. I don't care if you're sexy, and you can cook." She picked up a piece of toast and pushed away from the table. "Besides, Turner, I know the first thing you're going to do this morning is drive downtown and tell Monty."

He shrugged. "That's different."

"He's my partner," she said, mimicking him. "Is it another cop?" she asked quickly.

Turner shook his head, no. "Why don't you take your shower while I clean up?"

She kissed him on the back of his neck, touching his ear gently with her lips. "Do I know him?" she whispered.

He laughed and pushed her in the direction of the bathroom. When the kitchen was reasonably uncluttered again, he sat at the table and called Montgomery at home. He explained why he thought Wolinski was their murderer and said he wanted to show Crystal and White her photo. Although her hair was wrong, he was certain they'd identify Wolinski as the woman who'd hit Alexandra and the same one whom Dean had seen at the murder scene. Women have ways to change their hair, but that face would be difficult to forget.

They agreed to meet at Parker Center in an hour and drive to the White estate to interrogate Crystal again and show her Wolinski's picture. Katy could go to the institute later in the day and try to get an ID from White if he was coherent.

It was nearly 9 A.M. when Turner and Montgomery pulled into White's driveway. The maid let them in, and Chernack met them in the den. He was friendly and seemed more relaxed than the last time they'd been there. Turner explained why they had come.

"Sorry, you're too late," Chernack said. "I thought you knew. She's gone."

"Gone as in gave up the money?" Montgomery asked. "Where did she go?"

"Don't know. She said she was dying in this house and couldn't stomach another second in the company of either Phil or me," Chernack said without any emotion. "She packed all of her new clothes, a few of the family heirlooms she fancied, and left."

"She gave up all that money?" Montgomery repeated.

"Her exact words were, 'There ain't enough fucking cash in this world for me to waste another fucking minute of my life in this tomb,'" Chernack said, obviously enjoying the moment.

"Did she find a way to access the accounts and get the money?" Turner asked. He couldn't believe she'd left without trying to steal some of it.

"I checked. There isn't any money missing, and I've closed the accounts."

"Does Phil know?" Turner asked.

"Yes, but it's odd. When I told him, he said he was glad. As he gets healthier, I think Phil realizes how little she actually cares for him."

"We need to find her," Turner said. "Before she ends up like her sister."

"She spent most of the money she had but took her car and two suitcases and acted like a woman who had someplace to go."

"Exactly, what did she steal?" Turner asked. He wasn't surprised Crystal couldn't leave without pilfering something.

"A few small pieces of expensive porcelain and Mrs. White's cheaper jewelry. It only had sentimental value. The insured stuff is in the vault," Chernack said. "It was a small price to get her out of our lives."

"Did she make any calls right before she left?" Turner asked.

"You're joking. The woman was on the phone day and night."

Chernack found the latest phone bill. Crystal had her own line, so it was easy to search for numbers. Montgomery used his cell phone to call any number with a Hollywood area code. The last item was the business number for the manager of an apartment house on Franklin. The man wouldn't give him any information over the telephone but said he'd be happy to cooperate when he saw some police ID. Turner had a hunch they'd found Crystal's new residence.

Montgomery stuffed the phone bill in his pocket, and Chernack led them to the back of the house and Crystal's bedroom. It was clean. Not a scrap of paper had been left behind. She'd even taken the radio alarm clock and a small television that belonged to Phil's father.

"Not exactly the perfect house guest," Chernack said, holding the cable wire that had been attached to the new flat screen television.

"She never pretended to be anything but what she was," Turner said. He felt the same way about people who brought a python into their home and couldn't understand why the thing was having their kids for dinner.

"I know that, but you hope someone will appreciate it when you're trying to do something good and not screw you," Chernack said, throwing the cable back on the floor.

"All she knows is how to survive. Let's hope she can do that until we find her again." Turner had an uneasy feeling about Crystal being back in Hollywood, if that's where she'd gone.

"Why? What could happen to her?" Chernack asked.

"I think she knows who killed her sister. I'm hoping the killer hasn't figured that out."

"I can't believe I'm going to say this," Chernack said, shaking his head and struggling with the words. "If you're planning to interview her, I'm going with you. I guess I'm still sort of her attorney." He sat on the unmade bed. "You have no idea how much I hate that woman."

Montgomery laughed. "Then don't go," he said.

"If I want to sleep tonight, I have to go. How did I get involved in this? I'm a contract attorney."

"A lawyer who can't sleep at night—now I have seen everything," Turner mumbled to Montgomery as they left the bedroom.

Montgomery convinced Turner to let the lawyer ride with them to the apartment building in Hollywood. He wasn't as certain as Turner that they'd find Crystal at that location. It was a long shot but the only lead they had.

Driving through some of the worst traffic in Los Angeles, Montgomery reached West Hollywood in about an hour. He tried La Cienega to get away from the Santa Monica Boulevard lunch-hour crowd, turning east on Sunset, but it didn't matter. It was bumper to bumper everywhere he went. On Wilcox, the traffic had thinned out considerably. The apartment building was on the corner of Franklin and Highland in a surprisingly nice upscale neighborhood.

The Palms was a security building. Turner buzzed the manager's apartment. In a few seconds, a short overweight middle-aged man appeared at the front doors. Turner pressed his badge and ID against the glass, and the little man unlocked the door. The manager had a neat row of hair plugs lining the top of his forehead. His newly planted crop of hair was combed straight back. He wore a blue-striped long-sleeved shirt with Levi's and suspenders.

He gave each of them his business card before allowing them to follow him inside. His apartment was a few steps from the front door. He walked quickly, taking wobbly little duck steps like a wind-up toy. He invited them to make themselves at home in a room that was half office, half living space. Turner immediately felt comfortable. It was a pleasant place, and he could smell something roasting in the oven. The area occupied by a desk and file cabinets was probably originally intended to be the dining room.

The manager took a piece of paper off the desk and gave it to Montgomery. "I believe this is what you came for, officer," he said, giving him Crystal's tenant application. Turner read it over Montgomery's shoulder. Crystal had paid for the first and last month's rent and a substantial cleaning deposit. She was in one of the larger apartments and had already paid to have some minor changes in wall color and had also ordered new rugs. She had installed expensive window treatments. "I wasn't at ease with her at first, but she grows on you," he said. "Have I made a mistake?"

"No," Turner said quickly. "She hasn't done anything wrong. We just need to talk with her."

The fat man took his handkerchief out of his back pocket and dabbed at the sweat dripping from between his rows of hair and down his cheeks. "That's a relief," he said. "I'm not good at this judging-people thing." He stuffed the handkerchief back in his pocket. "Can I get you some coffee, something to drink?" he asked, moving toward the oven to check his roast.

"No," Turner answered. "Do you know if Crystal . . . Miss Moody is in?"

"As a matter of fact I do. We spoke just before you arrived. Naturally, I didn't mention your visit," he said, waiting for some recognition of his cleverness. When it didn't come, he added, "She's on the top floor, 407, last apartment."

He seemed eager to get them out of his apartment and couldn't understand why they refused to take the first-rate elevator. He pointed out the staircase after Turner insisted on walking and watched as they climbed to the fourth floor. Montgomery complained at the top of each landing and needed several minutes to catch his breath when they reached Crystal's floor.

"I'm getting a cold," he said, coughing until he could breathe again. "The elevator would have been nice."

Turner ignored him and found the door with the small gold numbers 407. He motioned for Chernack to move out of range of the peephole as he knocked and rang the doorbell. He could hear someone walking on what sounded like a tile entry. He stood directly in front of the door and stared at the peephole, which went dark for just an instant.

"Fuck," a woman's voice said from the other side of the door.

"Open the door, Crystal," Turner ordered.

The lock turned and the door opened. Crystal stood before them, wearing her tight hip-hugging Levi's, cowboy boots, and a shiny silver halter top.

"What the fuck do you want?" she asked, standing in the doorway. She finally caught a glimpse of Chernack. "That motherfucker is not coming near me." She tried to close the door, but Turner was too fast. He stepped inside the apartment, with Montgomery a step behind him.

Chernack stood in the hallway. He was obviously uncomfortable about forcing his way into anyone's home. Montgomery held the door open for him until, reluctantly, he entered.

Crystal stood in the middle of an elegant living room with plush carpeting and a velvety white couch and chairs. She folded her arms and glared defiantly at Turner. She had been rousted enough by the police to know she wasn't going to have her way.

"Sit down, Catherine," Turner said, pointing to one of the chairs. "We need to talk." He used her real name, hoping he could soften her a little.

"Why is he here?" she asked, indicating Chernack.

"He's your lawyer. He's here to make sure we don't violate your rights."

"You mean like breaking into my fucking place. He's doing a great fucking job so far." She stepped behind a well-stocked bar and poured herself a glass of red wine. She didn't bother to offer them anything.

"Sit down," Turner said again. "Don't make me ask again."

She held up her glass to him and came around the bar. She dropped onto the couch and sipped at the wine. "You can't prove the old man didn't give me that stuff."

"Nobody cares about the stuff you took. It's yours. Keep it. Sell it," Chernack said.

"Then why are you fucking with me? I'm not bothering anybody. I don't have drugs. Search the place."

"Let's calm down," Montgomery said. He sat on the couch. She put her drink on the end table and crossed her arms.

"The day after your sister was killed, Dean came to see you and Phil," Turner said.

"I already told you that," she said curtly. "Don't you people keep notes or nothing? That's when he gave me his shit and the

243

money." She sneered at Chernack. "But we all know that ain't important any more."

"He told you he'd been at Alex's Hollywood Hills house the night before, didn't he?"

"So what? He used her car and brought it back."

"Did Alex know he had it?" Montgomery asked.

"She let him use it to move girls around. That's all I know."

"Who was the woman at the house with Alex when Dean got there?"

"He didn't tell me nothing about no other woman." She took a deep breath and exhaled. "Who told you that? He didn't tell me every fucking thing he did or who he did it with." She looked at Chernack, who started to say something but changed his mind and sat quietly. "Just leave me alone," she said.

Turner was getting tired of her bullshit. "How are you paying for this place? You doing a little business in the back alley?"

"I have money the old man gave me," she said, and Chernack looked up as if he knew she was lying. She saw his expression and added, "I sold a few things, and I'll get a job waiting tables."

Suddenly, Turner realized that without saying much, she was telling them a lot. He wondered if Montgomery had the same thought. It was so bizarre, but something Crystal would do.

"If this woman killed your sister, she isn't going to let you live to identify her," Turner said. "My guess is she's already planning a way to dispose of you. She got lucky when Phil killed Dean, but you'll be easy. She can stand on the toilet in the stall next to you in the ladies' restroom at some restaurant and put a bullet in your brain. Or wait until you're sitting on your new balcony and shoot you from the roof of that building across the alley . . . drag you into some dark alley and cut your throat. You saw what she did to Alex, and Alex was a trained officer with martial arts skills."

Crystal stared defiantly at him. "He didn't tell me nothing about no fucking woman," she said, articulating every word.

Montgomery sighed and pushed himself off the couch. "You want to go it alone, fine. Maybe this time, when she kills you, she'll leave enough evidence so we can catch her. Come on," he said to Chernack. "We're out of here."

Chernack follow them into the hallway. When the door closed, he turned to Montgomery.

"Is that true what you told her? Is she in danger?" Chernack asked.

"If she's doing what we think she's doing, she might as well put a big red bull's eye on her forehead," Turner said, pushing the lawyer out of his way. He jogged down the stairs and into the lobby. When they were back in the car, he told Montgomery, "I'm getting surveillance on her."

"What's going on?" Chernack asked. He was confused and getting testy.

Montgomery turned and stared at him in the back seat. "She's blackmailing the killer," he said. He took a cell phone out of the glove compartment and gave it to Turner. "Call Katy. She'll have the surveillance squad move to this address."

"You know who the killer is?" Chernack asked. They didn't answer. "We need to get her out of there. Go arrest him."

"What if we're wrong and the real killer sneaks in here and kills her? It's just a hunch."

Chernack was squirming in the back seat. "I'll get Mr. White to press charges for robbing him. We can put her in jail. She'll be safe there."

"No," Turner said. He was angry. "We let you come along; don't screw up this case. Crystal's stupidity is going to bring this killer to us. Let us do it our way, and she might just live through this thing."

"You're using her as bait. What if you mess up and the killer gets past your surveillance? We need to protect her."

"Haven't you learned anything about this hooker?" Turner asked. "She's blackmailing the psycho that butchered her sister. She isn't going to hide. She's greedy, and she'll play this out one way or another. If you really want to help, let us catch the killer." He was through arguing. "I'll tell you this one time. Don't interfere, or you're responsible for what happens to her."

Chernack sank back into the seat. "You're right," he said. "I don't understand any of you. I've done some things I'm not proud of, but I can't comprehend inflicting pain and watching it happen." He opened the door and got out of the car. He stood on the curb and made a call on his cell phone. Within ten minutes, a black limousine drove up and parked in front of Montgomery's police car, and Chernack was gone. Turner watched as the limo disappeared westbound on Franklin.

"You think he'll drop a dime on us?" Montgomery asked.

"Don't know. Does it matter? She knows she's playing with fire. Wolinski probably gave her some money, like a down payment, to show good faith, make her lower her guard." Turner was thinking out loud. "Wolinski won't wait too long. She'll want Crystal gone as soon as possible."

Turner held up his hand to stop Montgomery's conversation so he could talk to Katy on his cell phone.

"I need to meet with Wolinski," Turner said when he had finished.

"Not a good idea, partner. In fact, it's a very bad idea. She's a smart lady. She's probably figured out we're getting close."

"Maybe I can encourage her to do something stupid on our time schedule. Then surveillance can close the trap when she goes after Crystal."

"She kills people, Mike."

"She's not going to kill me at Parker Center. She wants to interview me on this Elaine Miller thing. It's the perfect reason to spend time with her and plant some seeds."

"Some case we've got. We picked you, Lieutenant Wolinski, because you're the only one left. We can't prove anything, but if you kill Crystal, it would really, really help us."

Turner laughed. "She doesn't have to kill Crystal . . . just try to kill her."

"How much money you think Crystal wants?"

"How much is freedom and a career worth? Wolinski might agree to pay, but she has to kill Crystal. She isn't the kind of woman to let someone blackmail her."

"Fascinating, but at the risk of repeating myself, we can't prove any of this."

"Maybe, but we both know I'm right. Killing Alex was Wolinski's checkmate to McGann. He was ruined, and his only move was to go crawling back to her. Game's over. Wolinski wins because he needs her now."

Montgomery started the car. "District attorneys and juries don't want chess analogies. They want proof. Something we don't have."

TWENTY-TWO

Stevenson and Bell sat in the RHD captain's office and listened intently to Turner as he laid out his theory on who killed Alexandra Williams. It was difficult to explain a working cop's gut instinct to a man like Bell, who'd spent his career making his career, not doing police work.

His lips tightened as Turner explained why they had moved the surveillance team to Crystal's apartment.

"Another unsupported leap to a new high-profile suspect," Bell said when Turner had finished. "I agree the blood in the car and on the ground could've been staged, but anyone could've done it. Wolinski certainly is big enough and strong enough, but there's no physical evidence. Did that drag queen Sonny Fuentes ID her?"

Turner had to admit Sonny hadn't been able to identify Wolinski, but he had methodically eliminated every possible suspect until only Wolinski remained. Bell examined all the photos and carefully read the statements Turner had given him. When he'd finished, he sat back.

"Is that it?" Bell asked.

"We know there isn't anything solid to implicate Wolinski," Stevenson started to answer.

"Nothing solid," Bell said. "There's nothing, period, except some pretty huge leaps of faith."

"They think Crystal knows who the killer is," Stevenson said. "They want to set up on her and wait. We just told you about Wolinski because she's our best suspect. She had motive."

"This Sonny Fuentes said the killer was big, maybe a woman or a man, with wild brown hair. That isn't exactly Sally. Leave her out of this until you get something more. You can't damage her reputation on a wild hunch. Poor taste in men doesn't make her a killer. McGann is still a better suspect," Bell said. "At least, he had solid motive. I'll grant you the body in front of his house is peculiar, but killers aren't always rational."

"But don't you see? That's what I'm trying to tell you," Turner pleaded. "This killing was never about Williams. It was always about McGann."

Bell stood and picked up the homicide book on Alexandra Williams. "Someone had better explain that to Officer Williams's mother, because she felt it was very much about her dead butchered daughter." He dropped the book on Turner's lap. "You work on this, and next time give me more than your suspicions to take back to the chief. Without proof, your theory is a waste of my time." The mild-tempered man was irritated. "I don't like sloppy police work. Picking a suspect and making the evidence fit is not good police work." He left Stevenson's office and walked to the detective bay. He shook hands with one of the older detectives. The exchange seemed cordial and good-natured, as if the conversation in Stevenson's office had never happened. Bell had turned on a switch, and he was the friendly old man again—no hint of the anger he'd displayed just a few seconds ago. The detectives joked with him, and he patted several of them on the back before leaving.

Turner watched him, but Bell never looked back at the office window or seemed to give Turner or his wounded ego another thought. Turner, on the other hand, felt like a squashed bug on the bottom of the old man's shoe. He gathered his papers and photos that were scattered over Stevenson's desk and slid them into a large manila envelope.

Stevenson's face was flushed to a shade of pink. He was apparently feeling the fallout from Bell's rebuke. Turner knew why. Wolinski was a guess, and guesses were bad police work.

"Concentrate on Crystal and McGann," Stevenson told him.

Turner didn't argue, and Montgomery was quiet, too. All those bells and sirens that had gone off and pointed him toward Wolinski were Turner's experienced reactions and nothing more. As a street cop, he relied on those sensors—the hairs on the back of his neck, the tightness in his stomach, or the little voice that said, "Don't wait. Handcuff this guy now, or pat that guy down first." He listened to them on the street, and they kept him alive. He was smart enough to do what he had to do and explain it later. Trying to tell Bell about this investigation's equivalent of the hairs on the back of his neck convinced Turner it was time to revert to more reliable street tactics and worry about the consequences after they had their killer in custody.

He was out of the captain's office as quickly as he and Montgomery could collect the pieces of their investigation. Stevenson was upset but didn't have much to say to him, and he was grateful. They took all the paperwork back to Turner's office, where Katy had been working on deciphering Crystal's phone bills. She hadn't stayed to hear Turner's presentation and wanted to know Bell's reaction.

"I don't know. What would you say, Monty, kind of lukewarm?" Turner asked.

"Sure, you could say that, if puking all over your theory and calling us morons is lukewarm," Montgomery said. He was peering over Katy's shoulder. "Did you find anything interesting?"

"Bell might be right. Not about the moron thing, but about Wolinski not doing it. Look at this," she said, showing them a phone number she'd highlighted that appeared twice on Crystal's bill on two different days. "It's McGann's apartment."

Turner couldn't believe it. "She called McGann?" he asked, taking the bill out of Montgomery's hand.

"Twice, just before she moved. Every other call is related to her move or to girlfriends in jail or out of state. Two calls to her mother, but no calls to Wolinski."

Turner stared at the bill and shook his head. It didn't make any sense. He was certain Sonny Fuentes had seen a woman with Alexandra. McGann wouldn't have parked that car in front of his own house. He threw the bill on his desk and dropped into his chair. Why would Crystal call McGann? When he looked up, Montgomery and Katy were staring at him.

"I'm baffled," he said.

"We go back to basics," Montgomery said. "Follow the solid leads. I like traditional, plodding police work. We follow Crystal and let her take us to the killer. I never did like this movie detective stuff. Let the case take us where it takes us."

Turner was quiet. He knew Montgomery was giving him a not-so-subtle putdown. He wasn't a detective. He was an IA sergeant who had just embarrassed them, and maybe he should stand aside and let the real investigators take charge.

No fucking way, Turner thought.

TWENTY-THREE

Turner tried to avoid any contact with the occupants of the sixth floor at Parker Center, but it was impossible. He frequently needed something from one of the bureau offices or Press Relations, or he wanted to talk to Paula. That night, he wasn't surprised to see every office door still open and lights on. All the clerical help had gone home. With their heavy workloads and inadequate salaries, they didn't need to impress anyone.

Every adjutant, including Paula, was still sitting at his or her desk waiting for the boss to call it a night. Turner waved at Paula as he passed the chief of staff's office, but she didn't notice him. She was preoccupied with several people he didn't recognize, so he kept walking. He could see that the chief's office door was open. Martin had probably gone out to a meeting. His drivers and bodyguards always kept the door closed when he was there.

Turner had called Wolinski earlier and asked if she had some free time to discuss the Elaine Miller matter. He told her that it was a distraction and he wanted to get the interview out of the way so the chief could be comfortable that he hadn't talked to the IG and so he wouldn't be penalized any further in the lieutenant selections. Turner didn't like how easy it was for him to lie, but he couldn't exactly tell her that he thought she'd butchered Alex and that he was hoping to panic her enough so she'd try to kill Crystal sooner. He was surprised how pleasant and friendly she was on the telephone. She'd told him to come at his convenience because she'd be working at least another couple of hours and could stop whenever he arrived.

Martin's adjutant was in his glass-enclosed space just inside the chief's outer office. He directed Turner to the executive's niche, back out the door, and to the right. Wolinski was sitting at her desk, which was piled high with correspondence and stacks of projects nearly ready to be distributed. She was totally focused on the work in front of her and didn't notice when he walked in. He watched her for a moment. It was difficult not to stare. She was a very pretty woman. She wore a cream-colored pantsuit.

The jacket was hung over the back of her chair, and she'd rolled up the sleeves of a silky white blouse. Her dark blond hair was tucked back behind her ears, and, even hunched over the desk with her glasses set low on her nose, she was very attractive and classy. Paula always seemed flustered and overwhelmed by a heavy workload, but Wolinski gave the impression of someone who had everything under control. He stared at her delicate hands with the freshly manicured nails and suddenly felt very foolish. His perfect theory was disintegrating before his eyes; it didn't work with this sort of woman.

Finally, she looked up and smiled at him, the kind of smile that forces you to smile back, regardless of how you feel. Her blue eyes were lined with dark circles from too much reading, but they were still very nice. She stood and shook hands. Her skin was soft, but she had a man's firm grip. She pulled a chair over closer to her desk and invited him to sit. She was tall and slender and moved very gracefully. She pushed the paperwork on her desk aside and took a yellow tablet from her desk drawer. He waited for the girlish gestures and giggling that Paula always talked about, but Wolinski was subdued and professional. She chatted cordially about how hard he was working and how difficult it must be for him and Paula to maintain any kind of decent relationship. This wasn't the vacuous, promiscuous woman described by Paula and Brenda on so many occasions. He wondered if she was too tired to be silly or whether Paula and her friends had embellished their stories because they disliked her. She was different from the woman he'd imagined, the deranged lover who could have killed Alex.

"Mike, I'm sorry we have to do this," she said sweetly, hesitating before asking, "May I share something with you confidentially?" She seemed uncomfortable and moved closer to whisper.

Turner leaned on her desk and could smell her perfume, a sweet, clean odor that hung in the air for only a wonderful moment and then was gone. She glanced at the door before speaking.

"Nancy Connelly suggested to the chief that you were the one who gave that information to Elaine Miller," she said. He tried to remain expressionless. It was difficult, because neither the chief nor Connelly had any idea how much information he'd given Elaine. "Connelly is still angry with you because Stevenson kept you at RHD. When you gave Elaine the IA update, Connelly knew she should've done it. Connelly made herself and the chief look bad. She resents you, and I think she's jealous of Paula. This investigation is her way of getting back at you." When she finished, Wolinski sat back and smiled at him. "Just a heads up."

Turner smiled. "Thanks," he said. He hadn't expected her to confide in him, especially about her mentor, Connelly. Wolinski's charm and openness were a little disconcerting, but they seemed a bit rehearsed, too. He'd come here expecting a different kind of woman, one who was a little off-balance and capable of doing terrible things. This woman was just the opposite. She appeared centered and stable.

She asked him several questions about his relationship with Elaine Miller and his handling of confidential information. Her final question was whether or not he had given the IG any material other than the original IA investigation. He answered quickly. He looked into those beautiful blue eyes, and with all the sincerity he could muster, he lied again.

She jotted notes as he answered her questions. He was impressed with the way she'd organized the interview. She finished quickly and didn't try to be cute or clever. He was comfortable with her and liked her direct no-nonsense approach. Paula had told him Wolinski was smart, and he agreed. She talked easily and knowledgeably about department issues and, for that matter, every subject he broached. He wanted her to talk to him, open up to him, and she did.

He glanced at his watch and realized that they had been talking and laughing for over an hour. He apologized for keeping her.

"Don't worry about it," she said. "I needed a break, and you're good company." She removed her glasses and delicately replaced a strand of hair that had slipped out of her hair clip and hung over her right eye. She rubbed her temples gently. "I've got a headache. I think it's coffee deprivation."

"Why don't you let me buy you a real cup of coffee? The hotel on the corner has a coffee bar that stays open all night." Turner heard himself say the words before his mind had an opportunity to process the implications of what he was suggesting. "Mocha and vanilla biscotti will cure anything," he added. He knew he shouldn't do this without letting Monty know he was leaving the building, but there wasn't any practical way to tell him. Besides, he hadn't planted the seed of panic yet by giving her just enough information to let her think they were close to finding the killer. He was trying to convince himself that it was okay to be alone with her. It was just a cup of coffee, no big deal. He could feel a little dampness under the arms of his jacket. Maybe he was experiencing some guilt about using Crystal as a sacrificial lamb.

Wolinski didn't hesitate. She'd enjoy spending more time with him, she said. She rolled down her sleeves and slipped on her jacket. She put her glasses in the desk drawer and removed the two decorative clips that kept her silky hair away from her face. Her hair was cut to fall just below her ears. It looked soft and was styled to move gently as she turned her head. She smiled at him.

"Okay," she said, slipping the strap of her small purse over her shoulder. Without a moment's thought, she took the long way to the elevators by way of the north hallway. It meant they didn't have to pass by Paula's office. Wolinski didn't say anything, but Turner was impressed. She had anticipated a possible predicament and solved the dilemma without a word.

They talked easily in the elevator and during the half-block walk to the lobby of the Gardens Hotel. He left her at a clean table and went to the bar to order their drinks. There were only a dozen tables in the small room near the lobby. An Asian man sat by himself in the corner. The other places were empty and had been for some time, judging by the bored expression of the man behind the counter.

As the man poured their coffee, Turner understood how Wolinski manipulated everyone so easily. He had loved Paula a long time, and Wolinski was very different from everything he liked about Paula. Paula was natural and funny. She was smart, too, but not an intellectual. She liked Levi's and tank tops, chewed her nails, and never fussed with her naturally curly hair. Wolinski was tailored and manicured. She wore expensive clothes and quoted the department manual, *The Wall Street Journal,* and *The New Yorker* with equal ease. He knew he should tell her what he needed to tell her, take her back to her office, and go home, but he couldn't seem to disengage from this unique woman.

He knew she was subtly working him, too, with her sensuous movements and warm smiles, but it didn't matter. He was enjoying her company in a guilty, odd sort of way.

"Are you seeing anyone?" he asked, knowing he'd better start working before she completely distracted him.

"No," she lied, and she immediately became less fascinating.

"Really? I heard you were still dating McGann," he said innocently.

If someone had asked him to describe the change in Wolinski's expression when he mentioned McGann's name, he would've had a difficult time. It was hardly noticeable but still extraordinary. Her body barely moved, but her eyes could've turned Lot's wife to salt. He'd seen that look before—those cold, dead eyes, a predator's stare. As quickly as it came, it was gone. Within seconds, she was soft and lovely again, laughing and denying the rumors. Her behavior reminded him of someone. He'd heard the older detectives talk about Ted Bundy, the handsome, intelligent killer who could win a woman's confidence, entice her with his smile, then brutally strangle her without a moment's regret.

The IA sergeant came alive in Turner's brain. Why was she lying? Before he could give it much thought, she confided in him that she really didn't want coffee. She'd really like a brandy. Did he care to join her? Turner stood and offered his hand to help her up. She put her hand on his arm, and he escorted her to the hotel's bar.

Business in the glitzy bar, unlike that in the coffee room, was brisk. He found two stools near the piano. Multicolored chandeliers reflected off the mirror behind the long polished marble bar with gold-plated railing. Japanese businessmen in dark suits had invaded the place. They seemed at home in these gaudy surroundings in the middle of L.A.'s Little Tokyo, where most of the waiters and the bartenders spoke their native language. The piano player had a repertoire of familiar show tunes. Turner looked around for a microphone and said a quick prayer of gratitude that it wasn't a karaoke bar.

He ordered two cognacs, and he and Wolinski leaned closer to hear each other over the music. He had noticed the reaction of other men in the room as she entered—how they stared at her as she sat with her legs crossed. She probably wasn't beautiful in the classic sense, but she was one of those women who knew how to put the package together. She playfully twisted a strand of hair around her finger and had a sexy way of pushing her hair back with her fingertips, teasing but pretending not to care. She gave her full attention to Turner while her body performed for the masses. It was quite a show.

By 11 P.M., they had finished their second drink, and he ordered some snacks to keep his head from spinning. She didn't seem affected by the alcohol but ate hungrily. Turner admired her appetites. He told himself he was pretending to enjoy her company, but had to admit she did know how to make a man feel comfortable. Wolinski kept their conversation in a sexually neutral zone, but her subliminal messages were firing like an AK-47. He'd never even thought of cheating on Paula all the years they'd been together, and this night was no exception, but some strange feelings were beginning to stir in him. It was the way he'd felt when he'd had to put down a rare pedigreed German shepherd when it went crazy on him. It had to be done, but he always felt bad about it.

"I'm curious," he said, trying to get his mind back on business. "What kind of man is McGann?"

She cleared her throat and sipped her brandy. She stared at him and didn't blink. He'd seen men do this to intimidate or show superiority. It was a gimmick, but he looked away first, and she giggled for the first time that night.

"I don't know. He's a man. Is there more than one kind?"

"I hope so."

She was serious again. "He's weak, uncommitted . . . and pretty much ruined, from what I hear."

"Why would any woman be attracted to a guy like him?" He felt like one of those Italian anarchists taking a hammer to Michelangelo's *Pieta*. The perfect woman was fidgeting.

"Why do you care, Michael?" She tossed her hair back, exposing a long white neck. "He's sexy and smart but can't keep his hands off other women."

"He's married."

She laughed. "Hardly . . . Patricia doesn't want to be a wife or lover. He never wanted kids. He needs a woman who . . ." She stopped and looked confused, as if she were saying too much.

"Sorry, I thought as long as you were done with him, you wouldn't mind talking about him. He's such a degenerate." She blinked. He'd hit a nerve. "There's a witness that'll probably nail him. We're sure she knows what happened to Alex, and it's only a matter of time before we pick her up and she tells us everything. I

255

know Martin's already filled you in," he said, slurring just enough to let her think he'd drunk too much.

She nodded, but he knew that nobody had told her anything. If he was right, Wolinski should be getting a little uneasy about Crystal as a liability. "He's a complicated man," she said almost to herself.

"I think he's pretty ordinary . . . common in the basest sense of the word," Turner said, trying to provoke her.

Wolinski picked up her empty snifter and waved it at the bartender. "Would you like another?" she asked Turner without looking at him. "My treat."

Turner accepted her offer as he swallowed a shrimp on toast to keep himself from really getting drunk. The bartender placed two drinks in front of them. He made certain that Wolinski's drink was positioned just right and waited until she glanced up before taking her money. He ignored Turner and seemed annoyed that Wolinski wasn't alone.

"What do you think the deal was with Alexandra? You've got to admit that was pretty weird," Turner persisted. He could sense from her body language that she didn't know all the details but that she didn't want to talk about McGann or Alexandra. He was determined not to talk about anything else.

She turned on the barstool, and her knees rubbed against his thigh. She didn't try to move away. "Alexandra Williams was trailer trash. When it comes to sex, a man will go where a woman is willing to take him."

He shifted a little on the stool to give her more room.

"Do you think he killed her?" he asked.

She laughed again, but this time it was genuine. "I would imagine killing someone requires emotional commitment and considerable courage, two qualities one doesn't easily associate with Jim."

"So if he didn't, who did?"

"That's what you're supposed to figure out. I'd think the possibilities are endless."

"What do you mean?" he asked.

"The woman was a pervert and a criminal. She didn't care how she treated anyone. People like Alexandra make enemies," she said with a hint of a smile before draining the remainder of her brandy. She pulled on her jacket and tossed her hair away from her face with a jerk of her head, a gesture Turner had to admit he loved watching. He stood and helped her. They left the bar slowly, maneuvering around the crowded tables with friendly drunks. The piano player, who'd been staring at her all night, blew her a kiss, and she rewarded him with practiced indifference.

As they strolled back to Parker Center, she slid her arm through his and leaned slightly on his shoulder, the same way Paula always did. He was over six feet tall, and she was just slightly shorter, about the same size as Paula. It was a familiar fit but made him uncomfortable. He asked if she was all right to drive. She nodded and claimed it would take more than three or four brandies to make her drunk. She just felt good, she said. He escorted her back to her car, which was parked near the back door of the police building. It didn't surprise him that Wolinski had managed to finagle a premier parking space. He waited while she found the keys in her purse. She unlocked the driver's door and turned quickly, threw her arms around his neck, and kissed him—a long, sweet, passionate kiss. He was too surprised to react. He inhaled the fragrance of her perfumed hair and felt her soft warm body rubbing against his. He was trying to extricate himself when suddenly she pulled away and got into her car. She slammed the door and drove away, leaving him standing in the parking lot contemplating why he wasn't going with her. She didn't invite him.

Was it just him, or had the last few minutes been as strange as they seemed? Everything that had happened signaled that two people were about to spend the night together, or at least as long as it took to screw each other senseless. Yet there he was, standing alone in the nearly empty parking lot watching her drive steadily away. Turner didn't want anything to happen and had no delusions about his sexual appeal or prowess, but he was old enough and had had enough experience to know when all the indicators were blinking. She had not too subtly been telling him so all night, and definitely with that kiss she wanted him, but she drove away. He felt like a fly whose wings had just gotten pulled. At that moment he was more certain than ever that Wolinski was their killer. What she had just done was something Alexandra would've done to a man—toying with him, teasing him. Wolinski had learned from the best, or maybe she was the teacher. He wondered what she'd had in mind for McGann. Was she like a poisonous spider keeping him close in her web until the time was right for the kill?

He looked at his watch. It was nearly 2 A.M. He'd practically told Wolinski that Crystal would lead them to her. If he was right about Wolinski, she would somehow try to take out Crystal before she could talk. He'd meet with the surveillance team immediately to give them a heads up. Besides, if he went home right away, Paula would surely smell perfume on his clothes. He shook his head. He'd have a difficult time trying to explain how nothing had happened or what was intended to happen. He couldn't go home. He didn't want to contaminate his real life with whatever he'd just been doing. He had his cell phone in his pocket, so he called the surveillance team.

They were set up on Crystal's apartment. They'd followed her to several places during the day, and her light was still on. They figured she might still be doing some traveling that night. Turner said he'd join them for a few hours if someone could pick him up at Hollywood station in about twenty minutes.

When Turner drove into the Hollywood Division parking lot, he saw the supervisor's car tucked away in a dark corner. He flashed a small green light at him, or Turner would never have seen him. Uniformed officers in black-and-whites pulled in and out of the lot without noticing or challenging the suspicious-looking man slumped in his car. Turner waited for the lot to empty, and he slid into the passenger seat.

The supervisor put his headlights on and drove quickly to the exit, turning onto Wilcox and driving northbound toward Crystal's apartment.

"Why don't you get hassled when you sit like that in a station parking lot? You could be some kind of wacko terrorist or something."

"I could be a sniper, and none of these young coppers would challenge me. They look, but they don't see," he said.

"They probably think you're an old drunk sleeping it off and feel sorry for you."

"Bullshit," he said, looking at Turner, who was smiling. "You're an asshole."

"I won't argue with that. I might be the biggest asshole alive."

"I knew there had to be some reason you wanted to wander the streets in the middle of the night, besides my pretty face and charming conversation. What did you do?"

"Not sure. I might've set a killer in motion. You can't let Crystal out of your sight." He really didn't want to accuse Wolinski publicly, but he wanted the surveillance team to be aware that something might happen. "We think Crystal's contacted the killer, so be extra vigilant. She's smart enough to go after anyone who can identify her."

"Her?" he asked.

"We think the killer's a woman," Turner said. "What's our girl been up to today?"

"Moved around a lot. Nothing that helps you, but she's still awake." He reached over the seat and took a notebook out of the back seat. "Here's the log. See for yourself. We just continued from the McGann surveillance. I figured it's all part of the same investigation."

A female voice that Turner recognized as the assistant's came over the radio.

"She's still in there, boss. The point guy is in the tree next door, and he says she's dressed and seems to be waiting for something," she reported.

"Well, it's 3 A.M., so we can eliminate a pizza guy," he said. He leaned against his headrest, closed his eyes, and told Turner to wake him if anything important happened.

Turner thumbed through the pages of the surveillance log. He read the notes for the last few days that the squad had worked on McGann. The entries were the same almost every night. Wolinski arrived about 9 P.M. and stayed until midnight at the latest. As soon as she was out the door, McGann was on the road for an hour or two, visiting adult bookstores and adult theaters, but nothing illegal. Wolinski couldn't have been all that satisfying, or the guy would've been too tired to do all that traveling.

Then something struck him like a migraine. He fumbled through his pockets and found Crystal's phone bill.

"I'm so stupid," he said, slapping the dashboard. The supervisor woke up, startled. "Sorry," Turner said as he searched the phone bill, looking for the times Crystal had called McGann's apartment. On both days, the surveillance log put Sally Wolinski in McGann's apartment at the times Crystal called. Finally it made sense. She was talking to Wolinski. This woman was smart. To the whole world it looked like Crystal and McGann knew each other. But why?

His phone rang. It was Paula.

"What's wrong?" he asked, looking at his watch.

"Your girlfriend just left," she said, sarcastically. "Where are you?"

"I'm with the surveillance team. What are you talking about?"

"Wolinski was here looking for you."

The image of Alexandra's battered body popped in his head, and he felt real fear for the first time in years.

"Are you alright?" he asked. His voice was straining to stay calm, but he sounded distressed. The supervisor stared at him.

"What's going on, Mike?" Paula asked. She was angry, now.

"Are you sure she's gone?"

"I think I heard her drive away. What does she want?"

"Lock up and do not let her in if she comes back. She's dangerous, Paula. That's all I can tell you. Just do what I say. I'm sending a black and white to watch the place."

Paula hung up. She was pissed; he could tell. Turner's stomach felt queasy. He thought about Wolinski's strange kiss in the parking lot. What was going on in her head? While he was calling West Hollywood sheriffs, the point man was on the radio, telling them that Crystal had gotten a phone call. She finished her conversation, put on a jacket, and was out her apartment door, leaving all the lights on.

Anonymous voices broadcast her movement down the stairwell toward the building's back door. She was described as wearing dark clothes. She walked to a car parked half a block from her building. It wasn't the car Mr. White had given her, but she had the key. Without turning on the headlights, she drove away and around the corner, making turns until she was back in front of her building. Turner didn't hear another car move or see anyone, but the surveillance officers were reporting her every move. She drove around the block two more times before she continued eastbound on Franklin, obviously satisfied that no one was following her.

The officer in the lead car broadcast Crystal's direction and approximate speed. Turner never heard an engine start and didn't see another car on the street, but someone, maybe all of them, were following Crystal. The supervisor said he'd stay in the rear, since two white males in a car always looked like the police to criminals. He heard the assistant's voice as she took over as the lead car. This was usually a difficult surveillance time, because at 3 A.M. there wasn't a lot of traffic to hide behind. Luckily, they were in Hollywood. Street people and production workers were always moving around, so they had some cover. The surveillance officers deftly continued trading the lead position as they followed Crystal toward the Hollywood Hills. She wouldn't see the same car behind her for more than a few minutes, if she ever saw one of their cars.

Crystal drove around in circles for twenty minutes, up and down side streets and through gas station parking lots, finally stopping her car on a deserted cul-de-sac with the headlights off so she could watch traffic. This surveillance team was patient and seemed to know all the tricks. No one drove past that street, but one of those calm voices broadcast her every move or lack of movement. Eventually, she started the engine again and worked her way back to Franklin. She was going back toward her apartment. Turner guessed it was just a trial run to see if she was being followed. Then she made an abrupt right turn onto Cahuenga from the left turn lane. They were parked on Cahuenga quite a distance south, and Turner could see the tail lights on Crystal's car moving northbound. No other cars were close to her, but the point was broadcasting as if she were driving beside Crystal's car.

"Where's your girl?" Turner had to ask. "How can she be calling this? She's not on the street."

"No telling. She could be anywhere. The only thing I know for sure is she won't lose that car."

Crystal seemed to have a destination now. As she slowly drove her Toyota through the narrow winding streets of the hills, a tense male voice was calling the surveillance. He described Crystal's careful trip around the treacherous curves on a very dark night on secluded residential streets. He was driving on the same road with his headlights off.

Turner wasn't certain at first, but then he knew exactly where she was going. He gave them the address, and the supervisor ordered the point car to back off and two of his officers to go directly to the house. It was the murder site; Alexandra's bloody love nest in the Hollywood Hills was her destination.

She reached the house before the surveillance units could get there. She had the advantage of knowing where she was going. The new point man couldn't see any lights on in the house, but several cars were parked on the street. Members of the surveillance team scrambled to get up the hill and find places on foot or in their cars where they could watch the house or be close enough to respond if necessary.

Crystal sat in her car for several minutes. The point described her checking her watch frequently. Finally she got out and stood in the street, looking in both directions. It was quiet except for the crickets. The street was dark, with one or two dim lights over garage doors. Crystal was barely visible as she walked directly to the front of Alexandra's house.

The surveillance supervisor was restless and fidgeting. "Do we get some uniforms out here?" he asked. "It looks like a meet. My people can handle it, but it's up to you."

"I'd feel better with your crew rather than some baby-faced uniformed cop." Turner took his utility bag from the back seat and found his small flashlight. He reached into the glove compartment and retrieved an extra hands-free radio and put it in his jacket pocket. "I need to get closer. I've got to see what's happening in that house," Turner said.

"Let my guys do it. I don't need some out-of-shape middle-aged cop messing up my well-oiled machine. You know they won't do anything without checking with you." Turner was out the passenger door before the supervisor had finished talking. Turner heard him broadcasting to his people, telling them to watch for an old man stomping around in the bushes.

Turner adjusted the earpiece and keyed the radio. He gave the point man a test transmission. A calm voice acknowledged him and asked for his location. Turner was trying to make his way along the south side of the house, the same way he'd come the first time. The point reported that Crystal had entered the unlocked front door, and the lights inside went on immediately.

Stepping carefully between the house and wall, Turner reached the back corner of the structure in a few seconds. He peeked into the backyard. It was cavern-dark, but he could barely see what he thought was the hot tub outside the sliding glass doors. A little light filtered between the vertical slats covering the window. He took a deep breath and crouched as low as his back would allow. He ran awkwardly toward the hot tub and nearly fell as his hard-soled shoes skidded on water puddles left by the lawn sprinklers. He slid behind the spa and landed hard on his knees. He tried not to groan out loud, but he could see that his pants were torn, and he didn't know if the dampness he felt was water or his blood. He crawled to the edge of the tub and saw light coming from the living room. Two of the slats that covered the window were broken at the bottom. When he lay on his stomach, he could see most of the room.

Crystal was standing by the door. She still wore her tight Levi's and boots. A turtleneck sweater and a worn Levi's jacket had replaced the silver top. Her right hand was hidden inside a large leather purse that hung from her shoulder. She was arguing with someone. Turner pulled himself closer to the window. A female voice in his earpiece told him to look to his right. He did, and he saw a shadow in front of the stucco wall. She tossed something on the grass behind him. It landed with a muffled thud. He reached back to get it and felt a terrible pain in his knees. He picked up a pair of binoculars, and when he looked up again, she was gone. He knew she was somewhere close by.

As he focused on the room, the door to the bedroom opened, and someone wearing a long coat and gloves entered the room. At first he couldn't tell if it was a man or a woman. Long, brown hair hid the person's face. Turner put the binoculars on the ground and took a long deep breath. There was no mistaking that walk, those graceful movements. He rested his forehead on the cold cement. His stomach was churning from the brandy, and he thought he might vomit. Something crashed inside the house, and he looked up quickly.

Crystal had bumped into a table and knocked over a lamp. She seemed frightened, and she stared at the other woman's hands as she tried to back away. He saw the gun in the gloved hand and heard a female voice in his earpiece. The assistant was transmitting what he was seeing. He scrambled to his feet. This wasn't going to happen. He reached for the sliding glass doors as he heard yelling and kicking at the front door of the house. Someone grabbed his jacket from behind and pulled him away from the doors. He was knocked off balance. His damaged knees buckled, and he fell to the ground, with the female surveillance officer kneeling beside him. "Crossfire," she whispered, moving behind the hot tub for cover and staring at the door with her .45 pointed where he'd tried to enter. It was too late. He rolled over, and through the broken slats he saw the tall woman turn in the direction of the front door as it crashed open against the wall. At the same moment, two popping sounds and fiery flashes came from a gun in Crystal's hand. Four of the surveillance officers had forcibly entered the house. They were wearing raid jackets and yelling "police." Crystal let her gun fall to the floor and raised her hands. She was screaming hysterically, "Don't shoot; don't shoot."

Turner saw the officers check the other rooms while one of them came to the sliding glass door. "Code 4, it's me, the good guys," he shouted before opening the door.

The supervisor's assistant tried to help Turner to his feet. He pushed her hand away, but didn't say anything. He was angry. He knew it was a crossfire situation. He didn't care. He didn't want anyone to die, and he would've taken his chances. If she'd let him alone, he might've been able to stop Crystal.

He hobbled inside the house and saw Crystal in handcuffs, sitting on the floor near the couch. He moved carefully around the body lying near the bedroom door. The gloved hands were handcuffed, too, but it was a formality. She was dead. Both of Crystal's shots had found their mark, one through the heart and one that had pierced that long beautiful neck. The ugly brown wig had fallen off near her body, and her blond hair was spotted with her own blood.

Even in death, Wolinski was an intriguing woman. Turner stared at the slender figure, still dressed in the elegant pantsuit, lying peacefully on the floor. The blouse had a single spot of blood where the bullet had penetrated her heart, probably killing her instantly. The long black coat had opened wide like the back-drop for a gruesome piece of art. Someone had kicked the semi-auto Berretta away from her hand, and it lay a few feet from her body. She could've killed Crystal anywhere. Why would she have come back here? he wondered. He backed away from her and sat on the arm of the couch.

"You okay?" the surveillance supervisor asked, pointing at Turner's knees.

"Do me a favor and call Stevenson and Montgomery. They need to be here," Turner said. He wasn't okay, but it had nothing to do with his bruised knees.

"Already done. They're on their way. You want to talk to her before they get here?" he asked, looking down at Crystal, who was leaning against the couch with her head resting on her knees.

"Did you bag her hands? We'll need to do the gunshot residue," Turner said. He was trying to think like a detective again, but he couldn't shake the melancholy that overwhelmed him every time he glanced at Wolinski's lifeless body.

TWENTY-FOUR

It was early afternoon before the coroner removed Sally's body from the house. Chief Martin and several of his staff officers had visited the crime scene. The chief, dressed casually in a sweater and slacks, walked directly to Stevenson, declining to take a closer look at Wolinski's body. He was visibly shaken and disturbed by her death. The staff officers took a quick peek through the open door, then congregated on the sidewalk in front of the residence.

They left as soon as the chief had walked a block down the street to address the news media, which were huddled in a jungle of cameras and wires behind police tape. In an uncharacteristically concise statement, Chief Martin told the curious reporters that a police officer had been killed and that the suspect was in custody. He promised a formal news release later in the day or the next morning, when all the family notifications had been made. He turned away and got into his car before they could ask questions. His driver took him swiftly in the other direction.

Nancy Connelly was the last of the commanding officers to arrive. She wore dark glasses as she talked to Stevenson but refused to enter the house. She was angry at everyone and no one. She snapped at the young Asian officer trying to keep the log and criticized a sergeant who asked if she'd move her car. The Hollywood Division captain was telling Turner that he'd notified Jim McGann in person about the incident, but McGann declined to leave his apartment. Connelly interrupted their conversation to complain that McGann wouldn't return her messages left on his Blackberry. She cursed Wolinski's professor husband, who'd been separated from his wife for nearly a year. Connelly had called him, too, but the guy told her not to contact him again until he could bury his wife's body. He had no interest in knowing how she'd died, and he demonstrated no grief. He coldly thanked her for the notification and hung up. "Miserable fuck" were the last words Connelly spoke before she left. Turner was beginning to understand that Connelly might've been Sally's only real friend.

Crystal told Turner she'd talk to him if Chernack would come to the house and represent her. Turner called the attorney, and he reluctantly agreed. Turner wanted to get a statement from Crystal before she had a chance to make up another lie. In less than thirty minutes, Chernack was in the living room dressed in sweatpants and tennis shoes. He explained to Crystal that it was in her best interest to tell the truth about what had happened, including everything she knew about Alexandra's death. Crystal was stubborn and streetwise, but she was scared. She had shot a cop and had come very close to dying.

"Otherwise," Chernack said, yawning, "It looks like you just killed a cop for no particularly good reason."

After several minutes of trying to describe a simple self-defense scenario to the skeptical lawyer, Crystal relented and tearfully told the truth. She and Dean had recognized Wolinski from her visits to Alexandra's West L.A. bungalow. There were many visits and many fights between Alex and the jealous Wolinski over McGann. Her sister had told Crystal that Wolinski was an LAPD lieutenant. Crystal knew that the bloody knife left in the bungalow had been a warning to her and Dean not to talk about what they knew.

Dean had seen and recognized Wolinski in the Hollywood Hills house the night Alexandra was killed. Crystal insisted that Dean was the one who'd first suggested blackmailing Wolinski.

"Phil, the nut case, messed up the plan by killing Jimmy," Crystal said, and she admitted that she needed to revive the plan when she could no longer endure living at Phil White's father's house. She'd called Wolinski at work and demanded money to keep quiet about what she knew. "She got pissed off and only talked to me if I called her at that McGann guy's apartment," Crystal said. "She told me when I could call."

"I never got Alex fucking that psycho cop. I told her there was something wrong with that bitch. I know trouble, and that bitch was trouble," she said, pointing at the blood stain where Wolinski's body had been. "I knew she was setting Alex up for something. I warned her, but Alex, she don't care. She thought it was some kinda big joke having the psycho bitch and her boyfriend both fucking her. That bitch killed my sister to get back at some guy she didn't even want anymore, and Jimmy saw her do it."

"He saw it?" Turner asked.

"Yeah, he was standing there," she said, pointing toward the laundry room.

"What about Monkey? Was Fuentes there, too?"

"No way. He sent Sonny back to the car, but he stayed to watch. Fucker thought he was gonna see a couple of naked bitches get it on, right up to the minute they start arguing about the boyfriend. She gets behind Alex and puts the fucking wire around her neck and wraps it around the mirror. Jimmy said the blood was everywhere, but even with her throat cut, Alex was fighting, getting cut up with that knife, trying to get away from the wire." She stopped and wiped tears from her face with both hands. "Jimmy almost barfed all over himself, but he couldn't move." She was quiet again as she struggled not to cry, but tears continued to roll down her cheeks. Finally she managed to say, "I'm glad I shot the fucking bitch."

She told them Dean ran away while Wolinski cleaned up the bedroom. He couldn't believe the police had found Alexandra's body in the police car the next day. He was panicked that some-one might've seen him driving the car or that his fingerprints were all over it. When the police didn't come for him in a day or two, he knew Wolinski must've wiped the car clean, too.

"How much money were you getting from Wolinski?" Montgomery asked.

"She promised me $15,000 this morning, but she said I had to come here to get it. She said the money didn't matter because she did what she had to do."

"You didn't think she might want to kill you, too?"

"I wanted the money. I figured I got a gun, too, but she was gonna kill me when I walked in the room. When the door got busted down, she got distracted."

"So you killed her," Turner said.

"It was self-defense," she whined at Chernack. When he didn't react, she said, "Who cares what this fuck says? That's what it was."

Turner had had enough. He told Montgomery to have her transported to Van Nuys jail and booked for murder. They both knew that charge wouldn't get filed, and the DA prob-ably wouldn't even file for manslaughter. Turner didn't care. He wanted her out of his sight.

Chernack talked with Katy for a few seconds in the kitchen and then followed Crystal out of the house, somehow managing to avoid the media hounds. His parting words to Turner were, "I'm a corporate lawyer."

No one was surprised when Katy ran Crystal's gun and found it had been stolen. The DA would file that charge. They were all shocked to learn that Wolinski's gun belonged to McGann. It was his duty weapon, the final coffin nail in McGann's career and life. Wolinski had arranged phone calls from Crystal going to McGann's apartment, and it would've been McGann's gun that killed Crystal.

"I wondered how Wolinski got home after she dumped Alexandra's body that night," Katy said as they watched Crystal being driven away. "So I checked with the cab companies, and I got a guy who remembers picking up this tall woman with wild brown hair hiding her face in McGann's neighborhood the morning Alex got dumped. He delivered her a block from Parker Center."

"That explains the funky wig," Turner said. "No one could ID her."

Montgomery was staring at Turner's torn pants and bloody knees. Turner was dirty from crawling around in the backyard and knew his unshaven face probably made him look like a derelict.

"Why were you out here last night?" Montgomery asked him.

"Let's just say I had a feeling something might happen. That's a lot simpler than the truth."

The black detective looked around the living room and checked the rest of the house. Everyone was gone except the two of them.

"Okay, I'll buy that for now because you look so pathetic. But you owe me a real explanation."

Turner nodded. Suddenly, he was very tired, and he asked Montgomery to take him home. It was an effort to drag his battered body to the car. A few uniformed officers were still outside the house, cleaning up the yellow tape and other garbage. They stared at him and whispered to each other. Turner knew that their theories were probably close to the truth. Street cops understood instinctively those details that staff officers wrote endless reports about but never got quite right. Turner knew they were talking about him, so he stopped and waved at them and thanked them for their help. They hesitated, then waved back and wished him good luck. He smiled as he painfully folded his bruised legs into the passenger seat.

Montgomery locked the front door of the house and placed the evidence seals around the door frame. When he was certain everything was secure, he instructed the officers to open the narrow street and allow vehicle traffic again. Most of the reporters had left with the body. The rest had followed Crystal to Van Nuys.

During the drive home, Turner decided to give Montgomery some version of the truth about why he was riding with the surveillance team. He didn't mention the kiss or the drinks, instead claiming it was so late after the interview that he'd decided to stay with the surveillance team rather than go home. He did mention Wolinski's strange visit to his house but truthfully couldn't explain it. Montgomery didn't say anything but seemed to know he wasn't getting the whole story. He changed the subject and volunteered to write the follow-up for Stevenson so Turner wouldn't need to come in the next morning.

He helped Turner out of the car and into the apartment. Paula wasn't home, and Turner felt a little twinge of disappointment. Montgomery turned on all the lights and started filling the tub with hot water. While it was filling, he took a damp towel and told Turner to sit down. He put the hot wet towel on Turner's knees and gently lifted the soaked material away from the bloody skin. He had to do it several times before he loosened all the caked blood.

"It doesn't really look too bad," Montgomery said when he'd finished. "I do this for my kids all the time. It's the dried blood that causes most of the pain if you try to pull the material away."

"Thanks, Dad," Turner said as Montgomery helped him get up.

"Go soak, asshole. You'll feel better."

Turner closed the bathroom door and threw his clothes on the floor. He eased into the tub. He could barely hear the television in the living room and then Montgomery's voice talking on the phone to his wife. He was describing the day's events and telling her that Turner looked worse than he was. She'd seen him on television and was worried. They talked about Martin's press briefing and finally what their daughter had done at school. Turner listened, thinking how lucky Monty was to have someone who could bring him into a different world, a wonderfully ordinary place where people didn't hurt or kill each other but worried about homework and their daughter's new boyfriend.

"You okay in there?" Montgomery shouted from the other side of the door.

"Yes, thank you. Go home before your wife blames me for you missing dinner again."

"It's all right. I got a few minutes."

Turner managed to ease himself out of the tub. He knew Monty wouldn't leave unless he was certain there wasn't any permanent damage to his partner. He wrapped a towel around his waist and checked for any other bruises. His knees were clean and looked almost normal, but his legs had black-and-blue marks where he'd hit the cement when he got pulled down.

When he came out of the bathroom, Montgomery pointed at his knees and said, "Those are going to hurt like hell tomorrow."

"I put some stuff on that's supposed to keep it from drying out," Turner said as he poured two glasses of brandy. They drank and talked until Montgomery admitted he'd better go home. He'd tried several ways to get Turner to talk about the previous night, but Turner had skillfully avoided the subject. Turner had decided while he sat soaking in the tub that his few moments with Sally Wolinski and what he'd done to set her in motion would stay locked in his head. No one, not even Paula, especially Paula, would ever know about his time with the dead woman. What was the point? He would deny knowing why Wolinski came to his house. Actually, that would be the truth. He would tell Paula that Wolinski was a crazy woman, who did crazy, inexplicable things.

Turner woke up in bed at 6 the next morning and couldn't remember Montgomery leaving. Paula was already awake and in the shower. He found a note from Montgomery on the dresser explaining to Paula why Turner was passed out at 7 P.M. and probably shouldn't be disturbed. He sat up and was sore everywhere but felt like he was back in the land of the living. He put on his bathrobe and went to the kitchen.

He made coffee and poured himself a full mug. He felt better as he moved around, so he decided to make breakfast. When Paula finished her shower, she called for him and came into the kitchen to find him.

"There you are," she said, kissing him. She apologized for not being home to take care of him. Bell had kept her, she explained.

She was obviously uncomfortable until he insisted there had been no need for her to come home. He was lying again. It did bother him. She asked about everything that happened and finally brought up Wolinski's bizarre visit. He gave his rehearsed explanation. She watched him as he spoke and didn't pursue it, but he saw something unusual in her expression. She didn't believe him.

"Those pictures on the news last night scared me. You look good, except that," she said, pointing at his legs. "You okay?" She didn't wait for an answer before taking a piece of his toast.

"Little beat up, but mending." He smiled at her standing barefoot in the kitchen with wet curly hair and wearing that old bathrobe. She was beautiful and he loved her. He couldn't understand what had happened the night before, but he figured this was worth keeping even if she did put the job ahead of him. She gave him that Toscano smirk that always meant she knew more than he thought she knew, and she returned to the bedroom to finish dressing. She didn't ask questions. He didn't know if she'd seen him leave the building with Wolinski or if someone had told her they left together. She didn't ask why he was working with the surveillance detail. She didn't seem especially upset over Wolinski's death, but then they weren't really friends. He worried about all the questions she didn't ask. When Paula wasn't curious, she usually knew the answers—or thought she did.

Montgomery called and was on his way to the apartment to pick up Turner. He had the briefing paper for Turner to review in the car. They would meet with the chief about an hour later with Stevenson and Bell. Turner promised Paula he'd attend her badge ceremony later that day, when she'd be sworn in as a captain. She tucked Harry Sims's silver captain's bars in the pocket of his Levi's before she left home. She wanted Turner to put them on her uniform right before the ceremony.

When they arrived at Parker Center, Turner and Montgomery went directly to Turner's office in IA, where Katy and Stevenson were waiting. They all agreed that Turner should be the spokesperson after Stevenson made a few introductory remarks. They walked together to the chief's conference room, where the staff officers were seated around the horseshoe-shaped table. After a few minutes, Chief Martin entered with Sylvia Diaz and Elaine Miller. Bell trailed in behind them and closed the door. Turner saw Paula slip in the back door and sit in one of the extra chairs against the wall.

Stevenson began with a general overview of the investigation, beginning with Alexandra's murder and including the death of Dean. Turner completed the story with a step-by-step analysis of how they eventually focused on Wolinski as their primary suspect. Bell studied his hands as Turner gave the same information that Bell had rejected a few days earlier. Turner paused, giving Bell an opportunity to say something, but there was no apology, no acknowledgement that he might've been wrong in his hasty condemnation of Turner's theory. When the old man did look up, it was with indifference, as if the humiliating incident had never happened. Turner wasn't certain what he'd expected. He knew what he would've done in Bell's position, but the words "Sorry, I was wrong" apparently weren't in the old man's vocabulary.

During his summary, Turner referred to McGann on several occasions. He avoided the details of McGann's relationship with either Alexandra or Wolinski and only alluded to the sordid reason for the relationship.

Diaz listened intently. She turned her eyes away from the crime-scene photos of Alexandra and Dean but seemed fascinated by the pictures of Wolinski lying in a Hollywood pose with only slight traces of blood on her stylish pantsuit.

By the time Turner got to the point of explaining why the gun in Wolinski's hand belonged to McGann, he could feel a change in the demeanor of the staff officers. This crazy woman had targeted a deputy chief. It could've been any one of them. Many of them had a potential Wolinski in their past, and suddenly they became less judgmental of their colleague.

Elaine Miller asked about the status of the Internal Affairs investigation involving McGann. Martin interrupted Turner to answer the question. While Diaz nodded in agreement, the chief explained that the Police Commission and he felt that at this time it was in the best interest of the department to conclude the investigation with an official reprimand for McGann and to reassign him to South Bureau. Turner saw Paula's eyes roll back. She would be assigned to the 77th Patrol Division as her first command, and the 77th was in South Bureau. McGann would be her new boss. He knew Paula could fight her own battles, but it bothered him. He took the polished captain's bars out of his pocket and rolled them around in his hand. She saw them and smiled.

The other staff officers, facing their own mortality, readily agreed that McGann should be reinstated, especially the current South Bureau deputy chief, who most likely was picturing his cushy new job in the affluent West Bureau.

Elaine Miller looked at Turner for an instant, then closed her eyes for several seconds. When she opened them again, she stood, picked up her briefcase, and without a word left the conference room and Parker Center for what would be the last time. Turner wondered why she hadn't used all the incriminating information he'd given her. He'd expected her to throw it in Martin's face. She didn't, and she'd probably saved Turner's career, or what was left of it. He was relieved, but had to admit he was disappointed, too. By giving her those files, he had forfeited a piece of his honor, hoping to make McGann accountable. Now, nothing meaningful would come from that sacrifice.

After the two-hour briefing, Martin approved the press release drafted by Katy. It named Wolinski as Alexandra's killer and Crystal as the suspect in custody for the murder of Wolinski. It broadly described the blackmail scheme and named RHD as the division whose officers followed and arrested Crystal. McGann's name was not mentioned other than to say that Wolinski had killed Alexandra in a love triangle involving him. The story was confusing and bland enough to stay on the front page of the California section of the *L.A. Times* for only one day. A few days later, a single-paragraph blurb ran on the back page explaining why the DA wouldn't file a murder count on Crystal. She would go back to jail for probation violation and plead guilty to blackmail and possession of a stolen gun. She wouldn't require the services of Terry Chernack for at least another ten to fifteen years.

TWENTY-FIVE

The badge ceremony lasted less than thirty minutes. Turner carefully placed the captain's bars on Paula's uniform collar, and the chief of police handed her the badge. She raised her right hand and swore to uphold all those values no one seemed to care about any more. Martin said a few words of encouragement to his two new captains and disappeared down the hall and into his corner office. Bell hugged Paula and shook hands with Turner, as if the embarrassing scene in Stevenson's office had never happened. Turner was pleasant but walked away before the old man could engage him in conversation. He wasn't ready to forget how Bell had treated him.

"My condolences," Stevenson said, grinning at Paula. "I can't understand why anyone would want a command these days."

Paula touched the bars on her collar. "I know it won't be easy, but I'm counting on Harry to bring me luck."

"This is my last day," Stevenson said, patting her arm. "I signed my papers last night, so I'm counting on you to be better than Harry was."

"You actually retired?" Turner asked. He hadn't believed Stevenson would do it. The department seemed to be his life. Montgomery looked just as surprised. Apparently, Stevenson hadn't confided in him, either.

"Don't get all choked up, Turner. I did manage to piss off the chief one last time. I got you transferred into RHD as a detective. You start working homicides on Monday."

Turner caught a strange expression on Paula's face before she smiled as if she were pleased. He was happy. He liked doing police work and had stopped thinking about being promoted. She said she understood his desire to keep doing the work, but her strained reaction told him his promotion was still important to one of them.

He went with her to Bell's office so she could clean out her desk. She emptied her personal stuff into a large cardboard box. She'd already moved the contents of her locker and the bigger items from her office over to 77th or back to the apartment. Rose had given her a brass nameplate for her new desk. Paula put it in the box. She started to shut down her computer, and Turner noticed a message from Brenda.

"There's a Mafia meeting tonight in the commission board room," she said, deleting the message. "Would you rather just get dinner or something?"

"You should go," he said. "I'll grab a hamburger on the way home."

"No, come with me. It's a good excuse to leave early, and then we'll go to dinner."

The last place Turner wanted to be that night was in the Police Commission board room listening to Brenda and Paula's other high-powered female friends, but he was pleased with her offer and wanted to be with her. He waited while she changed into her jeans before they walked upstairs and found Brenda and Connelly already in the commission room. Connelly shook Paula's hand and congratulated Turner for going to RHD. She smiled but looked exhausted. She'd made all the arrangements for Wolinski's funeral earlier that day. She was bitter about McGann and complained to anyone who'd listen how he should've received harsher punishment.

"I intend to make his life miserable," Connelly said after Paula tried unsuccessfully to change the subject.

"Diaz has a special event for you tonight at her restaurant," Brenda said, interrupting and pushing Paula and Turner away from Connelly. "The woman's morbid," Brenda said when they were at a safe distance. "Did I mention everyone expects great things from you?"

"Wonderful," Paula said. "I can't make it. Mike and I are celebrating tonight." He smiled and Brenda laughed. "Can't miss the commissioner's party. It's a command appearance."

Several other women and Diaz entered the room, which was already crowded with female lieutenants and captains. Turner was bored but enjoying Paula's good fortune. He was proud of her but couldn't help noticing how much she relished all the attention, even though she claimed she didn't.

Finally Diaz made her speech, inviting everyone to her restaurant to continue the celebration. She praised Paula and talked about how the new captain would be the future of the department. Turner watched the faces around him, mostly women's. Some were older—the pioneers, the ones who'd come first, taken the abuse, and opened the doors. Some were younger, prettier, like Paula. They'd seen their chance and taken advantage of the opportunities. Paula never felt she owed anyone for her success. Maybe she was right, but she'd joined the club and was going places he couldn't or wouldn't want to go. He felt sad; a distance had grown between them. Some day she would feel it, too, and leave him—not intentionally, but there wouldn't be anything to keep them together. This high-profile world was and always would be essential to who and what she was. Despite Wolinski's political savvy and manipulations, Turner guessed that world really wasn't all that important to her. She would've taken love, any kind of love, over the day job. Maybe that's what kept him thinking about her. Sometimes it was difficult to find that softness in Paula, the kind of passion that makes a woman do stupid things.

"What are you thinking about?" Paula asked, standing beside him. She leaned over and kissed him on the cheek.

"Ready to go?" he asked, getting up and trying to clear his head.

"Would you mind if I went with Sylvia Diaz for a few minutes, half hour max? You can get something to eat, and I'll meet you at home. I feel funny not going, since the party's for me."

"Actually, I was thinking the same thing," he said. She hugged him and waved at Brenda.

"See you at home," she said without looking back at him. He watched her leave and wondered how long it would take him to finally pack his stuff and find a place to live.

FORTHCOMING SEQUEL BY
CONNIE DIAL

Mike Turner hates dirty cops worse than criminals. He's back in LAPD's Internal Affairs, assigned to a special surveillance squad where he encounters a trio of uniformed thugs who prey on the city they've sworn to protect and serve. Despite interference from department supervisors and betrayal by those closest to him, Turner pursues the dangerous, heavily-armed renegades until it nearly costs him the job he loves. He's a veteran street cop who follows a trail of death and violence from the environs of Los Angeles to its bloody conclusion in the mountains of central California.